"It's not just your baby—it's mine, too," Graham reminded her.

"But you never wanted one," Serena reminded *him*.

"You did?"

"Maybe I didn't expect it to be like this, to be by mistake. But I wouldn't give up this baby for anything."

Graham felt an intense stab of emotion in his gut. He wondered what it was like, to feel so positive about parenthood. He feared becoming the same kind of parent his mother and father had been. Selfish and negligent and uncaring. But if he walked away now, he made that a certainty. He had to try, at least, to be different. His baby deserved his best efforts.

Dear Reader,

Welcome to another month of life and love in the backyards, big cities and wide open spaces of Harlequin American Romance! When April showers keep you indoors, you'll stay snug and dry with our four wonderful new stories.

You've heard of looking for love in the wrong places—but what happens when the "wrong" place turns out to be the right one? In Charlotte Maclay's newest miniseries, two sisters are about to find out...when each one wakes up to find herself CAUGHT WITH A COWBOY! We start off this month with Ella's story, *The Right Cowboy's Bed*.

And hold on to your hats, because you're invited to a whirlwind *Last-Minute Marriage*. With her signature sparkling humor, Karen Toller Whittenburg tells the delightful story of a man who must instantly produce the perfect family he's been writing about.

Everyone loves the sight of a big strong man wrapped around a little child's finger, and we can't wait to introduce you to our two new fathers. Dr. Spencer Jones's life changes forever when he inherits three little girls and opens his heart to love in Emily Dalton's *A Precious Inheritance*. And no one blossoms more beautifully than a woman who's WITH CHILD... as Graham Richards soon discovers after one magical night in *Having the Billionaire's Baby* by Anne Haven, the second story in this extra-special promotion.

At American Romance, we're dedicated to bringing you stories that will warm your heart and brighten your day. Enjoy!

Warm wishes,
Melissa Jeglinski
Associate Senior Editor

Having the Billionaire's Baby

ANNE HAVEN

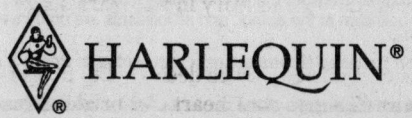

TORONTO • NEW YORK • LONDON
AMSTERDAM • PARIS • SYDNEY • HAMBURG
STOCKHOLM • ATHENS • TOKYO • MILAN • MADRID
PRAGUE • WARSAW • BUDAPEST • AUCKLAND

To Angela.
Thanks for being a great editor.
And thanks even more for your friendship!

ISBN 0-373-16824-1

HAVING THE BILLIONAIRE'S BABY

Copyright © 2000 by Anne Haven.

ABOUT THE AUTHOR

Anne Haven decided to be a writer when she was ten. She began with short stories and attempted her first full-length novel a couple of years later. Ah, the hubris of youth! Although that initial manuscript never made it to publication, she did continue to hone her craft and eventually coauthored several books. Anne likes to experiment with a wide range of writing styles, from deep and intense to light, fun, fantasy-based stories such as *Having the Billionaire's Baby*.

Dear Reader,

Some people enter into parenthood in a perfectly planned sequence of events. Usually they're involved in a long-term relationship and usually it takes a while for them to get pregnant or for an adoption to go through. They've designed their lives to be able to raise children. They've made a deliberate decision: *I'm ready. The time is right.*

Serena and Graham, the characters in this book, are not such people. As the story begins, having a baby is the last thing on their minds. But their lives take a few crazy turns and pretty soon they're expecting.

I hope their adventures in surprise parenthood entertain you and bring a smile to your day.

Anne Haven

Chapter One

May

He was getting married.

Serena Jones sat in the last pew of the beautiful old San Francisco church and gazed at the altar. The edges of her vision blurred as she watched the groom, Dirk Huntington Emerson III, the man of her dreams. The man *she* was supposed to marry.

But the bride at his side wasn't Serena. She was a blue-eyed, blond-haired, statuesque goddess. The kind of woman who made plain Janes like Serena feel about as attractive as a turnip.

Her head pounded. She hadn't gotten much sleep. She felt her eyes prickle with unshed tears.

No, she thought. *I'm not going to cry today. Not here. I'm not going to be so pathetic.*

But she fumbled with the latch on her purse and rummaged inside for the monogrammed handkerchief her stepmother had given her last Christmas. She held it in her hand just in case.

Dirk looked so good up there. So handsome in his tuxedo. His dark blond hair and extra-tall frame held Serena's gaze like a magnet. She wanted to ignore the woman clinging to his arm. Wanted to ignore the words of the priest conducting the ceremony.

Oh, God, Serena thought. *How can I let him do this? How can I let Dirk make this mistake?*

And it surely was a mistake. That picture-perfect Barbie doll, Elaine Richards, would never be able to love him like Serena did.

An image popped into her mind—Dustin Hoffman at the end of *The Graduate,* storming the church. Banging on the glass doors, then racing to the choir loft to call a halt to Katharine Ross's wedding.

He hadn't let the one he loved marry the wrong person.

Suddenly Serena knew she couldn't, either.

She'd always been the kind of person who stood by and let life happen *to* her. Passive. But this time she had to act. So much was at stake, so much more than ever before. She had to put herself on the line.

She had to stop this wedding.

And there wasn't a moment to lose. She had to

get to the altar. She would march right up there and tell Dirk once and for all how she felt.

With jerky movements Serena stood and stepped toward the side aisle.

And plowed into a broad male chest.

"Oh!" she gasped.

She glanced upward to meet the coolest, most enigmatic pair of gray eyes she'd ever seen. They regarded her from an incredibly attractive face with strong, sculpted features. Slowly her gaze dropped, taking in the sensuality of his full, unsmiling mouth and the clean-shaven skin of his jaw before aiming straight ahead at the knot of his dark red tie.

All at once she became aware of how her body was plastered against his hard, lean length. She took an awkward step back.

"Excuse me," she murmured.

The stranger reached out to steady her. His gaze recaptured hers and held it. "I'm afraid I can't let you do this," he said under his breath.

Serena heard the grim determination in his voice and shivered. This was not a man to be trifled with. He seemed like an immovable force and rather reminded her of a huge chunk of granite—cool, gray, impenetrable granite.

Except for the subtle scent of him, she noted. It was warm and sensual and masculine.

Not at all rocklike.

"Here." The man put a large hand on her shoulder and guided her stunned self toward one of the doors at the back of the church. "A bit of fresh air, I think."

She'd accompanied him all the way to a little courtyard outside before she realized what was happening. She didn't know this man from Adam. But somehow she'd let him smoothly and casually derail her attempt to stop Dirk's wedding. She hadn't even put up a fight. She hadn't kept her sights on her goal—on Dirk—on what she was supposed to do. This impossibly handsome, magnetic stranger had distracted her with appalling ease.

"Wait a minute," she mumbled, halfheartedly turning back to the door.

But she knew it was too late. Already she could feel her courage waning. Even if she went inside she wouldn't be able to finish what she'd started. She wouldn't try to stop the wedding. She would stand by and watch the man she loved marry someone else.

The stranger touched her arm, his grip gentle yet firm. "I think we'd better stay outside." His features remained expressionless, but underneath his surface calm Serena sensed that unyielding solidity.

Effectively dissuaded, she veered off course. She took a few small steps and sank onto a stone bench below an arch of trellised wisteria vines.

Who *was* this guy? And how had he known what she'd intended to do? Had her heartbreak and distress—and momentary recklessness—been so easy to read? Or was he some kind of apparition created by her sleep-deprived brain?

But no, he was very real, very much alive. He had a strong physical presence. And that sexy male scent—no apparition could smell that good.

She glanced more closely at him, taking in his well-cut dark hair, impeccably tailored suit and expensive Italian shoes.

This man, she decided, was as powerful in the world as his personal bearing implied. Powerful and sophisticated. And very, very wealthy. The kind of man her father and stepmother would respect, she realized with ambivalence.

He raised a sardonic eyebrow. "You're staring," he informed her.

Immediately she looked away. "I'm sorry." She gazed at her hands, which clutched her handkerchief and purse on her lap. "It's just that—I don't know who you are. Why you're doing this."

The man uncrossed his arms and slid his hands into his pockets. "I was trying to help you. Come tomorrow you might have regretted the scene you were about to make.'' He paused. "My name is Graham Richards.''

Serena glanced sharply at him. "The bride's last name is Richards.''

He nodded, not looking pleased with the connection she'd made. "Yes,'' he acknowledged.

Serena examined his features. He didn't look as if he could be Elaine's brother or any other type of blood relative.

"I'm her ex-husband,'' he said, answering her unspoken question.

"Oh.''

She pictured him and the Barbie doll together. They must have made a gorgeous couple. His dark good looks would have gone perfectly with Elaine's fair beauty. And both of them had a remote, almost untouchable air about them. She couldn't think of a more ideal pair.

"So why did you get divorced?'' The words popped out before she could censor them.

His expression revealed nothing, not even a flicker of reaction to her nosy question. "We had differences.''

"Differences,'' she repeated. How many separated spouses *hadn't* had differences? "I guess I was looking for something more specific.''

He raised an eyebrow. "We were emotionally incompatible,'' he said.

Serena wondered how they could have been emotionally incompatible when neither of the two seemed to *have* any emotions.

She thought of how he'd stepped in just now. Obviously he had enough loyalty to Elaine to make him want to protect her from a scene. And if he did, then he might be more attached to her than he realized.

"You're sure you didn't give up too soon?" She couldn't help asking. "I mean, suppose you'd been able to work things out?"

"Your life would have been a lot simpler, I take it." His tone was dry.

She grimaced, unable to deny that the thought had occurred to her. "How long ago was it?"

"Eight years. You probably didn't even know Dirk existed eight years ago."

Oh, she'd known he existed, Serena thought. Unfortunately Dirk hadn't known *she* existed. But she'd been well aware of him, her adolescent self overflowing with excitement every time he came home from university to visit his parents.

She straightened her spine, clutching her purse more tightly. "I met Dirk when I was ten. That was twelve years ago. Our parents were neighbors."

"Ah." Graham Richards watched her silently, his gray eyes cool and distant.

Serena felt a renewed despair. She'd known Dirk twelve whole years and loved him for most of those years. But not once had he noticed her romantically.

Maybe she should have studied the fashion magazines more carefully and learned to dress better. Maybe she should have dieted as religiously as her stepmother, Cassandra, and worn gobs of gooey makeup and forced herself to be more outgoing.

Or maybe not. She still doubted Dirk would have been interested.

Her father and Cassandra were probably right. She probably would have been happier if she could have fallen in love with Bob Bennington, her father's vice president's son. Their parents had arranged several dates between them over the years, and Serena had really tried to like Bob. He was nice enough, and he certainly liked *her*. But he had a breathy, ingratiating voice, wore too much hair gel and had the personality of a damp dish towel.

She gazed at Graham Richards, still looming by her side. Though implacable and aloof, he definitely didn't have the personality of a damp dish towel. His reserve only made him more intriguing. *Still waters ran deep,* she thought.

Not that she was convinced there *was* anything going on below the surface of him. But if there was, if anyone could access it, it would have to be intense.

Maybe too intense.

Serena abruptly shook herself. It was none of her business. Graham Richards meant nothing to her, and besides, he was way out of her league— another irrelevant fact because she was in love with Dirk.

Quite hopelessly, as it turned out. Even now the minister was probably pronouncing him and Elaine to be husband and wife.

Taking a deep breath, she told herself not to feel so devastated. Honestly, this day wasn't nearly as unexpected as she liked to pretend. Deep down she'd *known* she didn't stand a chance with Dirk. After twelve years she would have been stupid not to. And though she might be young and occasionally foolish, she wasn't stupid.

Her only truly stupid moment had been thinking she could stop the wedding. Now that the heat of the moment had dissipated she saw how disastrous it would have been. Dirk would not, as she'd convinced herself in her sleep-deprived state, have gone along with her as Katharine Ross had gone along with Dustin Hoffman.

What sentimental slop that had been!

This was real life, not some Hollywood movie. Her melodramatic outburst would only have caused a momentary delay—an incredibly embarrassing one—to Dirk and Elaine's marriage.

Graham watched the young woman's features grow flushed, as if she'd just realized the enormity of what she'd been about to do.

She looked horrified.

He felt a tug of sympathy in his chest—a sympathy that was out of proportion to the situation. After all, this person was a complete stranger to him. And although he wasn't an insensitive monster, he hadn't made Richards Enterprises into the flourishing multinational conglomerate it was by being sentimental.

That thought did nothing to lessen the odd sensation in his chest, however. Much to Graham's surprise.

"I should thank you," she said, mustering a brave smile. "For saving me from humiliating myself."

"Don't mention it."

She took a deep breath, then let it out slowly. "I wanted to stop Dirk from getting married."

"I know."

"It wouldn't have worked."

Graham inclined his head, silently agreeing with her assessment.

He observed how she held her demure little purse with both hands, how she sat on the stone bench with her spine so straight, looking prim and proper and miserable. Her light brown hair was pulled tightly into some kind of bun, and her features, which would otherwise have been pretty, were puffy and tense. Resignation had replaced the edge of desperation that had first caught his notice as he sat in the church, waiting for the wedding to start.

He'd only needed a moment to figure out she had feelings for Elaine's groom. He'd seen the adoration in her eyes as she'd watched Dirk Emerson, as well as her growing agitation throughout the ceremony.

That visible agitation was what had put him on his guard. Some sixth sense had told him she might do something extreme—such as try to stop the wedding.

By the time she'd risen to her feet he'd already left his pew and discreetly made his way to hers. He'd known he had to intercede.

Poor hapless, lovelorn fool, he thought now. Dirk and Elaine were so well matched and so besotted with each other that even Graham, with his cynical opinion of marriage, suspected the union would last.

And he hoped it did. Elaine deserved to be happy.

Despite their own failed three-year marriage, he

bore her no ill will. He only wished he'd been able to give her the love she'd craved. But that was the one thing he couldn't give.

The thought made his gut clench with guilt. A familiar sensation. No matter what he did or how much Elaine forgave him, the self-condemnation remained. Even after the way his parents had raised him, part of him felt he *should* have been capable of love.

His companion stood and offered her hand, interrupting his thoughts. "I'm Serena. Serena Jones."

Graham enfolded her small hand in his, feeling the smoothness of her skin. Her fingers were cool but not unpleasantly so, and she maintained the contact just long enough to be polite.

Yes, Serena Jones was polite, despite her misery. Suddenly a phrase came to his mind—*way too well behaved.* He'd read it in a business journal. A writer had used it to describe *him,* alluding to his eligible bachelorhood, lamenting that he didn't give the public more juicy romantic tidbits to fuel their gossip—didn't, in fact, give them anything but brilliantly calculated market strategies and astounding corporate takeovers. According to the journalist, Graham Richards had no personal life.

Just as Serena had no personal life—not with Dirk Emerson, anyway. Graham felt sure she'd kept her feelings to herself. Dirk had probably never dreamed he had such a devoted admirer.

But again, that was none of his business, Graham reminded himself.

He shoved his hands into his pockets. He murmured a courteous response to her introduction.

Where, he wondered, had his usual detachment gone?

And what was it about this woman that intrigued him so much?

SERENA FORCED HERSELF to attend the reception. She knew it would be agonizing to watch Dirk and Elaine together—but she had to do it before she could finally let go. It was, she thought with morbid irony, like going to the funeral of someone who'd died. It helped you to accept they were really, truly gone.

Graham drove her in his rental car from the church to the opulent old hotel where the reception was held. Like her, he'd come to the wedding alone. His original date had gotten sick at the last minute, and since he didn't live in San Francisco he wasn't in a position to find a last-minute replacement. His date's banquet seat was open, so he'd suggested Serena claim it instead of sitting at her assigned table in the back of the room.

Graham made sure to engage her in conversation

throughout the sumptuous dinner…which might as well have been sand, considering how much she tasted it.

Her inner despair hadn't dissipated.

She couldn't believe she'd tried to stop the wedding of someone with whom she hadn't even spoken in three years. Someone with whom she'd never really spoken, not in any meaningful way. She'd been invited today merely because their parents were neighbors.

Serena was only glad Graham had been the one to catch her on the verge of her horrendous mistake, and not someone like her father or stepmother.

At least Graham was kind about it.

After the meal he was accosted by a few acquaintances but soon caught up with her in a corner of the ballroom, where several large potted palms created a secluded alcove away from the noise and merriment of the other guests. He sat down on one of the red velvet chairs, his tall, imposing frame immediately making the space seem smaller.

"Hiding out, Serena?"

"Taking a quiet moment, but I'm going to stay until Dirk and Elaine make their exit. Then I'll go home."

He raised an eyebrow. "You haven't punished yourself enough for one day?"

"No." She smiled. "I like to twist the knife as much as possible. It's called masochism. One of my biggest skills."

He laughed softly, the sound low and masculine. Somehow he managed to be wryly sympathetic without making her feel pitiful. "You *will* get over him, you know. Give it a little time. You're still young. You're probably much more resilient than you realize."

She grimaced. "Young and resilient, hmm? If that's what I am, then what are you supposed to be? Let me guess. Old and decrepit?"

Of its own accord her gaze flicked over his elegant male form, which was anything but decrepit. Even through his dark tailored suit she could tell his body was all hard-packed muscle.

Strong.

Substantial.

Very, very virile...

A shiver of awareness traveled down her spine, startling her.

Luckily Graham didn't seem to notice. "I'm a bit older than you," he said. "And once you reach a certain age you become a lot more set in your ways. It gets harder to bounce back."

Serena ventured a curious glance at him. "Did you bounce back from your divorce to Elaine?" she asked.

Graham paused. "It wasn't that kind of divorce."

"Oh? What kind was it, then?"

He stared at her for a moment, his features expressionless. Finally the corners of his full, sensuous mouth quirked up. "Nosy tonight, aren't you?"

Serena nodded without remorse. She *did* feel nosy. Usually she would be much more reticent, but she wasn't ready to let him off the hook.

Tonight was her one chance to talk to Elaine's ex-husband. She wanted to know what kind of experiences he'd had with the woman who'd snagged Dirk.

"So," she continued as if he hadn't tried to deflect her, "it wasn't the kind of divorce you have to bounce back from. But you said you had differences, that you were emotionally incompatible. Wasn't it the least bit painful?"

"No, actually, it wasn't." He became silent again, but this time he didn't hold her gaze. He stared into his champagne glass. His expression turned brooding. "Not for me, in any case." He took a drink.

Serena watched him in surprise. Was that a small crack in his intimidating facade? Dear heavens, it was.

In the hours they'd spent together this was the

first time she'd detected one. She really had thought him completely unflappable.

"And Elaine?" she couldn't help asking.

"Was less detached," he answered. "But as you can see—" he waved to the wedding festivities on the other side of the potted palms "—she did recover. And it was still an amicable parting."

Serena frowned. Had his ex-wife been in love with him throughout their divorce? Was that why it had been painful for her? Perhaps she'd even wanted to stay together.

Serena had never imagined people like Elaine had to contend with things like heartbreak—or cramps or indigestion or bad hair days, either, for that matter.

But maybe the Barbie doll was more human than she looked.

As for Graham...

"Didn't you feel any love for her? In the beginning, that is?"

In the back of her mind Serena realized what a personal question it was—the kind of question she would normally never ask. But she didn't care. Nothing about her encounter with Graham Richards had been normal, so why start now?

She gave him an inquiring look.

One of Graham's eyebrows appeared as if it might disappear into his hairline. Obviously, she thought, few people dared to speak to him in such an impertinent manner.

And she couldn't quite believe that *she,* Serena Jones, was the one to do it.

Really, this man brought out the strangest side of her.

"I'm not sure this is a good line of conversation," he commented.

How typically understated of him, she thought. "You know, Graham, some people would have said it was none of my business and told me to butt out." She gave him a saucy grin. "But since you didn't, I'm going to ask again. Did you ever love Elaine?"

"I suppose you'll keep hammering away until I answer you."

"That's right."

"You might want to consider a career in espionage, Serena. You'd make a good interrogator."

"Thank you."

She would have repeated her question a third time but she suddenly realized she didn't need Graham to give the answer. She saw it in his gorgeous gray eyes. In the barely perceptible tension there.

Her own eyes widened. "You—you were never in love with her, were you?"

He didn't say anything.

"Oh, my God. You weren't." She shook her

head, her light mood evaporating. "I don't believe it. I mean, Elaine's so beautiful. So...perfect."

"As close to perfect as human beings get. Yes, I know. According to most people's standards she was a very, very good wife."

"And yet you..."

"I," he said, "was the problem. Not her. I wasn't a good husband." He finished his champagne.

She waited for him to continue, somehow knowing he had more to say.

He set down his glass. "I'm just not a family man. I'm not cut out for that kind of life—marriage, children, love, et cetera." He paused. "I'm too damned dispassionate. That's why it didn't work out."

Chapter Two

Serena silently processed Graham's disclosure. He was clearly unhappy with himself.

He sounded as if he felt guilty.

And bitter.

"You seem so sure about this," she said.

He shrugged. "I'm thirty-four. I've been around the block a few times. I've had enough experiences to know things won't change. So why not face the truth? I'm not good marriage material—or serious relationship material, either, for that matter."

How bleak and depressing, she thought. Just to give up on yourself like that.

True, not everyone saw marriage and family as the pinnacle of personal fulfillment. She could understand that. There were other things that made for a rich, meaningful life. Good friends, a career, somehow doing something to make the world a better place... But to rule out a relationship completely, to anticipate a lifetime of solitude, well, that was too much.

Biting her lip, she glanced through the potted palms at the rest of the party. Soft, jazzy music drifted to their secluded corner, and on the dance floor she could see couples swaying in time to the beat.

It was human nature, she thought, to want to pair up. Everyone craved closeness and connection, even people who were unconventional in other ways.

"Don't worry," Graham said, accurately reading her expression. "I've learned to accept it. It hasn't, as you probably imagine, ruined my life."

Well, now, that was debatable, wasn't it? Maybe he didn't feel dissatisfied now, but what about thirty years from now? Would he be lonely, regretting that he'd turned his back on love and intimacy? Would he wish he had grandchildren?

Maybe her dreams for a future with Dirk had been unrealistic, but at least she'd had them. At least she'd hoped to have a family someday with a special someone.

She knew Graham wasn't the only commitment-shy bachelor in the world—of course he wasn't—but it saddened her all the same.

"I'm flattered you're so concerned about my welfare," he said, "but I assure you it isn't necessary." His cool control had returned. After another pause he said, "Why don't you let me off the hook now and tell me about you and Dirk?"

She probably *had* done enough prying for one evening, she thought.

"I guess it's only fair to trade stories," she said. "Though I don't really know where to start."

Serena sighed. Her head was swimming a little, probably from her lack of sleep the night before, but it wasn't unpleasant. It made it easier for her to consider confiding in this handsome, undeniably sexy stranger whom she really *should* be keeping at arm's length.

"The truth is," she admitted, "there *is* no me and Dirk. Never has been. He never even knew I existed."

Graham watched her silently for a moment. "That's something you're sure about."

"Pretty much. After all, you've seen the man. He's better looking than most movie stars—the kind of man who can have a woman like Elaine. Why would he notice someone like me? I was just the shy girl next door."

"The shy, much *younger* girl next door," Graham pointed out. "That could account for a lot of it."

Serena shrugged. "Well, whatever it was, he didn't notice me." She laughed, suddenly able to see the humor in it. "Actually, it's pretty absurd. I worshiped him and he never had a clue."

She gave Graham examples.

She told him about the time she'd mooned over Dirk at a country-club party, hoping he would ask her to dance. He'd been so smart, so charming, the classic California golden boy. Everyone liked him, including Serena—who was already madly in love with him by then.

She'd been fourteen. He'd been in his early twenties and only had eyes for a beautiful red-headed restaurateur. The one boy with whom Serena had ended up dancing that night had been a year younger than her, a little carbon copy of Bob Bennington, her father's future handpicked suitor.

Forget Dirk—even boys her *own* age hadn't been interested! It hadn't done much to improve her flailing self confidence.

Looking back, of course, she wasn't shocked by her lack of social success. She'd had acne and bad posture, and her fashion sense had been ten times worse than it was now. Some maternal nurturing might have helped her adolescent self, but her mother had died when she was very young and Cassandra, who'd married her father several years later, was hardly the motherly type. So Serena had suffered through her teenage angst unassisted.

And all the while she'd pined for Dirk, steadfastly hoping he would look past her ugly-duckling exterior and see a magnificent swan.

Without stopping to wonder at her openness, she told Graham about her father and stepmother's roles in her love life—how they'd discouraged her, told her to get over Dirk and focus on someone more attainable.

It hadn't helped that they'd been right, of course, that Dirk really *had* been out of her reach.

As she talked about them Serena couldn't help wondering what her father and Cassandra, who were on vacation, would think if they could see her now. They'd probably be surprised that a man like Graham—a powerful, interesting, sophisticated man—was paying her any attention.

They might even be impressed enough to stop sending her on dates with Bob Bennington.

Graham, she thought again, was a very appealing man—despite his earlier self-condemnation. He might be a bit guarded, a bit enigmatic, but he was also kind and thoughtful and a very good listener.

In fact, she felt more comfortable with him than she had with anyone in a very long time.

Graham noticed her empty glass and, ever the gentleman, offered to replenish their drinks. Serena watched him stride toward the refreshments, noticing how he stood out, even in such an attractive, elegant crowd. She wasn't surprised to see quite a few heads turn in his wake—who wouldn't notice such a striking masculine figure?

She let her gaze trail over his broad shoulders and short, dark hair. What would it feel like, she suddenly wondered, to touch those strong, solid shoulders, to run her fingers through that thick hair? How many women had done so? Even if he did avoid commitment, did he ever indulge in brief affairs?

Her thoughts—which on any other night would have filled her with prudish horror—only made her tingle with excitement. Even as part of her recognized she wasn't quite herself, a bigger, more dominant part reveled in the unfamiliar, sensual feelings running through her. A subtle physical awareness had been growing between her and Graham all day, and she knew, just *knew,* it hadn't been one-sided.

At that moment she felt unbelievably daring, even reckless.

The chance to talk about her past angst had had a freeing effect, she realized. And why shouldn't she let go a little, stop keeping such a tight rein on herself—even if it was just for one night?

She had nothing left to lose.

It certainly wasn't as if she needed to keep saving herself for Dirk now, was it?

Serena chuckled at herself. What a foolish ninny she'd been!

She glanced over to where Dirk and Elaine talked with some of their guests, their arms lovingly curved around each other's waists. She felt an odd sense of detachment, as if it were a close friend who'd secretly admired Dirk so long and not herself.

Well, good, she thought defiantly. It was high time she got over the man.

And high time she took a risk with someone else.

THE PRIM little ingenue had turned into a siren.

At some point between the cutting of the cake and the tossing of the bridal bouquet, Serena Jones had metamorphosed into a sexy, womanly seductress.

And Graham was in trouble—because, as he whirled her around the polished parquet dance floor, he felt his common sense desert him like drops of water flying off lettuce in his housekeeper's salad spinner.

It was as if he and Serena stood inside their own private centrifuge.

No, that wasn't quite right, he thought dazedly. It was centripetal force, not centrifugal, that exerted itself on them. It drew them toward the axis, toward each other, rather than flinging them outward.

Yes. An irresistible pull that brought them closer and closer.

She met his gaze, her brown eyes as enticing as warm, melted chocolate. "You look different," she informed him. "Your hair's tousled. And your cheekbones are kind of flushed."

Why wasn't he surprised? He felt fevered. He didn't remember shoving his hands through his hair and he'd rarely allowed himself such a betraying action in the past. But tonight...

Tonight everything was going haywire. Turning itself inside out.

Demolishing his defenses.

"Is there something wrong?" she asked.

Of course there was. And if she moved any closer to him she'd be able to feel it, hard and throbbing against her belly....

It had been bad enough *before* she'd become a siren. Now it was pure, aching hell.

Graham forced himself to relax, to hide his turmoil and physical torment. He'd had years of practice at concealing his feelings, repressing them out of existence. Tonight it should have been easy.

But it damn well wasn't.

He muttered, "Air's a bit warm in here, I think."

Serena smiled at him. "Are you feeling hot under the collar, Graham? Here, let me help." Before he knew what she intended she'd reached up to grasp his tie. Boldly she loosened the knot, sliding it to the side in a slow, seductive motion and then returning it to the center. Still swaying in time to the music, she managed to release the top button of his shirt.

Graham was powerless to stop her. It was crazy. He felt dizzy. Giddy.

He felt like a naive schoolboy in the clutches of a wicked temptress.

He drew in a ragged breath. Instinctively he moved both of his hands to span the sides of her rib cage. With a low purr of approval she flattened her palms against his chest, her body heat seeming to singe him through the thin wool of his suit coat.

"There, that's better." She practically cooed.

Graham cleared his throat. "I don't know what you think you're doing...."

"Don't you?"

He struggled to regain his composure. "Serena, this isn't a game."

"Yes, I know that."

"You've had a rough day." He attempted a stern tone but failed. "You're not yourself...."

"Yes, well, I've considered that," she said, lifting her shoulders in a placid shrug. "It's not a problem."

If *he'd* been himself, Graham probably would have begged to differ.

But he wasn't.

Not at all.

His blood sang in his ears and he couldn't fight the desire surging through him. The overwhelming, forbidden desire that made him forget where they were, made the other dancers in their formal suits and colorful dresses recede from his awareness.

The damning truth was, his desire had been building all through the reception. All through the meal, when they'd had to make small talk with the other guests at their table. And all through their intimate little chat, when she'd forced him to reveal too much of his psyche and then proceeded to bare her soul to him.

She'd let him see the warm, intelligent, humorous woman inside her, making him resent anyone who hadn't appreciated her. Making him feel protective.

And attached.

And possessive.

She'd utterly enchanted him, put him under some mind-dimming spell.

And now his hormones were running rampant. They didn't care that she could never have a place in his life, nor he in hers. They didn't care that he was—despite her current behavior—way too old and jaded for such a young, inexperienced woman. They didn't care that the man she loved, for God's sake, had just married *his* ex-wife.

All his hormones cared about was getting that nubile body of hers into the nearest bed.

Sometime during the last half hour his ability to resist said hormones had markedly diminished. His infamous self-control had deserted him. And he couldn't even hide his desire from Serena anymore. The little minx had picked up on it and now she had him in the palm of her hand.

An explicit sexual image filled his mind. He felt himself harden even more.

Groaning, he couldn't help tightening his hold on her, pulling her closer.

She gave him a pleased, heavy-lidded look and brazenly fitted her body to his. "Mmm... Have I ever told you...?"

"Told me what?" Lord, but his voice was hoarse. He knew she could feel a certain part of him jumping against her, even though she didn't acknowledge it.

"That you're the most beautiful man I've ever seen?"

"No... No, you haven't."

"Well, you are. Especially now that you've

loosened up a bit.'' Her sultry gaze danced over him. "I like you all rough and tumble like this.''

Graham knew just whom he wanted to tumble.

Her.

Into bed.

"You would?''

Good God—had he spoken his thoughts aloud? He blinked at Serena's kittenish smile and realized he had.

What on earth had gotten into him? Everything had gone topsy-turvy, unreal.

"Because I'd like that, too." She arched into him in a provocative little movement that made him forget his train of thought. "I can feel you. I—I want you, too, Graham. I'm sick to death of being so straitlaced all the time. I'm sick of being so good and boring and polite!''

The journalist's description came back to him then, taunting and insistent. *Way too well behaved.*

And his spinning brain filled in a few more words.

Controlled.

Repressed.

Unadventurous.

All the things he secretly hated in himself. All the things Serena didn't want to be.

Two minutes later they were in an elevator, heading upstairs to Graham's hotel room.

SERENA AWOKE in stages.

The first thing she noticed was a feeling of warmth. She lay on her side, and the back of her torso and legs was suffused with a sweet, luxurious heat.

The next thing she noticed was an oncoming headache. For the second night in a row she'd hardly slept, and in a distant part of her brain she knew she'd have to face the consequences. She wouldn't be very functional today. Still half asleep, though, she tried to stay in that pleasant, slumberous state where she could feel the warmth at her back but ignore the incipient headache. But her body stretched and shifted without her volition. Infinitesimal movements, but enough for more sensations to filter into her mind, including the soreness from…

Oh, my God.

Her eyelids shot open. She hadn't…?

She had. This wasn't her bland beige bedroom in her bland beige condo in Pacific Heights. This was a very fancy hotel suite halfway across town.

Graham Richards's hotel suite.

Serena didn't move. She still lay on her side, and now she was conscious enough to know that the source of the pleasurable heat behind her was none other than…Dirk's new wife's ex-husband.

Graham's hand rested lightly on her hip, possessively cupping its curve.

The room was quiet. She could hear Graham's even breathing and thanked heaven he hadn't awakened yet. The only other sound was the ticking of his expensive wristwatch, which she'd tossed carelessly onto the nightstand last night when she'd undressed him.

She gulped.

When she'd undressed him. What a strange and horrifying phrase.

Tentatively she reached over and turned the watch face toward her. The cold metal chilled her fingers. She squinted to read the time. Seventwenty. My, she *hadn't* slept much. They'd only finished their long night of lovemaking a few hours ago.

She couldn't believe she'd done it. What on earth had possessed her? For twenty-two years she'd abstained from sex, hoping to lose her virginity with Dirk. Maybe that had been wrongheaded and old-fashioned—but to impulsively go to bed with Graham? What must he think of her? She remembered her behavior last night and felt her skin grow hot. Oh, how completely mortifying.

Not only had she been the one to make the first move, but once they'd gotten upstairs she'd acted like some kind of sex kitten. Passionate. Abandoned. Unfettered by troublesome things like, say...*her whole personality!*

Last night went against everything she wanted to believe about herself. And now, after being so intimate and uninhibited with Graham, she felt exposed and vulnerable. He'd seen a side of her she hadn't even known existed. They'd shared something so beautiful, so earth-shattering, and they'd only just met.

Panic zinged through her veins.

She didn't think she could face him this morning. Maybe that made her the world's biggest wimp, but she couldn't stand the embarrassment.

Graham stirred behind her, his hand sliding off her hip. This was her chance. Every second she lay here agonizing about it increased the likelihood of his waking up.

Serena inched cautiously forward. Ever so slowly she lowered her feet to the plush carpeted floor and sat up. She wore one of Graham's undershirts and nothing else. The sexy scent of him filled her nostrils, teasing her senses. Unable to resist, she turned her head and glanced at him over her shoulder.

He looked younger this morning. How old had he said he was? Thirty-four? His dark hair was tousled and his features had softened, making him seem like a different man from the huge chunk of granite she'd faced in the church yesterday.

Yesterday.

The reminder of their first meeting increased her sense of urgency, her need to escape. Her brain pounded as the headache gained force. She wasn't thinking coherently as she eased away from the bed and silently scampered around both of the rooms in the suite, retrieving bits of her clothing. Instinct and panic drove her.

In the bathroom she splashed cold water on her face and dressed clumsily.

When she finally slipped out of the suite into the hallway, she exhaled a sigh of relief.

THE SOUND of a distant click roused Graham out of the deepest, most peaceful sleep he'd enjoyed in months. He opened his eyes slowly, but it only took a second for him to remember where he was and what had happened last night. And to notice Serena was no longer with him.

He'd awakened to the sound of her leaving, of the door shutting behind her. He knew it instantly. The suite felt empty, drained of life.

Graham jumped out of bed. He was halfway across the outer room when he stopped himself, raking a hand through his hair. He couldn't go after her. He wasn't dressed. She must be on her way downstairs by now.

And he needed time to think.

What they'd shared last night. Erotic and intense, it had blown him away. Nothing had prepared him for it. He hadn't even believed such a consuming experience could happen, let alone to someone like him.

He felt shaken and overwhelmed.

It would have been easy if it had only been physical, but it hadn't. They'd made a deeper emotional connection with each other.

Graham muttered a gruff curse and strode into the bathroom, where he grabbed his robe off the hook. He shoved his arms through the sleeves and tied the sash, then leaned over the vanity, flattening his palms on the cool marble, and stared at his reflection in the mirror. Just as quickly he closed his eyes.

Last night. Big mistake. *Especially because she'd been a virgin.*

It couldn't lead to anything more. The connection between them was the kind that usually generated a serious relationship, family responsibilities. All the things he'd sworn off years ago. But he'd made his situation clear to Serena last night, hadn't he? He'd been up front, hadn't tricked her.

Yet she'd wanted *him* to be her first lover. He'd

known he should be strong and resist the temptation, yet he hadn't taken much convincing.

And now she'd chosen to leave without saying goodbye. Had she even left a note? Somehow he doubted it.

He wouldn't have wanted it this way. But perhaps it was for the best. At least it would buy him more time to come to terms with this experience— this strange, impossible, terrifying experience. More time to figure out what to do.

Graham straightened. Something made him cross the bedroom to the window. He pulled back the heavy drapes and looked several stories down to the city street below.

He hadn't expected to catch sight of Serena, but there she was. Her hair disheveled, her dress creased, she looked pretty and sexy and...much too young for him.

He watched her step gracefully into a cab. She had no idea how appealing she was, he thought.

An oppressive sense of loss assailed him as he watched her cab drive off down the street.

Chapter Three

July

"You're what?"

Serena faced her father and stepmother across the living room. They sat on her bland beige couch and looked deeply appalled. She repeated the announcement she'd made before her father's outburst. "I'm pregnant. I'm going to have a baby next February."

Cassandra's perfectly plucked eyebrows drew together. "But—but—but that's impossible!"

Serena shook her head. "It's a fact. My doctor confirmed it this week."

"I don't believe this," Harrison Jones said, red-faced. "Who's the father, for cripe's sake? Not Bennington's boy, is it?"

"No, it's not Bob," she said. "It's no one you know. He's from out of town."

"Out of town?" Cassandra echoed. "Then where does he live? How did you meet him?"

Serena shifted on her chair. "It's not important."

"Of *course* it's important."

"That's right," Harrison agreed. "This little weasel, whoever he is, is going to take responsibility for what he's done to you."

"He didn't do anything *to* me, Dad. I'm not a victim in this."

"No, you're certainly not," Cassandra said. She ran her fingers over her tight, bleached-blond chignon, looking harassed. "Oh, Serena, how could you let this happen? We expected better from you."

"It was a mistake," she said, wanting to beam herself to a different planet.

Please, she thought, *just let me get through the next ten minutes. Ten unpleasant, mortifying minutes. Then this will all be over.*

She sat up straighter. "We, um, took precautions. They failed. The doctor said these things happen."

"Not to my daughter, they don't."

Cassandra gave her husband a wifely pat on the shoulder. "It's all right, darling. They'll get married and everything will be fine. It's only July. There's still time for a wedding. It *will* be inconvenient, what with our trip to Milan, but if we make it a simple affair…''

Serena forced herself to speak. ''Um, actually…there's not going to be a wedding.''

Her father and stepmother looked confused. ''What do you mean?'' Harrison asked. ''You've eloped?'' He glanced around, as if expecting her new husband to pop out from behind a piece of furniture.

''No,'' she said quickly. ''I—I'm keeping the baby, but I'm not getting married.''

''Oh, yes, you are.'' He glowered at her. ''You and this little weasel—''

''Please stop calling him that. He's not a weasel.'' *He's a businessman from New York. A man you'd be overjoyed to have as your son-in-law. Unfortunately he's not the marrying kind.*

''Well, fine,'' Harrison said, ''but he's going to be your husband.''

This was one of the hardest things Serena had ever had to do. She couldn't remember a single time she'd ever stood up to her father, but now it was absolutely necessary. ''I'm sorry, Dad. That's impossible.''

''How can it be impossible?'' Harrison looked grim. ''Is he dead?''

''No, not as far as I know.''

She and Graham hadn't had any contact since

she'd made her hasty retreat from his hotel two months ago. At the reception he'd mentioned he would be overseas on an extended business trip for most of the summer, so she hadn't tried to call him in New York.

Then she'd learned she was pregnant.

"What do you mean, not as far as you know?" Cassandra repeated. "Who *is* this boy? I'm starting to feel concerned. Why won't you tell us his name?"

"Because it wouldn't make any difference."

From the moment she'd learned the stunning news that she was pregnant, Serena hadn't been able to stop thinking about Graham's assessment of himself at Dirk and Elaine's reception. Long before they'd wound up in bed together he'd told her he wasn't a family man, wasn't cut out to be a husband or father. That he was bad marriage material. A simple fact, one he'd confirmed and accepted.

And that meant he probably wouldn't jump for joy when he found out about their baby. Unlike her, he wouldn't be filled with awe and wonder at the prospect of parenthood. He'd only be filled with alarm.

Serena didn't want to deprive her baby of a father. But neither did she want the child to endure the pain of knowing Graham didn't love and value her or him. Though he'd warmed up later in the evening, Serena had initially glimpsed a cool, aloof side of him that triggered her protective instincts. What if he wanted his only involvement to be financial? Child-care money was the last thing she needed from him. It was certainly no substitute for a father's love and attention. After her own experiences of rejection, of not being wanted as a child, Serena knew she couldn't let her baby go through that, as well.

So she'd made a heart-wrenching decision. She wouldn't try to contact Graham. She wouldn't tell him about the new life they'd created together during their stolen night of passion. It was the best decision for all concerned.

Yet it made her heart ache.

And how could she explain everything to her father and stepmother?

Impossible. Maybe if they'd had a different kind of relationship she could have confided the truth. But she knew they would only become upset and judgmental. She didn't need that right now.

She met Harrison's gaze.

"So what exactly do you plan to do?" he demanded. "Have the child on your own? Be an unwed mother?"

"I'm sorry, Dad. But, yes."

Even as she spoke she felt another wave of disbelief. She still had moments when it all seemed unreal. She, Serena Jones, an unwed mother? The prim and proper good girl who'd never done anything naughty?

Except on that one unforgettable night, of course.

"Do you realize how embarrassing this will be?" Cassandra said.

"For whom?"

"For your father and me. When our friends and associates find out…"

"I don't see why they should care. It's none of their business. Most of them don't even know me."

Cassandra exhaled with unnecessary force. "That's a rather selfish attitude. Your actions *do* affect other people. You're not living in a vacuum. It's not right to pretend you're the only one involved in this."

Her stepmother, Serena thought, was quite a spin doctor. And a hypocrite, too. She and Harrison both. They always had been, but for most of her life Serena had simply put up with it.

Suddenly she found that much harder to do.

"If I'd thought I was the only one affected by this," she pointed out, "then I wouldn't have invited you and Dad over today. I wouldn't have bothered to inform you of my pregnancy."

"That's true," Cassandra said, "but things like this have a way of getting around. And it reflects badly on the whole family. That's just the way it is."

"Then I'm sorry about that. I guess I didn't realize people were old-fashioned enough to care. After all, it's not as if I'm fourteen. I'm a grown woman."

"This may be San Francisco," her stepmother replied, "but some people here still *are* old-fashioned." She paused, clasping her hands in her lap. "Serena, maybe you should think about going away for a while."

"I'm sorry?"

Harrison nodded at his wife. "Good idea," he muttered.

"Why would I go away?" She stared at them both, not comprehending their meaning. Then the penny dropped. "You mean to hide the pregnancy?"

Cassandra nodded.

"And then what—give the baby up for adoption?"

They didn't answer.

"I can't believe I'm hearing this."

Had she stepped into a time warp? It wasn't *that* scandalous for an adult woman to have a baby— and raise it—out of wedlock these days.

Serena cupped her belly, still flat because it was only her second month. She'd hoped that, after the shock wore off, her father and stepmother would express some joy or excitement about her pregnancy. The baby would be their grandchild, after all.

Instead they wanted her to consider giving it up for adoption.

Didn't they feel the least bit of attachment?

She'd wanted them to care about her and the baby more than they did. She'd wanted the arrival of her sweet little child to be more important than mean-spirited gossip.

Maybe that *was* immature and self-centered of her. But that was how she felt.

Serena stood and walked to her living room window, which gave a magnificent view of the city. Sunshine brightened the neighboring mansions, and flowers bloomed in the backyards and window planters.

"I'm going to have a baby," she stated. "Your grandchild. And she or he will be unspeakably dear to me. Adoption is out of the question."

Only then did she turn around to face her father and stepmother.

Maybe it was something in her voice, some unaccustomed tone of finality. But to her surprise neither of them said a word.

She realized she'd been bracing herself for more bullying. It didn't come. It was as if they'd worn themselves out during the course of the conversation and had finally realized she wasn't going to let them steamroll her—not this time.

They sat very still on her boring beige couch. Her father blinked at her, his mouth slightly ajar. Cassandra looked as if she'd encountered an alien life-form.

What an interesting experience, Serena thought.

She would have to try to assert herself with them again sometime.

She felt stronger and more rebellious than she had in years. This unexpected turn of events had called up some inner fire she'd thought long extinguished, stamped out in her early childhood. It might be just the push she needed to become more confident and self-sufficient as an adult. To stop letting her father and Cassandra oversee every detail of her life, from where she lived and worked to how she wore her hair to what kind of car she drove. To when and how she had a baby.

"Please don't bring up the subject of adoption again," she said.

Cassandra looked stung. A blotchy red flush showed through her foundation makeup. "It was only a suggestion. I didn't mean to offend you."

Not exactly a graceful apology, Serena thought,

but it would have to do. She was actually more upset with her father than Cassandra. It was his real grandchild he would have been losing.

"As long as you accept how I feel," she said, "we can put it behind us. I know neither of you is happy about this and I'm truly sorry if it affects your lives in a negative way." She paused, waiting as her father scowled, but he didn't reply. "And now, if you don't mind, I'd like to take a nap. Thank you for coming by today." She walked to the door and opened it for them.

For once in their lives they meekly complied with her wishes. They stood and trooped out to the exterior hallway. What an extraordinary role reversal! she thought. It felt good, though.

They managed to be polite as they bid their goodbyes and left. Serena closed the door and leaned against it, exhaling a long, relieved, satisfied sigh.

She hadn't been mild and obedient, hadn't done what she was told.

She felt proud of herself.

November

HE COULDN'T STOP thinking about her.

It had been six months now, and he couldn't get her out of his head.

Graham sat behind the slick glass credenza in his temporary London office and stared at the little monogrammed square of linen in his hand. When Serena Jones had fled his hotel room last May she'd left no note, but somehow she'd forgotten her hanky.

How very cute. And how very cute that he'd held on to it.

Months ago he'd decided he had to stay out of her life. For Serena's sake. After he'd left San Francisco reality had returned. He was still himself—a shell of a man who'd never been capable of feeling love. He still couldn't give her what she deserved.

A real future.

Marriage and a family.

But she had plenty of time to find someone else. She was twelve years younger than him. Just beginning her life as an adult. She could find someone who hadn't been around the block one too many times.

Yet the memory of his night with her haunted him. He'd taken her damned hanky all around the world with him, to Sydney, Tokyo, Paris, Madrid. And now London. He'd tried to fight this insanity. He'd extended his overseas business travels in a vain attempt to get her out of his system.

The more obvious method, sleeping with some-one else, was repellant, however. Impossible.

What a damned fool he was.

And it didn't matter where he went. The prob-lem was inside him. He couldn't run away from it.

Restlessly Graham dropped the handkerchief on the glass surface and pushed back his chair. He got up and strode across the plush carpet to the win-dow. Arms crossed, he stared out at the streets of London, awash with peach-tinted afternoon sun-light. Old stone buildings. Beautiful architecture...

Nothing to interest him. He wanted the city out-side to be San Francisco. Wanted to gaze out at the bay and the Golden Gate Bridge.

The intercom buzzed. Graham returned to the credenza and, still standing, pressed the button to talk. "Yes?"

"Mr. Richards, there's a call on line two. A woman from California."

His heart abruptly slammed into overdrive. He sank down onto the leather chair, cursing himself. It couldn't be Serena. Stupid to get so worked up. How many million-dollar business deals had he ne-gotiated without the slightest loss of equanimity?

And now he became a schoolboy at a simple phone call from Serena's home state.

He took the call, his voice more clipped than usual. "Graham Richards."

"Graham?" His ex-wife's melodious voice carried clearly across the Atlantic. "Is this a bad time?"

Immediately he softened his tone. "No, of course not. Hello, Elaine. How nice to hear from you."

"Yes, it's been a while. I tried to reach you in New York—and couldn't believe it when they told me you were still abroad. Everything okay?"

"Yes, but thanks for your concern. I've been working a little too hard lately."

"You? I'm stunned."

He chuckled. "How are you and Dirk?"

"Outrageously happy. Did you get my note last summer? We love the painting you gave us."

For their wedding gift Graham had sent them a modern still life by an up-and-coming New York artist. "Yes, I got your note. I'm glad you liked the painting."

They chatted a few more minutes like the old friends they were.

Graham never ceased to be amazed by his ex-wife's graciousness after their divorce. She hadn't tried to hide her hurt during their breakup eight years ago, but she hadn't focused on it, either. Hadn't pouted or sniveled or guilt-tripped him.

Yet he did feel guilty, and probably always

would. He shouldn't have married her without being madly in love with her.

At the time he'd told himself the feelings would come later, but after a few years it had become obvious they wouldn't.

Elaine paused in their conversation, her voice changing. "Look, it's delightful to get caught up, but that's not the only reason I've called. I thought I should spread some gossip."

"Now that sounds distinctly unlike you."

"I know," she said, "but this is a special situation. It's something I think you'll want to know."

"Nothing bad, I hope?"

"Oh, no. Not in my opinion, anyway. Though it is a bit—unexpected. Graham, I believe I saw you with a certain guest at my wedding reception. Serena Jones? Medium height, pretty brown eyes? Early twenties?"

"Yes, I...remember her."

Though remember seemed an insipid word for what he'd been doing all these months.

"Good, I thought you would. Well, it's like this. Dirk and I ran into her recently."

"Mmm?"

"And she didn't look the same. She was quite unmistakably pregnant. About six months, I'd say."

Graham lost the ability to breathe.

Oh, God. What did she just say?

He felt the way he had as a kid, when his father had driven the Camaro too fast. A lurching, dizzying sense of motion made him wonder if his stomach were still inside of his body.

"Graham? Are you there?"

He cleared his throat. "Yes, of course."

"I know it's none of my business, but I have a feeling you may know how Serena got that way. There's certainly no husband in evidence." Elaine paused meaningfully. "Call her, Graham. Or better yet, get on the next plane to San Francisco."

Chapter Four

Serena and her roommate of one month had just finished basting the pre-Thanksgiving turkey when the doorbell rang.

Meg O'Brien glanced at her watch. "About time," she said, affection in her voice. "Why don't you let them in while I put this bird back in the oven."

"Sure." Serena wiped her hands on a kitchen towel and walked around the corner and down the hallway to the entrance of the condo unit. Smiling broadly, she swung open the door. "Hey, guys!"

The smile froze on her face. It wasn't Meg's brother and his friend arriving for dinner.

It was *him.*

The father of her baby.

The man she'd never expected to see again.

Serena stared into his eyes and felt as if empty space had replaced the carpeted floor under her feet. It was like the dizzy spells she'd experienced a few months ago, early on in her pregnancy—only more acute.

She leaned against the door for support. "Graham." His name escaped her mouth in a low, breathy murmur.

Memories and unresolved emotions welled up inside her—attraction and dismay, longing and fear. Part of her wanted to slam the door in his face, but a bigger part of her knew she could simply never do that.

If possible, he was even more handsome than she'd remembered. Her gaze devoured the sight of him, the high, chiseled cheekbones, beautiful gray eyes, strong, masculine jaw. And his tall, lean body.

His face had a day's beard growth, she noted, and his dark charcoal suit was ever-so-slightly rumpled—but it didn't dim the overall effect of his person. He seemed to have a quality other men lacked—an extra bit of life force, a stronger physical presence.

It commanded attention and awe.

"Graham," she repeated. "What—what are you doing here?"

He stared at her swelled stomach. "You really are pregnant," he said in lieu of an answer.

As if he couldn't stop himself he reached out

and cupped her belly through the thin cotton fabric of her maternity dress.

His hand was big and warm, and she trembled at the contact. The moment was electric. Breathtaking. And much too intense.

His gaze met hers. "I'm the father?" He sounded sure of the answer and yet disbelieving at the same time.

She couldn't lie. There would be no point. "Yes," she admitted.

Meg called from the kitchen. "Hey, what's going on?" Her footsteps sounded in the hallway. "Where's that obnoxious brother of mine?"

Abruptly Graham pulled back his hand. Serena turned in time to see her pregnant friend round the corner and grind to a halt.

"Hello! Who's this? Not Daniel and Tom, obviously." Meg sized him up with a quick glance. Her auburn eyebrows shot up, as if she were impressed by what she saw.

"Graham," Serena said, "I'd like you to meet my roommate, Meg O'Brien. Meg, this is Graham Richards."

"Oh, my—it's the billionaire." She offered her hand. "Nice to meet you. I've read all about you in one of my brother's business journals."

She'd also relayed the information contained

therein to Serena—once she'd finally gotten her to say who the father of her baby was.

It had been startling, to say the least. Serena had suspected Graham was wealthy and powerful. But she'd never imagined he was a billionaire.

And it simply underscored the differences between them. They inhabited completely different worlds. Despite her newfound spunk, she was still essentially a quiet, low-profile person. She had nothing to offer a man like Graham.

Graham betrayed no surprise at Meg's bold statement—or at her equally rounded belly. "It's a pleasure," he said with a polite though unrevealing smile.

Serena watched the interaction with interest, thinking this was the cool, reserved, unruffled man she'd first met at Dirk's wedding.

"What brings you to San Francisco?" Meg asked.

"Serena, actually. Though I see I should have called first. This is clearly a bad time."

The aroma of hot, buttery turkey and other dishes filled the condo, and Serena saw Graham's gaze travel to the dining table set for four, which was visible through an arched doorway.

"Don't worry about it," Meg said. "My brother and his friend are just coming over for an early Thanksgiving. The meal won't be ready for over an hour, and I'm sure we can entertain ourselves if the two of you need to talk. You're also more than welcome to join us for dinner, Graham—there's plenty of food.''

''Thank you, but I've already eaten. I'll come back later.''

''Nonsense! Why don't the two of you go take a nice walk. I can tell Serena needs some fresh air, and there's a cute little park down the street.''

''And the rest of the cooking?'' Serena asked.

Meg waved off her concern. ''Daniel and Tom'll be here any minute. They'll help me in the kitchen.'' She reached into the closet for a windbreaker and thrust it into Serena's hands. ''Here, put this on. We don't want you catching cold, now, do we?''

She shooed them out of the condo.

Serena felt as if they were a couple of children being sent off to school. She glanced warily at Graham as they walked side by side to the elevator.

''I'm sorry,'' she said. ''Meg can be a bit of a whirlwind.''

He gave a slight shrug. ''She seemed very friendly. Have you lived together long?''

She shook her head. ''She moved in last month. We met in prenatal class.''

How odd it was, she thought, that she and Graham had made love, and yet he hadn't even known the most mundane details of her life—whether she'd lived with a roommate at the time, or even *where* she'd lived.

That thought made her realize he must have had to look up her address in order to find her, since she certainly hadn't given it to him.

Nor had she offered her phone number.

She wasn't listed in the directory, but obviously billionaires didn't have trouble getting people's addresses.

Shame filled her. She'd been panic-stricken when she'd woken up that morning in his hotel suite, but she shouldn't have cut and run before talking to him. At the very least she should have left him a note—and a way to get in touch with her.

Even if she'd never expected him to use it.

They entered the elevator. Graham pushed the button for the ground floor and the doors swished shut, enclosing them in temporary privacy.

She took a deep breath. "I behaved badly last May. I shouldn't have left without saying goodbye. It was cowardly and…and I'm sorry."

"You regretted what we'd done."

"I was confused." *Just like I am right now.*

"That's understandable."

They stared at the lighted panel that indicated

what floor they were on. Serena shifted, her hands going to her stomach in a protective pose.

Graham's gaze followed the movement. It lingered for a moment on her belly before returning to her face. "I'm the one who should apologize," he said. "I didn't intend things to go that far. I took advantage of your circumstances."

"No, you didn't."

His words didn't surprise her. She knew he was someone who judged himself harshly, having extremely high standards for his behavior.

But she didn't think he was right.

If anyone had been taken advantage of, it was him. *She'd* been the one to come on so strong on the dance floor. *She'd* been the one to proposition *him*.

Even now the memory made her blush. Her behavior that night had been brazen and outrageous.

She doubted she would ever overcome her embarrassment. Their lovemaking had given her a glimpse of a whole new world—but she couldn't quite accept the fact she'd experienced that world with someone she barely knew.

No matter how magnetic and handsome and irresistible he was.

She'd tried to tell herself there had been extenuating circumstances, and she'd been distraught that night, and sex between two single, consenting adults was hardly a crime. Not to mention that at twenty-two, she'd been more than old enough for a sensual awakening.

But none of that really mattered. It didn't erase her embarrassment.

Still, she had to take responsibility for her actions. All of them. It was part of growing up, standing on her own two feet—which had become extremely important to her.

She remembered her conversation with her father and Cassandra four months ago and the words she'd said to them. *I'm not a victim in this.*

"No one forced me to do what I did," she said.

The elevator dinged as they reached the first floor. They walked out, crossed the lobby and left the building.

Outside the sky was already darkening. The air had a slight coolness but no bite, and Serena was more than warm enough with the windbreaker. They headed down the hill, past the exclusive Pacific Heights homes to the playground where she sometimes went to watch children play and to dream about her baby's future.

"Your condo's charming," Graham said, joining her on a park bench under a lamppost. They sat in the circle of light it cast. Nearby, other lights illuminated the deserted play structures and reflected off the empty slides.

She glanced at him. "Not quite what you expected, though, is it?" she guessed. "Meg and I have done a lot of redecorating."

They'd gotten rid of the bland beige color scheme and replaced it with purples, sage green and terra-cotta orange. They'd bought new furniture and put paintings on the walls. Serena was still getting used to it—she'd never had so much color in her home.

Graham, having met her when she was still meek and staid and obedient, had probably expected the bland beige.

"I like it," he said.

They stared at each other without speaking. There was so much to say and it was hard to know where to start.

She was *afraid* to start. She really hadn't been prepared for this.

His gaze dropped to her stomach again. She knew he had to be affected by the sight, even though his expression gave nothing away.

Her pregnancy was striking. The shape of her body had completely altered since May. Not only had her belly expanded, but her normally small breasts had gained a couple of bra sizes. Her ankles and feet had swelled, too, so she'd had to buy larger shoes.

Every day Serena marveled at the changes. She

sensed the presence of her growing baby, and last month she'd felt its movements inside her for the very first time. That had been one of the most profound, heartrending moments of her life. She would never forget it.

Sure, she'd felt a pang of regret, wishing there were a father there to share the experience with her, but she'd known it was for the best.

She'd never expected Graham to reappear in her life.

"Graham, you have to understand—showing up on my doorstep like that—it's a bit of a shock."

"I know." His eyes met hers again. "I'm sorry I didn't call first."

She shrugged. It still would have been a shock. She hadn't expected their paths to cross again. He lived in New York, she lived in San Francisco. And they didn't exactly travel in the same circles.

"How did you find out about the baby?" she asked. Then, before he answered, she said, "Oh, God, it was Elaine, wasn't it?"

Serena shook her head at her own naïveté. She should have known. And she should have been prepared for this.

A few days ago she'd run into Dirk and Elaine on the street, but she'd barely had a chance to say hello because she'd been late for a doctor's appointment.

It hadn't occurred to her that Elaine knew or cared who she was, or that she would mention the meeting—and Serena's obvious pregnancy—to Graham. Serena hadn't thought the other woman had noticed what was going on between her and Graham at the wedding reception. She definitely hadn't expected her to put two and two together and figure out Graham was the baby's father.

She'd also been preoccupied by the revelation that it didn't bother her to see Dirk and his wife together—that she'd truly gotten over the man and that phase of her life was past.

"Elaine called me in London," Graham said.

"In London?"

"I've been overseas longer than I'd expected."

She calculated the travel hours in her head. He hadn't wasted any time getting here. Serena wasn't sure quite how that made her feel. Flattered, maybe. And a little bit worried.

"You could have just called."

"I could say the same for you."

She knew the words were a pointed reference to her silence about her pregnancy. "I'm sure you would have preferred that I'd told you about the baby myself," she said.

"Yes. I definitely would have preferred that. Did you think I'd never find out?"

"I don't know."

"So why did you keep it from me?"

Serena knew her choice was a departure from standard etiquette. She'd felt many pangs of conscience over the last six months.

But it was the best decision for all concerned, she reminded herself.

She clasped her hands together on her lap, her arms encircling the curve of her belly. She tried not to sound defensive. "I had my reasons. I knew how you felt about having children. I didn't want you to feel obligated."

"Does it matter how I felt about children before you got pregnant? That seems irrelevant now." He turned on the bench to face her more fully. His arm rested on the backrest, his hand almost touching her shoulder. "It seems to me I *should* feel obligated. I'm the baby's father."

"We used protection, though. It's not as if it's your fault."

"Nor is it yours—yet you're dealing with the consequences."

"I can handle it," she said.

She'd given it plenty of thought. She knew it was a lifelong commitment. She realized that as long as her child was alive, she would never stop being a parent.

"Do you think I can't?"

"It's what I want," she said, and meant it.

Graham studied her, his eyes unreadable. She noticed he didn't try to tell her it was what *he* wanted, but that came as no surprise. She appreciated his integrity, at least.

God, she thought, what an intimate thing it was to know you'd made a baby together. She couldn't quite wrap her mind around it. Without this man—this virtual stranger—the little being inside her womb wouldn't exist. She and Graham had created a new life together.

However unintentionally...

"My baby and I will be fine," she told him. They didn't need anything from him, least of all his billions. She had plenty of money in her trust fund, which had come into her control on her twenty-first birthday last year. Her baby would never want for clothing, or medical care, or money for an education.

"It's not just your baby, Serena. It's mine, as well."

"But you never wanted one."

"You did?"

"Maybe I didn't expect it to be like this, to be by mistake. But yes, I've always wanted children. I wouldn't give up this baby for anything."

As Graham watched her speak he felt an intense stab of emotion in his gut. He wondered what it was like, to feel so positive and untroubled about parenthood. He envied her lack of ambivalence. For him it seemed as if it would never be a simple or easy subject.

He wouldn't want to be the same kind of parent his mother and father had been. Selfish and negligent and uncaring. But if he walked away now, he made that a certainty.

He had to try, at least, to be different. His baby deserved his best efforts.

"Six months ago," he said, "I didn't plan to father any children. Ever. That's something I can't deny. But it no longer matters. I *have* fathered a child, and I'm not going to turn my back on her or him."

Serena lifted her chin. She met his gaze straight on, her brown eyes lively. "Is this where you suggest that we have a shotgun wedding? For the baby's sake?"

Her question startled him with its directness and its implicit denial. But he'd thought about exactly this issue all the way from London. They had explosive chemistry and a baby together. Those were reasons enough for a marriage.

The reasons against it didn't really matter. Not everything in life, he'd discovered long ago, was exactly what you would choose. You just had to do your best, anyway.

He wasn't the marrying kind. But when you had

a baby on the way, you got married. It was the only solution.

"What if I said yes?"

"Is that why you're here, Graham? Is that why you flew all the way here from London? To marry me?"

"Yes."

"Because we're having a child together?"

"Yes."

She met his eyes. "I don't believe in shotgun weddings or marriages of convenience. I don't think two people should become husband and wife if they're not in love."

And they weren't in love. Despite the connection they'd made at the wedding, they still knew relatively little about each other. They hadn't had *time* to fall in love—and Serena obviously didn't expect him to do so in the future, either. She just assumed he couldn't.

Smart woman, Graham thought.

He would never let himself forget what had happened with Elaine. He refused to fool himself, to hope that if they did have a shotgun wedding it would someday become a normal marriage.

And perhaps it went both ways. Perhaps Serena didn't think *she* could grow to love *him,* either.

Ironically, the thought stung.

"So, you're saying no."

"Yes."

"What about the baby?" he asked. "You don't think it would be better for our child to have two parents at home?"

"No—not if they don't love each other. And not if the father doesn't want to be one. Children pick up on that kind of thing, and it hurts them." She stared at the empty swing set several yards away.

He remembered enough of their conversation at the reception last May to know she spoke from experience. He had had a similar enough childhood to know she was right.

But to say that he didn't want to be a father…

"I realize you're trying to be honorable," she said. "You're trying to do your duty, and I appreciate it. But it isn't necessary."

"Wait." He slid closer and touched her shoulder, feeling her warmth through the fabric of her jacket. "What if I *do* want to be a father to this child?"

That gave her pause. She turned her head to examine his features. "What kind of father? A father who loves his child? Who'd do anything for him?"

He honestly didn't know. Could he possibly be capable of parental love, if not romantic love? Or would he turn out like his father and mother?

"I don't want to make empty promises," he said.

"The baby deserves more than a father who's just going through the motions, Graham. Honestly, I'd rather he or she didn't have any father at all than one who's cold and distant—and feels nothing for him."

Graham's tension rose. With a few short sentences she'd encapsulated his deepest fears and insecurities. He felt his face go slack, expressionless, in self-defense. What could he say in response?

She looked at him, clearly unhappy with what she saw. She lumbered to her feet, using the backrest to push herself up. "We should head back."

Silently he stood, frustrated with himself and the situation. He didn't *want* to feel those fears and insecurities, didn't want them to get the better of him. But there they were—impossible, for once, to ignore.

They'd walked halfway up the hill before he spoke. He stared straight up the hill and said in a low voice, "This isn't over, Serena. I'm not just going to disappear." *The way you disappeared last May.* "I have rights as the baby's father—and I won't let them be ignored."

A SHORT WHILE later Graham strode through the door of his hotel suite. He yanked off his suit coat and tossed it across the sofa, unknotted his tie and slid it from around his neck.

She wouldn't marry him.

He didn't know what would happen with Serena and the baby, but he knew he had to see this through. He was here to stay.

No other option existed.

He paced the room, one hand at his hip. With his other hand he rubbed his face and massaged his temples.

She wouldn't marry him.

In business he always had well-defined goals and could map out the steps to reach them. Here, though, he didn't. All he wanted was what was best for the child—but he had no idea, now, what that was.

The shock of finding out about Serena's pregnancy still hadn't worn off.

And the shock, to his system, of seeing her again…

During their conversation he'd kept remembering their night together. He'd remembered her body under his, the way she'd wrapped her arms around his neck and pulled him closer and whispered, ''I've never done this before,'' just as he'd begun to slide into her.

He still felt a mixture of primitive pleasure at having been her first—and consuming guilt, as well. In the back of his mind he'd suspected all along she was a virgin, but he hadn't wanted to face up to it. And then when she'd made her last-minute confession, he'd known he couldn't let himself continue.

But she'd told him not to stop, begged and urged and demanded, and it had been exactly what he'd wanted to hear.

And now there were consequences to deal with.

Maybe it *was* for the best she didn't believe in shotgun marriages. They hardly knew each other except with their bodies.

Graham abruptly sprung into action. He returned to the sofa, pulled his cell phone from the breast pocket of his coat and dialed his assistant, Jake Woo, who was still tying up loose ends in London.

It was the middle of the night there, but Graham paid Jake a very generous salary so he could call on him at times like this.

His assistant answered with only a hint of grogginess in his voice. "Hello?"

"Jake, it's me," Graham said. "Sorry about the hour."

"No problem. What's up, boss?"

Graham sat at the desk and unlatched his briefcase. "Care for a trip to San Francisco?"

"For business or pleasure? Never mind, forget I asked. What do you need?"

Graham shuffled through his papers as he reeled off a list of hard-copy documents and some extra office equipment. He had his laptop with him, and they made plans for him to receive some files by modem.

"I'll want a small staff—two more besides yourself. See if you can get Carita Lawrence. And maybe hire a temp from a local agency."

"Done."

Luckily, Graham thought, he didn't have a lot on his plate at the moment. Things always slowed down this time of year.

"Rent a couple of cars for yourself and Carita," he said. "Book a few more rooms here—and try to get a conference room downstairs if there aren't any more suites available."

"Done. I assume we'll be there a few weeks?"

"Maybe several months."

Jake expressed no surprise. "Fine. I'll fly to New York this morning and see you in San Francisco tomorrow. I probably won't be able to hire the temp or get Carita there until after Thanksgiving, though."

Graham realized he'd forgotten about the upcoming holiday. "Damn. You had plans, didn't you?"

"Nothing I'm not desperate to get out of," Jake said in a droll tone.

Jake openly acknowledged his desire to avoid his matchmaking family around the holidays, and

Graham knew he welcomed the excuse of work obligations. It was one of the reasons Jake was so perfect for the job—he thrived on the excitement and adventure of last-minute global travel.

"Need me to stop by your apartment for anything?" Jake asked. "Or shall I just bring the rest of the clothes you left in your room here?"

It was a good question. All Graham had with him were a couple of suits and some dress shirts. He'd left London yesterday in a bit of a hurry.

"Just bring whatever's there. When you get to San Francisco I may have you buy a few casual items for me."

"Like what—a sports coat and slacks off the rack?"

"Mmm, very funny. No, I was thinking more along the lines of jeans and T-shirts."

A brief silence ensued.

"Oh, sure. No problem," Jake said, as if he weren't well aware his employer hadn't worn jeans in years. He continued in a calm, casual tone, "Mind telling me what the hell is going on?"

"Serena Jones is having my baby."

Chapter Five

The day after Graham's reappearance in her life Serena lay on her side in her prenatal yoga class. Soft background music drifted across the peaceful, semidark room. This was supposed to be the final relaxation period, during which she let her mind empty of all her concerns and anxieties about her week.

But that was the last thing she was able to do today.

She couldn't stop thinking about Graham. And the fact that she had to call him.

When he'd left her condo last night he'd given her his business card, on which he'd written his private cell phone number.

"Call me when you're ready to talk," he'd said. "But don't wait too long."

How long was too long? she wondered.

Graham had also written down the hotel where he was staying, and his room number.

It was the same hotel, she couldn't help but notice, as the one where they'd had their little interlude. Not the same suite, thank goodness, but just seeing the hotel's name in Graham's strong handwriting was enough to make her pulse speed up.

She could picture the pristine suite at the moment she and Graham had first entered it. And she could see it the way it had looked a few hours later, in the morning.

Rumpled and disarrayed.

Clothing strewn everywhere.

A lamp knocked off an end table.

It was almost funny, she thought, that the suite had undergone a transformation that mirrored her own. In the morning it had looked as if it had been trashed by a bunch of rowdy rock musicians. Sometimes she felt her impulsive actions had done the same thing to her quiet existence. Overnight she'd gone from neat and tidy in her personal life, a prim virgin, to a sexually adventurous, unwed mother-to-be.

Her life had not been trashed. But it was definitely a lot messier than it had been before—even if she did want this baby more than anything in the world.

Some messes, she supposed, were preferable to perfect, antiseptic tidiness.

But then there was Graham. And the call she had to make to him. He'd left the ball in her court, but she knew he wouldn't allow her to ignore him for more than a few days. Every day that passed brought them another day closer to her due date—and their baby's arrival.

The tempo of the background music changed, signaling the end of the yoga class. Serena wiggled her fingers and toes and, at the instructor's prompting, pushed herself to a sitting position on her soft mat.

She glanced around the room at the other pregnant women, including Meg. They made a diverse group, being of all sizes and shapes as well as different ethnicities and backgrounds. A few of the women also attended the regular prenatal class where Serena and Meg had met.

"Ready to run some errands?" Meg asked.

Serena nodded, and they headed for the changing room. A minute later they stepped outside.

The street in front of the yoga center was bustling. It was the day before Thanksgiving, and some people were making their last trips to the grocery store for supplies while others strolled up and down the sidewalks, enjoying the sunny day. They were in the Marina district, close enough to the water that Serena could smell the saltiness of the bay in the breeze.

Their first stop was a flower shop around the corner.

"I have to get something for my parents," Meg said.

Meg was going to spend Thanksgiving with her parents in Palo Alto. Her younger brother and his wife would also be there. Daniel was spending his Thanksgiving in Las Vegas.

Meg wandered through the store, examining the loose flowers in galvanized buckets, and Serena decided she might as well choose something for her father and Cassandra. The shop was lush and humid, filled with the scents of flowers. Stacks of pine boughs for holiday decorating gave the air an unaccustomed spiciness.

Serena thought how glad she was to have Meg in her life. They'd hit it off right away during pre-natal class. The instructor had paired them for an exercise in which they talked about their feelings about being pregnant. Having heard her biological clock ticking for some time, Meg had decided on her thirtieth birthday to visit a sperm bank. She'd explained to a bemused Serena that she simply hadn't found a man she liked and respected enough to marry and she hadn't wanted to postpone parenthood any longer. She'd gotten pregnant on the first try.

A couple of weeks into the prenatal class, when Meg had spread the word that she was looking for a new apartment, Serena had immediately had the idea of inviting her to move into the condo and become her roommate. It was part of her ongoing attempt to broaden her horizons.

They were different in many ways and Meg was several years older, but they understood each other easily and could laugh together at the ridiculousness of life.

"And how about *your* Thanksgiving?" Meg said.

Serena shrugged. "Same old, same old. Just the three of us—and an unappreciated household staff that my stepmother micromanages and my father intimidates."

"Oh, dear." Meg clucked her tongue sympathetically. "What about the rest of the weekend? You still plan to work on your applications?"

Serena nodded. "I promise."

She'd decided to apply to graduate school. Last summer she'd quit her job in a gift boutique and taken a part-time position as a research assistant for one of her old college professors, with whom she'd kept up a correspondence since graduation. The woman taught geology, a subject Serena had loved even though her father and Cassandra had talked her into majoring in art history. Now she'd decided to pursue her true interests and perhaps become a geology professor herself someday.

Meg had selected a basket of flowers from the refrigerated case, done in fall harvest colors. She held it up, turning it this way and that. "What do you think?"

"Nice," Serena said. She held up the one she'd picked, which was almost identical. "What about this for my parents?"

"Nice." Meg's gaze went from one arrangement to the other. "A little bit boring, but they'll store well until tomorrow."

They set the baskets on the counter for the attendant to ring up.

"Wait," Meg said. "We should get some flowers for the condo, too. You know, to brighten the place up a little."

"Isn't it bright enough?"

"Never!"

Serena just rolled her eyes and went along with it. Meg went wild picking individual stems out of the buckets on the floor. Serena joined in, adding everything she could find in purple and orange, even varieties she never would have matched up together.

The assembled bouquets looked surprisingly good, she thought, if a bit unconventional.

"These will definitely liven up the apartment," she admitted as they paid for everything.

They left the shop, each carrying a shopping bag of carefully packed flowers, and headed for the French bakery a few doors down.

"So," Meg said. "You still trying to figure out what to do about the billionaire?"

Meg knew what had transpired last night after she'd sent Serena and Graham off to the park. Serena had told her as soon as their dinner guests had left at the end of the evening.

"Pretty much," Serena admitted.

She still had a hard time accepting that Graham was back in her life. That he'd found out about her pregnancy. That he'd expected her to marry him...

She'd made so many plans these past months. It had been hard enough to adjust to being pregnant and to being a single mom. Now all those plans had been changed, and she didn't know what the new plan was.

Meg pushed open the swinging door of the crowded bakery and they stepped inside. Serena inhaled the yeasty scent of baking bread, momentarily sidetracked from her troubled thoughts. The shop had an entirely different smell from the flower store but it was an equally pleasing one. She gave an appreciative sigh, wondering if her pregnancy hadn't intensified her senses.

"Maybe you shouldn't write him off so quickly," Meg said. She pulled a paper number from the dispenser and they stood to wait their turn. "Maybe you should spend some time with him, get to know him better. He *was* pretty hot, after all."

Serena stared at her in disbelief. "Wait a second. You're telling me I should let this man into my life just because he's good-looking?"

"I don't think you're going to keep him out of your life, no matter what you do. He wants to marry you."

"He wants to marry the mother of his child," Serena replied.

"He tracked you down as soon as he found out you were pregnant. That's got to count for something. A lot of men would have stayed away and kept their fingers crossed that you never got in touch with them."

Serena considered that. If Graham were as doubtful of his ability to have relationships as he'd claimed in May, he wouldn't have bothered to show up at all.

"It was just one night," Serena reminded her. "We got carried away. That's not a reason to be stuck with each other forever."

"So you *are* considering a shotgun wedding."

"Of course not! You know how I feel about that."

Meg shook her head, as if disappointed. "Well, spend some time with him, anyway. See what he's like when you're not trying to maneuver him into bed." She grinned saucily.

"*Meg.*" Serena glanced around to make sure no one had overheard.

"You might find you like more about him than his sexy body."

"And I might not," she muttered.

"In which case you've still got the sexy body to work with. Give it a chance."

Serena was grateful one of the clerks called their number, bringing the conversation to a pause. She let her friend do the ordering.

Meg had obviously done some thinking about the situation with Graham and come to her own conclusions. Serena was a little surprised Meg had encouraged her to be more open-minded about Graham, though.

Usually Meg was more interested in espousing female independence. She believed a woman didn't need a man to make her life complete, arguing it was perfectly possible for a woman to be happy alone.

And, unlike Serena's parents, she'd supported Serena's plan to be a single mom.

Meg turned to her while the cashier rang up their order. "Well, Graham's quite a male specimen," she remarked.

Something about her friend's expression made Serena laugh. With Meg she could never lose her good humor for long. "He *is* fairly attractive, isn't he?" she conceded.

Meg laughed. "Yeah, you could say that." She shook her head again. "Look at you. Pine secretly after one guy for years and then, wham, one day when you're not paying attention you land one of the most handsome and powerful men in the country."

"I haven't *landed* anyone."

"Fine, fine. But when are you going to call him?"

"I don't know."

"He'll call if you don't."

"I know."

"So *call* him."

IT WAS too much.

She wanted to strangle her father and Cassandra for this little stunt.

Sitting in the large, ostentatious drawing room Thanksgiving evening, a glass of mineral water in her hands, she tried to smile at Bob Bennington and his parents as they greeted her and made small talk. After all, it wasn't *their* fault their hosts had pretended to Serena this would be a private family dinner.

But really—if she'd known the Benningtons were coming, she never would have left home today. And if she'd never left home, she wouldn't have accidentally locked her keys in the car along with the flowers she'd bought.

Now she would have to take a taxi home. Or worse, catch a ride with Bob. Thank goodness Meg would be home from her Thanksgiving well before Serena left her parents' house.

She was sick to death of her father and step-mother's continuing attempts to marry her off to Bob. In September they'd talked him into offering to be her birth coach. She'd said no, of course, but that hadn't stopped them. Last month they'd sent him over to her condo to drop off some extra jars of marmalade they'd had sitting around the pantry. Marmalade! What was she supposed to do with four jars of the stuff? She hated marmalade, and so did Meg!

And tonight was the last straw. Had her parents somehow not really figured out she was pregnant?

Six months pregnant and they were still trying to fix her up with Bob.

Six months pregnant with another man's baby!

She reminded herself to breathe deeply, trying to employ some of the relaxation techniques she'd learned in her yoga class.

Cassandra was enthusing about some violin prodigy she'd seen perform. "Here, Bob," she said, producing the program. "You and Serena should see the selections he played. I think you'll be very impressed." She sat down on the sofa next to Serena and waved him over to the other end, so Serena was sandwiched between them.

Bob dutifully oohed and ahed over the program, which Cassandra rested on Serena's knees as she turned the pages. Serena leaned back against the sofa, trying to get some space for herself and her rounded stomach.

Her father and Mr. Bennington started talking about their latest golf game.

"He's giving a second performance next week," Cassandra said to Bob. "Perhaps you could take Serena to it."

"That would be a pleasure," he said in his breathy, overeager voice. He gave Serena a big smile.

Didn't *he*, at least, care that she was pregnant? Didn't that make him think twice about pursuing her?

Apparently not.

Apparently he was simply thrilled to go along with her parents' mission to marry her off before the baby was born.

Serena tried not to stare at his excessive application of hair gel.

The moment he got up to refill her glass of mineral water at the sideboard she turned to her stepmother. "I thought it was just going to be family tonight," she said under her breath.

"Yes, but this was a last-minute thing." Cassandra's voice was unnaturally high and cheerful.

Serena didn't believe her for a minute. "You said—"

"I know, dear, isn't it delightful? The Benningtons were able to come, after all. And you know how we always have such a big turkey every year. It was only a matter of setting a few more places at the table."

Serena trembled. She wondered if the hormones from her pregnancy were responsible for the sharp burst of outrage she felt.

She saw red. Bright, intense, ire-provoking red.

How could they think they would get away with this, that these manipulations would actually work? She couldn't take any more of this. She had to fight back!

Without pausing to consider the consequences, she impulsively shot to her feet. "Oh, good heav-

ens, that reminds me! What was I thinking? I totally forgot to tell you!''

Her father paused in the middle of a sentence.
Everyone stared at her.

She flashed a sheepish smile and rushed on.
''Pregnancy-induced memory loss, I guess. Just a
minute ago I locked myself out of my car, and now
this.''

''Well, what is it?'' her father demanded.

She glanced at Cassandra. ''You did say it was
just a matter of setting more places at the table,
right? Well, I forgot to tell you to set one more.
That won't be problem, will it?''

Her stepmother blinked. ''Excuse me? What do
you mean?''

''My boyfriend is coming, too.''

The moment she said the words, she realized
what a huge mistake she'd made. She'd lost her
head and done something crazy.

But it was too late to take it all back. She
couldn't back down now.

''What on God's green earth are you talking
about?'' her father said.

No choice but to press forward, she told herself.
She straightened her shoulders, standing as tall as
possible. ''I completely forgot to tell you. His
name is Graham. He's supposed to be here any
minute.'' She glanced at her watch. ''Er, maybe

I'd better go try his cell phone. It *is* getting a bit late, isn't it?''

"But—"

She quickly excused herself and fled from the room.

Oh, dear heaven, she thought, *what have I gotten myself into? I've well and truly lost my mind.*

Slipping into the downstairs guest room, she was glad she'd memorized Graham's number. She closed the door, sat on the edge of the bed and picked up the phone from the nightstand.

A sudden wave of nervousness made her fingers shake as she punched in the numbers, but she forced herself to complete the call and press the receiver to her ear.

He answered on the first ring. "Graham Richards."

She swallowed, almost losing her courage. God, maybe she should just hang up and tell everyone he'd had to cancel. That he'd had a family emergency. Or had come down with a sudden case of food poisoning.

But no.

Now that she'd started this snowball rolling, she realized, she wanted him to show up. She *wanted* to send a clear message to her parents that she didn't need their mercenary matchmaking.

"Graham," she said, "it's Serena."

"Serena." His voice conveyed no surprise, no pleasure, no relief—no anything at hearing from her.

Well, what had she expected? she asked herself. For him to sing out with joy?

"Listen," she began, ignoring the part of herself that felt irrationally disappointed, "I, um, need to talk to you about something. Not the, ah, something we..." She broke off as the door swung open and Cassandra glided into the guest room.

Cassandra offered no explanation for her presence, just gave a jaunty little wave and motioned for her to continue talking.

Serena couldn't believe the woman. Frantically she searched her mind for something to say—some way of getting Graham to understand she needed him here without raising her stepmother's suspicions as to what was really going on. She wasn't good at this kind of deception but she had to make her best effort.

"Um, where are you?" she said.

"At my hotel."

"No, I mean—where *are* you? I thought you were supposed to meet me here a few minutes ago."

There was a long pause on the line.

Across the room, Cassandra raised her eyebrows.

Serena felt even more determined to evade her stepmother's overbearing manipulations.

"Something's going on," Graham commented.

"You bet," she said into the phone. "And I understand completely. You got caught up in your work and forgot all about the time."

"Are you in some kind of trouble?"

"Uh-huh." Maybe it wasn't a life-or-death emergency, she told herself, but it was definitely trouble.

"Where?" he asked.

"Cassandra will be serving dinner soon," she said by way of an answer. "And I'm sure my father's dying to meet you. How soon can you make it?"

More silence. Serena put her hand behind her back and crossed her fingers, desperately hoping he would come through for her.

"Where do they live?" Graham asked.

She gave a lighthearted laugh, barely able to contain her relief. "You need the address *again?* Okay, but write it down this time, all right?" She gave it to him. "Will you be able to remember the directions I gave you earlier, or do you want me to repeat them?"

"Not necessary. I've been to that neighborhood before."

"Well, all right then. The drive shouldn't take you more than twelve minutes."

"I'll be there in ten," he said.

"That's great."

"And Serena?"

"Yes?"

"I'm going to want a really good explanation."

"Oh, you'll get that. And mashed potatoes and gravy to go with it."

Chapter Six

Serena placed the telephone receiver on its cradle. She met her stepmother's gaze across the guest room. "Yes?"

Cassandra's poise seemed momentarily to desert her. "Oh, well, I—I wanted to tell your, er, boyfriend not to bother to bring anything to dinner."

It was clearly a pretext to enable her to listen in. And a remarkably flimsy one, too, Serena thought.

"Then why didn't you do so before I hung up?" she asked.

Cassandra stammered ineffectually.

"Don't worry," she interrupted, "I'm sure he forgot to pick something up, anyway." She passed Cassandra near the doorway and started toward the drawing room. "He gets so involved in his work sometimes, the rest of the world just ceases to exist."

"And what kind of work would that be?"

"Oh, you know." Serena waved a hand in the air. "Business stuff."

About two dozen businesses, actually. Graham had his fingers in a lot of different pies. Since he'd shown up in her life again, Serena had read the business magazine articles about him.

Her stepmother trailed after her. "I have to say, Serena, your father and I are very surprised by all this."

"I'm sorry I forgot to tell you sooner." Her tone was blithe. "It was careless and inconsiderate. But of course, you don't mind unexpected guests, right? So it's not as if it's the end of the world."

Serena wondered where her words were coming from. But instead of feeling ashamed she felt...gleeful. This had probably been coming for a long time, she realized.

They entered the drawing room. The first thing Serena saw was her father's glowering face. Bob also looked a bit put out, and Mr. and Mrs. Bennington's features were decidedly tense.

Serena's glee deflated a bit. She wondered if she would really be able to handle them. She hoped Graham arrived as soon as he'd indicated.

"Well," Cassandra said with an excruciatingly gracious smile. "It appears we'll be able to sit down to eat in another twenty minutes or so. I'll go tell Mandy about our surprise guest...."

GRAHAM PARKED his rental car on the street outside the Jones residence exactly ten minutes after hanging up his cell phone. He'd been out the door of his suite the moment he'd realized Serena needed him and reached the hotel lobby by the time they'd ended their conversation.

He wasn't quite sure why he'd been so willing to drop everything and rush to her assistance....

Except, of course, that she *was* the mother of his child, he reminded himself. That should be reason enough, shouldn't it?

He got out of the car and strode to the front door of the big white house, carrying the bottle of wine the concierge had obtained for him in thirty seconds flat.

The facade of the house, he noted dispassionately, was halfway between being tasteful and being pretentious. Too many columns and curlicues, though it was all very well maintained. From Serena's description of them in May, he thought it probably matched her father and stepmother pretty closely.

Graham climbed the front steps and rang the bell. A woman in a starchy black and white uniform answered the door a few seconds later. He identified himself and she led him across the tiled entrance hall and around the corner to the living room.

"Graham!" Serena rushed forward as he stepped through the arched doorway.

"Hello, Serena."

She looked so glad to see him it almost made his heart stop. For a fraction of an instant he felt as if there truly were a bond between them, as if they were an intimate, loving couple.

His gaze drank in the sight of her. She wore a cream silk maternity dress that showed off her figure to advantage. She glowed with vitality.

Before this week he'd never stopped to consider whether pregnant women were attractive. The whole idea had been so removed from his life that it had never crossed his horizon.

But now...

Well, now he was damned sure that pregnant women were indeed attractive.

"Graham," she said again, rising on tiptoes to kiss his cheek. Her round belly brushed against him in the process. "I'm so glad you're here. Come meet my parents and their friends." She tucked her arm through his, leading him into the room.

The contact, simple as it was, did something to his chest. Made it feel constricted, and made his heart feel like it was beating too fast. They'd hardly touched the other night. And he'd been thinking about touching her for so many damned months....

Reality returned as soon as he focused on the room's other occupants. He could only assume these people were the reason Serena was so glad to see him—the reason she'd called him at all. He was only here to help her deal with them.

He wondered precisely what that would entail....

SERENA HID her frustration as she performed the introductions. Bob had disappeared to the rest room a moment ago, but she went through her parents and Mr. and Mrs. Bennington.

She'd *hoped* for a minute alone with Graham, a chance to give him the lowdown before they had to face everyone. At least a moment to agree on basic details.

But Cassandra had made that impossible, hovering by her side as soon as she'd returned from the kitchen. Serena had known that if she tried to wait for Graham outside, her stepmother would probably follow her—just as she'd followed her into the guest room to make her call.

Graham, of course, being Graham, took everything in stride, anyway, assessing the situation and remaining calm and composed when Serena made a point of introducing him as her new boyfriend. He shook hands with everyone and presented Cassandra with a bottle of wine—which he really shouldn't have been able to produce on such short notice, Serena thought.

Her father handed Graham a cocktail and ordered him to take a seat.

Serena sat beside him on the sofa, close enough to be convincing as his girlfriend, but not touching.

Harrison narrowed his eyes, sizing Graham up. If he was impressed by Graham's tailored suit and tie, he didn't bother to show it. "She hasn't introduced you to us before, has she? For some reason your face is familiar to me. But I can't place it."

"You haven't met him before, Dad. Graham and I haven't known each other very long."

"I hope not," he said, his voice becoming an aggressive growl. "Because if he's the little weasel who got you pregnant I'll make sure you're married by the end of the day, Thanksgiving or no Thanksgiving."

Serena cringed at her father's lack of tact. She hadn't expected it to be so extreme, especially because the Benningtons were here.

But then, he had *that* whole family under his thumb, didn't he? He could get away with anything in front of them. They were too busy trying to curry his favor to care if he acted obnoxiously.

"I'm sure than won't be necessary," Graham replied smoothly. "Serena invited me here as a dinner guest, not a future bridegroom." He smiled at her. "Isn't that right, Serena?"

"Uh, right."

"In fact, I'm sure marriage is the furthest thing from our minds at this point."

"Definitely."

Her father eyed them impatiently, as if he knew he was missing something about their interchange. "When you're a guest in someone's house," he broke in, "the least you can do is make sure the hostess knows you're coming. You've sent Cassandra into a fit with trying to figure out how to set another place. They even had to put an extra leaf in the table."

Graham inclined his head. "I apologize for the inconvenience."

"Fine, then. So tell me what you do for a living, Graham."

"Dad," Serena said. "He's just here for dinner. He doesn't need the third degree."

He shot her a quelling look. "If this man is important enough to you that you'll bring him to Thanksgiving dinner, then I have a right to be concerned. I want to make sure he's legitimate, that he's not just after our money."

Serena had to stifle a laugh.

It was ludicrous that someone would actually think Graham Richards, the ultimate self-made billionaire, corporate genius and sometime venture capitalist, could be a gold digger. And it was ludicrous to think she wouldn't spot a gold digger on her own.

Graham didn't laugh, however. He gave her father a blank stare. "Money is not the only reason a man might want to marry your daughter."

No, Serena thought. There was always the reason of making a baby together, though that wasn't a good enough one for her to take the plunge. And someday some different man might actually *want* to marry her—because he loved her.

"As for what I do," Graham continued, "well, I simply do whatever I please. Recently I've been moving around a great deal—Tokyo, Madrid, London."

Serena didn't know whether to be amused or annoyed at the picture of capricious, unfocused drifting he portrayed. It was the furthest thing from the truth, but it was also probably factually correct.

Just then Bob returned from the bathroom. He stopped in his tracks when he caught sight of Graham. "Oh, my God," he said.

No one paid him any attention.

Serena's father said, "Hmmph. Sounds like an unstable life-style."

Bob said, "He looks like…"

"And you should have shaved," Harrison admonished.

Serena glared at her father. It was a five o'clock shadow that dotted Graham's cheeks, nothing outrageously scruffy.

Bob stepped closer to the sofa. "Has anyone ever told you you bear an uncanny resemblance to Graham Richards of Richards Enterprises?"

"No," Graham said simply.

Bob shook his head. "Strange. I mean, I've only seen him in photographs, but he looks just like you. That is, you look just like him. No one's mentioned this before?"

"No."

"Oh, for heaven's sake," Serena said, butting in. "He *is* Graham Richards. The head of Richards Enterprises. He's a billionaire. So what. Big deal. I'm pregnant and I'm hungry and I would like to have some dinner. Now."

"Do you need anything, Graham? Salt, pepper? Cranberry sauce? More wine? Water? A few more slices of turkey?"

Cassandra was laying it on a bit thick, Serena thought. But then, the whole evening had gone haywire when she'd announced Graham's identity.

She should have expected this to happen. Graham was well known in certain business circles, even if he wasn't as famous as Bill Gates. It wasn't surprising, in a group their size, that someone would recognize him.

And once they'd done so...

Even her father had jumped on the bandwagon to flatter and fawn over him. He'd asked tons of awestruck questions, gushed about one or another of Graham's recent business ventures and made repeated comments about what an honor it was to have him in their home. His previous rude treatment had completely disappeared.

As for Cassandra, she played the role of attentive hostess to perfection, entertaining him as if he were visiting royalty.

Serena wanted to puke.

The only thing that appeased her was the fact that Graham did not seem particularly impressed by everyone's obsequious behavior. He responded to questions as briefly as possible and continually directed the conversation away from himself.

Cassandra had allowed them to sit next to each other, placing Bob on the other side of Serena and his parents opposite them.

Serena was amazed her father hadn't offered Graham the head of the table.

Around the time the pumpkin pie and ice cream were served, the topic finally rolled around to Serena and Graham's supposed relationship.

"Imagine my surprise," Harrison said. "Serena's never brought home anyone before, and then suddenly she shows up with someone of *your* stature."

Good grief, Serena thought. How much more pompous could he get?

"You never did say how long you've been dating," Cassandra remarked. She gave them a questioning smile.

"Oh, just a few weeks," Serena said quickly.

Graham nodded.

"And you really don't mind that Serena's, well, in her condition?" Cassandra said. "That's unusual—and so very charming."

Serena darted a quick glance at Bob, who looked a bit glum as he stared deeply into his pie. He had been the least effusive tonight. No doubt his fascination with Graham was balanced by the fact that he'd lost his already questionable status as her likeliest husband candidate—and her father's favorite pet.

"Of course I don't mind," Graham was saying. "Why should I?"

"Well, er, there *will* be a baby in the picture soon," Cassandra said as delicately as she could.

Graham shrugged. "If the baby takes after her mother I'm sure I'll adore her."

"It might be a boy, you know." Serena felt the need to point this out.

"Mmm. Then I'll adore him, as well."

"Babies are hard to resist, aren't they?" Mrs. Bennington said with a smile. Her features grew wistful. "I remember Bob's first year...."

Serena's eyes widened. Bob's mother hardly ever spoke, and it was never about anything personal. Usually she was one of those seen-and-not-heard wives. Quiet and demure, and always passing the salt and pepper before anyone even asked for it.

The kind of wife I'd probably be, she thought, *if I'd married Bob.*

It wasn't Bob's fault. Not exactly. It was just that he so unquestioningly wanted to follow in their parents' footsteps, while Serena wanted to live her life differently. Deep inside she'd always known that, even when she'd still been a mouse.

The conversation revolved around babies in general for a while before returning to Serena and Graham. Her father tried, she thought, to hide his dissatisfaction with her unwed state, but he didn't completely succeed.

"We would have preferred her to have a husband before getting pregnant," he said. "That just seems like the right way to do it." He sighed and lifted his demitasse cup of strong after-dinner coffee. "But some little weasel took advantage of my daughter."

"Dad, it wasn't like that."

"So you keep saying. But I say that if it wasn't, he would have taken responsibility for his child."

Graham raised an eyebrow. "Even if, for example, she neglected to inform the man of his paternity?"

Serena felt her hackles rise. She didn't want to get into this at the dinner table. "I've explained my reasoning," she said, her voice cool.

"Perhaps you should have more faith in men," Graham suggested.

"It's not a question of faith. I simply want the best for my child."

"Which is?"

"I want her to live in a loving household. The only way to guarantee that is to have a household of only two. Me and my child."

Cassandra gave a false, overly cheerful laugh, glancing around the table. "Well, dear, but there are no guarantees in life, are there?" She appeared confused and disturbed by the tension that had developed between Serena and Graham—and anxious to smooth things over. "You might just find the perfect stepfather for your child someday, Serena. Perhaps you'll realize a family of three can be even more stable than two."

I wonder who that perfect stepfather might be, Serena thought. *A certain someone sitting at this very table, perhaps?*

"Every child needs a father," Harrison said gruffly.

Bob took a long gulp of coffee.

Serena realized, then, what she'd done. She only intended to stop her parents from throwing her together with Bob. But, in doing that, she'd given them a new, infinitely more ambitious goal—to marry her off to a billionaire. Oh, heaven help her.

The evening was a total disaster.

Her father insisted they retire to his study for some brandy and cigars. Graham politely suggested the smoke might not be the best thing for the baby, so they settled on brandy alone.

Graham helped her out of her chair, continuing to act like her boyfriend.

Serena wanted him to stop. She felt aggravated, and all she wanted was for this evening to end.

Unfortunately, if she acted coolly toward Graham, her parents would no doubt try even harder to patch things up between them. They were most likely to feel content and leave her alone if she resumed the performance she'd given earlier—that of his sappy sweetheart.

Sure, she told herself, they would probably be obsessed for a while with getting her and Graham hitched. But eventually they would have to face the futility of it, wouldn't they?

For now she just needed to get through the rest of the night.

They filed into her father's study and took seats near the large fireplace. She sat beside Graham on the sofa, with Mr. Bennington on the other side of him.

Graham declined her father's offer of brandy, as did Serena. "I do have to drive home after this," he said. "And you were very generous with the wine this evening."

"Well, thank you for providing some of it," Cassandra said with a tinkling laugh. "So charming of you. And such a perfect selection to go with the bird."

Graham's comment reminded Serena that she'd locked her handbag and keys in her car. Great. It looked as if she would have to leave with Graham or risk a lot of irritating questions from the others. "Speaking of driving home," she said to Graham, "I guess I'll have to catch a ride with you." She told him what had happened.

"I'd be happy to take you to your condo," he said.

"It'll be nice for the two of you to have a private moment," Cassandra remarked with a benevolent smile. She looked thrilled with the idea. She looked as if she hoped an engagement would begin that very night.

Dream on, Serena thought.

Twenty minutes later they were finally out the door. Graham thanked her parents for their hospitality and bore their excessive good wishes with bland patience. He led her to a gray Lexus and politely handed her in. Without needing directions he headed toward her condo, which was only a short drive away.

She knew it was time for her to thank him for coming tonight.

Unfortunately, she felt distinctly ungrateful at the moment.

Leaning her head against the headrest, she closed her eyes, completely worn out.

And she wasn't just unhappy with Graham. She was unhappy with herself, as well. She regretted her behavior, regretted involving Graham in her family problems.

Instead of instigating their little charade, she should have found a way to assert herself firmly and directly—like she'd done several months ago when she'd told her parents she wouldn't put her baby up for adoption.

But she'd been so mad. And the Benningtons had already been there, and it had been too late to get rid of them—and she *hadn't* wanted to have to assert herself against a united group of five.

She could see why she'd done what she'd done. But she still should have resisted the temptation.

It seemed as if she'd taken two steps forward and one step back in her personal growth. But maybe tonight *was* still progress of a sort—and not a real step back. A year ago she would have sat miserably through the situation her father and Cassandra had orchestrated, doing nothing to resist it.

At least she was no longer being so hopelessly passive all the time.

She did have some inner fire, even if it had gotten a bit misdirected tonight....

"You're smiling," Graham remarked.

Her eyes snapped open. "Am I?"

"Feeling better now that you're out of their house?"

She glanced at him, expecting a wry expression on his face, but it wasn't there. Even his humor, she thought, was completely deadpan.

"I'm feeling better because I'll be asleep in bed in less than fifteen minutes," she said. "When you're pregnant and tired, the thought of bed can be Nirvana."

"Mmm."

The interior of the car was silent again. She

could hear a car honk in the distance, and an engine accelerating.

It was only nine-thirty or so, but it felt much later. Most people were in their homes, winding up their Thanksgiving holiday.

"I suppose I owe you my deepest gratitude." She forced herself to admit it.

He shrugged, letting the wheel slide under his fingers as they came out of a turn.

"It was great of you to come over tonight, and to go along with everything." She grimaced. "Sorry my father was such a beast at first."

"No problem," he said.

"And I'm sorry everyone became such simpering fools when they found out who you are. But I guess you're used to that kind of thing, aren't you?"

"Not particularly."

She groaned at the memory of it. "It was embarrassing."

"Don't worry about it," he advised.

They drove another block. At the end of it they paused briefly for a brightly lit city bus, empty but for a single passenger, to clear the intersection before they continued on their way.

She glanced around the rental car and said, "So, couldn't you have gotten, like, a Lamborghini or something? Or a Rolls and chauffeur?"

"You don't like the car?"

"No, it's fine. It just doesn't seem very billion-aire-ish. I'm sure Cassandra was disappointed when she saw us climb into it. Maybe she'll think you're an imposter, not really the illustrious Graham Richards of Richards Enterprises. Then all of her and Dad's hopes for my future would be brutally crushed."

He tilted his head to look at her. "Are you getting punchy, Serena?"

"Uh-huh. And you'd better watch out," she warned carelessly, "or I'll start berating you for those pointed comments you made over dessert."

"Hmm?"

She leaned against the headrest again. "You know what I'm talking about. I was pretty peeved about what you said, too."

He paused while he made the turn onto her street. "Was it because I said those things in front of the others," he asked, "or because I said them at all?"

"Both."

"I can't apologize for everything I said, Serena, but I shouldn't have spoken that way in front of your parents and their friends. I'm sorry." He pulled up outside her condo building, a converted four-story mansion, and cut the engine. "Forgive me?"

She glanced at him. The light from a nearby streetlamp illuminated his features, making them look even more chiseled. His short, dark hair was thick and surprisingly lustrous—and simply seemed to beg for a woman to run her fingers through it.

Lord, she thought, but he was handsome. How was she supposed to resist a man like this?

She turned her head and looked out the window. "Maybe," she said, not wanting him to figure out how easily he could distract her from being vexed with him.

"I guess that will have to do," he said, unperturbed and unruffled.

He helped her out of the car and accompanied her into the lobby.

From 8.00 p.m. to 8.00 a.m. the security door automatically locked, blocking access to the elevator. They walked to the panel of buttons for each of the units, and Serena reached for hers.

She pressed the button and waited.

Nothing happened.

Several seconds went by.

Meg wasn't home.

Chapter Seven

Forty-five minutes later Graham ushered Serena into his hotel suite.

He'd tried to find an open restaurant, but even the one downstairs had closed early.

Serena took off her coat and hung it over the back of a chair. She sat on the sofa, looking uncomfortable.

Graham shrugged out of his coat and hung it in the closet by the door.

The layout of the suite was reversed from the one he'd had in May, but other than that the spaces were identical. The same beautiful furniture, the same drapes at the windows.

Memories from May permeated the place.

He remembered the way she'd kicked the door closed behind them. Her body had been hot in his arms. They'd both been about to explode with the force of their desire for each other.

But not tonight. Now he and Serena were different. They had a baby between them, and things had gotten difficult. But he still wanted her.

"So," he said, "how long has Bob been after you?"

"Years."

He'd promised that he would extract an explanation from her of his presence at dinner, but such an explanation was completely unnecessary. Her family was not very subtle. "And you've never been interested? Even though your parents approve?"

"No. It's funny. My father was worried about you being after my money, but marrying me would secure Bob a piece of the company."

He sat on the couch beside her. "You don't think he likes you for yourself?"

"He doesn't even know me. Not the real me."

But I do, Graham thought. He had made love to the real Serena in a hotel suite just like the one they were in. He knew her passion and had also seen the inhibited side of her, the person she didn't want to keep on being.

"It's a good thing you won't end up married to him," Graham said.

"Yeah."

He checked his watch. "If Meg doesn't come home you can stay the night here."

"She'll be home."

"I can have an extra bed sent up."

"She'll be home."

They sat for a moment without saying anything. He wondered where the awkwardness had come from between them. At the reception they had talked so easily with each other.

He got up and fixed them both glasses of sparkling water from the refrigerator in the bar. When he came back she had turned on the television and was flipping through the channels.

Serena had hoped to find something interesting to watch to distract herself from her thoughts about Graham, but nothing on any of the fifty-six available channels held her interest for more than a few seconds. She got up, restless, and walked to the windows.

The hotel was on the hill above downtown. From the suite Serena could look out at the tall office buildings of the financial district. Between them she could see the lights on the span of the Bay Bridge. In the distance the East Bay hills were painted with the glow of houses and streetlamps.

She felt Graham rise and cross the room to stand near her. "Tell me about the last six months," he said. "About the baby."

Serena thought for a long moment before answering. So much of the past months had been about the baby, but not those first few weeks. In the days after she'd fled Graham's hotel room he had been on her mind constantly. She'd been overwhelmed by the remembered sensations of their lovemaking. It had made her feel flushed just to think about it.

The way she had responded to his caresses... The way all her inhibitions had just dropped away like her discarded clothes... She had felt like a different person.

Thinking about him, she'd felt an incredible craving to experience those sensations again. The temptation to want to have an affair with him was strong—even though it went against her principles. But there was no way she could have called him up to suggest such a thing, even if he hadn't been overseas. It would have been far too embarrassing.

And then, of course, she'd realized she was pregnant. That had changed everything. She couldn't possibly call him after learning that.

Graham was still waiting for her to speak.

"It's been...interesting," she began. "A big change."

"Did you have much morning sickness?"

"A little. It wasn't too bad. I was working mostly afternoons, so I was usually okay by the time I left the house."

She had spent a lot of time wondering what her

baby would look like and how he or she would behave. How much of Graham would the child have, and which traits? His sexy smile, his strong face, his mesmerizing eyes? She had sometimes wished it were possible for the child to have a father. But that pretty much meant that Graham would have to be a different person.

Because he seemed interested, Serena told Graham about the stages of her pregnancy, her appointments with the doctor, her first ultrasound.

He listened to her, attentive, and she looked at him and felt a momentary weakness. Would it be so awful to let herself have another chance with him, to let things go where they might?

Serena stopped talking.

They were staring at each other. Graham's eyes were dark in the dimly lit room. His gaze seemed to be fixed on her mouth, and she wondered whether he'd been having the same kind of thoughts she'd been having.

Without consciously meaning to, she licked her lips. She wanted him to kiss her. She couldn't help wanting it. At her parents' house it had felt so good to kiss his cheek and link her arm through his when he'd arrived, even though it was all an act. His body was so strong and so solid and so warm. And being next to him—it was like dancing with him

at the wedding reception. It felt sexy and dangerous. An adventure.

"Serena," Graham said.

Then he kissed her. His head descended, and she
couldn't have turned away even if she'd wanted to.
Desire drew them together. It was stronger than
common sense.

His lips were incredible. She flashed to their first
kiss in his suite in May. It had been all hunger and
desperation, the first step toward inevitable lovemaking. Even now she felt her body begin to yearn
for him. To want him to do more than just kiss
her. Far more.

With that came a sense of panic. A you-don't-
know-this-man kind of panic. And a fear of herself
and what might be unleashed. What had been unleashed the last time.

She resisted the feelings. *It's just a kiss,* she told
herself. *I'm not in danger from a kiss, especially
one that feels as incredible as this one does.* And
it was an unbelievably erotic kiss. Graham's lips
and tongue seemed to ignite her, and the kiss went
on and on.

He put his hand on her ribs, just below the curve
of her breast. She felt her breasts swell and her
arousal build. She wanted him to touch her there,
now.

And that realization changed everything. Because she *was* in danger from this kiss. This kiss wasn't going to end anywhere but in bed unless she stopped it right away. And if they ended up in bed things were going to be bad for her. She had to keep at least a vestige of control over the situation, over herself.

"No," she said, pulling back. "I can't do this."

Graham released her. He looked at her with eyes that were intense with interrupted passion.

Neither of them said anything for what seemed like a very long time. Serena tugged at her dress to straighten it. She rubbed the back of her hand across her tender lips.

"Why not?" Graham asked.

"Because I can't."

Common sense had returned in full force. They had too much between them to indulge themselves like this. *She* had too much at stake to indulge *herself*. She didn't know what to do about Graham's presence in her life, but she knew that sleeping with him wouldn't solve anything. It would probably just make things more difficult than they already were. By his own admission he didn't want to be a parent. She couldn't afford to have a man like that in her life. In her child's life. No matter how charming and magnetic and powerful he was.

"Serena, you weren't an unwilling participant in that kiss."

"I know. But I'm not ready for this. I—"

The phone rang.

Graham scowled at it, but answered it. "For you," he said a moment later.

It was Meg. She'd just arrived at the condo. Serena gathered her coat from the back of the chair.

"We still have a lot to talk about," Graham said.

"Tomorrow," Serena said. "Or over the weekend."

"Tomorrow. I'll make some time in the afternoon. Does that work for you?"

"Yes."

"Somewhere outside, I think. Safer that way."

"Okay."

"Serena?"

"Hmm?"

"We'll find a way to make this work."

MEG DROVE Serena to her parents' house on Friday morning so she could pick up her car. It was just a quick trip, but when they returned to the condo a large vase of purple orchids awaited Serena in the outer lobby.

"Hmm. I wonder who those could be from," Meg said, grinning. She'd arrived just a few seconds ahead of Serena.

Serena opened the card and read Graham's writing. *To working things out...*

Laconic and understated. As usual.

Meg was watching her. "Well? What did he say?"

She stuffed the card into her handbag and picked up the vase. "Not much. No declaration of love or anything."

"Is that what you were hoping for?"

"I'm not that foolish."

In the elevator Meg admired the bouquet. "They're beautiful," she said. "They smell divine. And they go with our color scheme."

"I noticed."

"Think he did that on purpose?"

"Wouldn't surprise me," Serena said.

The man was very observant. And he had impeccable taste in flowers—not that she was impressed, she assured herself.

Serena stared at the delicate purple flowers. With a finger she touched one smooth petal, marveling at its silkiness.

They reached their floor.

"Where are you going to put the orchids?" Meg asked as they entered the condo.

Serena walked to a vase of the flowers they'd bought the other day, sitting on a side table in the living room. "Maybe I'll put them in with these."

"Are you crazy? No, I can't allow that. You'd ruin the effect of his bouquet."

"But I thought you liked to mix and match stuff."

"Not when you've got a dozen stems of the most beautiful, most exotic orchids on the planet. Here, how about the coffee table?"

Meg took the orchids from Serena and set them on the coffee table, making a few slight adjustments to the arrangement and standing back to admire it.

"Now that your billionaire's back in the picture I suppose you'll be receiving flowers on a regular basis—and extravagant gifts for the baby, too."

"I hope not."

"And why's that?"

Serena shrugged. Graham had plenty of money to throw around, but if he thought it would influence her attitude toward him he was in for a surprise. "I don't want to be bought," she said. "And I don't want my child to be bought, either. Money's okay when it makes your life more comfortable. But it's not a substitute for love."

"I agree," Meg said, giving her a thoughtful look.

Serena wasn't sure Graham could offer anything *but* money—not after what he'd told her last spring. And she didn't want their child to be hurt by his emotional detachment. It made her afraid to let him into her baby's life.

GRAHAM ARRIVED in the early afternoon for their talk. The weather was perfect for a trip to the beach. Serena had insisted on driving, but since they would be going in the opposite direction from his hotel he'd offered to meet her at the condo.

Serena opened the door and stared at him.

He looked like a different person. She'd never seen him in anything but a suit. Now he wore jeans and casual brown shoes, and a texturized, charcoal heather cotton sweater.

He definitely looked younger. And extremely attractive. In business attire he looked devastatingly handsome and powerful, but like this he seemed more approachable, more accessible. Less detached and remote.

Like a real, flesh-and-blood human being.

It triggered a sense of yearning inside her. She wanted to feel his arms around her again and wrap her arms around him. And she wanted one thing to lead to another, just like things had threatened to last night.

Crazy.

And *not okay*. She had to learn to control her physical responses to him, no matter what. Even if he showed up wearing nothing but a fig leaf.

She swallowed. "Hi, come on in. I just need to get my shoes."

Leaving him in the living room, she went to her room and got a pair of canvas sneakers. She wore jeans, but they were a maternity style with a lot of elastic at the waist. On the way out the door she grabbed her oversize windbreaker from the hall closet.

A few minutes later they were belted into her blue Volvo and pulling out of the driveway.

She remembered to thank him for the orchids. They talked about innocuous subjects while she drove down the hill and out of Pacific Heights.

The day was exceptionally clear, with a bright blue sky and fresh, cool air coming in through the open car windows. They passed a row of old Victorian houses painted in charming pastels, then turned west onto Kennedy Drive, which wound through Golden Gate Park to the ocean.

On days like this Serena couldn't imagine living anywhere else on earth. She had never traveled much, but she still felt that San Francisco was her true home. She wouldn't be happy living anywhere else.

The subject made her wonder about Graham. And where he'd grown up. She felt overwhelmingly curious to learn more about him. She didn't want to feel that way, but she couldn't help it. And it couldn't hurt to ask a *few* questions.

"Have you lived in New York all your life?" she said when they'd almost reached the beach.

"No."

"When did you move there?"

She slowed the car for a red light where Kennedy Drive met the Great Highway. Ahead of them lay the Pacific Ocean. Gentle swells rolled toward the shore, and the wind kicked up an occasional whitecap.

"About twenty years ago," he said.

"So that's where you and Elaine lived together?"

"Mmm."

He wasn't the most forthcoming person when it came to personal information, she thought. She remembered their interactions at Dirk and Elaine's wedding reception. He'd been a little more open then, but it was only after she'd prodded him.

"Twenty years," she said. "So, Graham, where did you live before that?" When he didn't answer, she glanced at him in the passenger seat.

He sat watching her with his elbow resting at the open window, his right hand raised to the side of his face, two fingers pressed against his temple. A sexy, contemplative pose.

Ignore it, she ordered herself. *Don't let yourself*

dwell on your attraction to him. That will get you precisely nowhere, and you've got to keep a clear head.

The light changed and she drove on, turning north toward the Cliff House.

"Do we have to discuss this?" he asked after a long pause.

"You're my baby's father, as you've taken pains to point out. Don't you think I should know a *little* of your history? Anyway," she said, half teasing, "if you refuse to tell me yourself, I'll go to the library and look it up. I'm sure there's plenty of information on you."

"You do have a tenacious side, don't you?"

"That's right."

"Most of the information you'd find would be boring business details."

She gave an insouciant shrug. "I'll just dig a little deeper. Search the worldwide web. Maybe even hire a PI to check you out."

Graham raised an eyebrow. "My assistant asked me if I shouldn't have *you* checked out."

"Go right ahead. I have nothing to hide." She turned into the parking area, pulled into a spot and cut the engine. "Do you?"

She was teasing him, but Graham felt the tension in his body. Not that he did have something to hide—not in the sense she meant. But he never talked about his earlier years. He didn't want to relive them. As far as he was concerned they belonged in the past and were best forgotten.

If only he *could* forget them.

If only they didn't keep affecting the present.

Chapter Eight

Serena continued to watch him as they sat in her car, an inquiring expression on her face.

She was obviously a lot more comfortable prying into his past than discussing their present, he thought. Or their baby's future. Whenever those subjects came up she immediately closed down, but right now she was perfectly open and cheerful.

He forced himself to smile. "I'm not harboring any scandalous secrets, if that's what you're asking."

"Hmm..." She unfastened her seat belt.

Graham got out of the car and circled to help her, though she stepped out before he could reach her.

"What about the nonscandalous variety?" she asked, shutting the door.

They started toward the beach, which was separated from the parking area by a low cement wall.

On the ocean side the wall dropped a few yards to the sand, with steep staircases set at intervals. Sand had blown in small drifts over the bottom steps, but it wasn't too treacherous, so Graham resisted his urge to lend her a steadying arm. He did, however, walk slightly ahead of her to catch her if she tripped.

"Why don't you ask me what you want to know?" he suggested.

"All right. Where did you grow up?"

"A small town in Texas."

As they reached the beach she glanced at him, surprised. "But you don't have a drawl."

"I lost it real fast when I got to New York," he said.

"Oh. So you wouldn't be teased?"

"Mmm."

They crossed the soft, dry sand by the wall to the damp, harder packed sand near the low-breaking waves and started down the beach. Serena walked closest to the water, and the slope of the shore made her seem another inch shorter; the top of her head barely came to his chin.

"And you were, what—fourteen when you moved?" she asked.

"Right."

Though "moved" was hardly the word for it, he thought. He'd hitchhiked his way there, with nothing more than the shirt on his back and a few dollars he'd gotten from the pawnshop for the ten-speed bike his grandfather had gotten him before he died. It had taken Graham almost two months, and he'd gotten into some dangerous scrapes before getting there. Seventeen hundred miles was a long way for a boy that young to travel alone.

But he'd survived.

If his parents had taught him one thing, it was how to survive anything.

"Do your parents still live in New York?"

"No," he said. He could have told her they'd never lived there at all, but he didn't. Instead he said, "They died a long time ago."

"Oh... I'm sorry. I know how painful it can be when a parent dies." She gave him a sympathetic look.

Her sympathy was misplaced, but he couldn't make himself tell her the truth—that sadness and pain had not been a big part of his reaction. When he'd learned of their deaths in a drunk-driving accident—one they, of course, had caused—he'd hardly felt anything at all. Perhaps a slight sense of relief, and release, and the smallest bit of residual anger about all the things they'd done to him. And anger that they'd killed an innocent teenager in the accident. But no real sorrow or grief for them.

They hadn't deserved his grief, he'd told himself. They'd been irresponsible parents who never should have had a child in the first place. He was only glad they'd had the sense not to have any more children.

He and Serena reached a busier stretch of the beach, dotted with couples and teenagers and families, little children and senior citizens.

The wind was blowing, and although the sun shone it was still November, too chilly to take off their shoes—which was fine with Graham. But the thought made him realize he hadn't walked barefoot in the sand for years.

Would he do so again, though? Someday soon? Perhaps when their child learned to walk?

The idea of bringing their son or daughter here caused a strange sensation in his chest. Most of the time their child's physical being didn't seem real yet. Not even when he saw Serena's pregnant belly.

His brain didn't quite make the translation from her stomach to a live, separate human being.

But that was what they would soon have before them. In only a few short months.

It shouldn't have been so profound, but he felt as if his world were slowly turning upside down. The sound of the wind, of the waves crashing against the shore and a bird calling in the distance rushed in his ears.

They'd gone another fifty yards before he'd even begun to get hold of himself.

Serena glanced at him, her expression telling him she thought he'd been thinking about his parents' deaths the whole time. Her eyes were full of concern and empathy. As if she actually cared.

The woman he'd met in May hadn't been the type to go to bed with just anyone. There had been something between them that night. A connection that was more than just sexual. He caught a glimpse of it again.

Which made him wonder why she was working so hard to keep him at arm's length.

It seemed like a good moment to change the subject to the important one between them. "Why don't we talk about the baby?"

Instantly her expression changed. It was as if she'd withdrawn from him like a hermit crab retreating into its shell. And there was a discomfort in her eyes that looked almost like fear.

Vestiges of the old Serena, he thought. The one she'd told him about, who had been frightened by life, afraid of taking risks.

Some habits were hard to break.

"We'll need to work something out," he continued.

Serena turned her head away from him, staring toward the horizon. She sighed. "I wish we didn't have to go through this."

"Meaning you wish I hadn't found out about your pregnancy?"

She crossed her arms, still looking away. "I guess so. I don't know."

It wasn't what he wanted to hear, of course. He wanted her to regret that she hadn't told him months ago. But that wasn't where she was. And with the things he'd said in May…

Ahead of them on the beach a father and daughter were flying a kite together. Made in a bright and colorful butterfly design, the kite whipped and danced in the brisk breeze off the water. The man knelt beside his little girl, teaching her how to handle the line. They looked happy, as if they truly enjoyed being together.

The scene wasn't unusual, but it was totally foreign to Graham's childhood experiences. Seeing it so soon after his recent reflections, he was utterly captivated. He couldn't take his eyes off them.

They held the line together, father and daughter. Then the father said something in the girl's ear and released his hold. She held the line alone, and even from a distance Graham could see the look of exuberant pride on her face as she gripped the spool in her small hands. The man smiled at her with love and affection.

It was such a simple activity, Graham thought. Teaching your child to fly a kite.

But it was also much more.

Serena didn't think he would ever be able to establish that kind of connection with their child. And he understood her fears. Last May he'd painted a bleak picture of his abilities in the love and parenting department.

It was also true that if he did somehow fail as a father, she and the child would suffer for it.

But he wouldn't fail. Not if his son or daughter depended on him. Romantic love—the kind he'd never felt for Elaine—was one thing. But raising a child...

Well, he would never let a child feel the way he had when he was young. He would support, guide and encourage him or her. Teach and be there to listen when times got rough. He would do the right thing.

Serena broke the silence. "I'm starting to think some people aren't meant to be parents, Graham. And maybe you're one of them. If that's the case, then you shouldn't try to fight it. You should just accept it."

"I won't accept that. I'm going to be a parent no matter what."

"Biologically. But you don't have to be anything more," she reminded him.

How, he wondered, could she say that? And how could she be so clinical, so ultrarational about it? He wasn't a faceless sperm donor or some stallion put out to stud, dammit.

Women were supposed to be the emotional ones—so where was her emotion now?

Graham realized the irony of the situation. All his adult life he'd experienced himself as unemotional. And had been perceived that way, too. Now, when it came to his paternity, he experienced Serena that way.

And he didn't like it.

"You want to make that decision for me," he said. "You did make that decision when you opted not to tell me about your pregnancy."

The muscles around her mouth tightened. She didn't say anything.

"But that wasn't right, Serena. It's not your decision to make."

"It's my baby."

"Ours."

They'd been down this road before, he thought. And nothing seemed to have changed since the last time. The unusual experience they'd shared at Thanksgiving hadn't erased the deeper issues.

"All I can tell you," he continued, "is that I'm

not going to go away. That's something you'll have to accept, if nothing else.''

''And if I don't,'' she said, ''you can hire a whole army of lawyers to make me.''

''I wouldn't do that,'' he assured her.

She stopped walking and turned to face him. ''But what if I simply refused to compromise?'' she demanded, glaring at him. ''Would you be so calm and understated then, or would you give in to the need to bully me?''

Her sudden anger caught him off guard—and it made him realize how difficult it must be for her to face him. She was brave to stand up to him. He did have the power to bully her, if he so chose.

But he wouldn't. That would be a misuse of power. No, he would simply stick around until she changed her mind about him. He could be every bit as tenacious as she. He would wait her out, and eventually she would relent—without the use of force.

Somehow he would play a role in their child's life, a role that was good for all three of them.

Her expression changed, a flicker of something he couldn't identify passing over her features.

''What is it?'' he said.

She looked away. ''It's nothing.''

''Serena, tell me what it is.''

Her hands went to her stomach, cupping it.

"Is something wrong?" he asked. His insides lurched at the idea of danger for her or the baby. "Are you all right?"

"I'm fine." She sighed. "The baby just started to kick a lot, that's all."

That's all? He wanted to say. *Our baby is moving inside you and you tell me it's nothing?* "Just now?"

She nodded.

He felt a little light-headed. "Is this the first time?"

She shook her head, still not looking at him. "It started several weeks ago."

The wind lifted her honey-brown hair and blew a few strands across her cheek. He raised a hand and brushed them back, tucking them behind her ear.

Serena glanced at him, and their gazes held. He saw her eyes darken slightly, and it was like the night before. That sensual zing between them. Just touching her hair aroused him.

"I'd like to feel it," he said. He couldn't pretend not to be fascinated. "Let me?"

Slowly she nodded, as if she didn't really want to say yes but couldn't bring herself to say no. He moved to her side, placing one hand on her back and the other on the center of her belly.

"Show me where," he said.

She guided his hand to the lower left side—and then he felt it. A gentle, repeated fluttering sensation under his palm. Even through two layers of fabric he could feel it. Something primitive stirred inside him. God, he thought, that was their child in there.

In the past days he'd thought endlessly about parenthood. He'd dwelt on it and tossed it over in his mind. Until today nothing had crystallized.

But now, as he felt his child kick inside Serena's womb, the final pieces fell into place.

He did have fatherly feelings. Strong ones.

It was more than just a sense that he would be able to do the right thing, to raise his child properly. It was a sense that he could be a *real* father. A loving father. And it wasn't just a sense. It was bone-deep knowledge. He wanted to experience the kind of parent-child bond he'd seen between the man and girl with the kite. He wanted to be part of a continuum across the generations—to share and nurture and teach, and leave something behind when he was gone.

Those very feelings made him different from his parents, he realized. He doubted they'd been excited when he'd kicked in the womb. He'd been an accident, as they'd made sure to tell him—regretted as soon as he was conceived. He didn't think they'd ever looked forward to a single moment with him, ever thought their lives would be enriched by his presence. Or felt a need to make *his* life rich. They hadn't taught him to fly a kite, or to swim, or to ride that ten-speed bike from his grandfather.

They hadn't looked outside themselves long enough to do that. They'd been too busy partying, living it up, having a good time.

But he wasn't like his parents. He'd never valued personal enjoyment so much that nothing else registered in his awareness.

True, his attempt at romantic love with Elaine hadn't worked. But parental love was a different sort of phenomenon. And surely his response today, to feeling his baby's movements, showed he had more fatherly impulses than he or Serena had suspected.

He stared at his hand on her stomach, unable to speak. The fluttering had tapered off, yet he didn't pull away. He couldn't.

Serena was the one to end the contact, stepping back and forcing him to drop his hands. Her face registered discomfort. It must disturb her to share such an intimate moment with him, he thought. Especially when they hardly knew each other.

Abruptly she took off down the beach. He collected himself and went after her.

"Now you know what it's like when the baby kicks," she said when he caught up with her. She was trying to sound normal, casual, but didn't succeed. "It's not such a big deal, is it?"

They both knew it was a very big deal, but he didn't try to argue with her.

Instead he said, "I'm going to be around for the milestones, Serena. I don't want to miss out on the day our baby is born, or the first time he or she walks, or even the first time she gets an ear infection. I want to be there and I want to be a father to our child."

"You live in New York. What will you do, commute every week? I can't exactly make these meaningful little moments wait for the weekend so you can be there. What if the baby takes his or her first steps in the middle of the week?"

"I'm moving to San Francisco. I've already started the process."

She stared at him, eyes wide.

"So it's that easy? You can pick up and move from New York to San Francisco, just like that?"

"Yes."

Graham hadn't missed the critical edge in her tone. Though it would be better for their child for him to be in San Francisco, she seemed to think it should be harder for him to leave New York. That he should have stronger ties to a place he'd lived for most of his life.

He saw it through her eyes and he understood her concern. It made him seem indifferent, disconnected from his environment. He couldn't be that way and make a good father.

But he *wouldn't* be that way, not with his son or daughter, he vowed.

He slowed his steps and motioned the way they'd come. "Shall we head back?"

She nodded unhappily and turned. They walked north, retracing their footsteps in the sand.

"As I suggested the other night, the obvious way to raise our child is to get married and share a household. But since you won't agree to that, we'll have to set up some kind of schedule by the time the baby is born."

She didn't look at him. "For shared custody?"

"Visitation would be fine at first. I don't want to take her away from you when she's just a newborn."

"So it would be all three of us spending time together."

He smiled. "Would that be so awful?"

"I don't know, Graham," she said. "Do you even know how to take care of a baby?"

"No," he admitted. He hadn't spent much time

around babies during his thirty-four years of life. "But I'll learn how."

"I wouldn't want you just to hire a nanny to do everything."

"I'll take a class."

He would enjoy it, he thought. The idea of taking care of their child filled him with a sense of anticipation. Feedings and bath times and diaper changes—it all seemed more fascinating to him than the most intricate business deal.

Serena looked dubious. "The head of Richards Enterprises has time for that kind of thing? A run-of-the-mill baby-care class?"

"Yes."

The truth was, he had time for anything he wanted. He just hadn't taken it—not in the past. He hadn't had any reason to. But things had changed.

He could walk away from work any time he chose. Jake could take care of things. Graham no longer needed to devote all his energies to expanding his corporate empire. It was more than big enough.

And somehow none of that seemed to matter anymore—not as much as learning how to burp his baby after a meal.

"So you wouldn't hire a nanny?" Serena asked.

"I may hire one," he answered, "but only for backup. Not to be a primary caretaker."

She frowned and didn't speak for a moment. Then, almost grudgingly, she said, "I *was* planning on a small amount of day care next year. But not until I started school in September."

"School?" he repeated, surprised. She hadn't mentioned anything about school. And he knew she wasn't a student.

"I'm applying to some graduate programs."

Briefly she described her plans. She would only apply to universities in the Bay Area so she wouldn't have to relocate. Though she knew acceptance wasn't guaranteed, she felt very hopeful.

Her enthusiasm was obvious, and Graham thought it sounded like a great idea. "I'll take care of the baby while you're attending classes," he offered.

"The timing would be inconvenient. It would probably only be weekdays."

"No problem."

"It would be during your regular working hours," she said pointedly.

"Fine."

"Graham." She met his gaze. "Are you aware of what you'd be getting yourself into? What about your business? You wouldn't be able to look after the baby and get a lot of work done at the same time."

"Jake will handle business matters while I'm otherwise occupied. I've already been thinking about taking a bit of a breather the next few years."

She watched him for a long time before speaking, a faint frown creasing her brow. "Why? Why would you do that?"

"So I won't have to miss out on the formative years of our child's life. So I can be a good father."

She was reaching overload, he could tell. He knew her well enough to see the signs of stress around her eyes and mouth.

Time to back off for a while.

But they'd made progress, he thought. And someday soon he would get her to agree to having him around after the baby was born.

SERENA SAT on the sofa, applications spread before her on the coffee table, the vase of orchids pushed to one side. It was Saturday morning and she'd been there over an hour—ever since she'd given up on sleeping in.

She rubbed her tired eyes. "I would kill for a

cup of coffee right about now," she said to Meg, who was reading the paper in a nearby armchair.

"Me, too," Meg said.

They'd both decided to give up caffeine for the duration of their pregnancies. Most of the time they did all right without it, but Serena hadn't been able to sleep much lately and could have used the boost.

She was barely able to concentrate on her applications. Her thoughts kept drifting to her walk on the beach with Graham yesterday.

It had left her feeling bewildered and confused. Graham's attitude seemed to have undergone a subtle transformation since the night he'd come back, less than a week ago.

He still wanted her to respect his parental rights, but he hadn't talked about fulfilling obligations or dealing with consequences.

He hadn't seemed to be acting out of a dogged sense of duty.

Instead he'd truly seemed interested in their child and in being a real parent. He'd talked about the milestones of a baby's development—the same kinds of things she and Meg discussed.

And when the baby had kicked, he'd appeared to be deeply moved.

For her that had been an extremely unsettling moment. With Graham's large, solid hand cupping the curve of her abdomen, and their child moving inside her, she'd felt as if the three of them were going through the same experience. Almost as if they were sharing a tender moment of family togetherness.

But they weren't a family—not a real one. And she refused to let herself hope they could ever be.

Unfortunately, she saw no choice but to go along with Graham's plan for visitation and eventual shared custody. No matter what he'd said in May, he was obviously committed to his relationship with his child. If he didn't want to be involved he wouldn't have bothered to come to San Francisco. The fact that he had come, and hadn't left after her cool reception, boded well for his ability to stick it out. It wouldn't be right to deprive her child of a father, not unless he somehow demonstrated that he wasn't worthy of the role.

Having Graham present in her life was another issue altogether, though. Spending the next twenty years in close contact with him wouldn't be easy. She'd probably end up like Elaine had—in love with a man who couldn't love her back. Heck, she was probably already halfway there.

But she couldn't fool herself into thinking Graham's feelings might change. He was here because of the baby, *not* because of her. If she hadn't gotten pregnant she would never have seen him again.

The knowledge was starting to bother her. Part of her wanted his emotional investment and devotion to include *her.*

But she reminded herself that wishful thinking had gotten more than one woman into serious trouble in her relationships. She couldn't fall into that trap. She already knew she tended to try to get love from people who couldn't give it to her. To chase after the unattainable and glorify and romanticize—and overestimate—her feelings. Just look at her ridiculous crush on Dirk.

But the last several months had changed her, made her stronger and wiser—and she wouldn't let herself do that this time.

Meg folded her San Francisco *Chronicle* and tossed it onto the coffee table, covering some of Serena's papers. "You're obsessing about the situation with Graham again, aren't you?"

She nodded. "I can't help it."

"Maybe you should just relax for a while, see what happens. Go with the flow."

"Yeah, right. You sound like some kind of Haight Street hippy chick."

Meg grinned. "I do my best." She used the armrest to push herself to her feet. "Come on, let's go make some blueberry pancakes. If I can't have coffee right now I'd at least like a good breakfast.''

Serena gratefully accepted Meg's invitation, and they set to work on a big, elaborate meal to satisfy their pregnant selves. In addition to pancakes they cooked home fries and omelettes and bacon and toast.

Right before it was all ready, the doorbell rang. They looked at each other.

''You expecting anyone?'' Meg asked.

Serena shook her head. ''Mind getting it while I flip this omelette?''

Meg came back a couple of minutes later with a handsome Asian-American man in tow. Serena had heard the murmur of their voices by the door, and her curiosity had been growing.

The man carried several bags that appeared to be full of gifts.

''This is Jake,'' Meg said. ''Graham's assistant. He's staying for breakfast.''

Serena raised an eyebrow.

''If that's okay with you,'' Jake said, smiling.

He had a very nice smile, and Serena understood instantly why Meg had invited him to stay for a meal. Her roommate was obviously smitten. And if Jake had taken her up on the offer, he was probably interested, as well.

"Sure," she said. "There's plenty of food."

"That's what I was telling Jake, but he wouldn't believe me."

"It's true. We cooked enough for four pregnant women, not just two."

Jake set his bags down. "Then I'd love to stay. Is there anything I can do to help?"

"What's in the bags?" Serena asked.

"Things for the baby. From Graham."

"Here comes trouble," Meg murmured.

Chapter Nine

"I don't want your gifts."

Serena strode through the open doorway of the suite, past Graham and to the plush sofa, where she dumped her armload of packages and shopping bags. She glared at him over her shoulder.

Graham held his cell phone in his hand, the mouthpiece flipped out. He'd obviously been on the line when she'd pounded on his door. He brought the phone to his ear. "It's her. I have to go. Talk to the agent and get back to me." He hung up and set the thing on a table, then walked to her. "I'm sorry?"

It wasn't spoken as an apology, and Serena didn't take it that way.

She gestured at the jumble of items, all of which were still wrapped. "I don't want this stuff."

"How do you know?"

"What do you mean, how do I know? I just don't want any of it."

"You don't appear to have opened any of it," he commented.

"I don't have to. All I have to do is look at the pile and I can see twenty or thirty presents. That's too many. I don't want them."

"What's wrong with getting a few things for the baby?" he asked calmly.

"It's not a few things! That's the whole point." Turning away from him, she stalked around the elegant room.

She felt angry and irrational—probably more so than the situation warranted—but she didn't care.

And she couldn't have suppressed her feelings if she'd wanted to, anyway. They'd been stewing inside her all day, ever since Jake Woo's visit—until she'd finally tossed all the packages into her car and driven here.

"I don't want my child to be spoiled by extravagant gifts," she exclaimed.

Graham stood watching her, his arms crossed. "I'm the father. Is it such a big deal for me to get some clothes and blankets and baby supplies?"

"Yes!"

"Serena…it's not as if I bought the kid a yacht."

She wasn't amused. "We'll see what happens on his fourteenth birthday."

He raised an eyebrow but didn't respond. He was the same Graham Richards she'd met last May, implacable and aloof, she thought. It was almost worse than if he'd gotten mad. In a twisted way she felt disappointed.

Graham indicated a book lying open on the dining table. "That book contains a list of essentials for newborns. I didn't get anything that wasn't on it."

If he hadn't been so unbearably cool and collected when he said it, she might have forgiven him. But he was, and it only provoked her more.

"How do you know I haven't already gotten those things?" she demanded. "You should have checked with me first."

"If you already have something, we'll return it," he said simply.

"You bet we will." She paced some more. "*You* will." She corrected herself. "Not me and not your assistant, either. God, he's the one who bought all that stuff, isn't he? You didn't even bother to pick it out yourself."

"That's where you're wrong," Graham said.

She barely heard him. "I want my child to have a normal, healthy life. And you know what that means? Love from his or her parents. Not money or the material possessions it can buy. Love!''

Her father and Cassandra had provided her with plenty of money, and it had never made up for the lack of love. That was the thing they hadn't been able to give. The thing she'd craved more than anything else.

Would her child go through the same experience?

Not if she could help it!

''I was almost starting to wonder if you could be a good father,'' she blurted, the words tumbling out of her. ''But now I see that's ridiculous. A father has to be able to express his emotions directly—through affection and loving care. Not through buying everything in sight!''

''Serena—''

''Don't tell me I'm being too emotional. This is an emotional issue! And you know what? I'd rather be a raving, hysterical maniac than be like you. You're nothing but a—a big chunk of ice!''

Silence met her outburst.

Graham watched her from across the room, his face expressionless.

At that moment, and despite yesterday's evidence to the contrary, he seemed every bit as chilly and impenetrable as she'd accused him of being.

Yet she held her breath.

Ho, boy, she thought as reality rushed in on her.

She'd totally lost her temper. She'd yelled at him, and called him names, and it wasn't polite. It was rude and obnoxious. Just how much bad behavior, she wondered fleetingly, was Graham going to let her get away with?

Even as her mind formed the question, she saw a change in his eyes. Something fiery coming to life. All at once it was as if the air between them sizzled.

Serena felt her skin heat, the way it had when she sat too close to the fire pit at summer camp when she was nine. Blood pounded in her brain.

In the space of an instant the whole mood in the room shifted.

"A chunk of ice?" His voice was low and deceptively calm, but she could hear the difference in it. It had an angry, almost menacing undertone he couldn't hide. His lips curved in a mocking smile—mocking her or himself, she couldn't quite tell. He walked decisively toward her. "I'm inhuman, you think? No blood in my veins?"

Serena nodded without thinking, then quickly shook her head. She breathed again, but shallowly, as he moved inexorably closer.

He stopped a few inches from her protruding belly. She retreated a step until her back bumped into a wall. In her peripheral vision she saw Graham raise his arm and rest his hand on the wall, a few inches to the side of her head.

He leaned toward her. "A chunk of ice," he said, "would be a person who feels nothing." He raised his other arm and pulled her handbag from her shoulder. He dropped it to the floor and rested a second hand on the wall, on the other side of her.

She was trapped.

Graham said, "Not even desire…"

They didn't touch anywhere, but Serena felt his heat and his physical presence more intensely than she'd ever thought possible. She could smell his unmistakable personal scent, a mixture of soap and after-shave and sexy musk. Arousal simmered into being inside her, spreading throughout her body.

With someone else she might have felt physically threatened. Unsafe. But she knew Graham would never cause her bodily harm. He did seem sensually dangerous and explosive, but it didn't frighten her. Not really.

No, it excited her.

Her palms flattened against the wall behind her hips. *Oh, dear,* she thought, *why am I getting such a thrill out of this? Why do I want this to be happening?*

The next moment she forgot her dazed self-analysis when Graham brought his lips a mere inch from her own. She could feel his warm breath against her skin, and she felt so attracted to him she couldn't move.

She ached to do what they'd done six months ago.

And she suddenly, inexplicably, didn't care if it was wrong or unwise or inappropriate.

The emotional threat he posed to the rest of her life no longer mattered.

"Serena," he whispered. "I *do* feel desire. The most incredible, irresistible desire. For you. And you know that, don't you? You feel it, too."

She blinked heavily, feeling as if time had slowed down. A tiny, embarrassing moan escaped her throat. "Yes," she managed to say.

It seemed to be all the invitation he needed. His mouth caught hers, and they kissed urgently. They didn't touch anywhere else along their bodies, and the promise of more contact—the unbearable anticipation—only excited her. Their tongues explored each other's mouths and their lips left raw bruises.

It was even more exciting to be together than it had been in May. Six months had passed. They'd waited so long for this, pretended the attraction was no longer there. But they couldn't repress it.

It had to come out.

Now.

Graham cradled the nape of her neck in his

hand, angling her head so he could control his access. Without realizing she'd raised her arms, she felt herself fumbling with the buttons on his white dress shirt. One of the buttons popped off and flew across the room, but she barely noticed. She thrust aside the crisp fabric of his shirt and touched and stroked and kneaded his muscular chest.

His skin was so warm, his body so responsive to her every caress.

Not at all like a big chunk of ice would feel.

He drew his mouth slightly back from hers, and she heard him groan in a way that expressed both agony and pleasure. It filled her with gratification and pride in her own effect on him.

She felt greedy, aggressive, unapologetic as she traced her way to his nipples. Her fingertips brushed him lightly, eliciting another groan.

"God, Serena..."

Graham spun them around, still standing, so his back rested against the wall and her back was against his chest. She murmured a halfhearted protest but let him have his way. He slid his legs out so his torso was level with hers and his thighs gripped her legs. She had to kiss him over her shoulder but, surprisingly, the awkward position only made it seem more exciting. Her hands gripped his thighs, squeezing the powerful muscles there. Her bottom pressed into his erection, and she felt that part of him strain against her every time she made the smallest movement.

It felt naughty, daring. Just five minutes ago she'd had no idea they would be doing this. No idea she would give in to temptation this afternoon. But she couldn't have stopped for anything.

She simply had to have him.

Graham pulled the neckline of her shirt off her shoulder, along with her bra strap. He dropped a series of kisses down her neck and lightly bit her bared shoulder, then circled his tongue over the sensitized skin, soothing and inflaming it at the same time. He opened his lips against her, his mouth warm and wet, and applied a gentle suction that drove her completely wild.

"Graham..." It was almost a question, but it didn't ask anything. She didn't know why she spoke.

"Mmm." He kissed his way to the vulnerable spot right behind her ear.

The sensations made her shiver.

He paused, and she became aware of the labored sounds of their breathing. For a moment they were both utterly still. Time decelerated, ticking slowly after the frantic, sped-up passion that had overwhelmed them.

"I've been wanting to do this," he said, his voice hoarse, "for a very long time."

His hands cupped the lower curve of her belly. She longed for him to roam just a few inches lower, to slip between her legs and touch her the way he'd done last May.

But he didn't move.

"I like it," he told her, a primitive possessiveness in his voice, "that my baby's growing inside you. No other man's but mine."

Serena closed her eyes. A little spark of frustration flared inside her. She didn't want to hear about the baby right now. She was tired of his preoccupation with their child and with being a father. She wanted, just for a minute, for him to be fascinated with *her*.

It didn't make sense, considering she didn't want them to be involved with each other at all. Didn't want there to be fascination on either side.

But then, nothing about this encounter made sense.

Least of all the rush of renewed desire she felt when his hands skimmed up her stomach and found her breasts. Through the thin cotton of her shirt he grazed the hard, aching tips of them.

She couldn't help but arch her back.

"Tell me you've wanted this, too," he commanded softly. "Tell me you need this."

As if entranced, she turned her head to look over

her shoulder. She spoke an inch from his lips. "Yes. Yes, Graham. I've wanted this, too."

Their mouths met, and time sped up again. She turned toward him, but her stomach made complete contact difficult, so he led her quickly to the sofa. He brushed the baby gifts aside and pulled her onto his lap. Her arm went around his neck, her other hand touching his chest again as they kissed. She zeroed in on one of his nipples.

Graham's fingers encircled her wrist, stopping her. "No," he said against her mouth.

"Why not?"

"Because I don't want to lose control before it's time."

Rebelliously she twisted her hand out of his grasp. "I don't care."

Her movements impatient and a little rough, she brushed his shirt down his arms. She slid her tongue along his collarbone, leaving a slick trail in her wake, and was pleased when he couldn't suppress a moan.

"If you're not made of ice," she said against his throat, "you'll have to prove it."

She lowered her knees to the floor between his feet, her hands on his thighs as she leaned forward and boldly traced circles around each of his small nipples.

Graham drew in a sharp, ragged breath. "Serena—"

She pulled his shirt completely off his body and tossed it aside. Ignoring his objections, she splayed her hands on either side of his rib cage and sucked at one of his nipples, teasing it with her teeth.

Last May, she remembered, he'd gone a little wild. She would make him do so again. She needed to see him that way, especially today—after he'd been so damned cool and collected.

"Serena—"

He gripped the hem of her full maternity shirt and pulled it over her head. Their gazes locked, and the heat between them went up another degree.

She watched with satisfaction as his gray eyes flicked to her breasts, still concealed by the black lace of her bra, and his pupils, already big, enlarged further. His hands shook, and he reached for the front clasp and released it. Her breasts, fuller than they'd been before, spilled freely out.

His appreciation and arousal made her feel as if her body were an exquisite work of art. She knew some women felt self-conscious and unappealing during their pregnancies—they'd discussed the phenomenon in prenatal class—but at that moment Serena experienced the opposite. The lush curves of her body made her feel *more* sexy and womanly than usual.

She stopped minding Graham's preoccupation with her pregnancy then—she was glad he was one of the men who could see beauty in it.

Bracing her hands on the large square coffee table behind her, she slowly levered herself up and sat on the edge of it.

They faced each other, both naked from the waist up.

Graham reached for her. Leaning forward, he stroked her curves. With the pads of his thumbs he caressed the tips of her breasts until the most intense liquid fire pooled between her legs. She let herself cry out, overcoming her inhibitions because she knew, from experience, that it would torment him even more.

Graham knelt on the floor between her legs, copying her earlier position. His gaze, heavy-lidded and starkly sexual, met hers.

Yes, she told him with her eyes. *You can do it. I'll let you do what you want.*

Maybe he was exacting his own small form of revenge, but he didn't kiss her breasts right away. He brushed his lips over her arms, her shoulders, the base of her throat. When she thought she would burst with yearning, he tasted the outer curves of her breasts, staying clear of the darkened areolae. Serena trembled with anticipation. She braced her hands on the solid wood tabletop behind her and let her head tilt back provocatively.

It was as if she'd become a new being. She'd only had this experience once before—six months ago—and it was strange and bewildering at the same time as it was secretly familiar.

And exhilarating.

Finally, with one strong arm supporting her back, Graham closed his lips over the tip of one of her breasts. Her body jerked and bowed as if electrified.

He did things that made her moan, and gasp, and curl her fingers against the table.

"You taste so good, Serena." His voice had a rawness she'd never heard before.

He *had* lost control. It was a distant thought.

She raised her hands to his strong, supple shoulders and let her nails dig into his flesh. "Don't stop," she said, and he didn't, not for several minutes.

Suddenly she couldn't stand to have any more barriers between them. He seemed to get the same idea, because he stopped and tugged at the waistband of her black leggings.

"Lift your hips," he urged.

Serena obliged, and he yanked down the leggings and her lacy panties at the same time. She reached for his belt buckle with unsteady hands but was able to release it quickly. Next came the button on his slacks. His zipper sounded unnaturally loud in the room as she slid it downward. In moments they were both completely naked.

She pushed him back so he sat on the couch, and she straddled his lower thighs. Reaching down, she held the hard length of him with both of her hands.

He groaned. "You've got to—"

"Stop this? I don't think so, Graham. Tell me how this feels," she demanded, and stroked up and down.

"You know how it feels." He ground the words out.

"Good?"

"Too good. You're going to make me—"

He writhed under her ministrations. He groaned. He even swore.

Serena felt the dampness between her legs and knew they both needed release. She raised herself on her knees, positioned him at just the right spot and slowly lowered herself.

For a moment the feeling of sweet perfection was so strong she froze. It felt as if they belonged together, even though she didn't believe that at all. But the force of the illusion overwhelmed her.

She stared into Graham's beautiful gray eyes and slowly, ever so slowly, started to rock her hips.

His hands held them, aiding her movements, encouraging her to move faster and faster.

It only took a minute before they both teetered on the edge. Graham rasped her name, throwing his head back, and they both came at the same moment.

Serena felt as if the rest of the world had disintegrated. Only they were left, their trembling bodies entwined.

When the last aftershocks began to die down, she buried her face in the curve of his neck and inhaled deeply. A fine sheen of perspiration covered his skin, and her tongue darted out to taste the saltiness of it.

Her limbs felt replete, her whole body spent, and she allowed herself to go completely slack. Graham gently stroked her hair, smoothing it from her flushed face and neck.

ONCE, OF COURSE, could never be enough. Graham took her to the bedroom, where he made incredibly slow, tender love to her all over again. After that they ordered room service dinners, and Serena left a vague phone message for Meg, saying she wouldn't be home that night. She and Graham ate, then made love a third time, then finally slept.

Chapter Ten

Graham awoke early the next morning with a strong sense of déjà vu. The bed was empty except for him. Once more, he thought, Serena had left.

Except she hadn't gotten too far away.

Not this time.

He heard noises through the closed bedroom door, and it was too early for housekeeping.

Graham got out of bed, surprised he hadn't wakened sooner. He usually wasn't a heavy sleeper. But there was something about making love to Serena and having her beside him all night....

He crossed the room in a few quick strides and grabbed his robe from a chair. He thrust his arms through the sleeves and was tying the belt as he stepped through the door.

Serena stood by the window, looking out. Just as *he'd* done last May, he thought distractedly.

And she hadn't dressed yet. She wore a white

hotel robe that matched his. She'd tied the belt low on her hips, under her expanded middle.

She turned toward him as he approached.

"I thought you had run away again." He didn't mean to say the words aloud, but they were out before he realized he was speaking.

He remembered the profound sense of loss he'd felt six months ago, watching her on the street as she stepped into a cab and drove off. He hadn't thought about that particular moment in months, but this morning it came back to him in precise detail.

And he suddenly realized it wasn't the first such experience he'd had.

The other incident had happened twenty-five years ago. He'd barely been nine. Much too young to be left home alone for several days, yet that was what his parents had done. They'd ignored his quiet anxiety—even then he'd known how to keep a lid on his feelings—and skipped off to some exciting beach party to which they'd received a last-minute invitation. He remembered watching from his bedroom window as they threw their bags into the car and left, not once looking back at the house.

And forgetting to say goodbye.

Serena hadn't moved from the window. Her arms were crossed in front of her, on top of her stomach. "I'm not the same person I was six months ago, Graham. I don't run away from difficult situations anymore."

He managed a smile. "Going to bed with me is a difficult situation?"

"I don't have much experience with this kind of thing. I suppose you do, though."

"A little."

In his teens and early twenties he'd sown most of his wild oats. It seemed like a century ago. Since his divorce he'd had a few discreet affairs, but they weren't the sort that required spending the whole night together—hence there had been few mornings after.

He looked into her eyes, suddenly feeling acutely aware of their twelve-year age difference.

Six months ago she'd been a virgin.

She seemed to read his thoughts. "Please don't apologize for taking advantage of me again," she said. "You're not the only one responsible for what happened yesterday."

"No, but I—"

"Was seriously provoked by a furious female." She stood back from him. "Each of us could have stopped it from getting out of control, but neither of us did. I think subconsciously we've wanted it to happen all along. We were just waiting for the opportunity."

He raised an eyebrow. "You've given this a lot of thought, have you?"

She shrugged, amazingly nonchalant. "It was bound to happen again, even though we pretended otherwise. Maybe it wasn't the wisest thing to do, but that's life."

"That's life?"

"Yeah. We can't change the past so we might as well go forward."

"And what exactly does that entail?" he asked, nonplussed by her attitude and a little uneasy.

She turned toward the window. "I won't try to keep you out of our baby's life, Graham. We need to make plans for visitation and discuss how we want to bring up our child. I have an ultrasound appointment on Thursday. I think you should come. Now that we've gotten this—" she waved her hand in the air "—desire out of our systems, we can start making the necessary choices."

Graham stared at the curve of her neck. That incredible skin he'd kissed over and over in the night. "It may be out of your system, but it's not out of mine."

Never before had he experienced the kind of overwhelming sexual intensity he felt with Serena. *Ever.*

"I'm not interested in a relationship, Graham. I just want what's best for our child." She paused.

"I guess we could be lovers for a while... A temporary thing."

Interesting, he thought, that she was willing to be his short-term mistress but not his shotgun wife.

"I don't think that would be a good idea," he said. No matter how tempting he found her....

"No, me neither."

In his mind he heard the same click of the door closing, like in May. She was gone, like she had been then. Not in body, but she was holding herself back from him, withdrawing. It was ironic. She'd just granted him what he wanted—a place in his child's life. But it felt incomplete, and a temporary fling wouldn't change that.

He told himself not to dwell on that. She had agreed to stop shutting him out, even if only on one level. And maybe with time she would realize *he* wasn't the same person he'd been six months ago, either. That something had changed in him. Visitation could turn into shared custody, and he could give his child the kind of support his own parents had never given him.

He would be a good parent, even a loving one. He believed that, despite her skepticism. He couldn't forget the emotional response he'd had the other day to feeling the baby kick. Or the fatherly anticipation he'd felt about his or her birth when he'd gone shopping for baby supplies.

It was unfortunate that Serena had only perceived his gifts as an excessive display of wealth.

But perhaps now that her anger had cooled she would let him explain his motives.

"What about the things I bought for the baby? Do you still refuse to accept them?"

They both turned to look at the sofa. The gifts still sat there, though a few had tumbled to the floor when he'd brushed them aside yesterday. Yesterday, when they'd been caught in the heat of passion.

"I may have overreacted a little," she confessed after a moment.

"Oh?"

"Yeah. It, um, probably had a lot to do with the whole sex thing. I was just…tense and…trying to find another outlet." She blushed.

"So you'll accept the baby things?"

She walked to them. Sitting on the sofa, she picked up a red-wrapped box and turned it over in her hands. "Maybe these aren't as extravagant as I thought—not if they're all from a list in a baby book." She met his gaze, her eyes serious. "But I still don't want you to take care of everything…."
She sighed. "It was a nice gesture, though. Thank you, Graham. And I'm sorry I yelled at you."

They spent the next ten minutes opening the packages together. To his gratification Serena did like the baby clothes he'd picked out. Only a few of the items were duplicates of things she'd already bought, and he promised to return them himself— a task that appealed to him. He would enjoy going to the stores and looking around some more.

Afterward he asked if she were hungry.

"Famished," she said.

"Room service again?"

She nodded.

While Serena went to freshen up he called down and ordered a large breakfast, then decided to ring Jake, as well.

"Hey, boss. I was wondering when I'd hear from you. Sleep in?"

Graham sat at the desk in the corner. He glanced at the carriage clock that rested on its surface. It was almost nine. Well past his normal waking time, even on a Sunday. "Apparently so."

"Well," Jake said, "I hope you had a good night."

"Mmm."

"Did you get my voice mail messages?"

"Haven't checked."

When Serena had arrived yesterday he'd turned off his cell phone.

After they'd eaten dinner he'd put out the Do Not Disturb sign.

He hadn't been very accessible.

But Jake didn't complain, and Graham had a feeling his assistant had figured out the reason for his seclusion.

"I'll save you the trouble," Jake said. "I found a good real estate agent. She's waiting for your call." He gave Graham the number. "I told her what you wanted and she's pulled out some listings."

"Sounds good."

Jake cleared his throat. "There's something else. Trouble brewing at BradleyTech. A little dissension in the ranks. Kurt Jackson heard rumors of it yesterday afternoon while playing golf...."

Graham listened to his assistant's analysis of the situation, which was a very typical split in the board of directors.

It had always been the kind of situation in which Graham thrived. He'd relished the challenge of bringing a board, or a group of managers, together so they could focus on business instead of internal squabbling. His ability to analyze business situations and bring other people into line behind him was a large part of his success, and one of the things he enjoyed most in his work.

But he had no interest in spending the rest of the day on the telephone.

Or in flying to Oregon to hold the hands of mature adults who really should have known better.

Unbelievably, he much preferred to spend his day reading baby books.

"Jake," he said, "I trust you more than anyone else who works for me."

"Thank you."

"You've been my assistant for, what, five years?"

"Just about."

"Well, it's time you got a promotion."

LATER THAT WEEK Serena and Meg attended their weekly yoga class and spent the rest of the evening at home. They popped a big bowl of popcorn and sat on the sofa watching a bad movie on television.

"So," Meg said as the credits started rolling. "How are things with you know who?"

Serena looked at her. "Okay, I guess. I'm trying to stay on an even keel."

It hadn't been easy. When she'd woken up in Graham's suite the other morning she'd felt an instinctual swell of panic. It had been crazy to get physically involved with him again, and she'd called herself all kinds of a fool.

She had no more gotten the desire out of her system than he had. It continued to be present between them, and it impeded her ability to function.

But she told herself to accept the inevitable. Once Graham had returned, she couldn't have gone long without repeating the night they'd shared last May. And now that they'd repeated it her lust for him was stronger.

And it *was* just a physical thing, just lust. It had to be. She wouldn't let it be anything else, wouldn't let herself form an emotional attachment.

No more hopeless, self-sabotaging situations, she'd promised herself.

No more loving people who couldn't love her back.

And that was one of the things, she'd realized, that had set her off about the baby gifts. Graham seemed to have figured out how to love the baby, but with *her* there was nothing deeper than desire. She'd been jealous of her own child, for goodness sake!

Beside her, Meg reached for the remote and switched off the television. "I noticed you've spent the last several evenings together," she commented.

Serena had gone to dinner with him three nights in a row, to talk about the baby. They'd had a good time, but she'd made sure to keep her distance from him. "Sorry to leave you alone so much," she said.

"That's okay. I've been busy at work." Meg paused. "Actually, I haven't been completely alone...."

"Oh?" Serena asked, glad to change the focus from herself to her friend.

"I did go out on a date last night."

Serena's eyes widened. Meg had stopped dating when she'd gotten pregnant. "With whom?"

"Jake Woo."

Of course, Serena thought, remembering the interactions she'd witnessed last weekend. All during breakfast the two had exchanged flirtatious repartee.

At the time Serena had been a little distracted by her reaction to Graham's baby gifts, but she hadn't missed the chemistry.

She knew Jake had had to fly up to Oregon but had gotten home yesterday. He certainly hadn't wasted any time asking Meg out.

"How did it go?" she asked.

"It was a very nice dinner."

"Just dinner?"

"Just dinner."

"But you want to see him again."

Meg grinned. "I'd be crazy not to. He's funny and smart—and a total babe."

Serena returned her smile. Jake was definitely all those things. He didn't get her blood going like Graham did, but she could see the appeal. "I thought you weren't looking for love these days?"

"I wasn't. I'm not."

"But you're not going to say no if it comes knocking on your door?"

"Maybe." Meg sighed. "It's complicated, though. He lives in New York and he travels a lot. He's a very busy guy."

"And my pregnancy seems to have increased his workload."

Meg shrugged. "It's because of your pregnancy that I met him in the first place," she said.

"Speaking of pregnancy," Serena said, "does he know how yours came about? Have you told him about your visit to the sperm bank?"

"Of course."

"What did he think?"

"That I'm an adventurous woman. Which I am."

GRAHAM CAME BY an hour early for their ultrasound appointment. "There's something I want to show you," he said. "Down the street."

Once downstairs, she started to head for his car.

"No, we can walk," he said. "If you get cold I'll lend you my sweater, all right?"

They'd only taken a couple of steps down the street before she figured out where they were going.

"You've bought a house."

He shook his head. "Not yet. I wanted you to see it first."

Serena had mixed feelings about him living so close by. It would be convenient, but it made her nervous.

Still, she let him take her to the house.

It was better than she'd expected. Much better. Just a few blocks down the street and around the corner, it was relatively humble. *Relatively.* Though still a nice Pacific Heights home, it didn't scream that its inhabitant was a billionaire. It wasn't a huge mansion at the end of Broadway with servants' quarters and a five-car garage.

Walking through the airy interior, she could see their child spending time there. It would provide a relatively normal environment. More affluent than the majority of houses on the planet, yes, but not relentlessly, coldly ostentatious and opulent.

The place was unoccupied and empty of furniture, but she could feel a sense of warmth. It was the kind of place that could be turned into a real home.

The backyard was wonderful, too, full of flowers and a nice stretch of grass for a child to play on. In one corner a swing hung from a tall tree.

It was the kind of place she wouldn't mind living in herself. A great house to raise a child in.

Graham locked the house and they headed down

the sidewalk to her condo. "You like it," he said, accurately gauging her response.

"You're the one who would be buying it," she responded noncommittally. "Do you?"

"Yes." He pulled out his phone. "I'll be just a moment," he told her, and placed his call. When the other party answered he spoke without any preamble. "I'll take it," he said.

Serena waited while he finished the call, her gaze wandering around the neighborhood. The street was wide and clean, with a few London plane trees spaced at intervals, their branches bare for the upcoming winter and leaves scattered over the sidewalks.

She glanced at Graham as he put away his phone. "You didn't have to show me the house," she told him.

He gave her an odd smile. "Since our child will spend some portion of her life there, I thought you should have some say in the selection."

"You keep referring to the baby as a she. What makes you think that's what it will be?"

He shrugged. "Something tells me it'll be a girl."

"Oh? And what would that be?"

"Father's intuition." He put an arm around her shoulders, and they walked the rest of the way to her condo.

"So, DO YOU WANT to know the baby's sex?" the sonographer asked an hour later.

Serena was on the examining table. The sonographer had completed the initial part of the ultrasound exam. "I'd rather be surprised."

The woman smiled. "So would a lot of other people these days. Are you ready for your husband to come in?"

Serena nodded, ignoring the woman's mistaken assumption about her relationship with Graham. "Sure."

She was appropriately covered for modesty. Having Graham view the ultrasound was no big deal, she told herself. Just as she'd been telling herself ever since she'd mentioned it on Sunday morning.

But it was a big deal. She felt like there was no going back. Talking about how to raise a child was one thing, but this seemed like the first concrete step of being parents together.

Even if they didn't have a relationship of their own, they would be parents of the same child. Sharing a huge part of their lives with each other.

Graham came in. He sat down on a stool close to her, with a clear view of the monitor. The sonographer once again held the ultrasound unit on Serena's belly and explained the images on the video screen as she did so.

The baby's shape was clearly visible. Serena stared at the monitor, transfixed. Long moments passed. It was just so incredible to see that little being move inside her.

Graham squeezed her hand. She hadn't even realized he'd been holding it, but for some reason it felt natural.

"We made that," he said, his voice full of awe.

"Yeah."

She looked over and saw that his eyes were damp. It amazed her. Graham Richards, the man who seemed so remote and unreachable when she first met him, who described himself as too dispassionate to be able to have a family, was almost crying at the sight of his child in her womb.

It had been the right decision to bring him into their child's life.

But now she had to keep herself from falling in love with him.

Chapter Eleven

That weekend, Meg went to Carmel with her brother.

Feeling protective, Graham had insisted on staying at Serena's in case anything went wrong. It had been hard to convince her, but he'd promised not to touch her.

And he hadn't.

He awoke on the couch, missing the feel of her body in his arms. A week ago, during their night together, he'd awakened briefly in the early morning and lain on his back with Serena turned toward him, hugging his left side. The even rhythm of her breathing told him she still slept. Her head rested on his shoulder, her body in the crook of his arm. Her round stomach pressed against the side of his torso, and one of her arms stretched possessively across his chest. He had savored the experience.

The sound of his cell phone broke the stillness

of the morning. Briefly he considered ignoring it, but it was almost eight, and he might get more calls which, sooner or later, would disturb Serena's slumber.

The digital display identified Jake as the caller.

"This had better be good," he said.

"Graham," Jake said. "How's it going? Sleep well?"

"Not really."

"So how's Serena this morning?"

Graham abstained from answering. "Aren't we chatty today." It was his only remark. He headed to the kitchen for a glass of water.

Jake chuckled. "I stopped by your suite a few minutes ago. No one answered...."

"Get to the point, Jake, or you're fired."

"Sure thing, boss." Jake was unfazed. "Er, I thought I should give you a heads-up."

"About what?"

"Have you seen the morning paper?"

"No." Graham took a long drink of water, the phone still pressed to his ear.

"Well, I think you'll want to check it out." Jake told him the page number to go to. "It's very interesting," he added.

"I'm not going to like this, am I?"

"Hard to say. I was a bit startled when the concierge here pointed it out to me. But maybe you'll find it amusing...."

They ended the call. Graham took a moment to put away the sheets and blankets he'd used, then went in search of the paper.

He knew Serena and Meg subscribed to the *Chronicle,* but it wasn't in the hallway outside their door, which meant it must be delivered to the condo's lobby. He dressed, not bothering to button his shirt, grabbed Serena's keys and took the elevator downstairs.

On the ground floor he let himself out through the glass door to the exterior lobby. A short stack of newspapers sat near the front entrance. He knelt and picked one up.

He was about to stand when the outer door flew open. Harrison Jones barreled through, heading for the button panel, then stopped in his tracks as he caught sight of Graham. His features hardened into anger.

Graham stood up. He knew how it must look for him to be in Serena's lobby at this hour of the morning, unshowered and unshaven.

It looked as if he'd spent the night.

Which, of course, he had.

And he doubted Serena's father would be terribly enthusiastic about that fact. Not that it mattered what Harrison thought—his daughter was an adult, and perfectly capable of making her own choices. But Graham would have to deal with the man for a long time to come. Harrison would be his child's grandfather.

No, Graham thought, looking at the man's eyes, Harrison wasn't happy. His old-fashioned morals had clearly been scandalized. He looked as if he could have a stroke any minute if he weren't careful.

"Good morning," Graham said.

"You little *weasel!*"

Graham stared at him. "I'm sorry?"

"Being sorry won't cut it. Care to explain this?" Harrison brandished a rolled-up copy of the *Chronicle.*

"It's a newspaper," Graham said, his voice bland. "I was just collecting Serena's copy." He held it up. "I've been told there's something I should read."

"Well, then, read it!"

Graham started to flip to the page Jake had indicated, but Harrison impatiently ripped the paper out of his hands and replaced it with his own, which was already folded to the right spot.

It was a gossip column, Graham realized, and not the business section, as he'd expected.

"Go on!" Harrison ordered.

Graham obligingly scanned the print.

Business whiz Graham Richards is back in town, but this time it's not a corporate take-over he's got in mind. He's been seen around San Francisco with a sweet young thing named Serena Jones, daughter of cosmetic king Harrison Jones, Jr. Rumor has it he even went to Thanksgiving dinner at the Jones residence in Presidio Heights.

Has the billionaire bachelor set his sights on our local girl?

The plot thickens. Serena Jones is visibly pregnant—due in, say, February?—and our loyal sleuths couldn't identify a likely father candidate. Until they realized Richards's last appearance in the City by the Bay was at the May wedding of Dirk Emerson III and Elaine Richards—who is none other than the billionaire's ex-wife.

Go ahead and do the math yourself, but it sure looks to me as if Richards and the lovely Serena need to get to the altar ASAP.

Graham grimaced as his eyes reached the end. Damn. It had been inevitable that he would draw notice at some point, but he hadn't expected it to happen yet. He'd only been here a couple of weeks.

Since he neither sought nor shunned publicity—

nor conducted, until recently, a very interesting personal life—the mainstream media had mostly left him alone.

But his few appearances with Serena were obviously too much for the local gossips to pass up.

He remembered the day he and Serena had met, and his near obsession with the business article that had chided him for having no personal life.

Way too well behaved. That was how the writer had described him.

And it had stuck in his craw.

Well, he doubted the writer would have the same complaint now. As portrayed in the *Chronicle,* he was definitely *not* well behaved. Or boring or tame. He was an amorous playboy with a love child on the way.

"What have you got to say for yourself?" Harrison demanded.

Graham folded the paper. "I had nothing to do with this."

Harrison grunted. "Of course you didn't. Only a damned fool would plant a story like that about himself. What I want to know is exactly what did you have to do with my daughter's pregnancy?"

"That's a question you should ask Serena," Graham said evenly.

Serena was the one who'd decided not to reveal his paternity to her parents. Though he didn't like to play around with the truth, this was a matter for her to decide, not him.

"I'm not asking Serena. I'm asking you. Did you or did you not get my daughter pregnant?"

The door opened again. Cassandra bustled in, looking harried and disarrayed. "Oh, there you are, Harrison. It took me forever to find a parking space—" She stopped as she registered Graham's presence. Clearly she hadn't expected to see him there. Her gaze flicked to his chest. "Oh. Oh, my."

"Hello, Cassandra."

She composed her face into a smile. "Hello, Graham. Fancy running into you here."

"Mmm." Different approach from her husband but probably the same objective, Graham surmised. This was not the morning he'd envisioned when he'd woken up. "I think we'd all better go upstairs."

The glass door that led to the elevator was locked. He had Serena's keys, but it struck him that if they used the intercom she could get a few moments' notice about the chaos that was about to descend on her.

"I forgot to bring the keys down with me," he said, ignoring his discomfort at the lie. "She'll have to buzz us in."

He went to the button panel and pressed the one for Serena's unit.

Nothing happened.

"Here, let me do it." Harrison elbowed Graham aside and leaned heavily on the buzzer.

Half a minute later Serena finally answered. "Graham?" she asked, her sleepy and somewhat confused voice crackling through the speaker.

"It's your father," Harrison barked. "And Cassandra. We've got the weasel with us."

There was a long silence.

"Graham?"

He stepped to the microphone. "I locked myself out. Your parents are here. There's something they want to discuss with us."

Chapter Twelve

Oh, my God, Serena thought. She stood in the hallway by the intercom, momentarily inert after buzzing them all in. What the heck was going on? If her father was calling Graham a weasel that could only mean one thing.

But Graham had agreed not to reveal his paternity to her parents before she was ready.

So how had they figured it out?

She realized she didn't have time to stand there wondering about it—they would be upstairs in another minute. She had to shake off her early-morning fog and get her butt in gear.

Returning to her bedroom, Serena threw on the first clothes that came to hand—a pair of sweatpants and an oversize T-shirt.

She hurried to the entryway as someone pounded vigorously on the door.

She forced a smile as she opened it. "Dad," she said. "Come on in. Hi, Cassandra."

Her parents swept past her into the condo. Graham, half-dressed, followed and closed the front door.

She tried to read his expression. "What's going on?"

Her father glowered at her. "That's just what I intend to find out!"

Cassandra took him by the elbow. "Now, darling… Let's go sit down in the living room before you get any more worked up." To Serena she said, "Maybe you and Graham could make some coffee?"

"Good idea," Graham said.

Serena's father hadn't moved. "Harrison?" Cassandra prompted.

He reluctantly let her pull him toward the living room. "You know they'll just use the time to get their stories straight," he grumbled.

Cassandra patted him on the arm as they went. "Yes, dear."

Serena and Graham went to the kitchen. She didn't really want to make coffee, since she couldn't drink it and the smell drove her crazy—but she figured that was the least of her worries.

She met his gaze. "What happened? Why are

they here—and how did they find out you're the baby's father?''

Graham unfolded a newspaper she hadn't noticed he'd been carrying. ''We made the society page.'' He led her to a chair. ''You might want to sit down.''

Eyes wide, she did as he advised. ''Oh, no.''

''Exactly. Where do you keep the coffee?'' he asked, handing her the paper.

She glanced at it, immediately spotting his name in the column of text. ''I think there's some in the freezer,'' she said distractedly, ''but it's old.''

''Fine. I doubt anyone will notice how it tastes today.'' He opened the freezer door as she started to read.

Serena felt her stomach sink lower with every sentence. *Dear heaven,* she thought. It didn't seem real. It was too appalling to be real. Reaching the bottom, she couldn't help reading it again—and again—just to make sure she wasn't hallucinating.

''Good grief,'' she murmured. ''This is…unbelievable.''

She felt exposed.

Vulnerable.

Violated.

It was such an invasion of their privacy.

Graham leaned against the counter, arms crossed, watching her. He had buttoned his shirt and looked less like someone who'd just gotten out of bed.

"You're used to this kind of thing, aren't you?" she said, wonder in her voice.

"Not exactly. But I've certainly seen my name in print before."

Graham had to deal with being in the public eye. That was just a reality.

And now it looked as if her child would have to deal with that, too—now that his or her parentage was no longer a secret.

She would have to deal with it....

Thousands of people all over town had been apprised of her situation.

"Oh, God," she mumbled. "What a mess. Everyone will know...."

"Let's don't worry about everyone yet. I think we've got more pressing problems."

"My parents."

He nodded. "In particular your father, who'd obviously like to wring my neck."

The coffeemaker hissed and gurgled as it reached the end of its cycle. Serena was so preoccupied she barely noticed the aroma.

"Okay, then," she said, standing up. "We'll deal with him."

"How, exactly?"

"I don't know. But we'll get him to back off. Somehow... Just follow my lead."

Graham inclined his head. "As you wish." He switched off the machine. While she'd read the column he'd set three cups on a tray and found a small carton of cream in the fridge. "Milk for you?" he asked.

"Just water." She got it herself.

"Serena?"

"Yes?"

"I'm sorry your name got dragged into this. I'd hoped the press would leave you alone."

She grimaced. "Thanks, but it's not your fault."

Not really, she thought. Graham couldn't help being who he was—the kind of person who naturally sparked other people's interest.

True, this wouldn't have happened if he'd never come back to San Francisco, but she couldn't blame him for that. She hadn't exactly refused to have contact with him during the last few weeks. And she hadn't worried about being seen with him in public.

They brought the coffee to the living room and found her father and Cassandra sitting on the sofa.

"Well?" Harrison said.

Serena took a chair a few feet away from them. "Graham is the father of my baby," she said as calmly as she could.

Her father clenched his jaw. His lips compressed into a tight line at her confirmation.

Cassandra blinked several times very rapidly.

"I meant to tell you in a different way," Serena continued, "at a different time. But the society page beat me to it."

"Oh, my," Cassandra said. "He really is the father of your baby?"

"Yes."

Harrison made a sound like a discontented boar. "I knew it the minute I saw him."

"Now, honey," Cassandra murmured. "Try to be nice."

"I *am* being nice," he growled. He turned his attention to Graham, who'd taken the second armchair. "You're the lowest kind of scoundrel to do this to my daughter. Of all the gall. To get her pregnant and then come waltzing back into her life a few months later and try to set her up as your…your mistress. Have you no shame?"

Cassandra coughed politely. "I think Harrison means to say that you young people seem to live by a slightly different moral code than we're accustomed to."

Her stepmother didn't seem to have forgotten for a moment who Graham was. She didn't want to alienate him, even if he couldn't be talked into the wedding Serena was sure her parents wanted.

Harrison, on the other hand, didn't seem to care *whose* toes he stepped on at the moment.

"My God, man," he said. "How could you come to our home, eat our food and take advantage of our goodwill when you knew your baby was in there?" He pointed to Serena's stomach with two quick jabs of his finger. "You lied to us! You told us you'd only met her a few weeks ago!"

"No, Dad." Serena cut in before Graham could reply. "I did. I'm the one who said all that, not him."

"He went along with it."

"Because I needed him to. I was tired of you and Cassandra freaking out about my pregnancy and trying to marry me off to Bob. I wanted it to stop, so I dragged Graham to dinner. And I didn't tell you he was the father because I didn't want you to try to pressure us into marriage."

"Well, *somebody* needs to do it!"

Graham inserted himself into the conversation. "Speaking of Thanksgiving, I notice the gossip columnist seems to have a lot of information about intimate family details."

Serena latched on to the change of topic. "I know neither of you wants me in the limelight right now, so it wouldn't make sense for you to call the paper about Thanksgiving." And none of the Benningtons would have dared to do that, either, she thought. "But Graham does have a point...."

Cassandra flushed. "I certainly didn't call the person who wrote that column. I've never done that in my life." She paused. "But I—I think I did happen to mention something about Thanksgiving to one or two friends. I didn't mean to call any public attention to us. But I was just so proud of you, Serena. I mean, it's not just any girl who can bring a billionaire home to dinner."

Her stepmother was still convinced, Serena thought, that a woman's basic function in life was to catch the wealthiest man she could.

Graham ignored Cassandra's ongoing awe. "Obviously one of your friends, or your friends' friends, couldn't resist the temptation to pass along the news to the paper," he observed. "It wouldn't take much digging for the columnist to uncover the rest. A few judicious phone calls to people with loose tongues, and the story would be complete."

"I—I'm so sorry, Graham. I didn't mean any harm."

"No, I don't imagine you did. In any case, I should have realized something like this was bound to happen eventually. If the initial information hadn't come from you it would have come from someone else."

Harrison shifted impatiently. "None of this de-

lightful chitchat gets to the basic issue. Marriage.''
He addressed Graham. "Get on your nice clothes,
boy. You're going to a wedding.''

"Serena and I have discussed marriage, and it's
not an option.''

Harrison narrowed his eyes. "Don't you dare
tell me she's not good enough for you.''

"On the contrary," Graham said.

Serena watched him, expecting more, but he
didn't offer any explanation.

What, she wondered, did he mean? That *he*
wasn't good enough for *her?* But that was ridiculous. He was a brilliant, handsome, fascinating
man. And a wealthy one. He could have any
woman in the world.

As long as she didn't need to be loved....

Was that what he was saying—that his inability
to feel love made him unworthy of her?

For the first time Serena wondered what had
caused that deficiency in him. Nobody was born
not knowing how to love. Somewhere along the
line, sometime before Elaine, Graham must have
been seriously scarred. But where and how? With
his parents' deaths? Or before that? She thought
back to their conversations about his past. He'd
revealed so very little about himself.

Her father continued to bluster. "Fine, then.
Whatever. But there's going to be a ceremony.''

"I'm afraid you're mistaken," Graham said. "Your daughter won't have me."

"Why ever not?" Cassandra broke in. "You're not—not committed to someone else, are you?" She looked horrified by the possibility.

"No," he assured her, "that's not the problem. It's the fact that your daughter refuses to have a shotgun wedding. She doesn't believe in them. Or in marriages of convenience, I believe she called them."

Cassandra turned to stare at Serena. Finally she said, "Serena?"

"Yes?"

"Serena, dear?"

"Yes."

"Are you feeling okay?"

"Yes."

"Because I'm not sure you are."

"I am."

Cassandra got up and walked to Serena's chair. She knelt beside it and spoke in a hushed tone. "Let's go through this one step at a time, shall we? First, Graham is the father of your child. Second, he seems willing to take responsibility for it. Third," she said, lowering her voice even more, "judging by Graham's attire earlier he seems to have spent the night here."

"All of those things are true, Cassandra." She

didn't bother to explain that Graham had slept on the couch.

"Then what's the problem? Why didn't you get the man to the altar months ago?"

Serena suspected Cassandra would never understand her reasons, no matter how carefully she presented them. It wasn't in the woman's nature. But she tried, anyway. "I want to marry for love."

"So love him."

"It's not that simple."

Not if you didn't want to wind up with a broken heart. Not if you were determined to break the old patterns of your past and become a happier, stronger, more fulfilled human being.

"What about the baby?" Cassandra asked. "Can't you do it for the baby?"

"If I thought that would be the best thing for my child then I might. But I don't. No one needs the emotional baggage of growing up in a household where his or her parents married only because their birth control failed." Serena took a deep breath and turned to her father. "Dad, you're not going to force me into this. I'm twenty-two years old and it's entirely my decision. I know this is difficult for you and I know you don't approve of my actions, but you'll just have to get used to it."

"Now, Serena—"

"I mean it, Dad. I know you think you know

what's best for me, but there's no way you could. There's no way you can know the whole story. I appreciate your concern, though. I'm sure you and Cassandra have done this today because it's the only way you know how to express your love for me."

As she said the words Serena realized the truth of them. Her father and stepmother *did* care about her in their mixed-up way. They wanted what they thought was best for her, and they could even be protective.

And protectiveness was why her father had spoken so harshly to Graham, even though it would have been more strategic to act polite.

Cassandra had tried to look out for her interests, too, even though she had an inaccurate idea of what those might be.

Yes, her parents' love was clouded by their needs and desires and flaws, and they had a terrible way of showing it.

But it did exist.

Serena looked from one to the other of them. They both looked uncomfortable, as if love was a little too unseemly to discuss. They'd never been able to express their feelings in an open, vulnerable way, she thought. But it didn't change the truth she saw in their eyes.

With her greater understanding she was able to

forgive them a little for being so annoying and controlling and smothering over the years. They were just doing the best they knew how.

She pushed herself to her feet. "Thank you for trying to help me. I appreciate your efforts even though I can't go along with them."

She seemed to have gotten through to them. Within minutes her parents were out the door. Their moods were a bit subdued, but Serena detected a real respect for her in their expressions.

They were disappointed, she realized, but they respected her for standing up to them. It was a continuation of the process she'd begun several months ago, when she'd first told them about her pregnancy.

She closed the door and turned to face Graham, who stood a few feet away. "Well," she said. "This was an interesting way to start the day."

"I'm sorry I didn't see it coming. I should have been thinking more clearly and taken better steps to protect you from the media."

She led him into the living room. "Graham, you're being too hard on yourself. It's not your fault," she said, and meant it. She collapsed onto the sofa, relaxing for the first time since the intercom buzzer had woken her up. "Well, I'm zapped. Eight-thirty in the morning and I feel as if I need a nap."

He sat next to her. "Do you need to go back to bed?"

"I don't think I'd be able to sleep. Not after this." She looked at the tray Graham had set on the coffee table. No one had touched the coffee. "It would have been nice," she said, "if this had happened on a morning when you hadn't stayed over, no matter how innocently."

"It wasn't too bad," Graham said. "Just a little awkward."

Actually, he thought, he was glad he'd been here to run a little interference. He knew Serena was capable of dealing with her parents alone, but why *shouldn't* he have to face up to them with her when he was the reason the column had been printed?

A few minutes later Serena went to freshen up. He took the coffee cups to the kitchen. Dumping their lukewarm contents down the drain, he reviewed the morning's events.

He wouldn't be able to shield Serena and the baby from attention. Only a quick wedding would help the current furor die down. But Serena had just confirmed, decisively, her position on the matter.

Which was too bad. Because they could probably have a pretty good marriage.

The thought startled him.

Since when had any marriage involving him

seemed even remotely positive? And when had
marriage become less of a necessary duty in his
mind and more like something he might actually
look forward to?

It was disturbing. Very odd and unexpected.

Graham made a fresh pot of coffee and drank a
cup, standing at the counter in his shirt and jeans.
He stared into space, his brain not quite making
sense of his new discovery.

Chapter Thirteen

The next day Graham was once more contemplating marriage—instead of attending to business—when Elaine called his cell phone.

"Just wanted to check up on you," she said. "I assume you saw yesterday's paper."

"Sadly, yes."

He sat in a downstairs conference room with piles of uninspiring paperwork spread out on the table before him. Carita Lawrence and the temp, who'd become a permanent employee, sat in the next room. Jake had left to round them up some lunch at a Thai restaurant he'd discovered and raved about. Next week they would move into their new office downtown.

He and Elaine discussed the society page.

"Your name was mentioned, too, I believe," he said.

She didn't seem to care. "Yes, but they left my

private life alone. You, on the other hand… I'm so sorry you have to go through this kind of thing.''

''Can't be helped.'' He pushed back his chair and walked to the door, which he shut quietly.

''So how did Serena take it?''

''Not particularly thrilled,'' he said. ''Her parents even less so. She hadn't told them who the father of her baby was. I'd met them on Thanksgiving, but she introduced me as her new boyfriend.''

''Did she now? What an interesting young woman…. The paper must have been quite a shock for the Joneses, then.''

''Mmm.''

''So, did they wave a figurative shotgun in your face?''

''How did you guess?''

''And will they achieve their objective?'' Elaine wanted to know. She'd never been shy with him. Diplomatic if it were called for, but never shy.

''Probably not,'' he said. ''Serena's not amenable.''

''Is that so?'' Elaine paused. ''What about you? Are *you* amenable?''

Graham took a moment to answer. He sat down, knowing he couldn't lie to her. Once more he recalled that moment in Serena's kitchen, the strange thoughts he'd had. ''I can't exactly say.''

"Oh, really?" Elaine's voice had a teasing note. "How fascinating…"

"How are you and Dirk?"

"Great," she said, laughing at his change of subject. "We'll have you over to dinner sometime. I assume you'll be in town a while longer?"

"Yes."

"You wouldn't happen to be moving to San Francisco, by any chance?"

"Yes. I would."

"Oh, good. I hoped you would say that. Now back to the reason why. What's going on between you and Serena Jones?"

Graham wondered what would happen if his ex-wife and the mother of his child ever got together on something. Between the two of them they would be more relentless than a squad of Marines.

"Graham?"

"I don't know what to tell you."

"You're going through some confusion these days, aren't you?"

"Yes, I suppose you could say that."

"It's because you're falling in love with her, isn't it?"

It was the strangest thing. When he heard Elaine say the words, the words he hadn't quite allowed into his conscious mind, Graham felt a jolt of recognition. It was a little like the moment on the beach when he'd first felt the baby kick in Serena's belly, and just as profound. Everything he believed about himself shifted—coming more into line with reality.

The reality of the transformation that had begun last May, the moment he'd spotted Serena in the church.

Some frozen part of him had melted.

And Serena had caused that. Something about her had triggered the process, changing him irrevocably. Her spirit, perhaps, or the genuine, lively way she related to other people. Her strength and intelligence. Or some indefinable quality of her overall being, the sum total of her personality.

He couldn't help but...

Love her?

Sitting at the conference table with the phone clamped to his ear, Graham ran a hand through his hair. He thought about the time he'd spent with Serena. In her arms he'd never been the cold, aloof, emotionless person he'd always considered himself. His tight self-control deserted him.

And it wasn't just when they were in bed, he realized. He felt powerful feelings with her when they were doing other things—taking a walk, sharing a meal, simply talking.

She did make him feel things.

Attachment.

Intimate vulnerability.

A soul-deep affinity.

That was why he wanted to marry her, wasn't it? It wasn't just to provide their child with a solid home. It was so much more than that.

Parental love wasn't the only type of love he could feel, after all.

He'd been wrong about himself. He wasn't a hopeless case, spoiled goods, way too old and jaded to fall in love. He'd just needed the right woman to come along.

"You've been silent an awful long time," Elaine commented. "Are you all right? I didn't just give you a shock, did I? No, never mind. I can tell I did. You hadn't figured it out yet, had you?"

"Why," he murmured, barely aware of the words, "is this happening?"

It hadn't happened with Elaine. Why not? She was a fine person. A kind, generous, exquisitely beautiful person. Yet she'd never made him feel the way Serena did.

She seemed to understand his train of thought. "You and I weren't meant to be together, Graham. You and Serena are."

"How do you know that?" His voice was low and husky and raw.

"I can just tell."

He stood up, a restless energy spreading through

his limbs. Aimlessly he paced around the room. "I don't know what to say."

"Don't say anything. Not to me. It's Serena you need to speak with. You need to tell her you love her."

"I don't think she would believe me."

She'd bought his assessment of himself just as fully as he had. And, he realized, she'd protected herself accordingly. That was why she'd spent so much energy pushing him away. She didn't want to get hurt by him. But did that mean what he hoped—that she was capable of being hurt because she loved him, too?

Even if she hadn't faced it yet...

"I don't think she's ready to hear the words," he told Elaine.

His ex-wife wasn't concerned. "*Show* her, then," she urged. "By your actions. This is someone you need to fight for, Graham. She's the mother of your child and the woman you love. Don't let her slip away again."

Chapter Fourteen

Serena stayed busy. The gossip column blew over, but she still obsessed about the future it foretold for her and the baby. A life of total anonymity was no longer a likely possibility—but she told herself they would be all right no matter what. She could handle whatever publicity debacles occurred. She was strong enough and confident enough to meet them head-on.

She shopped for the nursery with Meg and did some Christmas shopping by herself. She went for walks. She signed up for a new class, titled Baby Care Basics, at the hospital.

Graham signed up for the class, too. He came around often with things for the baby, or to discuss what he'd been reading in his child-rearing books.

He had closed on the house almost immediately, and had moved into one of the bedrooms as soon as he could get the electricity and telephone running. A decorator had jumped at the chance to work on the house and had thrown herself into the task of making the house habitable in record time. Every day Graham brought paint samples and swatches of fabric to show Serena.

Something had changed in him. Serena couldn't quite put her finger on it and she was afraid to speculate on what it might be. She didn't want to forget the lessons of the past. But his permanent presence in her life was unavoidable.

And acceptance was the only mature and reasonable response.

One night, a couple of weeks after the gossip column had appeared, she went shopping with Graham. He took her to an antique store and showed her a beautiful child's bed, with an intricate inlaid headboard.

"I know this kind of bed is a few years off, but I want our child to have a good place to nap when he or she is over at the house."

She noticed he said nap instead of sleep, as if he expected their arrangement wouldn't involve overnight custody.

She'd been trying to put thoughts of the future to the back of her mind. It was enough that she and Graham had agreed to participate jointly in raising their child. The small details could wait a few months.

But seeing the beautiful bed made her consider the ridiculousness of the arrangement they were trying to create. Constant shuttling between her condo and his house wouldn't be the best thing for their child. Nor would seeing Graham on an intermittent basis.

Maybe it would be best if she could just let go of her need for love. She and Graham liked each other pretty well. They spent many hours together without friction. Why not marry him and share a house with him? God knew the house was big enough that they wouldn't be under each other's feet all the time. And their child would have a better start in life because of it. She knew they both loved the child enough that they wouldn't let their lack of a real marriage get in the way of nurturing him or her.

Just as quickly the idea passed.

It was a crazy idea, and it went against everything she'd been telling herself for so many months. She was nervous about the future, that was all. It was too easy to want to rely on Graham, to get used to having him in her life. And soon that would turn sour. She would begin to truly love him, just as Elaine had. Then she'd not only have a broken heart, but she'd be stuck with Graham in her life because of their child.

Better to let things continue as they were.

Graham bought the bed and took her back to her condo.

He fixed her a light supper and then offered to stay to help her with her grad school applications. She didn't protest.

It had been a busy week, and she was more tired than she'd realized. Her hands and face felt a bit puffy, and her head had been aching off and on all day, though it had stopped for a while in the afternoon.

They pulled out her virtual dinosaur of an electric typewriter and set it up at the dining room table. Graham typed in the initial pages of biographical information while she worked on revising her statement of purpose, eschewing her laptop for a good old notebook and pen, which were easier on her tired eyes.

At one point she stopped and lightly massaged her lids.

"I'm going to need a really good night's sleep," she told him.

He paused in his typing. "Should we stop?"

"No. I want to get these done."

She returned to her writing. But she couldn't concentrate. She did enjoy having Graham around. More than was wise. It was hard to keep him at a distance, hard to restrict his involvement in her life solely to their child. Here she was, after all, letting him into the other areas of her life. She didn't know what it would lead to and didn't like many of the possibilities.

Graham finished typing the forms and put away the typewriter. He returned with a cup of herbal tea for her.

"How's it going?" he asked.

She leaned back in her chair. "This is getting kind of blurry." She indicated her writing in the notebook. "I'm practically seeing spots. And my head hurts and I'm bloated and tired." She couldn't help complaining.

"Time to go to bed, then."

She didn't need him to tell her that, she thought with a flicker of annoyance.

Briefly she closed her eyes.

When, she wondered, had she suddenly become so whiny and cranky? She didn't like it. It confused her.

Part of her would have liked to let him take care of her, she realized. Pamper her a bit. But she told herself she wasn't willing to pay the price in emotional vulnerability.

"I'll get you something for your headache," he said, then strolled into the bathroom and searched through the medicine cabinet as if he owned the place.

Graham gave her a couple of pregnancy-safe

acetaminophen pills and put her to bed. She hardly ever went to sleep before Meg got home—even on days like today, when Meg worked an evening shift at the record store—but she felt completely beat.

Maybe she was coming down with a cold, she thought vaguely.

"I'll see you at the baby-care class tomorrow night," Graham said as she lay curled on her side in the blessedly dark room. "You're sure you don't want me to drive you there?"

"No," she mumbled. "I'll be fine. I just need some rest."

"GOOD EVENING. My name is Julie Greenfield, and I'm going to teach you how to take care of your new little bundle of joy. This class is called Baby Care Basics and it meets for four sessions...."

Graham sat at the last bank of tables, unable to focus on the nurse at the front of the room.

Serena was late. Only a little late, but he wondered if she'd forgotten about the class. She *had* had some memory problems lately....

He waited another ten minutes, but Serena still didn't show up. He couldn't concentrate on a word Nurse Greenfield said.

Perhaps Serena still wasn't feeling well, he thought. She'd been headachy and pretty out of it last night. Perhaps he should call and check in with her. See if she needed him to take her some chicken soup for dinner.

It was preferable to sitting here worrying.

He stood and headed for the door. As he left, his gaze fell on a familiar pregnancy book a young couple had brought to the class with them. It sat on a corner of their table. Graham owned a copy and had read the thing from cover to cover.

Including the section on possible complications...

Suddenly something clicked in Graham's mind. He recalled Serena's physical complaints last night and realized he'd read about those symptoms before—in the pregnancy book. They could signal a serious medical condition. Headache...blurred vision...seeing spots. And she'd mentioned she felt bloated, too....

All signs of something called preeclampsia— pregnancy-induced hypertension. Which could lead to eclampsia, an even more serous condition.

The survival rate for eclampsia, he remembered, was *not* one hundred percent.

Unacceptable odds.

Graham felt as if someone had socked him in the gut. As if he'd gotten the wind knocked out of him. He had to get Serena to a doctor. If anything happened to her or the baby...

It was too much to contemplate.

He'd been standing in the hallway, stunned, but suddenly he sprung into motion. Striding quickly in the direction of the parking garage, he dialed her home number on his cell phone. The four long rings before the answering machine picked up felt like an eternity.

Thankfully the outgoing message was brief and to the point. After the beep he spoke urgently, hoping she was screening her calls.

"Serena? Serena, if you're there, please pick up!" He waited a few seconds before repeating the words, but nothing happened.

Damn.

He cut the connection as he hurried down a flight of stairs. His shoes clattered on the steps as he descended.

He punched in Serena's cell phone number.

It rang a couple of times before a woman answered it, sounding flustered. "Serena?" he asked.

"No, it's Meg."

"This is Graham. Where's Serena?"

"Graham. Thank God," she said. "Serena wouldn't tell me your number. I was just about to call Jake to get it."

"Is she okay?" His voice sounded hoarse with anxiety in his own ears.

"I—I don't really know," she said. "We're at the hospital. They're running some tests."

Fear struck, piercing deeply. "Which hospital?"

She told him. It was the one he was in. He stopped on the stairs.

"Emergency room?" he asked.

"No, they transferred her upstairs to the birthing center."

"God—she's not... But it's too soon."

"I don't know. I think they're just better equipped to deal with her up here. At least that's what one of the nurses said. It's been a little crazy and overwhelming. I'm kind of in shock."

"What floor?"

"Seventh."

Graham took off up the stairs. "I'll be there in two minutes."

He flipped off the phone and ran up the five flights to the seventh floor. He turned two corners and found himself in the waiting area of the birthing center. Meg was there, standing by a chair that held two handbags.

Neither Meg nor Serena was supposed to have visited this part of the hospital for a couple of months yet. The large room was empty except for Meg, one nervous young man chewing his fingernails and an older couple who were probably about to become grandparents.

"I forgot you had that birthing class," Meg said. "I didn't know where you were."

"It's okay. What do the doctors say?" Graham asked.

"They haven't told me anything. I thought it might be preeclampsia but there's no confirmation yet."

Graham muttered a curse under his breath.

"I should have called you earlier," Meg said. "You have a right to know about any complications."

"I'm here now," he said.

"Serena was so adamant. She didn't want to depend on you. She kept babbling some nonsense about letting you take care of her too much and then something about history repeating itself and how she wasn't going to let that happen."

Meg was babbling, too. "Have you called her parents?"

"No," she said, straightening. "I'll do that."

"And I'll go see if I can find a doctor."

SERENA LAY on her left side in the observation room, staring at the light green wall a few feet from her bed. One of the nurses had hooked her up to the monitors with two beltlike contraptions that went around different parts of her middle, digging uncomfortably into her skin. One of the monitors made a whirring sound as it printed out some kind of a graph.

In the initial flurry of activity they'd checked her vitals, taken blood and a urine sample and done a bunch of other things she didn't understand.

But everything was calmer now. They'd confirmed that she had pregnancy-induced hypertension, which probably also meant preeclampsia. They wouldn't be able to get the lab work until the morning, and they wanted to keep her overnight for observation. But her life and the baby's weren't in any immediate danger. They'd caught her condition before it had escalated.

She felt less terrified than she had earlier. Less physically at risk.

Emotionally, however, she still felt distraught. Never in her life had she felt as strong a need for another person as she'd felt that evening for Graham. She'd wanted him by her side. Desperately.

Too desperately.

She wasn't supposed to be that emotionally attached to him.

And she wasn't supposed to have fallen in love with him, either....

But she had.

At some point in the middle of this crisis she'd realized the truth. She loved him. Irrevocably.

She'd let him into her life and her heart—even

though she *knew* she had a tendency to get herself into hopeless situations, ones where the other person couldn't return her feelings. Even though she'd vowed not to set herself up for heartbreak again.

She'd convinced herself it was okay to get increasingly involved with him. She'd convinced herself she could do it and not fall in love, and they could be all nice and cozy with each other and she could keep her emotions just as separate as he could.

What hogwash.

She had it bad, and the realization filled her with a total and complete panic.

She didn't know what to do.

But she knew she couldn't see Graham. Not right now. Not when her new knowledge of her love for him had left her so raw and vulnerable.

Chapter Fifteen

She refused to see him.

Graham paced the waiting area like a caged tiger. Nurse Columbo behind the counter gave him a narrowed-eyed, warning look, as if she expected him to bolt down the hall for Serena's room at any moment.

But he didn't know where it was.

No one would tell him.

He was ready to try bribery any minute. He would trade away his whole investment portfolio at the moment just for a chance to see her. To reassure himself she was okay.

He didn't believe the doctor. If Serena was really doing fine they wouldn't have kept her overnight. There was something they weren't telling him. There had to be.

He couldn't think straight.

Serena's roommate walked up to him, putting a

hand on his arm. He shook it off before he realized what he was doing.

She raised an eyebrow. "My, aren't we surly this morning...."

He ran a hand through his hair. "I'm sorry Meg. I'm just so—"

"Tense. Yeah, I figured that out." She gestured to the rows of seats—where Harrison and Cassandra looked inappropriately comfortable and calm, he thought. "Why don't you go sit down. Rest for a while. You look awful."

Graham frowned. He'd sat on one of those damn chairs half the night.

"No," he said, and left it at that.

He continued to pace. Meg gave up on him and wandered off.

He felt an irrational surge of anger toward the woman. Why had Serena allowed *her* to visit her room, and not him? *He* was the father of Serena's baby, for cripe's sake! *He* was the man who loved her and wanted to spend his life with her. Not Meg.

Even Serena's parents had been allowed in to see her. Last night *and* this morning. And so had a couple of other people who'd stopped by.

It wasn't fair, dammit.

And he sounded like a petulant little boy, complaining about fairness when all he really needed was to see Serena.

His conversation with Elaine kept running through his head. "Don't let her slip away," she'd said, but he'd never imagined the choice to do so might be taken out of his hands. He'd felt there was plenty of time to show her how he felt, to bring her slowly around to a place where she wouldn't be so fearful, where she could accept the fact that he loved her.

He loved her, dammit.

Which meant he should be in there, at her side. Holding her hand and comforting her. Reading her a funny magazine article, kissing her temple, giving her strength.

It never should have come to this. He should have seen the symptoms for what they were the other night. Should have brought her to the doctor before she had to spend a night and a day moving closer to the danger zone. And if he'd been the one to spot her illness, he thought selfishly, there would be no way she could keep him out of her room.

"Graham?"

He turned to find Cassandra looking at him.

"I need a cup of coffee," she said. "Why don't you walk me down to the cafeteria?"

"No, thanks," he said immediately. Automatically.

"She's fine," Cassandra told him. "It's okay for you to leave for a few minutes."

"No."

Cassandra stepped in front of him. "Come walk with me," she said.

It wasn't a question, and there was something about her tone that made him look closely at her.

She met his eyes full on, and he was surprised to see something in them he'd never seen before in their brief interactions. Some kind of inner strength and self-knowledge. Courage. Pride.

She'd struck him as a weak woman, someone who had trampled on Serena in subtle and not-so-subtle ways in order to secure her own place in the Jones household. Honestly, he didn't like her very much, but what he saw in her eyes made him want to give her one chance to say whatever it was she needed to say.

They left the birth center.

Graham stopped on the other side of the door. "I know this isn't about getting coffee, Cassandra." He wasn't in any mood to be any more polite than minimally necessary.

She nodded in acknowledgment of his assessment. "You're right. I want to talk to you about Serena."

"Go on."

"She's a very lucky young woman."

"How so?" Personally, he didn't see it right now.

"She's okay, for one thing. This could have been a lot more dangerous, but the doctors say it's all under control, and she'll be fine if she takes care of herself. All she needs now is bed rest."

"And the other thing?"

"She has you."

"Sure she does," he muttered. For all that she actually wanted him. Anyway, he knew exactly what Cassandra meant, and he didn't like it. "But no amount of money is going to buy her health."

"I'm not talking about money."

"Uh-huh."

Cassandra hesitated. She reflexively patted her hair, which was slightly less well put together than usual. "I know you think badly of me. To be honest I haven't given either you or Serena many reasons to think well of me. But there's nothing like finding out someone is in the hospital to knock some sense into you." She paused again. "Ever since she got pregnant Serena has been a different woman."

"She's changed me, too," Graham admitted.

"Of course she has. She does that to everyone. It just takes a lot longer with some of us."

Graham glanced at the door to the waiting area. "If you're not talking about my money, then what?"

"You love her."

"Yes." It felt strange to admit it to this woman so easily when he'd had such trouble admitting it to himself. But he'd had a few days to get used to the idea.

"You love her for herself, not for how she looks on your arm, or because of her money, or anything else. Just for herself."

"Yes."

"And not just because she's having your baby."

"No."

Cassandra smiled, but it was a little watery. "I thought so."

GRAHAM LOOKED LIKE HELL, Serena thought. Just as Cassandra and Meg had told her when they'd come in to urge her to accept his visit.

His clothes were rumpled. His once crisp dress shirt lay open at the collar—not just open but showing a slice of skin and chest hair. His eyes had dark circles under them. Stubble covered his cheeks and jaw, lending him a haggard look.

And his gray eyes seemed washed out as they scanned her thoroughly from head to foot when he entered the room.

It was obvious he hadn't slept. Serena felt a wave of guilt. Meg and Cassandra had told her about the uncomfortable chairs in the waiting area, and said Graham had spent the night on one of them. But she hadn't realized what bad shape he would be in.

Maybe she should have seen him last night, after all—if only to show him she was all right. Instead she'd pushed him away for her own selfish reasons. Just because she loved him. And because he didn't—and couldn't—love her back.

He had every right to be concerned about the baby, and about her health, as well.

Graham walked to her bed. He took a seat on the rolling stool the nurses used and came right beside the bed. Up close he looked even worse, if that were possible.

They looked at each other for a long moment.

"How are you, Serena?" he asked at last.

"I'm okay."

"Are you in pain?"

She shook her head. "Just uncomfortable."

"I've been worried."

"The doctors told you I was okay, right?"

"I needed to hear it from you." His voice seemed raw.

"I'm fine, Graham."

Those gray eyes of his raked her again. "You don't look that fine to me."

"I'm just tired. That's all." She pointed at the machinery and monitoring equipment around her. "The baby's fine. That's what's important."

He held her gaze for a long moment. She felt as if he could see right through her. He must be able to see the depth of her feelings, she thought, as clearly as if they were written in lights on a billboard.

Finally he reached out his hand and took hold of hers. "I'm glad about the baby," he said. "Very glad."

Of course he was, she thought. That was the only reason he'd come back to San Francisco in the first place. Because of the baby. Because of his sense of responsibility.

Oh, he liked her well enough. He'd told her that the other night, and of course she'd known it already. You didn't have sex as good as theirs without at least liking the person.

But love was a whole different ball game.

Graham squeezed her hand. "I'm glad about the baby," he repeated, "but not any more than I am that you're okay."

That stopped her. "Really?"

"Really."

She bit her lower lip. That couldn't possibly mean what she wanted it to. She would be a foolish pregnant ninny to hope.

They sat that way for what seemed like an age. She kept thinking he was going to say something more, but he didn't. It was as if he was searching for words but couldn't find them.

Beside her, the machines whirred as they printed out another chart. She wanted to look at it, wanted to be reassured that everything was fine with her baby, but she knew she wouldn't be able to read it. She had to trust in the monitoring equipment. Someone would come in if there was any trouble.

Graham squeezed her hand and released it. "I never told you about my parents." His voice was flatter than it had been.

"Yes, you did," she answered. "You told me how they lived in Texas for a while and died a long time ago. Their deaths seemed to scar you pretty deeply."

He shook his head and smiled a little, sadly. "My parents weren't nice people, Serena. They lived just for themselves, never for anyone else." He looked at her belly for a long moment. "I was a mistake," he said, "just like our little friend in there. But our baby has two parents who value her already, and will do so as long as they live."

"You didn't?"

He shook his head. "I had a couple of drunken partyers who didn't even bother to look after my basic needs for food and shelter, much less love me. I didn't know any differently, so I thought every child hated his parents the way I hated mine.

I hated them for ignoring me, abandoning me, sometimes even for having me.''

He paused. "When you asked me about them, I let you think we moved to New York when I was fourteen. We didn't. *I* went to New York. Alone. I ran away and never looked back. And they never tried to find me. I knew they wouldn't, so I didn't even bother to conceal my identity once I finally made it to the city. They died a year later, and the sheriff tracked me down within a couple of weeks to tell me.''

"How did they die?''

"They plowed their Camaro into oncoming traffic. Drunk. Killed a teenage boy.''

"How awful.''

"I just felt free,'' he admitted.

Serena's heart went out to the little boy who'd had to be so brave—and so alone. She could only imagine what a scarring experience his childhood must have been. It made her eyes prickle with tears just to think about it.

She reached out her hand, hoping he would give his back to her. He did. She held it gently in hers, interlacing their fingers.

"What did you do? How did you survive?''

"I was a scrapper.'' He told her briefly of the jobs he'd taken, the places he'd stayed. "At one point I worked in the mailroom of an investment bank during the day and ran my own business—delivering takeout food—at night. I learned how to invest in the stock market and got my GED so I could continue my education.''

He'd also spent a lot of nights on the streets and he hadn't trusted anyone enough to accept their assistance. He'd gotten by on his own, worked his way to the top on his own.

Alone and lonely, Serena thought.

Knowing his background only made her love him more. To know what he had overcome to get where he was today...to know why he was the kind of person he was and why he faced the challenges he did. She knew that his confession was a rare one, a precious extension of trust and honesty.

He was a good man. She couldn't think of a better one with whom to share the upbringing of her child, even if they could never have anything more than that between them. She could trust him implicitly with her child's physical and emotional safety. She knew he would do anything in his power to make sure his child's experience of life was vastly different from his own.

''I'm not telling you this for sympathy,'' Graham said, as if he had noticed the dampness in her eyes. ''It's just so you know where I'm coming from. My background.''

''I understand,'' she said, forcing her voice not

to waver. "Your background." She swallowed, trying to return his honesty with all the courage she had at her disposal. "And the reasons you can't love me."

He shook his head. "The reasons I do love you."

It's okay, she almost started to say. *I understand. It doesn't matter. We can still raise our baby right, and I won't make a big deal of the fact that I'm in love with you.*

But then she caught herself.

"You love me?"

"I love you."

She couldn't speak. Her brain seemed to have frozen, and she couldn't trust her sensory input.

"I know you don't believe me," Graham said. "And there's no reason you should, considering the things I told you last May. But you've changed me somehow. You and the baby."

She started to cry.

She couldn't help it. There were times when you just had to cry, and this was one of them. She tried to stifle it, absurdly worried that it would set off the monitors and send a nurse running in, but then she just gave in to the emotions.

Graham handed her a handkerchief. She wiped the tears from her eyes and blew her nose loudly and inelegantly into it.

As she wadded it up, she noticed her monogram in the corner.

"This is mine. Where did you get it?"

He met her gaze. "You left it at the hotel."

"And you decided to carry it with you?" She smiled, a little embarrassed by her crying jag.

"Last May."

He said it quietly, seriously.

"Last May," she said, "but that means..."

"That I've been carrying your damned handkerchief all around the globe with me," he said affectionately.

"Since last May?"

He nodded.

"But it's just a handkerchief."

"It was the only part of you that you left me."

"You were carrying that silly little hanky around the globe for all those months?" she asked.

"Thinking of you every time I touched it."

She put her hand on her belly between the monitoring straps. She thought of all the months she'd spent alone, planning for her baby's arrival, being strong all by herself. "And you never bothered to call me?"

"Don't be angry."

She blew out a stream of air. "I'm not. I just don't understand this. You only came back because of the baby."

He shook his head. "I should have come back sooner, but I thought I had nothing to offer you. You were so young, so vibrant, and you had your whole life in front of you. I couldn't face putting you in a situation where I knew you wouldn't get what you wanted so badly."

"Love."

"Right."

"Because you were so old and decrepit and incapable of loving anyone?"

"I thought I was. No, scratch that. I was. Not necessarily old and decrepit," he said with a smile, "but certainly not capable of love. You changed that, though. You unlocked something inside me. I don't know how you did it, but you changed me. Made me feel whole. Opened me up so I could fall in love with you."

"Oh, my."

"Is that all you can say?"

"I didn't think you ever would. I'd pretty much given up hope."

"You hoped?"

"Of course I hoped! I'm madly in love with you, you big fool."

"Oh," he said. "I hoped you were."

"Is that all you can say?" she asked, laughing.

"No." Graham took both her hands in both of his. He pushed the stool aside and got down on his knees on the hard linoleum floor. He looked straight into her eyes, his gray eyes warm with love. "Serena, will you marry me?"

"Yes," she answered immediately. "Oh, yes."

He leaned in and kissed her then, a long, luxurious, sexy kiss that set her heart to racing and was probably just about to sound the alarms when he broke it off.

He smiled at her, and she smiled at him. "But no shotgun wedding," she said mischievously. "You know how I feel about those...."

Epilogue

April

They were getting married.

It was a beautiful, warm spring afternoon, and Serena stood near the house, gazing across the garden and past the rows of seated guests to her bridegroom. Graham, in an elegant linen suit and a dark, stylish tie, held their healthy two-month-old daughter, Claire, in a small receiving blanket in his arms.

"Ready to get this show on the road?" Meg whispered by Serena's side.

She nodded but couldn't speak—her heart felt so full of love and tenderness for the pair who awaited her at the other end of the garden. Graham and Claire, father and child. Her family.

Serena's eyes prickled with emotion and she blinked, trying to hold back the tears. She'd done an awful lot of that in the last few months.

"Oh, no, don't start that again—you'll make me cry, too." Meg gave her shoulder a warm, sisterly squeeze.

"I'm okay," Serena managed to say in a low, husky voice. "I'm just—just—"

"Happy. Very, very happy." Meg finished for her with a grin. "I know. And I'm so happy for you." Holding her bouquet of tiger lilies, she stepped forward as the string quartet finished one musical selection and began the next. "There's my cue." She glanced back with a wink. "I'll meet you at the top of the aisle."

Serena watched as her friend, wearing a surprisingly demure, drop-waist pale peach dress, slowly traversed the brick walkway that ran down the center of the garden.

Her own dress was a pale, silvery purple and a little whimsical, in a style that made her look a bit like a twenties flapper. She held a bouquet of the same fragrant purple orchids Graham had sent her after Thanksgiving. She also wore a few of the exotic blossoms in her hair, forgoing a veil.

Beside her stood her father, who would give her away. It was Serena's one concession to his old-fashioned sensibilities. Though she hadn't seen it as necessary—she was hardly a traditional bride—she hadn't been averse.

Lightly she held her father's arm. She glanced

sideways and smiled when she detected a hint of nervousness in his face.

He wasn't perfect, and they still had a lot of work to do on their relationship—but he was her father. She couldn't help loving the man.

Meg reached the end of the brick path, taking her position on the opposite side of the minister from Graham and Jake, his best man.

Harrison smoothed the front of his conservative navy suit. "All right, girl. Now it's our turn."

They moved forward, and the guests rose to watch them advance. Serena looked slowly from side to side, smiling at the small assembly of guests. Her gaze landed on Daniel, Meg's brother, who was watching Meg's dozing baby boy for her. And Dirk and Elaine, who stood holding hands on the other side of the aisle.

Dirk and Elaine would never know exactly *how* she and Graham had met at their wedding—that was a secret that would never be known by anyone else but Meg. But as Serena's mind flashed back to that long ago day, when she'd tried to call a halt to the ceremony, she felt amusement and affection for the inexperienced young woman she'd been— and she was profoundly thankful for the twist of fate that had landed Graham at just the right place and time to intervene.

If not for that one single moment, her life would

be completely different. She wouldn't have Graham, or her daughter, or even Meg. She might still be a meek little mouse.

Thank God it had all unfolded as it had, she thought. She wouldn't trade her life now for anything. Not only did she have the most wonderful family and friends, but she'd also recently gotten into a graduate studies program—at the top school she'd applied to.

Serena raised her gaze to Graham's as he stood before her, waiting with their daughter who, like Meg's son, happily snoozed away. She saw love in Graham's eyes, and passion and warmth.

He wasn't a huge chunk of ice, or granite, or any other inanimate substance. He was a breathing, flesh-and-blood man who loved her—she now understood—with all the intensity and passion inside him.

Imagine that.

They smiled at each other. She felt a tear escape her eye and trickle down her cheek, but she didn't care. And she wasn't the only one crying, she noticed wryly. Several of the guests, and Meg, as well, had succumbed to the power of the moment.

She and her father reached the front, and he gave her a kiss on the cheek as he left her with Graham and Claire. The minister began the ceremony.

Serena eagerly awaited the chance to speak her

vows, and after she finished them she waited just as eagerly for Graham to speak his. His simple "I will" held a wealth of meaning, a depth and emotional charge only he could give to it.

Someone else might take the phrase "to love, honor and cherish" lightly, but not the Graham who stood beside her. Serena knew how much of a miracle it was that he was finally in a position to pledge to do those things. A total turnaround, she thought, from last spring.

Meg took her bouquet, and Jake held Claire so they could exchange rings and a kiss—a long, sweet, tender kiss filled with the promise of many years to come.

They were husband and wife.

The reception took place inside the house, with a buffet of delicious food, which Serena managed to taste—despite all the happy distractions of the day—and dancing in the center of the living room.

Her father and Cassandra, finally able to embrace their roles as grandparents, looked after Claire while Serena and Graham took several turns on the floor. Their friends and family surrounded them, and the room was filled with the sounds of celebration—but as they danced they only had eyes for each other.

"I love you," he told her in a husky voice. "You and Claire. More than anything."

"And I love you," she said, her arms tightening around his neck.

He was her husband now. The father of her child and the man she wanted to wake up next to for the rest of her days. How incredible and divine.

Serena smiled. She knew they had forged a love—and a family—to last a lifetime.

Sometimes yours truly thinks she ought to get out of the gossip racket and into the fortune-telling trade. A few months ago I suggested that a certain billionaire bachelor might want to marry one of our local girls.

And guess what?

The deed's been done, and with all the style and personal flair one would expect from one of San Francisco's most interesting couples. A quiet garden wedding—so hush-hush, I'm almost afraid to say, that my loyal spies didn't even get word of it until *after* the event— recently took place at the couple's Pacific Heights home.

Yes, Graham Richards and Serena Jones have indeed tied the knot, and their adorable baby girl, Claire, was apparently right in the middle of the ceremony. There's more to the tale, of course, but everyone deserves a little it up for everyone to see. "It's a set of English razors." he said and grinned at Dan. "The waiter must have got the labels mixed. Thanks again, Dan."

Abruptly Pierce sat down. He was smiling.

Jennie felt them all watching her. She raised her head and looked around the table. It was as if she knew what they were thinking. Of the twelve other couples seated around the large table, she had known five of the men before she'd made the test. Irving Schwartz, Bonner, three others, who were top-ranking executives with other companies. The other seven men all knew. Some of their wives, too. She could see it in their eyes. In only two of the men could she see any sympathy. David and Nevada Smith.

David she could understand. But she did not understand why Nevada should feel sorry for her. He scarcely knew her. He had always seemed so quiet, even shy, when they met at the studio. But now there was a wild sort of anger deep in his black Indian eyes as he looked from her to Dan Pierce.

Thirteen men, she thought, and all but one of them knew her for what she'd been. And the thirteenth was the unlucky one. He was going to marry her. She felt a light touch on her arm. Rosa's voice broke the silence that threatened to engulf her. "I think it's about time we went to the little girl's room."

Jennie nodded dumbly and followed her from the table silently. She could feel the eyes of other diners following her. Without even returning their glances, she recognized several other men she had known and saw their wise, knowing smiles. She began to feel sick. Rosa drew the curtain in front of the small alcove in the corner as Jennie sank silently onto the couch. Rosa lit a cigarette and handed it to her.

Jennie looked up at her, the cigarette in her fingers already forgotten. The tears started to come into her eyes. "Why?" she asked in a hurt, bewildered voice. "I don't understand. What did I ever do to him?"

She began to cry silently as Rosa sat down beside her and drew her head down to her shoulder.

Dan Pierce chuckled to himself as he threaded his way to his car through the dark and deserted parking lot. Wait until he told the story in the locker room at Hillcrest tomorrow morning. The men would laugh their heads off. None of them really liked Jonas, anyway.

True, they tolerated him. But they didn't accept him. There was a difference. They all respected Jonas' success but they wouldn't lift a finger to help him. Not like they would for Dan Pierce if he needed their help, which he didn't. He was one of them, he'd grown up in the business with them. They had their rules. They stuck together.

Wait until he told them how the broad looked. Like she was ready to sink through the floor, while all the time, Jonas stood there like a *shmuck*, smiling and thinking how nice everybody was. It would break them up.

A dark figure suddenly appeared out of the shadows in front of him. He peered anxiously through the darkness as it silently came closer. "Oh, it's you, Nevada. I didn' know who it was."

Nevada stood there silently.

Dan laughed aloud as he remembered. "Wasn' that a bitch, though?" He chortled, reaching out a hand toward Nevada to steady himself. "I thought she'd bust when she opened the case and saw the razors. An' Jonas, the jerk, he don' even know what he's gettin' into—"

Dan's voice suddenly choked off in a grunt of pain as Nevada sank his fist into his belly. He fell back against a car, clutching at it to hold himself up. He stared at Nevada. "Wha' you go an' do that for?" he asked in a hurt voice. "We're ol' buddies."

He saw Nevada's hand coming toward his face and tried to duck. He wasn't quick enough and felt the pain explode in his eyes. Again the hammer tore into his belly. He bent over, retching, and another blow on the side of his face sent him sprawling into his own vomit. He looked up at Nevada with frightened eyes.

It was not until then that Nevada spoke, and an icy fear came up and clutched at Dan's heart. "I should've done this a long time ago," Nevada said, looking down at him. "I oughta kill you. But you ain't worth goin' to the gas chamber for."

He turned his back contemptuously and walked away. Dan waited until the sound of the high-heeled boots faded away. Then he put his face down on his hands against the cold concrete. "It was only a joke," he cried drunkenly. "It was only a joke."

Jonas followed Jennie into the darkened house. "You're tired," he said gently, looking down at her white face. "It's been a big night. Go on up to bed. I'll see you tomorrow."

"No," she said flatly. She knew what she had to do. She turned and walked into the living room, switching on the light. He followed her curiously.

She turned, slipping the ring from her finger, and held it out to him. He looked at it, then at her. "Why?" he asked. "Is it because of anything I did tonight?"

She shook her head. "No," she said quickly. "It has nothing to do with you at all. Just take the ring, please."

"I'm entitled to know why, Jennie."

"I don't love you," she said. "Is that reason enough?"

"Not now it isn't."

"Then I have a better reason," she said tightly. "Before I made that screen test, I was the highest-priced whore in Hollywood."

He stared at her for a moment. "I don't believe you," he said slowly. "You couldn't have fooled me."

"You're a fool," she said sharply. "If you don't believe me, ask Bonner or any of the other four men at the table who laid me. Or any of a dozen other men I saw in the restaurant tonight."

"I still don't believe you," he said in a low voice.

She laughed. "Then ask Bonner why Pierce gave me that present. There wasn't any mix-up, he meant the razors for me. The story was all over Hollywood, the morning after Bonner left here. How I shaved all the hair off his body, then blew him in a bathtub filled with champagne."

He began to look sick.

"And why do you think I asked you to let me do *Aphrodite?*" she continued. "Not because I thought it was any good. It was to pay Pierce off for this." She walked quickly to the desk and took out two small reels of film. She spun one out at him, the film unwinding from the reel like a roll of confetti. "My first starring role," she said sarcastically. "A pornographic picture."

She took a cigarette from the box on the desk and lit it. She turned back to him. Her voice was quieter now. "Or maybe you're the kind of man who enjoys being married to that kind of woman, so that every time you meet another man, you can wonder. Did he or didn't he? When, where and how?"

He took a step toward her. "That's over now. It doesn't matter."

"It doesn't? Just because I was a fool for a moment, you don't have to be. How much of tonight do you think you'd have been able to take if you'd known what you know now?"

"But I love you!"

"You even kid yourself about that. You don't love me. You never have. You're in love with a memory. The memory of a girl who preferred your father to you. The first chance you had, you tried to make me over in her image. Even in bed—the things you wanted me to do. Did you really think I was so naïve I didn't know those were the things she did to you?"

The ring was still in her hand. She put it on the table in front of him. "Here," she said.

He stared down at the ring. The diamond seemed to shoot angry sparks at him. He looked up at her, his face lined and drawn. "Keep it," he said curtly and walked out.

She stood there until she heard his car pull out of the driveway. Then she turned out the light and walked upstairs, leaving the ring on the table and the film, like confetti after a party, on the floor.

She lay wide-eyed on her bed staring up into the night. If she could only cry she would feel better. But she was empty inside, eaten away by her sins. There was nothing left for her to give anyone. She had used up her ration of love.

Once, long ago, she had loved and been loved. But Tom Denton was dead, lost forever, beyond recall.

She cried out into the darkness, "Daddy, help me! Please! I don't know what to do."

If she could only go back and begin again. Back to the familiar Sunday smell of corned beef and cabbage, to the gentle sound of a whispered morning Mass in her ears, to the sisters and the hospital, to the inner satisfaction of being a part of God's work.

Then her father's voice came whispering to her out of the gray light of the morning, "Do you really want to go, Jennie Bear?"

She lay very still for a moment thinking, remembering. Was that time forever gone? If she were to withhold from confession that part of her life which no longer seemed to belong to her it need not be. They would not know. It was her one real transgression. The rest of her life they already knew about.

To do so would be a sin. A sin of omission. It would invalidate any future confession that she might make. But she had so much to give and without giving it she was denying not only herself but others who would have need of her help. Which was the greater sin? For a moment she was frightened, then decided that this was a matter between her and her Maker. The decision was hers, and she alone could be held responsible, both now and at any future time.

Suddenly she made her mind up and she was no longer afraid.

"Yes, Daddy," she whispered.

His soft voice came echoing back on the wind. "Then get dressed, Jennie, and I'll go with you."

16

IT WAS ALMOST TWO YEARS FROM THE NIGHT OF THE party before Rosa heard from Jennie again. It was almost six months from the time she received the dreaded impersonal message from the War Department that David had been killed at the Anzio beachhead in May of 1944.

No more dreams, no more big deals, no more struggles and plans to build a giant monument of incorporation that would span the earth, linked by thin and gossamer strands of celluloid. They had come to a final stop for him, just as they had for a thousand others, in the crashing, thundering fire of an early Italian morning.

The dreams had stopped for her, too. The whisper of love in the night, the creaking of the floor beneath the footsteps on the other side of the bed, the excitement and warmth of shared confidences and plans for tomorrow.

For once, Rosa was grateful for her work. It used her mind and taxed her energy and consumed her with the day-to-day responsibilities. In time, the hurt was pushed back into the corner recesses of her mind, to be felt only when she was alone.

Then, bit by bit, the understanding came to her, as it always must to the survivors, that only a part of the dreams had been buried with him. His son was growing and one day, as she saw him running across the green lawn in the front of their home, she heard the birds begin to sing again. She looked up at the blue sky, at the white sun above her head, and knew that once again she was a living, breathing human being with the full, rich blood of life in her body. And the guilt that had been in her, because she had remained while he had gone, disappeared.

It all happened that day after she read Jennie's letter. It was addressed to her in a small, feminine script that she did not recognize. At first, she thought it another solicitation when she saw the imprimatur on the letterhead.

†

Sisters of Mercy
Burlingame, California

October 10, 1944

DEAR ROSA,

It is with some trepidation and yet with the knowledge that you will respect my confidence that I take my pen in hand to write. I do not seek to reopen wounds which by this time have already partly healed but it is only a few days ago that I learned of your loss and wanted to extend to you and little Bernie my sympathy and prayers.

David was a fine man and a genuinely kind human being. All of us who knew him will miss him. I mention him in my prayers each day and I am comforted by the words of Our Lord and Saviour: "I am the resurrection and the life; he who believes in me, even if he die, shall live; and whoever lives and believes in me shall never die."

Sincerely yours in J. C.
SISTER M. THOMAS
(JENNIE DENTON)

It was then, when Rosa went outside to call her son in from his play, that she heard the birds singing. The next weekend, she drove to Burlingame to visit Jennie.

There were tiny white puffballs of clouds in the blue sky as Rosa turned her car into the wide driveway that led to the Mother House. It was a Saturday afternoon and there were many automobiles parked there already. She pulled into an open space some distance from the sprawling building.

She sat in the car and lit a cigarette. She felt a doubt creeping through her. Perhaps she shouldn't have come. Jennie might not want to see her, wouldn't want to be reminded of that world she'd left behind. It was pure impulse that she had followed in driving here and she couldn't blame Jennie if she refused to see her.

She remembered the morning after the engagement party. When Jennie hadn't shown up at the studio, no one had thought very much about it. And David, who been trying to reach Jonas at the plant in Burbank, told her that he couldn't locate him, either.

When the next day and the day after that had passed and there was still no word from Jennie, the studio really began to worry. Jonas had finally been located in Canada at the new factory and David called him there. His voice had been very curt over the telephone as he told David that the last time he'd seen Jennie was when he left her home the night of the party.

David immediately called Rosa and suggested she run out to Jennie's house. When she got there, the Mexican servant came to the door. "Is Miss Denton in?"

"Señorita, she not in."

"Do you know where she is?" Rosa asked. "It's very important that I get in touch with her."

The servant shook her head. "The señorita go away. She not say where."

Deliberately Rosa walked past her into the house. There were packed boxes all along the hallway. On the side of one was stenciled *Bekins, Moving & Storage*. The servant saw the surprise on her face. "The señorita tell me to close the house and go away, too."

Rosa didn't wait until she got home, but called David from

the first pay telephone she came to. He said he'd try to speak to Jonas again.

"Did you reach Jonas?" she asked, as soon as he came in the door that evening.

"Yes. He told me to close down *Aphrodite* and have Pierce thrown off the lot. When I said we might wind up with a lawsuit, he told me to tell Dan that if he wanted to start anything, Jonas would spend his last dollar to break him."

"But what about Jennie?"

"If she doesn't show up by the end of the week, Jonas told me to have her put on the suspended list and stop her salary."

"And their engagement?"

"Jonas didn't say, but I guess that's over, too. When I asked him if we should prepare a statement for the press, he told me to tell them nothing and hung up."

"Poor Jennie. I wonder where she is?"

Now Rosa knew. She got out of the car and started to walk slowly toward the Mother House.

Sister M. Thomas sat quietly in her small room, reading her Bible. A soft knock came at the door. She got to her feet, the Bible still in her hand, and opened it. The light from the window in the hall outside her room turned her white novice's veil a soft silver. "Yes, sister?"

"There's a visitor to see you, sister. A Mrs. David Woolf. She's in the visitors' room downstairs."

Sister Thomas hesitated a moment, then spoke. Her voice was calm and quiet. "Thank you, sister. Please tell Mrs. Woolf that I shall be down in a few minutes."

The nun bowed her head and started down the corridor as Sister Thomas closed the door. For a moment, she leaned her back against it, weak and breathless. She had not expected Rosa to come. She drew herself up and crossed the small room to kneel before the crucifix on the bare wall near her bed. She clasped her hands in prayer. It was as if it were only yesterday that she had come here, that she was still the frightened girl who had spent all her life trying to hide from herself her love for God.

She remembered the kind voice of the Mother Superior as she had knelt before her, weeping, her head in the soft material across the Mother Superior's lap. She felt once again the gentle touch of the stroking fingers on her head.

"Do not weep, my child. And do not fear. The path that leads to Our Lord may be most grievous and difficult but Jesus Christ, Our Saviour, refuses none who truly seeks Him."

"But, Reverend Mother, I have sinned."

"Who among us is without sin?" the Reverend Mother said softly. "If you take your sins to Him who takes all sins to Himself to share, and convince Him with your penitence, He will grant you His holy forgiveness and you will be welcome in His house."

She looked up at the Reverend Mother through her tears. "Then, I may stay?"

The Mother Superior smiled down at her. "Of course you may stay, my child."

Rosa rose from the chair as Sister Thomas came into the visitors' room. "Jennie?" she said tentatively. "Sister Thomas, I mean."

"Rosa, how good it is to see you."

Rosa looked at her. The wide-set gray eyes and lovely face belonged to Jennie, but the calm serenity that glowed beneath the novice's white veil came from Sister Thomas. Suddenly, she knew that the face she was looking at was the same face she had once seen on the screen, enlarged a thousand times and filled with the same love as when the Magdalen had stretched forth her hand to touch the hem of her Saviour's gown.

"Jennie!" she said, smiling. "Suddenly, I'm so happy that I just want to hug you."

Sister Thomas held out her arms.

Later, they strolled the quiet paths around the grounds in the afternoon sunlight and when they came to the top of a hill, they paused there, looking down into the green valley below them.

"His beauty is everywhere," Sister Thomas said softly, turning to her friend, "I have found my place in His house."

Rosa looked at her. "How long do you remain in the novitiate?"

"Two years. Until next May."

"And what do you do then?" Rosa questioned.

"If I prove worthy of His grace, I take the black veil and

go forth in the path of the Founding Mother, to bring His mercy to all who may need it."

She looked into Rosa's eyes and once again Rosa saw the deep-lying pool of serenity within them. "And I am more fortunate than most," Sister Thomas added humbly. "He has already trained me in His work. My years in the hospital will help me wherever I may be sent, for it is in this area I can best serve."

JONAS—1945

Book Nine

1

OUTSIDE, THE WHITE-HOT MID-JULY SUN BEAT DOWN on the Nevada air strip, but here in the General's office, the overworked air-conditioner whirred and kept the temperature down to an even eighty degrees. I looked at Morrissey, then across the table to the General and his staff.

"That's the story, gentlemen," I said. "The CA-JET X.P. should reach six hundred easier than the British De Havilland-Rolls jet did the five-o-six point five they're bragging about." I smiled at them and got to my feet. "And now, if you'll step outside, gentlemen, I'll show you."

"I have no doubt about that, Mr. Cord," the General said smoothly. "If there'd been any doubts in our minds, you never would have got the contract."

"Then what are we waiting for? Let's go."

"Just a moment, Mr. Cord," the General said quickly. "We can't allow you to demonstrate the jet."

I stared at him. "Why not?"

"You haven't been cleared for jet aircraft," he said. He

looked down at a sheet of paper on his desk. "Your medical report indicates a fractional lag in your reflexes. Perfectly normal, of course, considering your age, but you'll understand why we can't let you fly her."

"That's a lot of crap, General. Who the hell do you think flew her down here to deliver her to you?"

"You had a perfect right to—then," the General replied. "It was your plane. But the moment she touched that field outside, according to the contract, she became the property of the Army. And we can't afford the risk of allowing you to take her up."

I slammed my fist into my hand angrily. Rules, nothing but rules. That was the trouble with these damn contracts. Yesterday, I could have flown her up to Alaska and back and they couldn't have stopped me. Or for that matter, even catch me. The CA-JET X.P. was two hundred odd miles an hour faster than any of the conventional aircraft the Army had in the air. Someday, I'd have to take the time to read those contracts.

The General smiled and came around the table toward me. "I know just how you feel, Mr. Cord," he said. "When the medics told me I was too old for combat flying and put me behind a desk, I wasn't any older than you are right now. And I didn't like it any more than you do. Nobody likes being told he is growing older."

What the hell was he talking about? I was only forty-one. That isn't old. I could still fly rings around most of those damp-eared kids walking around on the field outside with gold and silver bars and oak leaves on their shoulders. I looked at the General.

He must have read the surprise in my eyes, for he smiled again. "That was only a year ago. I'm forty-three now." He offered me a cigarette and I took it silently. "Lieutenant Colonel Shaw will take her up. He's on the field right now, waiting for us."

Again, he read the question in my eyes. "Don't worry about it," he said quickly. "Shaw's completely familiar with the plane. He spent the last three weeks at your plant in Burbank checking her out."

I glanced at Morrissey but he was carefully looking somewhere else at the time. He'd been in on it, too. I'd make him sweat for that one. I turned back to the General. "O.K., General. Let's go outside and watch that baby fly."

Baby was the right word and not only for the plane. Lieutenant Colonel Shaw couldn't have been more than twenty years old. I watched him take her up but somehow I couldn't stand there squinting up at the sky, watching him put her through her paces. It was like going to a lot of trouble to set yourself up with a virgin and then when you had everything warmed up and ready, you opened the bedroom door and found another guy copping the cherry right under your nose.

"Is there anywhere around here I could get a cup of coffee?"

"There's a commissary down near the main gate," one of the soldiers said.

"Thanks."

"You're welcome," he said automatically, never taking his eyes from the plane in the sky, while I walked away.

The commissary wasn't air-conditioned but they kept it dark and it wasn't too bad, even if the ice cubes in the iced coffee had melted before I got the glass back to my seat. I stared morosely out of the window in front of my table. Too young or too old. That was the story of my life. I was fourteen when the last one ended, in 1918, and almost over the age limit when we got into this one. Some people never had any luck. I always thought that war came to every generation but I was neither one nor the other. I had the bad fortune to be born in between.

A medium-size Army bus pulled up in front of the commissary. Men started to pile out and I watched them because there was nothing else to look at. They weren't soldiers; they were civilians, and not young ones, either. Most of them carried their jacket over their arm and a brief case in their free hand and there were some with gray in their hair and many with no hair at all. One thing about them caught my eye. None of them were smiling, not even when they spoke to one another in the small groups they immediately formed on the sidewalk in front of the bus.

Why should they smile, I asked myself bitterly. They had nothing to smile about. They were all dodoes like me. I took out a cigarette and struck a match. The breeze from the circulating fan blew it out. I struck another, turning away from the fan and shielding the cigarette in my cupped hands.

"Herr Cord! This is indeed a surprise! What are you doing here?"

I looked up at Herr Strassmer. "I just delivered a new plane," I said, holding out my hand. "But what are you doing out here? I thought you were in New York."

He shook my hand in that peculiarly European way of his. The smile left his eyes. "We, too, made a delivery. And now we go back."

"You were with that group outside?"

He nodded. He looked out through the window at them and a troubled look came into his eyes. "Yes," he said slowly. "We all came together in one plane but we are going back on separate flights. Three years we worked together but now the job is finished. Soon I go back to California."

"I hope so," I laughed. "We sure could use you in the plant but I'm afraid it'll be some time yet. The war in Europe may be over but if Tarawa and Okinawa are any indication, we're good for at least six months to a year before Japan quits."

He didn't answer.

I looked up and suddenly I remembered. These Europeans were very touchy about manners. "Excuse me, Herr Strassmer," I said quickly. "Won't you join me in some coffee?"

"I have not the time." There was a curiously hesitant look in his eyes. "Do you have an office here as you do everywhere else?"

"Sure," I said, looking up at him. I'd passed the door marked *Men* on my way over. "It's in the back of this building."

"I will meet you there in five minutes," he said and hurried out.

Through the window, I watched him join one of the groups and begin to talk with them. I wondered if the old boy was going crackers. You couldn't tell, but maybe he had been working too hard and thought he was back in Nazi Germany. There certainly wasn't any reason for him to be so secretive about being seen talking to me. After all, we were on the same side.

I ground my cigarette into an ash tray and sauntered out. He never even glanced up as I walked past his group on my way to the john. He came into the room a moment after I

had got there. His eyes darted nervously toward the booths.
"Are we alone?"

"I think so," I said, looking at him. I wondered what you
did to get a doctor around here if there were any signs of
his cracking up.

He walked over to the booths, opened the doors and
looked. Satisfied, he turned back to me. His face was tense
and pale and there were small beads of perspiration across
his forehead. I thought I'd begun to recognize the symptoms.
Too much of this Nevada sun is murder if you're not used
to it. His first words convinced me I was right.

"Herr Cord," he whispered hoarsely. "The war will not be
over in six months."

"Of course not," I said soothingly. From what I had heard,
the first thing to do was agree with them, try to calm them
down. I wished I could remember the second thing. I turned
to the sink. "Here, let me get you a glass of—"

"It will be over next month!"

What I thought must have been written on my face, for
my mouth hung open in surprise. "No, I'm not crazy, Herr
Cord," Strassmer said quickly. "To no one else but you would
I say this. It is the only way I can repay you for saving my
life. I know how important this could be to your business."

"But—but how—"

"I cannot tell you more," he interrupted. "Just believe me.
By next month, Japan will be *verfallen!*" He turned and almost ran out the door.

I stared after him for a moment, then went over to the sink
and washed my face in cold water. I felt I must be even
crazier than he was, because I was beginning to believe him.
But why? It just didn't make any sense. Sure, we were pushing the Nips back, but they still held Malaya, Hong Kong
and the Dutch East Indies, and with their kamikaze philos-
ophy, it would take a miracle to end the war in a month.

I was still thinking about it when Morrissey and I got on
the train. "You know who I ran into back there?" I asked.
I didn't give him a chance to answer. "Otto Strassmer."

There seemed to be a kind of relief in his smile. I guess
he'd been expecting to catch hell for not telling me about
that Air Corps test pilot. "He's a nice little guy," Morrissey
said. "How is he?"

"Seemed all right to me," I said. "He was on his way back

to New York." I looked out the window at the flat Nevada desert. "By the way, did you ever hear exactly what it was he was working on?"

"Not exactly."

I looked at him. "What was it you did hear?"

"I didn't hear it from him," Morrissey said. "I got it from a friend of mine down at the Engineers' Club, who worked on it for a little while. But he didn't know very much about it, either. All he knew was that it was called the Manhattan Project and that it had something to do with Professor Einstein."

I could feel my brows knit in puzzlement. "What could Strassmer do for a man like Einstein?"

He smiled again. "After all, Strassmer did invent a plastic beer can that was stronger than metal."

"So?" I asked.

"So maybe the Professor got Otto to invent a plastic container to store his atoms in," Morrissey said, laughing.

I felt a wild excitement racing inside me. A container for atoms, energy in a bottle, ready to explode when you popped the cork. The little man hadn't been crazy. He knew what he was talking about. I'd been the crazy one.

It would take a miracle, I'd thought. Well, Strassmer and his friends had come into the desert and made one and now they were going home, their job done. What it was or how they did it I couldn't guess and didn't care.

But deep inside me, I was sure that it had happened.

The miracle that would end the war.

2

I GOT OFF THE TRAIN AT RENO, WHILE MORRISSEY went on to Los Angeles. There was no time to call Robair at the ranch, so I took a taxi to the factory. We barreled through the steel-wire gate, under the big sign that read **CORD EXPLOSIVES,** now more than a mile from the main plant.

The factory had expanded tremendously since the war.

For that matter, so had all our companies. It seemed that no matter what we did, there never was enough space.

I got out and paid the cabby and as he pulled away, I looked up at the familiar old building. It was worn now, and looked dingy and obsolete compared with the new additions, but its roof was gleaming white and shining in the sun. Somehow, I could never bring myself to move out of it when the other executives had moved their offices into the new administration building. I dropped my cigarette on the walk and ground it into dust beneath my heel, then went into the building.

The smell was the same as it always was and the whispers that rose from the lips of the men and women working there were the same as I always heard when I passed by "*El hijo.*" The son. It had been twenty years and most of them hadn't even been there when my father died and still they called me that. Even the young ones, some of them less than half my age.

The office was the same, too. The heavy, oversized desk and leather-covered furniture now showed the cracks and wear of time. There was no secretary in the outer office and I was not surprised. There was no reason for one to be there. They hadn't expected me.

I walked around behind the desk and pressed the switch down on the squawk box that put me right through to Mc-Allister's office in the new building, a quarter of a mile away. The surprise echoed in his voice as it came through the box. "Jonas! Where did you come from?"

"The Air Corps," I said. "We just delivered the CA-JET X.P."

"Good. Did they like it?"

"I guess they did," I answered. "They wouldn't trust me to take it up." I leaned over and opened the door of the cabinet below the telephone table, taking out the bottle of bourbon that was there. I put the bottle on the desk in front of me. "How do we stand on war-contract cancellations in case the war ends tomorrow?"

"For the explosive company?" Mac asked.

"For all the companies," I said. I knew he kept copies of every contract we ever made down here because he considered this his home office.

"It'll take a little time. I'll put someone on it right away."

"Like about an hour?"

He hesitated. When he spoke, a curious note came into his voice. "All right, if it's that important."

"It's that important."

"Do you know something?"

"No," I said truthfully. I really didn't know. I was only guessing. "I just want it."

There was silence for a moment, then he spoke again. "I just got the blueprints from Engineering on converting the radar and small-parts division of Aircraft to the proposed electronics company. Shall I bring them over?"

"Do that," I said, flipping up the switch. Taking a glass from the tray next to the Thermos jug, I filled it half full with bourbon. I looked across the room to the wall where the portrait of my father looked down on me. I held the glass up to him.

"It's been a long time, Pop," I said and poured the whisky down my throat.

I took my hands from the blueprints on the desk and snapped and rolled them up tight, like a coil spring. I looked at McAllister. "They look all right to me, Mac."

He nodded. "I'll mark them approved and shoot them on to Purchasing to have them requisition the materials on stand-by orders, to be delivered when the war ends." He looked at the bottle of bourbon on the desk. "You're not very hospitable. How about a drink?"

I looked at him in surprise. Mac wasn't much for drinking. Especially during working hours. I pushed the bottle and a glass toward him. "Help yourself."

He poured a small shot and swallowed it neat. He cleared his throat. I looked at him. "There's one other postwar plan I wanted to talk to you about," he said awkwardly.

"Go ahead."

"Myself," he said hesitantly. "I'm not a young man any more. I want to retire."

"Retire?" I couldn't believe my ears. "What for? What in hell would you do?"

Mac flushed embarrassedly. "I've worked pretty hard all my life," he said. "I've got two sons and a daughter and five grandchildren, three of whom I've never seen. The wife and I would like to spend a little time with them, get to know them before it's too late."

I laughed. "You sound like you expect to kick off any minute. You're a young man yet."

"I'm sixty-three. I've been with you twenty years."

I stared at him. Twenty years. Where had they gone? The Army doctors had been right. I wasn't a kid any more, either. "We'll miss you around here," I said sincerely. "I don't know how we'll manage without you." I meant it, too. Mac was the one man I felt I could always depend on, whenever I had need for him.

"You'll manage all right. We've got over forty attorneys working for us now and each is a specialist in his own field. You're not just one man any more, you're a big company. You have to have a big legal machine to take care of you."

"So what?" I said. "You can't call up a machine in the middle of the night when you're in trouble."

"This machine you can. It's equipped for all emergencies."

"But what will you do? You can't tell me you'll be happy just lying around playing grandpa. You'll have to have something to occupy your mind."

"I've thought about that," he said, a serious look coming over his face. "I've been playing around so long with corporate and tax laws that I've almost forgotten about the most important part of all. The laws that have to do with human beings." He reached for the bottle again and poured himself another small drink. It wasn't easy for him to sit there and tell me what he was thinking.

"I thought I'd hang my shingle outside my house in some small town. Just putter around with whatever happened to come in the door. I'm tired of always talking in terms of millions of dollars. For once, I'd like to help some poor bastard who really needs it."

I stared at him. Work with a man for twenty years and still you don't know him. This was a side to McAllister that I'd never even suspected existed.

"Of course, we'll abrogate all of the contracts and agreements between us," he said.

I looked at him. I knew he didn't need the money. But then, neither did I. "Why in hell should we? Just show up at the board of directors' meeting every few months so at least I can see you once in a while."

"Then you—you agree?"

I nodded. "Sure, let's give it a spin when the war is over."

The sheets of white paper grew into a stack as he skimmed through the summary of each of the contracts. At last, Mac was finished and he looked up at me. "We have ample protective-cancellation clauses in all the contracts except one," he said. "That one is based on delivery before the end of the war."

"Which one is that?"

"That flying boat we're building for the Navy in San Diego."

I knew what he was talking about. *The Centurion*. It was to be the biggest airplane ever built, designed to carry a full company of one hundred and fifty men, in addition to the twelve-man crew, two light amphibious tanks and enough mortar, light artillery, weapons, ammunition and supplies for an entire company. It had been my idea that a plane like that would prove useful in landing raiding parties behind the lines out in the small Pacific islands.

"How come we made a contract like that?"

"You wanted it," he said. "Remember?"

I remembered. The Navy had been skeptical that the big plane could even get into the air, so I'd pressured them into making a deal predicated on a fully tested plane before the war ended. That was over seven months ago.

Almost immediately, we'd run into trouble. Stress tests proved that conventional metals would make the plane too heavy for the engines to lift into the air. We lost two months there, until the engineers came up with a Fiberglas compound that was less than one tenth the weight of metal and four times as strong. Then we had to construct special machinery to work the new material. I even brought Amos Winthrop down from Canada to sit in on the project. The old bastard had done a fantastic job up there and had a way of bulling a job through when no one else was able to.

The old leopard hadn't changed any of his spots, either. He had me by the shorts and he knew it. He held me up for a vice-presidency in Cord Aircraft before he'd come down.

"How much are we in for up to now?" I asked.

Mac looked down at the sheet. "Sixteen million, eight

hundred seventy-six thousand, five hundred ninety-four dollars and thirty-one cents, as of June thirtieth."

"We're in trouble," I said, reaching for the telephone. The operator came on. "Get me Amos Winthrop in San Diego. And while I'm waiting to talk to him, call Mr. Dalton at the Inter-Continental Airlines office in Los Angeles and ask him to send down a special charter for me."

"What's the trouble?" Mac asked, watching me.

"Seventeen million dollars. We're going to blow it if we don't get that plane into the air right away."

Then Amos came on the phone. "How soon do you expect to get *The Centurion* into the sky?" I asked.

"We're coming along pretty good now. Just the finishing touches. I figure we ought to be able to lift her sometime in September or early October."

"What's missing?"

"The usual stuff. Mountings, fittings, polishing, tightening. You know."

I knew. The small but important part that took longer than anything else. But nothing really essential, nothing that would keep the plane from flying. "Get her ready," I said. "I'm taking her up tomorrow."

"Are you crazy? We've never even had gasoline in her tanks."

"Then fill her up."

"But the hull hasn't been water-tested yet," he shouted. "How do you know she won't go right to the bottom of San Diego Bay when you send her down the runway?"

"Then test it. You've got twenty-four hours to make sure she floats. I'll be up there tonight, if you need a hand."

This was no cost-plus, money-guaranteed project, where the government picked up the tab, win, lose or draw. This was my money and I didn't like the idea of losing it.

For seventeen million dollars, *The Centurion* would fly if I had to lift her out of the water with my bare hands.

3

I HAD ROBAIR TAKE ME OUT TO THE RANCH, WHERE I took a hot shower and changed my clothes before I got on the plane to San Diego. I was just leaving the house when the telephone rang.

"It's for you, Mr. Jonas," Robair said. "Mr. McAllister."

I took the phone from his hand. "Yes, Mac?"

"Sorry to bother you, Jonas, but this is important."

"Shoot."

"Bonner just called from the studio," he said. "He's leaving at the end of the month to go over to Paramount. He's got a deal with them to make nothing but blockbusters."

"Offer him more money."

"I did. He doesn't want it. He wants out."

"What does his contract say?"

"It's over the end of this month," he said. "We can't hold him if he wants to go."

"To hell with him, then. If he wants to go, let him."

"We're in a hole," Mac said seriously. "We'll have to find someone to run the studio. You can't operate a motion-picture company without someone to make pictures."

That was nothing I didn't know. It was too bad that David Woolf wasn't coming back. I could depend on him. He felt the same way about movies that I did about airplanes. But he'd caught it at Anzio.

"I want to make San Diego tonight," I said. "Let me think about it and we'll kick it around in your office in L.A. the day after tomorrow." I had bigger worries on my mind just now. One *Centurion* cost almost as much as a whole year's production at the studio.

We landed at the San Diego Airport about one o'clock in the morning. I took a taxi right from there to the little shipyard we had rented near the Naval base. I could see the lights blazing from it ten blocks away. I smiled to myself. Leave it to Amos to get things done. He had a night crew working like mad, even if he had to break the blackout regulations to get it done.

I walked around the big old boat shed that we were using for a hangar just in time to hear someone yell, "Clear the runway!"

And then *The Centurion* came out of the hangar, tail first, looking for all the world like an ugly giant condor flying backward. Like a greased pig, it shot down the runway toward the water. A great roar came from the hangar and I was almost knocked over by a gang of men, who came running out after the plane. Before I knew it, they'd passed me and were down at the water's edge. I saw Amos in the crowd and he was yelling as much as any of them.

There was a great splash as *The Centurion* hit the water, a moment's groaning silence as the tail dipped backward, almost covering the three big rudders, and then a triumphant yell as she straightened herself out and floated easily on the bay. She began to turn, drifting away from the dock, and I heard the whir of the big winches as they spun the tie lines, drawing her back in.

The men were still yelling when I got to Amos. "What the hell do you think you're doing?" I shouted, trying to make myself heard over the noise.

"What you told me to do—water-test her."

"You damn fool! You might've sunk her. Why didn't you get a pressure tank?"

"There wasn't time. The earliest I could've got one was three days. You said you were taking her up tomorrow."

The winches had hauled the plane partly back on the runway, with her prow out of the water. "Wait here a minute," Amos said, "I gotta get the men to work. They're all on triple time."

He went down the dock to where a workman had already placed a ladder against the side of the giant plane. Scrambling up like a man half his age, Amos opened the door just behind the cabin and disappeared into the plane. A moment later, I heard the whir of a motor from somewhere inside her and the giant boarding flap came down, opening a gaping maw in her prow that was big enough to drive a truck through. Amos appeared at the top of the ramp inside the plane. "O.K., men. You know what we gotta do. Shake the lead out. We ain't paying triple time for conversation."

He came back up the dock toward me and we walked back into his office. There was a bottle of whisky on his desk. He took two paper cups from the wall container and began to pour whisky into them. "You mean it about taking her up tomorrow?"

I nodded.

He shook his head. "I wouldn't," he said. "Just because she floats don't mean she'll fly. There's still too many things we're not sure of. Even if she does get up, there's no guarantee she'll stay up. She might even fall apart in the sky."

"That'll be rough," I said. "But, I'm taking her up, anyway."

He shrugged his shoulders. "You're the boss," he said, handing me one of the paper cups. He raised his to his lips. "Here's luck."

By two o'clock the next afternoon, we still weren't ready. The number-two starboard engine spit oil like a gusher every time we started it up and we couldn't find the leak. I stood on the dock, staring up at her. "We'll have to pull her off," Amos said, "and get her up to the shop."

I looked at him. "How long will that take?"

"Two, three hours. If we're lucky and find what's wrong right away. Maybe we better put off taking her up until tomorrow."

I looked at my watch. "What for? We'll still have three and a half hours of daylight at five o'clock." I started back toward his office. "I'm going back to your office and grab a snooze on the couch. Call me as soon as she's ready."

But I might as well have tried to sleep in a boiler factory, for all the shouting and cursing and hammering and riveting. Then the telephone rang and I got up to answer it. "Hello, Dad?" It was Monica's voice.

"No, this is Jonas. I'll get him for you."

"Thanks."

Laying the telephone down on the desk, I went to the door and called Amos. I went back to the couch and stretched out as he picked up the phone. He shot a peculiar look at me when he heard her voice. "Yes, I'm a little busy." He was silent for a little while, listening to her. When he spoke again, he was smiling. "That's wonderful. When are you leaving? . . . Then I'll fly to New York when this job is finished. We'll have a celebration. Give my love to Jo-Ann."

He put down the telephone and came over to me. "That was Monica," he said, looking down at me.

"I know."

"She's leaving for New York this afternoon. S. J. Hardin just made her managing editor of *Style* and wants her back there right away."

"That's nice," I said.

"She's taking Jo-Ann back with her. You haven't seen the kid for a long time now, have you?"

"Not since the time you walked the two of them out of my apartment at the Drake in Chicago, five years ago."

"You oughta see her. The kid's turning into a real beauty."

I stared up at him. Now I'd seen everything—Amos Winthrop playing proud grandpa. "Man, you've really changed, haven't you?"

"Sooner or later, a man has to wise up," Amos said, flushing embarrassedly. "You find out you did a lot of fool things to hurt the people you love and if you're not a prick altogether, you try to make up for them."

"I heard about that, too," I said sarcastically. I wasn't in the mood for any lectures from the old bastard, no matter how much he'd reformed. "They tell me that generally happens when you can't get it up any more."

A trace of the old Amos came into his face. He was angry, I could see it. "I got a mind to tell you a couple of things."

"Like what, Amos?"

"Ready to remount the engine, Mr. Winthrop," a man called from the doorway.

"I'll be there in a minute." Amos turned back to me. "You remind me of this after we get back from the test flight."

I grinned, watching him walk out the door. At least, he hadn't gone so holy-holy that I couldn't get his goat. I sat up and started looking under the couch for my shoes.

When I got outside, the engine was turning over, sweet and smooth. "She seems O.K. to me now," Amos said, turning to me.

I looked at my watch. It was four thirty. "Then, let's go. What're we waiting for?"

He put a hand on my arm. "Sure I can't make you change your mind?"

I shook my head. Seventeen million dollars was a lot of argument. He raised his hands to his mouth, making a megaphone of them. "Everybody off the ship except the flight crew."

Almost immediately, there was a silence in the yard as the engine shut off. A few minutes later, the last of them came down the boarding flap. A man stuck his head out of the small window in the pilot's cabin. "Everybody off except the crew, Mr. Winthrop."

Amos and I walked up the flap into the plane, then up the small ladder from the cargo deck to the passenger cabin and on forward into the flight cabin. Three young men were there. They looked at me curiously. They were still wearing the hard hats from the shipyard.

"This is your crew, Mr. Cord," Amos said formally. "On the right, Joe Cates, radioman. In the middle, Steve Jablonski, flight engineer starboard engines, one, three and five. On the left, Barry Gold, flight engineer port engines, two, four and six. You don't have to worry about them. They're all Navy veterans and know their work."

We shook hands all around and I turned back to Amos. "Where's the copilot and navigator?"

"Right here," Amos said.

"Where?"

"Me."

"What the hell—"

He grinned at me. "You got anybody knows this baby better? Besides, I been sleeping every night with her for more than half a year. Who's got a better right to get a piece of her first ride?"

I stared at him for a moment. Then I gave in. I knew exactly how he felt. I felt the same way myself yesterday, when they wouldn't let me fly the jet.

I climbed up into the pilot's seat. "Take your stations, men."

"Aye, aye, sir."

I grinned to myself. They were Navy men, all right. I picked up the check list on the clip board. "Boarding ramp up," I said, reading.

A motor began to whine beneath me. A moment later, a red light flashed on the panel in front of me and the motor cut off. "Boarding ramp up, sir."

"Start engines one and two," I said, reaching forward and flicking down the switches that would let the flight engineers turn them over. The big engines coughed and belched black smoke. The propellers began to turn sluggishly, then the engines caught and the propellers settled into a smooth whine.

"Starboard engine one turning over, sir."

"Port engine two turning over, sir."

The next one on the check list was a new one for me. I smiled to myself. This wasn't an airplane, it was really a Navy ship with wings. "Cast off," I said.

From the seat to my right, Amos reached up and tripped the lever that released the tow lines. Another red light flashed on the panel before me and I could feel *The Centurion* slide back into the water. There was a slight backward dip as she settled in with a slight rocking motion. The faint sound of water slapping against her hull came up from beneath us. I leaned forward and turned the wheel. Slowly the big plane came about and started to move out toward the open bay. I looked over at Amos. He grinned at me.

I grinned back. So far, so good. At least we were seaborne.

4

A WAVE BROKE ACROSS THE PROW OF THE PLANE, throwing salt spray up on the window in front of me, as I came to the last item on the check list. There had been almost a hundred of them and it seemed like hours since we'd started. I looked down at my watch. It was only sixteen minutes since we'd left the dock. I looked out the windows. The six big engines were turning over smoothly, the propellers flashing with sun and spray. I felt a touch on my shoulder and looked back.

The radioman stood behind me, an inflatable Mae West in one hand and a parachute pack hanging from the other. "Emergency dress, sir."

I looked at him. He was already wearing his; so were the other two men. "Put it behind my seat."

I looked across at Amos. He already had the vest on and was tightening the cross belt of the parachute. He sank back into his seat with an uncomfortable grunt. He looked at me. "You ought to put it on."

"I've got a superstition about 'em," I said. "If you don't wear 'em, you'll never need 'em." He didn't answer, shrugging his shoulders as the radioman went back to his seat and fastened his seat belt. I looked around the cabin. "Secure in flight stations?"

They all answered at once. "Aye, aye, sir!"

I reached forward and flipped the switch on the panel and all the lights turned from red to green. From now on, they'd only go back to red if we were in trouble. I turned the plane toward the open sea. "O.K., men. Here we go!"

I opened the throttle slowly. The big plane lurched, its prow digging into the waves then slowly lifting as the six propellers started to chew up the air. Now we started to ride high, like a speedboat in the summer races. I looked at the panel. The air-speed indicator stood at ninety.

Amos' voice came over to me. "Calculated lift velocity, this flight, one ten."

I nodded without looking at him and kept opening the throttle. The needle went to one hundred, then one ten. The waves were beating against the bottom of the hull like a riveting hammer. I brought the needle up to one fifteen, then I started to ease back on the stick.

For a moment, nothing happened and I increased our speed to one twenty. Suddenly, *The Centurion* seemed to tremble, then jump from the water. Free of the restraining drag, she seemed to leap into the air. The needle jumped to one sixty and the controls moved easily in my hands. I looked out the window. The water was two hundred feet beneath us. We were airborne.

"Hot damn!" one of the men behind me muttered.

Amos squirmed around in his seat. "O.K., fellers," he said, sticking out his hand. "Pay me!" He looked over at me and grinned. "Each of these guys bet me a buck we'd never get off the water."

I flashed a grin at him and kept the ship in a slow climb until we reached six thousand feet. Then I turned her west and aimed her right at the setting sun.

"She handles like a baby carriage." Amos chortled gleefully from his seat.

I looked up at him from behind the radioman, where I had been standing as he explained the new automatic signaling recorder. All you had to do was give your message once, then turn on the automatic and the wire recorder would repeat it over and over again until the power gave out.

The sun had turned Amos' white hair back to the flaming red of his youth. I looked down at my watch. It was six fifteen and we were about two hundred miles out over the Pacific. "Better turn her around and take her back, Amos," I said. "I don't want it to be dark the first time we put her down."

"The term in the Navy, captain, is 'Put her about'." The radioman grinned at me.

"O.K., sailor," I said. I turned to Amos. "Put her about."

"Aye, aye, sir."

We went into a gentle banking turn as I bent over the radioman's shoulder again. Suddenly, the plane lurched and I almost fell over him. I grabbed at his shoulder as the starboard engineer yelled, "Number five's gone bad again."

I pushed myself toward my seat as I looked out the window. The engine was shooting oil like a geyser. "Kill it!" I shouted, strapping myself into my seat.

The cords on Amos' neck stood out like steel wire as he fought the wheel on the suddenly bucking plane. I grabbed at my wheel and together we held her steady. Slowly she eased off in our grip.

"Number five dead, sir," the engineer called.

I glanced out at it. The propeller turned slowly with the wind force but the oil had stopped pouring from the engine. I looked at Amos. His face was white and perspiration was dripping from it, but he managed a smile. "We can make it back on five engines without any trouble."

"Yeah." We could make it back on three engines, according to the figures. But I wouldn't like to try it. I looked at the panel. The red light was on for the number-five engine. While I was watching, a red light began to flicker on and off at number four. "What the hell?"

It began to sputter and cough even as I turned to look at it. "Check number four!" I yelled. I turned back to the panel. The red light was on for the number-four fuel line.

"Number-four fuel line clogged!"

"Blow it out with the vacuum!"

"Aye, aye, sir!" I heard the click as he turned on the vacuum pump. Another red light jumped on in front of me. "Vacuum pump out of commission, sir!"

"Kill number four!" I said. There was no percentage in leaving the line open in the hopes that it would clear itself. Clogged fuel lines have a tendency to turn into fires. And we still had four engines left.

"Number four dead, sir!"

I heaved a sigh of relief after ten minutes had gone by and there was nothing new to worry about. "I think we'll be O.K. now," I said.

I should have kept my big fat mouth shut. No sooner had I spoken than the number-one engine started to choke and sputter and the instrument panel in front of me began to light up like a Christmas tree. The number-six engine began to choke.

"Main fuel pump out!"

I threw a glance at the altimeter. We were at five thousand and dropping. "Radio emergency and prepare to abandon ship!" I shouted.

I heard the radioman's voice. "Mayday! Mayday! Cord Aircraft Experimental. Going down Pacific. Position approx one two five miles due west San Diego. I repeat, position approx one two five miles due west San Diego. Mayday! Mayday!"

I heard a loud click and the message began over again. I felt a hand on my shoulder. I looked around quickly. It was the radioman. There was a faint surprise in the back of my mind until I remembered the recorder was now broadcasting the call for help. "We'll stay if you want us, sir," he said tensely.

"This isn't for God and country, sailor! This is for money. Get goin'!"

I looked over at Amos, who was still in his seat. "You, too, Amos!"

He didn't answer. Just pulled off his safety belt and got out of his seat. I heard the cabin door behind me open as they went through to the emergency door in the passenger compartment.

The altimeter read thirty-eight hundred and I killed the one and six engines. Maybe I could set her down on the water if the two remaining engines could hold out on the fuel that would be diverted from the others. We were at thirty-four hundred when the red light for the emergency door flashed on as it opened. I cast a quick look back out the window. Three parachutes opened, one after the other, in rapid succession. I looked at the board. Twenty-eight hundred.

I heard a noise behind me and looked around. It was Amos, getting back into his seat. "I told you to get out!" I yelled.

He reached for the wheel. "The kids are off and safe. I figure between the two of us, we got a chance to put her down on top of the water."

"Suppose we don't?" I yelled angrily.

"We won't be missing much. We ain't got as much time to lose as they have. Besides, this baby cost a lot of dough!"

"So what?" I yelled. "It's not your money!"

There was a curiously disapproving look on his face. "Money isn't the only thing put into this plane. I built her!"

We were at nine hundred feet when number three began to conk out. We threw our weight against the wheel to compensate for the starboard drag. At two hundred feet, the number-three engine went out and we heeled over to the starboard. "Cut the engines!" Amos yelled. "We're going to crash!"

I flipped the switch just as the starboard wing bit into the water. It snapped off clean as a matchstick and the plane slammed into the water like a pile driver. I felt the seat belt tear into my guts until I almost screamed with the pressure, then suddenly it eased off. My eyes cleared and I looked out. We were drifting on top of the water uneasily, one wing pointing to the sky. Water was already trickling into the cabin under our feet.

"Let's get the hell out of here," Amos yelled, moving toward the cabin door, which had snapped shut. He turned the knob and pushed. Then he threw himself against it. The door didn't move. "It's jammed!" he yelled, turning to me.

I stared at him and then jumped for the pilot's emergency hatch over our heads. I pulled the hatch lock with one hand and pushed at the hatch with the other. Nothing happened. I looked up and saw why. The frame had buckled, locking it in. Nothing short of dynamite would open it.

Amos didn't wait for me to tell him. He pulled a wrench from the emergency tool kit and smashed at the glass until there was only a jagged frame left in the big port. He dropped the wrench, picked up the Mae West and threw it at me. I slipped into it quickly, making sure the automatic valve was set so it would work the minute I hit the water.

"O.K.," he said. "Out you go!"

I grinned at him. "Traditions of the sea, Amos. Captain's last off the ship. After you, Alphonse."

"You crazy, man?" he shouted. "I couldn't get out that port if they cut me in half."

"You ain't that big," I said. "We're going to give it a try."

Suddenly, he smiled. I should have known better than to trust Amos when he smiled like that. That peculiarly wolfish smile came over him only when he was going to do you dirty. "All right, Gaston. You're the captain."

"That's better," I said, bracing myself and making a sling step with my hands to boost him up to the port. "I knew you'd learn someday who's boss."

But he never did. And I never even saw what he hit me with. I sailed into Dream Street with a full load on. I was out but I wasn't all the way out. I knew what was going on but there was nothing I could do about it. My arms and legs and head, even my body—they all belonged to someone else.

I felt Amos push me toward the port, then there was a burning sensation, like a cat raking her claws across your face. But I was through the narrow port and falling. Falling about a thousand miles and a thousand hours and I was still looking for the rip cord on my parachute when I crashed in a heap on the wing.

I pulled myself to my feet and tried to climb back the cabin wall to the port. "Come on out of there, you no-good, dirty son of a bitch!" I yelled. I was crying. "Come on outa there and I'll kill you!"

Then the plane lurched and a broken piece of something came flying up from the wing and hit me in the side, knocking me clear out into the water. I heard the soft hiss of compressed air as the Mae West began to wrap her legs around me. I put my head down on those big soft pillows she had and went to sleep.

5

In Nevada, where I was born and raised, there is mostly sand and rocks and a few small mountains. But there are no oceans. There are streams and lakes, and swimming pools at every country club and hotel, but they're all filled with fresh, sweet water that bubbles in your mouth like wine, if you should happen to drink it instead of bathe in it.

I've been in a couple of oceans in my time. In the Atlantic, off Miami Beach and Atlantic City, in the Pacific, off Malibu, and in the blue waters of the Mediterranean, off the Riviera. I've even been in the warm waters of the Gulf Stream, off the white, sandy beach of Bermuda, chasing a naked girl whose only ambition was to do it like a fish. I never did get to find out the secret of how the porpoises made it, because somehow, in the salt water, everything eluded me. I never did like salt water. It clings too heavily to your skin, burns your nose, irritates your eyes. And if you happen to get a mouthful, it tastes like yesterday's leftover mouthwash.

So what was I doing here?

Hot damn, little man, all the stars are out and laughing at you. This'll teach you some respect for the oceans. You don't like salt water, eh? Well, how do you like a million, billion, trillion gallons of it? A gazillion gallons?

"Aah, the hell with you," I said and went back to sleep.

I came trotting around the corner of the bunkhouse as fast as my eight-year-old legs could carry me, dragging the heavy cartridge belt and holstered gun in the sand behind me.

I heard my father's voice. "Hey, boy! What have you got there?"

I turned to face him, trying to hide the belt and gun behind me. "Nothin'," I said, not looking up at him.

"Nothing?" my father repeated after me. "Then, let me see."

He reached around behind me and tugged the belt out of my grip. As he raised it, the gun and a folded piece of paper fell from the holster. He bent down and picked them up. "Where'd you get this?"

"From the wall in the bunkhouse near Nevada's bed," I said. "I had to climb up."

My father put the gun back in the holster. It was a black gun, a smooth, black gun with the initials M. S. on its black butt. Even I was old enough to know that somebody had made a mistake on Nevada's initials.

My father started to put the folded piece of paper back into the holster but he dropped it and it fluttered open. I could see it was a picture of Nevada, with some numbers above it and printing below. My father stared at it for a moment, then refolded the paper and shoved it into the holster.

"You put this back where you got it," he said angrily. I could tell he was mad. "Don't you ever let me catch you taking what doesn't belong to you again or I'll whomp you good."

"Ain't no need to whomp 'im, Mr. Cord." Nevada's voice came from behind us. "It's my fault for leavin' it out where the boy could get to it." We turned around. He was standing there, his Indian face dark and expressionless, holding out his hand. "If you'll jus' give it to me, I'll put it back."

Silently my father handed him the gun and they stood there looking at each other. Neither of them spoke a word. I stared up at them, bewildered. Both seemed to be searching each other's eyes. At last, Nevada spoke. "I'll draw my time if you want, Mr. Cord."

I knew what that meant. Nevada was going away. Immediately, I set up a howl. "No," I screamed. "I won't do it again. I promise."

My father looked down at me for a moment, then back at Nevada. A faint smile came into his eyes. "Children and animals, they really know what they want, what's best for them."

"They do say that."

"You better put that away where nobody'll ever find it."

The faint smile was in Nevada's eyes now. "Yes, Mr. Cord. I sure will."

My father looked down at me and his smile vanished. "You hear me, boy? Touch what isn't yours and you'll get whomped good."

"Yes, Father," I answered, loud and strong. "I hear you."

I got a mouthful of salt water and I coughed and choked and sputtered and spit it out. I opened my eyes. The stars were still blinking at me but over in the east, the sky was starting to turn pale. I thought I heard the sound of a motor in the distance but it was probably only an echo ringing in my ears.

There was a pain in my side and down my leg, like I'd gone to sleep on it. When I moved, it shot up to my head and made me dizzy. The stars began to spin around and I got tired just watching them, so I went back to sleep.

The sun on the desert is big and strong and rides the sky so close to your head that sometimes you feel like if you reached up to touch it, you'd burn your fingers. And when it's hot like that, you pick your way carefully around the rocks, because under them, in the shade, sleeping away the heat of the day, are the rattlers, coiled and sluggish, with the unhappy heat in their chilled blood. They're quick to anger, quick to attack, with their vicious spittle, if by accident you threaten their peace. People are like that, too.

Each of us has his own particular secret rock, under which we hide, and woe to you if you should happen to stumble across it. Because then we're like the rattlers on the desert, lashing out blindly at whoever happens to come by.

"But I love you," I said and even as I said them, I knew the hollowness of my words.

And she must have known, too, for in her scathing self-denunciation, she was accusing me with the sins of all the men she'd known. And not unjustly, for they were also my sins.

"But I love you," I repeated and as I said it, I knew she recognized the weakness in my words. They turned empty and hollow in my mouth. If I had been honest, even unto my secret self, this is what I would have said: "I want you. I want you to be what I want you to be. A reflection of the image of my dreams, the mirror of my secret desires, the face that I desire to show the world, the brocade with which I embroider my glory. If you are all these things, I will grace you with my presence and my house. But these are not for what you are, but for me and what I want you to be."

And I did little but stand there, mumbling empty platitudes, while the words that spilled from her mouth were merely my own poison, which she turned into herself. For unknowing, she had stumbled across my secret rock.

I stood there in the unaccustomed heat and blazing brightness of the sun, secretly ashamed of the cool chill of the blood that ran through my veins and set me apart from the others of this earth. And unprotesting, I let her use my venom to destroy herself.

And when the poison had done its work, leaving her with nothing but the small, frightened, unshriven soul of her beginnings, I turned away.

With the lack of mercy peculiar to my kind, ⊤ turned my back. I ran from her fears, from her need of comfort and reassurance, from her unspoken pleading for mercy and love and understanding. I fled the hot sun, back to the safety of my secret rock.

But now there was no longer comfort in its secret shade, for the light continued to seep through, and there was no longer comfort in the cool detached flowing of my blood. And the rock seemed to be growing smaller and smaller while the sun was growing larger and larger. I tried to make myself tinier, to find shelter beneath the rock's shrinking surface, but there was no escape. Soon there would be no secret rock for me. The sun was growing brighter and brighter. Brighter and brighter.

I opened my eyes.

There was a tiny pinpoint of light shining straight into them. I blinked and the penetrating pinpoint moved to one side. I could see beyond it now. I was lying on a table in a white room and beside me was a man in a white gown and a white skullcap. The light came from the reflection in a small, round mirror that he wore over his eye as he looked down at me. I could see on his face the tiny black hairs that the razor had missed. His lips were grim and tight.

"My God!" The voice came from behind him. "His face is a mess. There must be a hundred pieces of glass in it."

My eyes flickered up and saw the second man as the first turned toward him. "Shut up, you fool! Can't you see he's awake?"

I began to raise my head but a light, quick hand was on my shoulder, pressing me back, and then her face was there.

Her face, looking down at me with a mercy and compassion that mine had never shown.

"Jennie!"

Her hand pressed against my shoulder. She looked up at someone over my head. "Call Dr. Rosa Strassmer at Los Angeles General or the Colton Sanitarium in Santa Monica. Tell her Jonas Cord has been in a bad accident and to come right away."

"Yes, Sister Thomas." It was a young girl's voice and it came from behind me. I heard footsteps moving away.

The pain was coming back into my side and leg again and I gritted my teeth. I could feel it forcing the tears into my eyes. I closed them for a moment, then opened them and looked up at her. "Jennie!" I whispered. "Jennie, I'm sorry!"

"It's all right, Jonas," she whispered back. Her hands went under the sheet that covered me. I felt a sharp sting in my arm. "Don't talk. Everything's all right now."

I smiled gratefully and went back to sleep, wondering vaguely why Jennie was wearing that funny white veil over her beautiful hair.

6

FROM OUTSIDE MY WINDOWS, FROM THE STREETS, bright now with the morning sun, still came the sounds of celebration. Even this usually staid and quiet part of Hillcrest Drive skirting Mercy Hospital was filled with happy noises and throngs of people. From the Naval Station across the city of San Diego came the occasional triumphant blast of a ship's horn. It had been like this all through the night, starting early the evening before, when the news came. Japan had surrendered. The war was over.

I knew now what Otto Strassmer had been trying to tell me. I knew now of the miracle in the desert. From the newspapers and from the radio beside my bed. They had all told the story of the tiny container of atoms that had brought mankind to the gates of heaven. Or hell. I shifted in my bed to find another position of comfort, as the pulleys that suspended my leg in traction squeaked, adding their mouselike sound to the others.

I had been lucky, one of the nurses told me. Lucky. My right leg had been broken in three places, my right hip in another, and several ribs had been crushed. Yet I still looked out at the world, from behind the layer of thick bandages which covered all of my face, except the slits for my eyes, nose and mouth. But I'd been lucky. At least I was still alive.

Not like Amos, who still sat in the cabin of *The Centurion* as it rested on the edge of a shelf of sand, some four hundred odd feet beneath the surface of the Pacific Ocean. Poor Amos. The three crewmen had been found unscathed and I was still alive, by the grace of God and the poor fishermen who found me floating in the water and brought me to shore, while Amos sat silent in his watery tomb, still at the controls of the plane he had built and would not let me fly alone.

I remembered the accountant's voice over the telephone from Los Angeles as he spoke consolingly. "Don't worry, Mr. Cord. We can write it all off against taxes on profits. When you apply the gross amount to the normal tax of forty per cent and the excess-profits tax of ninety per cent, the net loss to us comes to under two million—"

I had slammed down the phone, cutting him off. It was all well and good. But how do you charge off on a balance sheet the life of a man who was killed by your greed? Is there an allowable deduction for death on the income-tax returns? It was I who had killed Amos and no matter how many expenses I deducted from my own soul, I could not bring him back.

The door opened and I looked up. Rosa came into the room, followed by an intern and a nurse wheeling a small cart. She came over to the left side of my bed and stood there, smiling down at me. "Hello, Jonas."

"Hello, Rosa," I mumbled through the bandages. "Is it time to change them again? I didn't expect you until the day after tomorrow."

"The war is over."

"Yes," I said. "I know."

"And when I got up this morning, it was such a beautiful morning, I decided to fly down here and take off your bandages."

I peered up at her. "I see," I said. "I always wondered where doctors got their logic."

"That isn't doctor's logic, that's woman's logic. I have the advantage of having been a woman long before I became a doctor."

I laughed. "I'm grateful for the logic, whichever one of you it belongs to. It will be nice to have the bandages off, even for a little while."

She was still smiling, though her eyes were serious. "This time, they're coming off for good, Jonas."

I stared at her as she picked up a scissors from the cart. I reached up and stayed her hand. Suddenly, I was afraid to have her remove the bandages. I felt safe having them wrapped about my face like a cocoon, shielding me from the prying eyes of the world. "Is it soon enough? Will it be all right?"

She sensed my feeling. "Your face will be sore for a while yet," she said, snipping away at the cocoon. "It will be even sorer as the flesh and muscles take up their work again. But that will pass. We can't spend forever hiding behind a mask, can we?"

That was the doctor talking, not the woman. I looked up at her face as she snipped and unwound, snipped and uncovered, until all the bandage was gone and I felt as naked as a newborn baby, with a strange coolness on my cheeks. I tried to see myself reflected in her eyes but they were calm and expressionless, impersonal and professionally detached. I felt her fingers press against my cheek, the flesh under my chin, smooth the hair back from my temples. "Close your eyes."

I closed them. I felt her fingers touch the lids lightly. "Open."

I opened them. Her face was still quiet and unrevealing. "Smile," she said. "Like this." She made with a wide, humorless grin that was a slapstick parody of her usual warm smile.

I grinned. I grinned until the tiny pains that came to my cheeks began to burn like hell. And still I grinned.

"O.K.," she said, suddenly smiling now. Really smiling. "You can stop now."

I stopped and stared up at her. "How is it, Doc?" I tried to keep it light. "Pretty horrible?"

"It's not bad," she said noncommittally. "You were never

a raving beauty, you know." She picked up a mirror from the cart. "Here. See for yourself."

I didn't look at the mirror. I didn't want to see myself just yet. "Can I have a cigarette first, Doc?"

Silently she put the mirror back on the cart and took a package of cigarettes from her coat pocket. She sat down on the edge of my bed, put one in her mouth, lit it, then passed it to me. I could taste the faint sweetness of her lipstick as I drew the smoke into me.

"You were cut pretty badly when Winthrop pushed you through that port. But fortunately—"

"You knew about that?" I asked, interrupting. "About Amos, I mean. How did you find out?"

"From you. While you were under the anesthetic. We kept getting the story in fragments, along with the fragments of glass we were picking out of your face. Fortunately, none of your important facial muscles were severely damaged. It was largely a matter of surface lesions. We were able to make the necessary skin grafts quickly. And successfully, I might add."

I held out my hand. "I'll take the mirror now, Doc."

She took my cigarette and handed me the mirror. I raised it and when I looked into it, I felt a chill go through me.

"Doc," I said hoarsely. "I look exactly like my father!"

She took the mirror from my hand and I looked up at her. She was smiling. "Do you, Jonas? But that's the way you've always looked."

Later that morning, Robair brought me the papers. They were filled with the story of Japan's capitulation. I glanced at them carelessly and tossed them aside. "Can I get you something else to read, Mr. Jonas?"

"No," I said. "No, thanks. I just don't feel much like reading."

"All right, Mr. Jonas. Maybe you'd like to sleep some." He moved toward the door.

"Robair."

"Yes, Mr. Jonas?"

"Did I—" I hesitated, my fingers automatically touching my cheek. "Did I always look like this?"

His white teeth flashed in a smile. "Yes, Mr. Jonas."

"Like my father?"

"Like his spittin' image."

I was silent. Strange how all your life you tried not to be like someone, only to learn that you'd been stamped indelibly by the blood that ran in your veins.

"Is there anything else, Mr. Jonas?"

I looked up at Robair and shook my head. "I'll try to sleep now."

I leaned back against the pillow and closed my eyes. I heard the door close and gradually the noise from the street faded to the periphery of my consciousness. I slept. It seemed to me I'd been sleeping a great deal lately. As if I was trying to catch up on all the sleep I'd denied myself for the past few hundred years. But I could not have slept long before I became aware that someone was in the room.

I opened my eyes. Jennie was standing next to my bed, looking down at me. When she saw my eyes open, she smiled. "Hello, Jonas."

"I was sleeping," I said, like a child just waking from a nap. "I was dreaming something foolish. I was dreaming I was hundreds of years old."

"It was a happy dream, then. I'm glad. Happy dreams will help you get well faster."

I raised myself up on one elbow and the pulleys squeaked as I reached for the cigarettes on the table next to the bed. Quickly she fluffed the pillows and moved them in behind me to support my back. I dragged on the cigarette. The smoke drove the sleep from my brain.

"In another few weeks, they'll have the cast off your leg and you can go home."

"I hope so, Jennie," I said.

Suddenly, I realized she wasn't wearing her hospital white. "This is the first time I've seen you in a black veil, Jennie. Is it something special?"

"No, Jonas. This is what I always wear, except when I'm on duty in the hospital."

"Then this is your day off?"

"There are no days off in the service of Our Saviour," she said simply. "No, Jonas, I've come to say good-by."

"Good-by? But I don't understand. You said it would be a few weeks before I—"

"I'm going away, Jonas."

I stared up at her stupidly. "Going away?"

"Yes, Jonas," she said quietly. "I've only been here at Mercy Hospital until I could get transportation to the Philippines. We're rebuilding a hospital there that was destroyed in the war. Now I am free to leave, by plane."

"But you can't, Jennie," I said. "You can't leave the people you know, the language you speak. You'll be a stranger there, you'll be alone."

Her fingers touched the crucifix hanging from the black leather cincture beneath her garment. A quiet look of calm deepened in her gray eyes. "I am never alone," she said simply. "He is always with me."

"You don't have to, Jennie," I said. I took the pamphlet that I'd found on the table by my bed and opened it. "You've only made a temporary profession. You can resign any time you want. There's still a three-year probationary period before you take your final vows. You don't belong here, Jennie. It's only because you were hurt and angry. You're much too young and beautiful to hide your life away behind a black veil."

She still did not answer.

"Don't you understand what I'm saying, Jennie? I want you to come back where you belong."

She closed her eyes slowly and when she opened them, they were misted with tears. But when she spoke, her voice was steady with the sureness of her knowledge and faith. "It's you who don't understand, Jonas," she said. "I have no place to which I desire to return, for it is here, in His house, that I belong."

I started to speak but she raised her hand gently. "You think I came to Him out of hurt and anger? You're wrong," she said quietly. "One does not run from life to God, one runs to God for life. All my years I sought Him, without knowing what I was seeking. The love I found out there was a mere mockery of what I knew love could be; the charity I gave was but the smallest fraction of the charity in me to give; the mercy I showed was nothing compared with His mercy within me. Here, in His house and in His work, I have found a greater love than any I have ever known. Through His love, I have found security and contentment and happiness, in accordance with His divine will."

She paused for a moment, looking down at the crucifix in her fingers. When she looked up again, her eyes were clear and untroubled. "Is there anything in this world, Jonas, that can offer more than God?"

I didn't answer.

Slowly she held out her left hand toward me. I looked down and saw the heavy silver ring on her third finger. "He has invited me into His house," she said softly, "and I have taken His ring to wear so that I may dwell in His glory forever."

I took her hand and pressed my lips to the ring. I felt her fingers brush my hair lightly, then she moved to the foot of my bed, where she turned to look at me. "I shall think of you often, my friend," she said gently. "And I shall pray for you."

I was silent as I ground my cigarette out. There was a beauty in Jennie's eyes that had never been there before. "Thank you, Sister," I said quietly.

Without another word, she turned and went out the door. I stared down at the foot of the bed where she had stood, but now even the ghost of her was gone.

I turned my face into the pillow and cried.

7

I LEFT THE HOSPITAL EARLY IN SEPTEMBER. I WAS SITting in the wheel chair, watching Robair pack the last of my things into the valise, when the door opened. "Hi, Junior."

"Nevada! What are you doing way down here?"

"Came to carry you home."

I laughed. Funny how you can go along for years hardly thinking about someone, then all of a sudden be so glad to see him. "You didn't have to do that," I said. "Robair could have managed all right."

"I asked him to come up, Mr. Jonas. I figured it would be like old times. It gets mighty lonely out there at the ranch with nothing to do."

"An' I figured I could use a vacation," Nevada said. "The war's over an' the show's closed down for the winter. And there's nothin' Martha likes better than to do a little invalidin'. She's down there now, gittin' things ready for us."

I looked at the two of them and grinned. "It's a put-up job, huh?"

"That's right," Nevada said. He came over behind the wheel chair. "Ready?"

Robair closed the valise and snapped it shut. "All set, Mr. Nevada."

"Let's go, then," Nevada said, and started the wheel chair through the door.

"We have to stop off at Burbank," I said, looking back at him. "Mac has a flock of papers for me to sign." I might be laid up, but business went on.

Buzz Dalton had an ICA charter waiting for us at the San Diego airport. We were at Burbank by two o'clock that afternoon. McAllister got up and came around his desk when they wheeled me into his office. "You know, this is the first time I can remember seeing you sit down."

I laughed. "Make the most of it. The doctors say I'll be moving around as good as new in a couple of weeks."

"Well, meanwhile, I'm going to take advantage of it. Push him around behind the desk, fellows. I've got the pen ready."

It was almost four o'clock when I'd signed the last of a stack of documents. I looked up wearily. "So what else is new?"

Mac looked at me. He walked over to a table against the wall. "This is," he said, and took the cover off something that looked like a radio with a window in it.

"What is it?"

"It's the first product of the Cord Electronics Company," he said proudly. "We knocked it out in the converted radar division. It's a television set."

"Television?" I asked.

"Pictures broadcast through the air like radio," he said. "It's picked up on that screen, like home movies."

"Oh, that's the thing that Dumont was kicking around before the war. It doesn't work."

"Does now," Mac said. "It's the next big thing. All the radio and electronics companies are going into it. RCA, Columbia, Emerson, IT&T, GE, Philco. All of them. Want to see how it works?"

"Sure."

He walked over and picked up the phone. "Get me the

lab." He covered the mouthpiece. "I'll have them put something on," he said.

A moment later, he went over to the set and turned a knob. A light flashed behind the window, then settled into a series of circles and lines. Gradually, letters came into view.

CORD ELECTRONICS PRESENTS—

Suddenly, the card was replaced by a picture, a Western scene with a man riding a horse toward the camera. The camera dollied in real close on the face and I saw it was Nevada. I recognized the scene, too. It was the chase scene from *The Renegade*. For five minutes, we watched the scene in silence.

"Well, I'll be damned," Nevada said, when it was over.

I looked across at Robair. There was an expression of rapt wonder on his face. He looked at me. "There's what I call a miracle, Mr. Jonas," he said softly. "Now I can watch a movie in my own home without goin' to sit in no nigger heaven."

"So that's why they all want to buy my old pictures," Nevada said.

I looked up at him. "What do you mean?"

"You know those ninety-odd pictures we made and I own now?"

I nodded.

"People been after me to sell 'em. Offered me good money for 'em, too. Five thousand dollars each."

I stared at him. "One thing I learned in the picture business," I said. "Never sell outright what you can get a percentage on."

"You mean rent it to 'em like I do to a theater?"

"That's right," I said. "I know those broadcasting companies. If they'll buy it for five, they plan to make fifty out of it."

"I'm no good at big deals like that," Nevada said. "Would you be willin' to handle it for me, Mac?"

"I don't know, Nevada. I'm no agent."

"Go ahead and do it, Mac," I said. "Remember what you told me about making a point where it counts?"

He smiled suddenly. "O.K., Nevada."

Suddenly, I was tired. I slumped back in my chair. Robair was at my side instantly. "You all right, Mr. Jonas?"

"I'm just tired," I said.

"Maybe you better stay at the apartment tonight. We can go on out to the ranch in the morning."

I looked at Robair. The idea of getting into a bed was very appealing. My ass was sore from the wheel chair.

"I'll order a car," Mac said, picking up the phone. "You can drop me at the studio on your way into town. I've got some work to finish up there."

My mind kept working all the time we rode toward the studio. When the car stopped at the gates, suddenly everything was clear to me.

"We'll have to do something about a replacement for Bonner," Mac said, getting out. "It isn't good business having a lawyer run a studio. I don't know anything about motion pictures."

I stared at him thoughtfully. He was right, of course. But then, who did? Only David, and he was gone. I didn't care any more. There were no pictures left in me, no one I wanted to place up there on the screen for all the world to see. And back in the office I'd just left, there was a little box with a picture window and soon it would be in every home. Rich or poor. That little box was really going to chew up film, like the theaters had never been able to. But I still didn't care.

Even when I was a kid, when I was through with a toy, I was through with it. And I'd never go back to it. "Sell the theaters," I whispered to Mac.

"What?" he shouted, as if he couldn't believe his ears. "They're the only end of this business that's making any money."

"Sell the theaters," I repeated. "In ten years, no one will want to come to them, anyway. At least, not the way they have up to now. Not when they can see movies right in their own home."

Mac stared at me. "And what do you want me to do about the studio?" he asked, a tinge of sarcasm coming into his voice. "Sell that, too?"

"Yes," I said quietly. "But not now. Ten years from now, maybe. When the people who are making pictures for that little box are squeezed and hungry for space. Sell it then."

"What will we do with it in the meantime? Let it rot while we pay taxes on it?"

"No," I said. "Turn it into a rental studio like the old Goldwyn lot. If we break even or lose a little, I won't complain."

He stared at me. "You really mean it?"

"I mean it," I said, looking away from him up at the roof over the stages. For the first time, I really saw it. It was black and ugly with tar. "Mac, see that roof?"

He turned and looked, squinting against the setting sun.

"Before you do anything else," I said softly, "have them paint it white."

I pulled my head back into the car. Nevada looked at me strangely. His voice was almost sad. "Nothing's changed, has it, Junior?"

"No," I said wearily. "Nothing's changed."

8

I SAT ON THE PORCH, SQUINTING OUT INTO THE AFTER-noon sun. Nevada came out of the house behind me and dropped into a chair. He pulled a plug out of his pocket and biting off a hunk, put the plug back. Then from his other pocket, he took a piece of wood and a penknife and began to whittle.

I looked at him. He was wearing a pair of faded blue levis. A sweat-stained old buckskin shirt, that had seen better days, clung to his deep chest and broad shoulders and he had a red-and-white kerchief tied around his neck to catch the perspiration. Except for his white hair, he looked as I always remembered him when I was a boy, his hands quick and brown and strong.

He looked up at me out of his light eyes. "Two lost arts," he said.

"What?"

"Chewin' an' whittlin'," he said.

I didn't answer.

He looked down at the piece of wood in his hands. "Many's the evenin' I spent on the porch with your pa, chewin' an' whittlin'."

"Yeah?"

He turned and let fly a stream of tobacco juice over the porch rail into the dust below. He turned back to me. "I recall one night," he said. "Your pa an' me, we were settin' here, just like now. It'd been a real bitcheroo of a day. One of them scorchers that make your balls feel like they're drownin' in their own sweat. Suddenly he looks up at me an' says, 'Nevada, anything should happen to me, you look after my boy, hear? Jonas is a good boy. Sometimes his ass gets too much for his britches but he's a good boy an' he's got the makin's in him to be a better man than his daddy, someday. I love that boy, Nevada. He's all I got.' "

"He never told me that," I said, looking at Nevada. "Not ever. Not once!"

Nevada's eyes flashed up at me. "Men like your daddy ain't given much to talkin' about things like that."

I laughed. "He not only didn't talk it," I said. "He never showed it. He was always chewing on my ass for one thing or another."

Nevada's eyes bore straight into mine. "He was always there whenever you were in trouble. He might have hollered but he never turned you down."

"He married my girl away from me," I said bitterly.

"Maybe it was for your own good. Maybe it was because he knew she never really was for you."

I let that one go. "Why are you telling me this now?" I asked.

I couldn't read those Indian eyes of his. "Because your father asked me once to look after you. I made one mistake already. I seen how smart you was in business, I figured you to be growed up. But you wasn't. An' I wouldn' like to fail a man like your father twice."

We sat there in silence for a few minutes, then Martha came out with my tea. She told Nevada to spit out the chaw and stop dirtying up the porch. He looked at me almost shyly, got up and went down to get rid of the chaw behind the bushes.

We heard a car turn up our road as he came back to the porch. "I wonder who that is?" Martha asked.

"Maybe it's the doctor." I said. Old Doc Hanley was supposed to come out and check me over once a week.

By that time, the car was in the driveway and I knew who it was. I got to my feet, leaning on my cane, as Monica and Jo-Ann approached us. "Hello," I called.

They'd come back to California to close up their apartment,

Monica explained, and since she wanted to talk to me about Amos, they'd stopped off in Reno on their way back to New York. Their train wasn't due to leave until seven o'clock.

I saw Martha glance meaningfully at Nevada when she heard that. Nevada got to his feet and looked at Jo-Ann. "I've got a gentle bay horse out in the corral that's just dyin' for some young lady like you to ride her."

Jo-Ann looked up at him worshipfully. You could tell she'd been to the movies from the way she looked at him. He was a real live hero. "I don't know," she said doubtfully. "I've never really ridden a horse before."

"I can teach you. It's easy, easier than fallin' off a log."

"But she's not dressed for riding," Monica said.

She wasn't. Not in that pretty flowered dress that made her look so much like her mother. Martha spoke up quickly. "I got a pair of dungarees that shrunk down to half my size. They'll fit her."

I don't know whose dungarees they were but one thing was for sure. They'd never been Martha's. Not the way they clung to Jo-Ann's fourteen-year-old hips, tight and flat with just the suggestion of the curves to come. Jo-Ann's dark hair was pulled back straight from her head in a pony tail and there was something curiously familiar about the way she looked. I couldn't quite figure out what it was.

I watched her run out the door after Nevada and turned to Monica. She was smiling at me. I returned her smile. "She's growing up," I said. "She's going to be a pretty girl."

"One day they're children, the next they're young ladies. They grow up too fast."

I nodded. We were alone now and an awkward silence came down between us. I reached for a cigarette and looked at her. "I want to tell you about Amos."

It was near six o'clock when I finished telling her about what happened. There were no tears in her eyes, though her face was sad and thoughtful. "I can't cry for him, Jonas," she said, looking at me. "Because I've already cried too many times because of him. Do you understand?"

I nodded.

"He did so many things that were wrong all his life. I'm glad that at last he did one thing right."

"He did a very brave thing. I always thought he hated me."

"He did," she said quickly. "He saw in you everything that

he wasn't. Quick, successful, rich. He hated your guts. I guess at the end he realized how foolish that was and how much harm he'd already done you, so he tried to make it right."

I looked at her. "What wrong did he do me? There was nothing but business between us."

She gave me a peculiar look. "You can't see it yet?"

"No."

"Then I guess you never will," she said and walked out onto the porch.

We could hear Jo-Ann's shout of laughter as she rode the big bay around the corral. She was doing pretty good for a beginner. I looked down at Monica. "She takes to it like she was born to the saddle."

"Why shouldn't she?" Monica replied. "They say such things are inherited."

"I didn't know you rode."

She looked up at me, her eyes hurt and angry. "I'm not her only parent," she snapped coldly.

I stared at her. This was the only time she'd ever mentioned anything about Jo-Ann's father to me. It was sort of late to be angry about it now.

I heard the chug of Doc Hanley's old car turning into the driveway. He stopped near the corral and getting out of the car, walked over to the fence. He never could drive past a horse.

"That's Doc Hanley. He's supposed to check me out."

"Then I won't keep you," Monica said coolly. "I'll say good-by here."

She went down the steps and started walking toward the corral. I stared after her bewilderedly. I never could figure her out when she got into those crazy moods. "I'll have Robair drive you to the station," I called after her.

"Thanks!" She flung it back over her shoulder without turning around. I saw her stop and talk to the doctor, then I turned and walked back into the house. I went into the room that my father used as his study and sank down on the couch. Monica always did have a quick temper. You'd think by now she'd have learned to control it. I started to smile, thinking of how straight her back was and how sassy she'd looked walking away from me, her nose in the air. She still looked pretty good for a woman her age. I was forty-one, which meant she was thirty-four. And nothing on her jiggled that shouldn't.

The trouble with Doc Hanley is that he's a talker. He talks you deaf, dumb and blind but you don't have much choice. Since the war started, it's been him or nothing. All the young docs were in the service.

It was six thirty by the time he'd finished his examination and begun to close up his instrument case. "You're doin' all right," he said. "But I don't hold with them newfangled notions of getting you out as soon as you kin move. If it'd been up to me, now, I'd have kept you in the hospital another month."

Nevada leaned against the study wall, smiling as I climbed into my britches. I looked at him and shrugged. I turned to the doctor. "How long now before I can really begin to do some walking?"

Doc Hanley peered at me over the edges of his bifocals. "You kin start walkin' right now."

"But I thought you didn't agree with those city doctors," I said. "I thought you wanted me to rest some more."

"I don't agree with them," he said. "But since you're out, an' there ain't nothin' that can be done about that, you might as well git to movin' about. There ain't no sense in you jist layin' aroun'."

He snapped his case shut, straightened up and walked to the door. He turned and looked back at me. "That's a right pert gal you got there, your daughter."

I stared at him. "My daughter?"

"That's right," he said. "With her hair tied back like that, I never seen a gal who took so after her father. Why she's the spittin' image of you when you was a boy."

I couldn't speak, only stare. Had the idiot gone off his rocker? Everybody knew Jo-Ann wasn't my daughter.

Doc laughed suddenly and slapped his hand on his thigh. "I'll never forget the time her mother came down to my office," he said. "She was your wife then, of course. I never seen such a big belly. I figured, no wonder you got married so sudden like. You'd been doin' your plantin' early."

He looked up at me, still smiling. "That was before I examined her, you understand," he said quickly. "You could have knocked me over with a feather when the examination showed her only six weeks gone. It was just one of those pe-culiar things where she carried real high. She was so nervous an' upset just about then that she blew up with gas like a balloon. I even went back to the papers an' checked your weddin' date just to make sure. An' dang my britches if it weren't a fact you'd knocked her up at most two weeks after you were married. But there's one thing I got to say for yuh, boy." He turned back at the door "When you ram 'em, you ram 'em good. Right up the ol' gazizzis, where it sticks!" And still laughing lewdly, he walked out.

I felt the tight, sick knot ball up inside me. I sat down on the couch. All these years. All these years and I had been wrong. Suddenly, I knew what Amos had been going to tell me after we returned from the flight. He'd seen how crazy I'd been that night and turned my own hate against me. And there was little Monica could have done about it.

What a combination, Amos and me. But at least, he'd seen the light by himself. No one had to hit him over the head with it. And he'd tried to make up for it. But I—I never even turned my head to seek the truth. I'd been content to go along blaming the world for my own stupidity. And I was the one who'd been at war with my father because I thought he didn't love me. That was the biggest joke of all.

Now I could even face the truth in that. It never had been his love that I'd doubted. It had been my own. For deep in-side of me, I'd always known that I could never love him as much as he loved me. I looked up at Nevada. He was still leaning against the wall, but he wasn't smiling now. "You saw it, too?"

"Sure." He nodded. "Everybody saw it—but you."

I closed my eyes. Now I could see it. It was like that morn-ing in the hospital when I looked into the mirror and saw my father's face. That was what I'd seen in Jo-Ann when I thought she looked so familiar this afternoon. Her father's face. My own.

"What shall I do, Nevada?" I groaned.

"What do yuh want to do, son?"

"I want them back."

"Sure that's what you want?"

I nodded.

"Then get 'em back," he said. He looked at his watch. "There's still fifteen minutes before the train pulls out."

"But how? We'd never get there in time!"

He gestured to the desk. "There's the phone."

I looked at him wildly, then hobbled to the phone. I called the stationmaster's office at Reno and had them page her. While I was waiting for her to come on, I looked at Nevada. Suddenly, I was frightened, and when I'd been little, I'd always turned to Nevada when I was frightened. "What if she won't come back?"

"She'll come back," he said confidently. He smiled. "She's still in love with you. That's something else everybody knew but you."

Then she was on the phone, her voice worried and anxious. "Jonas, are you all right? Is there anything wrong?"

For a moment, I couldn't speak, then I found my voice. "Monica," I said. "Don't go!"

"But I have to, Jonas. I have to be on the job by the end of the week."

"Screw the job, I need you!"

The line was silent, and for a moment, I thought she'd hung up. "Monica, are you there?"

I heard her breathe in the receiver. "I'm still here, Jonas."

"I've been wrong all the time. I didn't know about Jo-Ann. Believe me." Again the silence.

"Please, Monica!"

Now she was crying. I could hear her whispered voice in my ear. "Oh, Jonas, I've never stopped loving you."

I looked up at Nevada. He smiled and went out, closing the door behind him.

I heard her sniffle, then her voice suddenly cleared and filled with the warm sound of love. "When Jo-Ann was a little girl she always wanted a baby brother."

"Hurry home," I said, "I'll do my best."

She laughed and there was a click as the line went dead in my hands. I didn't put the phone down because I felt that as long as I held it, she was close to me. I looked down at the photograph of my father on the desk.

"Well, old man," I said, asking his approval for the first time in my life, "did I do right?"

SYDNEY'S SCENE

In the decades-old feud between the world's richest gem dealers, nothing, apparently, is taboo. For the Hammonds and Blackstones, all's fair in love and business—and has been since Howard "King of Diamonds" Blackstone allegedly schemed to wrest control of old man Jebediah Hammonds' diamond mines and Oliver Hammond allegedly stole the world's most recognizable necklace, the Blackstone Rose.

But yesterday's gossip pales in comparison to today's 40-carat gem: Millionairess and daughter non grata Kimberley Blackstone was on the arm of Blackstone's leader, Ric Perrini. The same Kimberley Blackstone who'd defected to the rival House of Hammond

jewelers in New Zealand ten years ago.

According to an industry insider Kimberley was seen entering the Blackstone estate on the gold coast of Vaucluse—a place she reportedly described as off-limits mere months ago. Rumor has it Sydney's No. 1 player, Perrini, keeps a room there, too.

"If Perrini has any say," says one source, "they won't be separated for long."

Dear Reader,

It is my great pleasure and privilege to introduce a new Desire continuity series, DIAMONDS DOWN UNDER. A series set in Australia and New Zealand was suggested in early 2006, and the idea of developing a six-book continuity with my friends and fellow Down-Under Desireables excited and thrilled—and occasionally overwhelmed—me. Over the ensuing twelve months thousands of e-mails blazed back and forth across the Tasman as we brainstormed and fine-tuned the underlying premise, the locations, the characters, the conflicts and storylines.

We chose diamonds as the heart of our series for their connection to wealth and glamour, to romance and commitment…and for the cold, hard qualities beneath the surface sparkle. Everything is not how it first appears. We started with a rare pink diamond known as the Heart of the Outback, a stone which built one man's wealth and rent a family in two.

For thirty years the Hammonds and the Blackstones have remained at odds, and creating causes of all that simmering animosity was almost as much fun as researching the glamorous homes, boutiques, jets, cars, clothes and jewellery. ☺ I hope you enjoy the roller coaster of passion, drama, secrets and scandal that commences in *Vows & a Vengeful Groom* and continues—with some unexpected twists—over the next five months.

Cheers from Down Under,

Bronwyn Jameson

You can share the fruits of our research at the series Web site www.diamonds-downunder.com which features behind-the-books information, character profiles, missing scenes and chances to win dazzling prizes.

BRONWYN JAMESON

VOWS &
A VENGEFUL
GROOM

Silhouette®

Desire

Published by Silhouette Books
America's Publisher of Contemporary Romance

With heartfelt thanks to Melissa Jeglinski
for her faith in and support of our author-led series
from start to finish. Thank you, MJ, you are a gem!

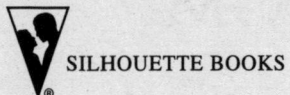 **SILHOUETTE BOOKS**

ISBN-13: 978-0-373-76843-1
ISBN-10:   0-373-76843-5

VOWS & A VENGEFUL GROOM

Copyright © 2008 by Bronwyn Turner

Visit Silhouette Books at www.eHarlequin.com

Printed in U.S.A.

BRONWYN JAMESON

spent much of her childhood with her head buried in a book. As a teenager she discovered romance novels, and it was only a matter of time before she turned her love of reading them into a love of writing them. Bronwyn shares an idyllic piece of the Australian farming heartland with her husband and three sons, a thousand sheep, a dozen horses, assorted wildlife and one kelpie dog. She still chooses to spend her limited downtime with a good book. Bronwyn loves to hear from readers. Write to her at bronwyn@bronwynjameson.com.

THE HAMMOND~BLACKSTONE FAMILY TREE

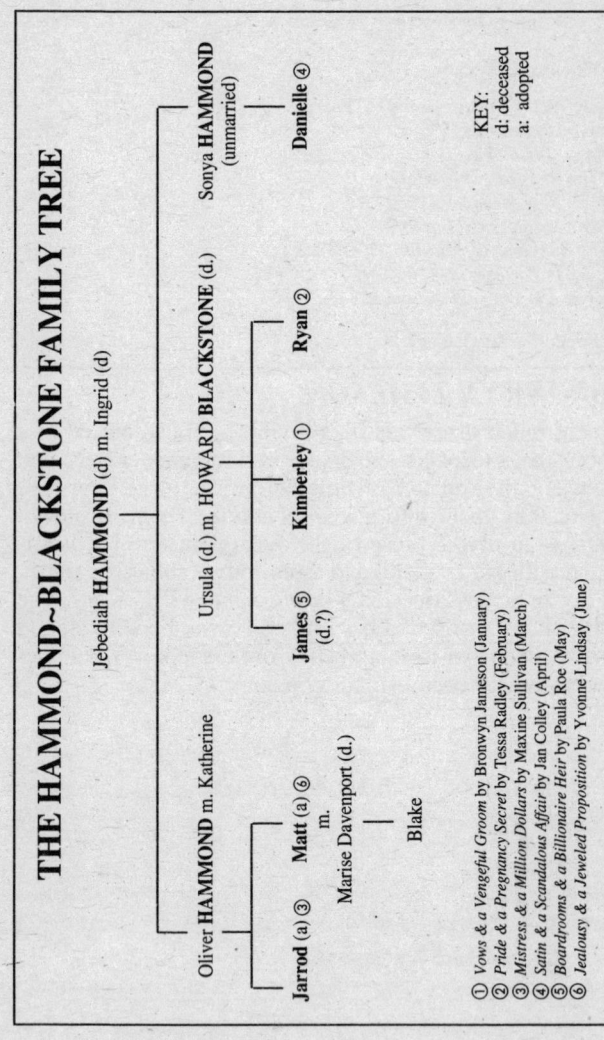

Jebediah **HAMMOND** (d) m. Ingrid (d)

Oliver **HAMMOND** m. Katherine

Ursula (d.) m. HOWARD BLACKSTONE (d.)

Sonya **HAMMOND** (unmarried)

Jarrod (a) ③

Matt (a) ⑥
m.
Marise Davenport (d.)

Blake

James ⑤ (d.?)

Kimberley ①

Ryan ②

Danielle ④

KEY:
d: deceased
a: adopted

① *Vows & a Vengeful Groom* by Bronwyn Jameson (January)
② *Pride & a Pregnancy Secret* by Tessa Radley (February)
③ *Mistress & a Million Dollars* by Maxine Sullivan (March)
④ *Satin & a Scandalous Affair* by Jan Colley (April)
⑤ *Boardrooms & a Billionaire Heir* by Paula Roe (May)
⑥ *Jealousy & a Jeweled Proposition* by Yvonne Lindsay (June)

One

Kimberley Blackstone's long stride—and the Louis Vuitton suitcase she towed in her wake—gathered momentum as she left customs at Auckland's international airport and headed toward the exit. Despite the handicap of her three-inch heels, she hit the Arrivals hall at a near jog, her focus on grabbing the first taxi in the rank outside, her mind making the transition from laid-back holiday mode to all that awaited her at House of Hammond on her first workday after the Christmas-New Year's break.

She didn't notice the waiting horde of media until it was too late. Flashbulbs exploded around her like a New Year's light show. She skidded to a halt, so abruptly her trailing suitcase rammed into her legs.

Surely, this had to be a case of mistaken identity. Kimberley hadn't been on the paparazzi hit list for close to a decade, not since she'd estranged herself from her billionaire father and his headline-hungry diamond business.

But, no, it was *her* name they called. *Her* face the focus of a swarm of lenses that circled like avid hornets. Her heart started to pound with fear-fuelled adrenaline.

What did they want?

What the hell was going on?

With a rising sense of bewilderment she scanned the crowd for a clue and her gaze fastened on a tall, leonine figure forcing his way to the front. A tall, familiar figure. She stared in stunned recognition and their gazes collided across the sea of heads before the cameras erupted with another barrage of flashes, this time right in her exposed face.

Blinded by the flashbulbs—and by the shock of that momentary eye-meet—Kimberley didn't realise his intent until he'd forged his way to her side, possibly by the sheer strength of his personality. She felt his arm wrap around her shoulder, pulling her into the protective shelter of his body, allowing her no time to object, no chance to lift her hands to ward him off.

In the space of a hastily drawn breath, she found herself plastered knee-to-nose against six feet of hard-bodied male.

Ric Perrini.

Her lover for ten torrid weeks, her husband for ten tumultuous days.

Her ex for ten tranquil years.

After all this time, he should not have felt so familiar but, oh, dear Lord, he did. She knew the scent of that body and its lean, muscular strength. She knew its heat and its slick power and every response it could draw from hers.

She also recognised the ease with which he'd taken control

of the moment and the decisiveness of his deep voice when it rumbled close to her ear. "I have a car waiting. Is this your only luggage?"

Kimberley nodded. A week at a tropical paradise did not require much in the way of clothes. Especially when she was wearing the one office-style dress and the only pair of heels she'd packed. When he released his grip on her shoulder to take charge of her compact suitcase, she longed to dig those heels into the ground, to tell him exactly what he could do with his car, and his presumptuous attitude.

But she wasn't stupid. She'd seen Perrini in action often enough to know that attitude yielded results. The fierce expression and king-of-the-jungle manner he did so well would keep the snapping newshounds at bay.

Not that she was about to be towed along as meekly as her wheeled luggage.

"I assume you will tell me," she said tightly, "what this welcome party is all about."

"Not while the welcome party is within earshot."

Barking a request for the cameramen to stand aside, Perrini took her hand and pulled her into step with his ground-eating stride. Kimberley let him because he was right, damn his arrogant, Italian-suited hide. Despite the speed with which he whisked her across the terminal forecourt, she could almost feel the hot breath of the pursuing media on her back.

This was neither the time nor the place for explanations. Inside his car, however, she would get answers.

The initial shock had been blown away—by the haste of their retreat, by the heat of her gathering indignation, by the rush of adrenaline fired by Perrini's presence and the looming verbal battle. Her brain was starting to tick now. This had to be her father's doing. And if it was a Howard Blackstone publicity ploy, then it had to be about Blackstone Diamonds, the company that ruled his life.

The knowledge made her chest tighten with a familiar ache of disillusionment.

She'd known her father would be flying in from Sydney for today's opening of the newest in his chain of exclusive, high-end jewellery boutiques. The opulent shopfront sat adjacent to the rival business where Kimberley worked. No coincidence, she thought bitterly, just as it was no coincidence that Ric Perrini was here in Auckland ushering her to his car.

Perrini was Howard Blackstone's right-hand man, second in command at Blackstone Diamonds and head of the mining division, that position of power a legacy of his short-lived marriage to the boss's daughter. No doubt her father had sent him to fetch her; the question was why.

On his last visit to Auckland, Howard had attempted yet again to lure her back to Blackstone's, to the job she'd walked away from the day she walked out on her marriage. That meeting had escalated into an ugly word-slinging bout and ended with Howard vowing to write her from his will if she didn't return to Blackstone's immediately.

Two months later Kimberley was still here in Auckland, still working for his sworn enemy at House of Hammond. They hadn't spoken since; she hadn't expected any other outcome. When her father said he was wiping his hands of her, she took him at his word.

Yet here she was, being rushed toward a gleaming black limousine by her father's number-one henchman. She had no clue why he'd changed his mind or what the media presence signified, apart from more Blackstone headlines and the certainty that she was being used. Again. Sending Perrini was the final cruel twist.

By the time they arrived at the waiting car, her blood was simmering with a mixture of remembered hurt and raw resentment. The driver stowed her luggage while Perrini stowed her. She slid across the silver-grey leather seat and the door closed behind her, shutting her off from the cameras that seemed to be multiplying by the minute.

Perrini paused on the pavement beside the hired car, his hands held wide in a gesture of appeal as he spoke. Whatever he was saying only incited more questions, more flashbulbs, and Kimberley steamed with the need to know what was going on. She reached for her door handle, and when it didn't open she caught the driver's eye in the rearview mirror. "Could you please unlock the doors? I need to get out."

He looked away. And he didn't release the central locking device.

Kimberley's blood heated from slow simmer to fast boil. "I am here under duress. Release the lock or I swear I will—"

Before she could complete her threat, the door opened from outside and Perrini climbed in beside her. She'd been closer inside the airport terminal, when he'd shielded her from the cameras with the breadth of his body, but then she'd been too sluggish with disbelief to react. Now she slid as far away as the backseat allowed, and as she fastened her seat belt the car sped away from the kerb.

Primed for battle, she turned to face her adversary. "You had me locked inside this car out of earshot while *you* talked to the media? This had better be good, Perrini."

He looked up from securing his seat belt and their eyes met and held. For the first time there was nothing between them—

no distraction, no interruption—and for a beat of time she forgot herself in those unexpectedly blue eyes, in the unbidden rush of memories that rose in a choking wave.

For a second she thought she saw an echo of the same raw emotion deep in his eyes but then she realised it was only tiredness. And tension.

"I wouldn't be here," he said, low and gruff, "if this wasn't important."

The implication that he would rather be anywhere but here, with her, fisted tightly around Kimberley's heart. But she lifted her chin and stared him down. "Important to whom? My father?"

He didn't have to answer. She saw it in the narrowing of his deep-set eyes, as if her comment had irritated him. Good. She'd meant it to.

"Did he think sending you would change my mind?" she continued coolly, despite the angry heat that churned her stomach. "Because he could have saved himself—"

"He didn't send me, Kim."

There was something in the delivery of that simple statement that brought all her senses to full alert. Finally she allowed herself to take him all in. He was not lounging with his usual arrogant ease but sitting straight and still. Sunlight spilled through the side window onto his face, highlighting the angles and planes, the straight line of his nose and the deep cleft in his chin.

And the muscle that ticked in his jaw.

She could feel the tension now, strong enough to suck up all the air in the luxury car's roomy interior. She could see it, too, in the grim line of his mouth and the intensity of his cobalt-blue eyes.

Despite the muggy summer morning Kimberley felt an icy

shiver of foreboding. Beneath the warmth of her holiday tan her skin goose-bumped. Something was very, very wrong.

"What is it?" Her fingers clutched at the handbag in her lap, gripping the soft leather straps as if that might somehow anchor her against what was to come. "If my father didn't send you, then why are you here?"

"Howard left Sydney last night. Your brother received a phone call in the early hours of this morning when the plane didn't arrive in Auckland."

"Didn't arrive?" She shook her head, unable to accept what he wasn't telling her. "Planes don't just fail to arrive. What happened?"

"We don't know. Twenty minutes out of Sydney it disappeared from radar." His eyes locked on hers, and all she needed to know was etched in their darkened depths, and in the dip of his head and the strained huskiness of his next words. "I'm sorry, Kim."

No. She shook her head again. This couldn't be happening. How could her all-powerful, larger-than-life father be dead? On the eve of his greatest moment, the day when he'd vowed to rub the Hammonds' faces in his accomplishments right here on their home turf.

"He was coming for the opening of the Queen Street store," she said softly.

"Yes. He was due to leave at seven-thirty but there was a delay. Some contracts to be signed."

There always were. Every childhood memory of her father concerned business papers, negotiations, dealing in the fabulous wealth of the diamonds that underpinned it all. She couldn't remember ever seeing him dressed in anything other than a business suit. That was his life.

Diamonds and contracts and making headlines.

"When I saw you at the airport," she said, "with all the cameras and media hubbub, I thought it was to do with the opening. Some strategy he'd come up with to grab attention for the new shop." The awful reality of tomorrow's headlines churned through her, tightening her chest in a painful vise. "They were there because they knew."

While she'd been enjoying her last walk on the beach, her last breakfast of papaya and mango and rambutan, while she'd laughed with the resort staff and flirted with the twenty-year-old charmer seated next to her on the flight home—

"I didn't know," she said on a choked whisper. Despite their bitter estrangement of the past decade, despite everything she held her father accountable for, she'd grown up adoring the man and vying with her brother to win his favour. For thirty-one years he had shaped her decisions, her career, her beliefs. For the last ten of those years she'd done everything she could to distance herself, but he was still her father. "I walked out of the terminal and into those cameras…. How did they know?"

"About your father?" He exhaled, a rough sound that doubled as a curse. "I don't know. They shouldn't have had names this quickly. They sure as hell shouldn't have known you were coming through the airport this morning."

The sick feeling in Kimberley's stomach sharpened. She hadn't worked her way around to that, but now he'd brought it up. Her forehead creased in a frown. "How did *you* know where to find me?"

"When you didn't answer your phone, I called your office."

"Last night?"

"This morning."

Kimberley digested that information. Obviously he didn't

mean in the predawn hours when her brother Ryan first received the news, otherwise he wouldn't have called her office. Wouldn't have found someone—Lionel, the office manager, no doubt—to point him in the direction of the airport. "You didn't call me as soon as you heard?"

"No." His voice dropped to the same harsh intensity that darkened his eyes to near black. "This wasn't something to hear over the phone, Kim."

"You thought it might be better if I heard from a news crew?" she asked.

"That's why I flew over here. To stop that happening."

"Yet it almost did happen."

"Because Hammond's office manager wouldn't give me your flight information over the phone." Ric ground out that information with barely leashed restraint. He didn't need her derisive tone reminding him of his impotent frustration on the drive to and from the city, not knowing if he'd make it back in time to meet her flight. Not knowing if the media would discover her whereabouts when that information had been deliberately withheld from him.

It hadn't been a surprise, just a damn aggravation.

There was no love lost between the employees of House of Hammond and Blackstone Diamonds. The enmity of a thirty-year feud between the heads of the two companies—Howard and his brother-in-law, Oliver Hammond—had spilled over and tainted relationships into the next generation. Kimberley had re-ignited the simmering feud when she took a position assisting Matt Hammond, the current CEO of House of Hammond.

"You can't blame Lionel for exercising caution," Kim said archly, as if she'd read his mind.

There was something in that notion and in her tone that trampled all over Ric's prickly mood. Ten minutes together and despite the gravity of the news he'd brought, they teetered on the razor's edge of an argument. He shook his head wearily and let it roll back against the cool upholstery. Why should he be surprised? From the moment they'd met, their relationship had been defined by fiery clashes and passionate making up.

He'd never had a woman more difficult than Kim...nor one who could give him more pleasure.

When the phone call about Howard came in, he'd made the decision to fly to her without a second's hesitation. As much as he hated what had brought him here, he relished the fact it would bring her home. She belonged at Blackstone's. Ric sucked in a deep breath, and the scent of summer that clung to her skin curled into his gut and took hold.

Just like she belonged in his bed.

"You must have left very early this morning," she said.

"I was on my way back to Sydney from the Janderra mine when Ryan called. An emergency trip, last minute, so I took the company jet. When Howard knew I wouldn't be back, he chartered a replacement for his trip."

"You were already in the air. That's why you were the one to come."

Ric turned his head slowly and found himself looking right into her jade-green eyes. They were her most striking feature, not only because of that dramatic colour offset by the dark frame of her brows, but because of how much they gave away. The trick, he'd learned, was picking the real emotion from the sophisticated front she used to hide her vulnerabilities.

Not that Kim ever admitted to any weakness. She was her father's daughter in that regard. And right now she was working overtime to keep both him and the shock of the news he'd delivered at arm's length.

"It didn't matter where I was," he said, strong and deliberate. "I would have come, make no mistake."

"To tell me my father was d—"

"To take you home."

"To Sydney?" The notion appeared to surprise her, enough that she huffed out an astonished breath. "You're forgetting, my home is here now."

"I haven't forgotten."

After she'd walked out on him, he'd allowed her time to cool down. To think about her hotheaded accusations and to realise they belonged together. Four long dark months of silence passed before he'd come after her…only to find that she hadn't cooled down one degree or come to any realisation other than the certainty their marriage had been a colossal mistake and that her new home was here, in Auckland, New Zealand.

With Matt Hammond as her boss and her protector.

No, he hadn't forgotten anything and the power of those memories fired his temper and sparked between them in the close confines of the slowly moving car. She knew he was remembering that last heated clash in her workroom at Hammonds. The knowledge glittered in her eyes and brought out colour along her high cheekbones as she lifted her chin to speak.

"You said you would never come after me again."

And he hadn't. Pride and the finality of divorce papers hadn't allowed him, but this was different. "This isn't about us," he said tersely. "This is about your father and your family."

Kimberley held the narrowed anger of his gaze for another second before looking away. She closed her mouth on the

instant comeback that flew to her tongue, the very inconvenient truth that the Hammonds were her family, too.

Her mother, Ursula, who'd died when Kim was a toddler,
was Oliver Hammond's sister. Because of the animosity
between the Blackstones and the Hammonds, she'd grown up
with a tremendously biased view of her New Zealand uncle
and aunt and their adopted sons, Jarrod and Matt. Yet when
she'd needed a new job, they'd welcomed her into their
business and into their home. Matt had been her friend when
she'd badly needed one. His wife, Marise, had never exactly
warmed to her, yet Matt had insisted on having her as god-
mother to their little son, Blake.

For the past ten years these Hammonds had been more her
family than anyone on the Blackstone side of the Tasman, but
she refrained from saying this out loud. If she'd read the tur-
bulence in Perrini's eyes correctly, then mentioning Matt's
name would be like red-flagging a bull. He'd never forgiven
Matt for offering her an easy escape from Blackstone's with
the plum position at House of Hammond, and the pair had
almost come to blows in the Hammond workroom the day
Perrini had tried to talk her in to taking him back. Anything
she said now would only lead to more hot words and this
wasn't the place.

This isn't about us. This is about your father.

How right he was…on more levels than the present.

Their relationship had never been about just them. Therein
lay the problem. They'd met at Blackstone Diamonds, they'd
bonded while working together to sell the retail jewellery
business plan to the board and they'd fallen into bed in a
wildly spontaneous celebration of their success.

But Perrini had wanted more. He'd married her to get it,

and his proud new father-in-law had delivered everything an ambitious young marketing executive could want. Power, prestige, a prominent bay in the executive parking lot…and entrée into one of Sydney's richest and most socially prominent families.

In the same sweet deal, he'd won the job of launching the retail business, Blackstone Jewellery, the job Kimberley had been promised and which she'd worked her backside off to earn. The killer blow? When she expressed her disappointment, Perrini sided with her father when he told her she didn't have the necessary skills or experience.

In time she'd come to accept their point, but at twenty-one she'd been wildly, madly in love, and she'd felt only a crippling sense of betrayal over what had led to that point. He'd pursued her; he'd married her; and all to serve his own ambitions.

Today he'd come to take her home to her family in Sydney, but could she trust his motives?

The farther they travelled in silence, climbing familiar streets toward her One Tree Hill town house, the more she realised that his motives didn't matter. The cold, hard reality of his news was finally beginning to pierce her armour of denial.

This isn't about us. This is about your father and your family.

Her father's plane was missing and even without the media's eagerness for photos of his anguished family, she couldn't go to work. Nor could she sit around her house going stir-crazy as she waited for news. With Matt away on a business trip she had no one to call on, no arms to hold her steady, no shoulder to cry on.

From the corner of her eye she could see Perrini's outstretched legs and the memory of his solid support at the airport ambushed her for a moment. A bad, unnecessary moment. She didn't need the comfort of his arms, not anymore, but she did need to go back to Sydney. She needed to be there when news came in of her father's fate.

And she needed to see the rest of her family, to make amends for the years of her absence.

Just the thought of seeing her brother Ryan and her Aunt Sonya, who'd been the closest thing to a mother figure in her upbringing, caused a tight ache in her belly and her chest and the back of her throat. She took a tighter grip on the bag in her lap and on her emotions. Tears would come, she knew, but never in front of Perrini.

"This is your place?"

Perrini's head tilted with what looked like curiosity as he surveyed the neat exterior of her stucco town house from the street where the limo had pulled up. Kimberley nodded abruptly in reply. He'd given the driver this address, so he knew without asking. And now that they'd arrived a new nervous tension gripped her insides with platinum claws.

This was her domain, a haven she'd created for herself away from the craziness of her busy business life. She didn't want Perrini prowling around, casting his long shadow over her privacy, leaving an impression she knew would stick like superglue to her visual memory.

Yet how could she not invite him in, when he'd flown through the early morning hours on top of a return flight to Blackstone's outback mine? Being one of her father's toys, the company jet would be furnished with every amenity and then some, but still…

"Would you like to come in?" she asked quickly, before

caution or nerves could change her mind. "I won't be long. I just need to repack and water my plants and call work to let them know."

One dark eyebrow arched. "You've decided to come?"

"Was there any doubt?"

"With you, Kim…always."

The wry tone of his comment surprised a short laugh from Kimberley and their eyes met with that sound still arcing between them. A hint of the Perrini smile that could render smart women senseless hovered at the corners of his mouth and the blue of his eyes suddenly seemed richer, deeper, sultrier. Everything inside her stilled…everything except the elevated beat of her heart.

Damn him. It wasn't even a proper smile. He wasn't even trying to charm her.

"I'd best get organised," she said briskly, breaking that moment of connection with a rush of smart-woman willpower.

She reached for her door just as his mobile phone buzzed. Leaving him to his call, she let the driver haul her luggage up the steep rise of steps to the closed-in portico that sheltered the front door. She rummaged in her bag for her keys and phone. Walking and talking would save precious minutes and by the time she'd unlocked and waved the driver inside, she'd also apprised Hammond's office manager that she was taking a week of personal leave.

Next, Matt. He needed to know, as her friend and her boss, but she'd barely dialled his number before a hand closed around her wrist, capturing her arm and her attention. Perrini. She recognised the span of his hand, the smattering of dark hair, the scar on his middle knuckle. The black-sapphire cuff links Howard had given him as a Christmas gift.

"Is that your boss you're calling?"

His voice was as tight as his grip and Kimberley blinked her attention away from his hand and on to the terse words he'd spoken. Her jaw tightened with irritation. She was in no mood for another go-round about the nature of her relationship with Matt. "So help me, Perrini, if you still can't accept that I wouldn't sleep with my—"

The rest of her reproach froze on her lips when she looked up into his face. Stark, taut, leached of colour. He exhaled a breath and the harsh sound echoed through the enclosed space. "I wish that were all, Kim."

The phone call.

He had news about the plane, about her father.

Panic beat hard in her veins but she straightened her shoulders in preparation for the blow.

"They've found debris," he said grimly, confirming her worst fear. "Off the Australian coast."

Debris. Kimberley assimilated the innocuous-sounding word. Not wreckage. Not bodies. "Just…debris?"

"No." He shook his head. "They also found one person. Alive. A woman."

A soft sob escaped her lips and she started to tremble somewhere deep inside. Perrini's arm came around her, lending her strength when she might have fallen.

"Who?" she breathed. "Please God, not Sonya, too."

"No, not your aunt." He took the phone from her limp fingers and flipped it shut. "According to Ryan, there's a chance it may be Marise Hammond. Your boss's wife."

Two

Marise Hammond may have been on Howard Blackstone's charter flight?

It made no sense in Kimberley's shock-muddled brain. Yes, Marise had been in Australia for the past month tying up estate matters following her mother's death. Yes, Marise was capricious and self-absorbed, but not to the extent that she would hitch a ride home with her husband's bitter enemy. She knew how Matt felt about Blackstone Diamonds, and all because of Howard.

Why would she choose to be in his company?

Perrini had no answer and the question had been wiped from Kimberley's mind, temporarily, by the rest of the details he passed on from that phone call. He stressed that the woman hadn't been identified, that Marise hadn't been confirmed as a passenger, that the information was unsubstantiated.

But his contact was a senior officer in the Sydney police force. Surely he wouldn't tell them a woman had been pulled from the water alive without concrete information. Surely he wouldn't provide a name without confidence in her identity.

Surely he wouldn't build up false hope that Howard, too, might have survived the crash.

That notion only struck her while she was packing—if you could call throwing random clothes into a suitcase "packing." There was no rhyme or reason to the process. She didn't want to deliberate over what she might need in the coming week beyond clean underwear, although she made a conscious choice to shed the austere black dress she'd been wearing for work in favour of a pretty white sundress.

She didn't want to contemplate the outcome of this trip.

She didn't want to think about the need to pack sombre black.

Then she caught sight of herself in the mirror and saw that her face contained little more colour than her dress and possibly less than the creamy South Sea pearls in her ears. But it wouldn't have mattered what she wore, her face would be a pale, haunted contrast to the dark hair she'd pulled back in a ruthlessly tight ponytail. Her eyes would still look dazed and lost.

In that instant the last of the indignation that had carried her through the past half hour deflated like a pin-pricked balloon. Weak-kneed, she collapsed to the edge of her mattress amid the bright heap of floral-hued clothes she'd tipped from her holiday suitcase.

From the living room she heard Perrini's deep voice, a low, mellifluous sound that worked its magic on her shattered senses and pulled her back from the abyss. He had to be on the phone—a reminder of the previous phone call he'd taken in the limo—and now that her head was clearer she made the connection.

Marise was alive. Perhaps she wasn't the only survivor.

That faint hope flickered like a slow flame in the centre of her chest. It was okay. She was going home and it would all be okay.

Perrini appeared at her bedroom door, the phone still in his hand. The way he looked at her made her heart skip a beat. "Was that more news?" she asked, eyes wide and fixed on his face.

"No. It was my pilot. The jet is fuelled and ready to go when you are."

Kimberley released the breath she hadn't known she was holding and nodded. "Once I decide what to wear, I'll be ready."

Given the circumstances, it was a ridiculous thing to say. She regretted it even more when Perrini surveyed her, and the haphazard contents of her suitcase, with ruthless focus. Then, with his trademark decisiveness, he crossed the room and pulled her up from the bed and onto her feet. Slowly he surveyed her, from her toes all the way up to her eyes.

"You'll do in what you're wearing," he said, and his eyes smoked with a hint of what she might do *for*. "I always liked you in white."

Kimberley blinked with astonishment. *He was flirting with her? Half an hour after delivering news of her father's possible demise? Unbelievable.*

"I'm not dressing to impress you, Perrini," she said sharply.

He almost smiled and that tightened the screws on her incredulity.

"Give me five minutes—and some privacy—and I'll change."

"No, you won't." He took hold of her hand. "I've put some colour back in your face and some life in your eyes. Now let's go before you start thinking too much and lose it again."

* * *

The trip from Auckland to Sydney passed in a slow-moving daze despite the swift efficiency and supreme comfort of flying in the Blackstone corporate jet. A Gulfstream IV, it was the exact same model of aircraft her father had chartered for his ill-fated flight. She'd asked Perrini about that, after they boarded. After she noted the rich mahogany paneling, the luxurious cream-colored leather seats, the fully stocked galley and ornately appointed bathroom.

Right after he'd pointed out the bed and said, "Feel free to use it. I'm happy to share."

No doubt he was trying to get the spark back in her eyes by employing the same diversionary tactics as back in her bedroom, but that didn't dull the electric awareness that shimmered between them. Was he remembering another private flight they'd taken together?

There'd been no bed on that charter flight from San Francisco to Vegas but it hadn't mattered. They'd improvised. And before she'd come down from that incredible high, Perrini stunned her with a proposal she'd thought as wildly impulsive and wickedly romantic as making love with him a mile up in the sky.

That weekend had been the zenith of ten blissful weeks as Ric Perrini's lover. She'd become his wife in a wedding chapel only Vegas could love, and afterward they'd spent three decadent days in a Bellagio suite ordering room service and indulging themselves in every way possible. She hadn't realised a wedding band would make such a difference, but oh, how it had. It was the difference between good champagne and the vintage French they quaffed that weekend. Another level, impossible to describe or define, that filled her senses and her heart until she wondered if they would explode.

On their return to Australia, they had.

Everything inside Kimberley contracted painfully as she recalled the bliss. She didn't want to remember the freefall plunge that followed their return home...or the shattering pain of hitting rock bottom. So she'd focused on the here and now, and asked Perrini mindless questions about the jet's inclusions and capabilities, and she'd learned that her father had chartered the same model.

Clinging white-knuckled to the armrests during takeoff with the high-pitched wail of the engines in her ears, feeling the forward thrust suck her back into her seat, she could not shut out the image of her father and Marise experiencing the same sensation fourteen hours earlier. Nor could she eradicate the image of all that power and speed crashing from the sky and hitting the sea with devastating impact.

The flicker of hope in her chest wavered and died, and Kimberley's emotions spent the three-hour flight seesawing between numbed disbelief and intense dread of what lay ahead. She took up Perrini's suggestion to lie down because she couldn't bear the thought of looking out the window at the stretch of sea where the plane had gone down. He'd told her that Australian search-and-rescue had mounted an extensive search, but she didn't want to see the evidence.

It wasn't denial, it was self-preservation.

She felt she'd done a decent job of disguising her turmoil. She hadn't succumbed to tears. She'd even managed to feign the easy breathing of sleep when Perrini came to check on her.

It was one of the hardest things she could remember doing, lying there controlling her breathing while he stood in the open doorway staring down at her. Then he'd pulled the light blanket over her prone body. If he'd spoken, if he'd touched her with more than the velvety brush of his knuckles, she might have given in and asked him to stay. To share the bed, to hold her, to distract her in any way he chose.

That's how fragile and alone she'd felt at that moment.

But he'd left as quietly as he'd come and she'd curled up tightly and hugged herself, the same as she'd done so many nights as a child when she would sneak down from her bedroom and hide in a quiet corner of the foyer in their Vaucluse home, waiting for her father to come home from a long working day or a week at the mine or at the end of another overseas business trip.

Now, as they neared that home, the thought that he'd never come home again sunk diamond-sharp talons into her heart. It shouldn't hurt this much, not when she'd come to hate everything about the way he operated, including his screwed-up ethics and his treatment of the Hammonds, who were his wife's family. Not to mention the manipulation of her marriage to suit his own self-centred ends.

Maybe she needed to focus on *that* son of a bitch, instead of a childhood ideal of a father who had never existed except in her imagination.

"Okay?" Perrini asked from behind the wheel of his Maserati. The coupe was all sleek, blue style and eye-catching looks on the outside, with an engine that purred deceptively until provoked. Then it roared to life with impressive power and drive.

This car is your perfect match, she'd told him a couple of miles back. Now, the thick ache in her throat made it impossible to answer his question.

At the next red light he reached across and put his hand over hers, where they lay tightly clenched in her lap. The unexpected gesture was so comforting and so strengthening that she immediately found her voice. "I wish you'd stop being so nice," she snapped. "It makes me nervous."

He cut her an inscrutable look from behind his sunglasses. "A temporary aberration. Don't get too used to it."

"Thanks for the warning," she said dryly. Then she shook her head when she realised that once again he'd shocked her out of her wretchedness. "Thank you," she repeated, this time with sincerity.

"For?" The lights changed and he took his hand back, using it to guide the powerful sports car through the gears as they climbed the curves of New South Head Road.

"For breaking the news to me in person. For rescuing me at the airport and bringing me home. For keeping me together along the way. I do appreciate it, Ric. Thank you."

"You're welcome." They travelled another block before he added, "You called me Ric. I must be making progress."

She'd called him Perrini from their very first meeting, a ruse to remind him of their business relationship because she hadn't trusted his smooth moves or her body's unruly responses to him. They'd had to work together and she'd wanted to keep it professional. She'd fought the good fight for almost two months. And after they'd hooked up she kept on using his surname out of habit—and to tease him when he got all he-man insistent about her calling him Ric.

Now she'd done so to show the sincerity of her thanks. "It was a temporary aberration," she said coolly. "Don't get too used to it."

He laughed, a two-note snort of amusement that pierced Kimberley's numbed senses. It was dangerous, letting him charm her so easily, so quickly, but this was a temporary situation. A week at most, and she would be returning to Auckland. And right now she needed that charm and the sound of laughter because they'd arrived in Vaucluse and were climbing the street lined with multimillion-dollar homes to the most spectacular of all.

Miramare.

For the first twenty years of her life the three-storey white mansion had been Kimberley's home. She'd never been struck by its majesty, its size, its opulence, until now as Perrini downshifted gears to negotiate the thick cluster of news teams waiting outside the security gates, and turned into the driveway. And there it was, rising before them like a Venetian palace. A home fit for the man the media dubbed Australia's King of Diamonds.

A man who'd forbidden her from ever darkening this doorstep again when she defied his will and refused to return to work for Blackstone Diamonds.

A maelstrom of conflicting emotions—resentment, anguish, anticipation, anxiety—stormed through her as Perrini parked beneath the *porte cochere*. Although her gaze was fixed on the steps leading to the grand entrance, she heard the subtle scrunch of leather and sensed him shifting in his seat to face her. Her heart beat like a tom-tom drum high in her chest.

"Good to be home?" he asked.

Now there was a question! Was this home? Would her family welcome her back into their home?

When she'd quit her job at Blackstone's and joined House of Hammond, she'd also deserted her family. That's how it was between the two sides of the family. You chose your team: Blackstone or Hammond. There was no common ground, no fraternity, and it had never been as simple as birth name.

Sonya Hammond was the perfect example. Her mother's much younger sister moved in with the Blackstones as a teenager. Staying after Ursula's death completed her estrangement from her brother Oliver Hammond and his family.

But Kimberley was more worried about Ryan's reception than Sonya's. Her younger brother had endured his ups and downs with Howard but now he headed the Blackstone Jewellery chain, which placed him very firmly in the Blackstone camp. He didn't approve her defection—his word, used when he'd called to try his hand at changing her mind—any more than he'd approved of her affair with, and subsequent marriage to, Perrini.

And Perrini's question still stood unanswered.

Good to be home?

"I'm feeling many things," she said frankly. "Good is not one of them."

"Care to elaborate?"

Slowly she turned to face him. "I wouldn't be here but for one thing."

Their eyes met, the knowledge a shock of understanding that sharpened his expression into tight lines and shadowed planes. If Howard were here, she wouldn't be. It was as simple—and as complicated to her psyche—as that.

Before Perrini could respond, something distracted him and the atypical hesitation caused her to turn back toward the house. Sonya stood on the top step, her willowy figure framed by the open front door. Kimberley's heart beat even harder in her chest.

"She hasn't changed," she murmured.

Still tall, slender, beautiful, her aunt Sonya was dressed elegantly in a skirt and heels, her brown hair pulled back in the same conservative style. A warm smile graced her lips as she lifted her hand in welcome.

She looked so heartwrenchingly familiar, so *Sonya,* that Kimberley struggled to contain the squeal of joy that exploded inside her. Reflexively her hand lifted to the chatelaine necklace she wore around her neck, Sonya's gift on her twenty-first birthday. Each exquisitely crafted antique charm was a symbol. Love. Fertility. Protection. Strength. Eternity.

After the dissolution of her marriage she'd put it away in its box, unworn but not forgotten. Until recently when she'd started wearing it again. She wiped away the tears that blurred her vision, then allowed Perrini to help her from the low-slung car so she could run up the stairs and into her aunt's open arms. Then she knew why she wore the necklace.

It was her connection to home, to Sonya, whose embrace reminded her what it should feel like to come home. Tears she'd refused to cry for her father fell unrestrained as she breathed the familiar scent of her aunt's Chanel No. 5 and felt the comforting pat of her hand on her arm.

I should not have let Perrini and my father keep me away this long. I should not have given them that power.

"I'm sorry," she choked out fiercely through her tears. "I'm so very sorry."

Sonya's hug tightened for a moment as she whispered, "We all are, honey. About everything."

Long before Kimberley was ready her aunt broke the embrace. Taking a half step back Sonya smiled through her own tears as she took Kimberley's hands in hers. "It is so good to have you back home again, Kim, and to see you looking so beautiful…despite the circumstances."

"It is so good to be here, despite everything that has kept me away."

Rough emotion dimmed the light in Sonya's warm hazel eyes. "Let's not talk about that now. Come inside. Your brother is out on the terrace with Garth. I'm sure you can't wait to see them both again. And Danielle arrived a little while ago, too. She flew down from Port Douglas as soon as she heard."

Danielle was Sonya's daughter, and she must have been waiting just inside the door for the perfect moment to make her appearance. She *had* changed. Between seventeen and twenty-seven Danielle Hammond had grown into a copper-haired beauty with her mother's willowy build and a tan befitting her Port Douglas, Queensland home.

Golden eyes welling with tears, she hurried over to embrace Kimberley with the same warmth as her mother and her own special brand of exuberance.

"You brought her," Danielle said fiercely over Kim's shoulder. "I will never doubt your genius again."

"I'm only the chauffeur," Perrini drawled, downplaying his role in the prodigal's homecoming, "and the sometime porter. Where do you want me to take these?"

Kimberley saw that he toted her matched set of luggage, but before she could answer, Sonya stepped into her customary role as hostess. "Take them up to Kim's room, please, Ric. You know where it is."

How? Kimberley wondered, frowning. Afraid of awkward encounters with her father or her brother, she had never brought him home when they'd been lovers. They'd met at his house and they'd kept their relationship quiet at work for as long as they could. Yet out of all the bedrooms and suites spread through the mansion's upper wings, he knew where to find hers?

He disappeared into the house with Sonya, and Danielle's voice cut through her distraction. "How are you coping, Kim...or is that a stupid question?"

"I'm fine."

Danielle's eyes narrowed in a way that demanded the truth, and Kimberley decided that her cousin hadn't changed so much after all. Up close she noticed that beneath the big smile and light sprinkling of freckles, Danielle's complexion was blotchy and her eyes red-rimmed from crying. She had grown up in this house, too, with Howard a larger-than-life presence in her upbringing. She was more a Blackstone than a Hammond, although she'd struck out and started her own jewellery design business as Dani Hammond since moving to the tropical north of Australia.

"I can see that the Port lifestyle agrees with you, but how are you doing beneath the smile and suntan? Is everything working out for you?"

"Don't change the subject," her cousin fired back. "You're the one under inquisition right now."

"I told you, I'm fine," Kimberley assured her, but tears were brewing in her eyes as she reached out to hug Danielle again. A couple of seconds was all she needed to restore her composure and in that time she realised that she'd spoken no less than the truth. Being here, with the people she'd grown up with—the people she loved—she *was* fine. "Has there been any more news?" she asked, straightening and wiping moisture from her eyes. Again.

"No...at least none that your brother is passing on."

Kimberley stilled. "Do you think Ryan heard something he isn't sharing?"

"I had that feeling but when I asked he just about bit my head off. I don't know what's going on with him, Kim. Oh, I know he's shattered about his father, and this waiting around for news is *so* not his style. Mum told me he's been trying to line up extra search aircraft and vessels, despite all that AusSAR is doing. That was *after* he went down to water police headquarters to demand full disclosure. I wouldn't be surprised if he tried to get a spot on one of the search vessels, as well."

Kimberley well knew of her brother's tenacity. "That would have been interesting."

"No kidding."

"Do you think they told him anything new?"

Danielle released her breath on a heavy sigh that blew an errant curl from her face. "Honestly, I don't know. He is just so antsy, I can't help thinking there is more."

"More than his father being missing and him stuck here unable to charge to the rescue?"

"I guess you're right," Danielle mused aloud, although she didn't sound convinced. She tucked her arm through Kim's and tugged her toward the front door. "Let's go in. Knowing Mum, she will be putting together a late lunch for you and Ric as we speak. I bet you haven't had anything to eat all day."

"True, but food is the furthest thing from my mind."

"Do try and have something if only to please Mum. Fussing over us all day is the only thing that's keeping her together. Let her do the same for you."

"I will, but there's something I need to do first."

"Ryan?" her cousin guessed astutely.

Kimberley nodded. *Yes—Ryan.*

Returning from his porter's errand to the second floor, Ric was halfway down the ornate marble staircase that rose from the grand foyer when Danielle and Kimberley came through the front door arm-in-arm. But he only saw one woman.

Dark hair slicked back in an efficient ponytail. Green eyes so recently awash with tears now clear and sparking with renewed resolve.

She'd rebounded from the tearstorm. Good. Bringing her home had not only been necessary but also essential, for her, for Sonya, for all the family. And now that she was here, she was staying. Whatever it took.

"There you are." Danielle released her hold on her cousin's arm as Ric descended the last of the stairs. "I was just taking Kim out to the terrace to find Ryan."

He knew this would be the difficult part of this reunion, hence the warrior-woman look on her face. "I'll take her," he said, smoothly stepping in to claim her hand. "Could you let Sonya know to bring our coffee out there?"

Danielle left them alone, but only after a raised-eyebrow look that took in his proprietary clasp on Kim's hand and a murmured comment he lip-read as "Nice work."

By the darkness that suddenly appeared in Kim's eyes and the jerk of her hand against his, he gathered she didn't miss that knowing look, either. "There's no need to take me anywhere," she said frostily. "I know my way to the terrace."

"I didn't imagine you wouldn't."

"Then let go of my hand. You've already given Danielle the wrong impression."

He raised an eyebrow. "That being…?"

"Don't pretend to be dense, Perrini. It's not becoming."

"Are you still hung up on what your brother thinks about us together?"

"Since we're not together anymore, no." She narrowed her eyes at him. "And wasn't it *you* who said this wasn't about us?"

"Throwing my words back at me? That's not like you, Kim."

Her emerald eyes shot fire at him and she tugged harder at her hand. Ric didn't let go. Instead he used the leverage to pull her closer, close enough that the flared skirt of her dress brushed his thighs and her eyes widened with apprehension. In the cool quiet of the atriumlike foyer he imagined he could hear the wild race of her heartbeat…or perhaps it was his own.

He thought about kissing her. When her mouth opened on a silent note of outrage, he ached to bend into that kiss. He imagined he'd get slapped for his efforts, but fear of that didn't stop him. The flicker of vulnerability in her eyes did.

The fierce determination was just a front for facing her brother. Beneath the veneer she was emotionally exhausted by the day's revelations and he knew there would be more to come, if not today then tomorrow or the next day. It was only a matter of time before the wreckage was located and the bodies recovered.

No, he couldn't take advantage of her weakness. Not now. As a compromise he lifted the hand trapped in his toward his lips. He felt her resistance, saw it snap in her eyes even as he turned her arm and delivered a chaste kiss to the inside of her wrist. Briefly it crossed his mind that she might slap him anyway, with words at the very least, but the sound of rapidly approaching footsteps broke the tension and he released her hand as Garth Buick strode into view.

Kim gasped, her surprise this time tainted with delight as

she launched herself at the Blackstone company secretary who was Howard's closest and oldest friend. The fact that they'd remained friends for so long was a testament to Garth's character and loyalty and remarkably even temperament.

He wrapped his arms around Kim with genuine affection, but the eyes that met Ric's over her head were shadowed with gravity. "Ryan's just taken a call from Stavros."

Their contact at police headquarters. Ric's heart stilled. "Bad news?"

"Nothing on Howard," Garth assured them both. "But we finally have confirmation of the passenger list."

"Was it Marise they found?" Kim asked. "Was she on the plane?"

The older man nodded heavily. "Yes. They've just brought her body in to the morgue."

Three

"Her body?" Kim's voice rose on a note of shock. Confusion clouded her expression as she looked from Garth to Ric. "You said she was alive. A survivor. You said they—"

"She passed away on the rescue boat," Garth said gently, "shortly after they took her on board. I'm sorry, Kim. I know you were close."

"No, not really."

A deep sadness imbued her comment and Ric wondered if she was thinking about Marise or her husband Matt, the Hammond Kim *was* close to. Or perhaps the couple's son. His jaw tightened. Dammit, he'd hoped there'd been a mistake. That they'd learn the woman wasn't Marise Hammond, the mother of a small boy, too young and innocent to be the victim of such a tragic loss.

"Are they certain it was Marise Hammond?" he asked.

"Certain enough that Stavros told us before the formal identification process. Unofficially, of course," Garth added.

"When you called me in New Zealand, you mentioned a foul-up with the passenger list."

"Initially there was a Blackstone employee listed," Garth said. "Jessica Cotter. She manages the Martin Place store and was supposed to be going to Auckland for the opening."

The name wasn't familiar to Ric, but he hadn't worked in the jewellery side of the business for almost eight years. "She couldn't be the one they found in the sea?"

"Wrong build, wrong hair colour, wrong clothing. It seems Ms. Cotter had a change of mind and got off the plane at the last minute. Hence the initial confusion over the passenger list."

"So it was Marise Hammond." Sonya's voice cut into the conversation, and Ric swung around to find her standing in the archway leading toward the kitchen. Although her eyes looked shell-shocked, she stood tall and poised and even managed a passable attempt at a smile. "Why don't you go through to the living room? Danielle and Ryan are there and I think we should all be together to talk about this. I've made tea and coffee but if anyone would prefer something stronger, please let me know."

Ryan Blackstone looked like he needed something stronger.
Ric eyed the younger man narrowly, taken aback by the gaunt grey cast to his normally tanned features. It was never a surprise to see Ryan wound tighter than a newly forged spring, especially in Ric's presence, but in all his years at Blackstone's Ric had never seen him unravel once.

Today, as his stark green gaze met his sister's across the wide expanse of the mansion's living room, he looked perilously close to that point.

"Coffee, Ric?"

Sonya distracted him with the proffered cup—black, strong, welcome—for only a second, and he turned back to see Kim bound so tightly in her brother's arms that he thought she might snap. It was a brief, silent embrace with none of the exuberant warmth of her reunion with Sonya or Danielle or Garth, but what it lacked in length and words it more than made up for in intensity.

Feeling like an intruder on this deeply private moment, he looked away and saw that Danielle had done the same. The significance of this particular reunion hit him suddenly and with all the force of a runaway ore truck.

It had nothing to do with their chequered history or Ryan's disapproval of Kim's defection. Nothing to do with any prior competition for their father's approval and affection. Nothing to do with her taking the Hammond side in the long-running family conflict.

Kim and Ryan were all that remained of their family unit. First their elder brother, James, abducted and never seen again. Then their mother's suicide. Now they faced the probable loss of their seemingly indestructible father.

No wonder they clung to each other so tenaciously.

The room where the family gathered opened onto the terrace and front gardens, and rose up through the second storey to a thirty-foot ceiling. Light and air spilled into the vast space via the opened banks of French doors and the stacked windows above, yet the atmosphere strummed with the dark tension of a mausoleum, until it was broken by the faint rattle of cup against saucer.

From the corner of his eye Ric saw Garth quietly take

Sonya's coffee and set it down on a side table. Her quiet "Thank you" broke the silence.

"I'm very sorry to hear about Marise," she continued with a calm composure that belied her distress.

Danielle, sitting beside her, took hold of her hand. "We can't be certain it was her...can we?"

"It was," Ryan said with surprising force. "The passenger list is confirmed. An all-male crew. Howard. His lawyer. Marise Hammond. She was the only female on the plane."

"Well, what was she doing on the plane?" Danielle fired back, undeterred. "I didn't think she would even know Howard, let alone be on speaking terms with him."

Ric put his untouched coffee down. The same question had been circling his head all day, and he didn't like any of the answers he'd come up with. But he could respond to the second part. "She worked at Blackstone's as Marise Davenport before she married Matt Hammond. And unless the tabloids are doctoring pictures now, she was still on speaking terms with Howard in December."

"What are you talking about?"

Danielle asked the question, but Kim studied him with equal bewilderment. Living so far from Sydney, neither woman would have seen the scurrilous piece run by a high-profile society columnist a couple of weeks back. A piece that could easily have been dismissed if not for the accompanying photo.

"*Scene* published a picture of them dining together," Sonya explained, "and hinted that they might be involved... personally."

Danielle's eyes widened with astonishment on her mother's careful choice of description. "Howard and Marise were having an affair? You have got to be kidding!"

"Of course it's not true," Sonya said with some heat. "That magazine is renowned for printing outrageous scuttlebutt and getting away with it by using broad hints rather than actual claims. Marise is married—she has a child. Whatever Howard's involvement with this woman, it was not an affair!"

Sonya's passionate declaration hovered for a long moment unanswered and uncontested, but when Ric caught Garth's eye he knew they were on the same wavelength. Howard's wealth and power and charismatic good looks had always attracted pretty go-getters—reportedly before, during and after his only marriage—and he'd never been averse to casting aside his current mistress in favour of a dazzling new model.

And Marise Davenport Hammond had always been a dazzler. From her time working at Blackstone's, Ric recalled her as a go-getter, as well. She'd put the moves on him and Ryan, too, before striking gold when she met the heir to the Hammond jewellery business at a diamond trade show. But now that she had Hammond's wealth at her disposal, why would she need to turn her eye elsewhere?

"Did your father say anything to you about meeting with Marise?" Ric directed his question at Ryan.

A distracted frown creased Ryan's forehead as he flipped shut the cell phone he'd been checking, but when he looked up his gaze focused razor-sharp on Ric's. "Not a word."

"Garth?"

"I asked him about the photo when it surfaced," the older man replied, "and he told me to mind my own business. In so many words."

Ric could imagine. Howard never minced words and the ones he chose were always colourful. "So you don't think they were discussing business that night?"

Garth shook his head. "I doubt it."

"No way in hell," Ryan added with force.

"Perhaps she was trying to broker harmony," Danielle suggested. "On behalf of Matt and the Hammonds."

Ric's gaze flicked to Kim, who'd sat through the exchange in uncustomary silence. One hand twisted at the charm pendant she wore around her neck and her dark brows were drawn together in a frown. He didn't have to say a word to garner her attention. Slowly her gaze lifted to his. Strikingly green. Pensive. Troubled.

"Marise wasn't involved with business at House of Hammond," she said. "And, no, she wasn't a peacemaker."

"So why was she meeting with Howard and flying on his plane?" Danielle exhaled on a note of frustration. "I guess we might never know."

"Does it matter?" Ryan pocketed his phone, his scowl forbidding. "The gutter press will jump all over this and you can bet they'll rehash that photo and every other sordid detail they can dig up."

Sonya made a soft sound of distress. She knew—hell, they all knew—that the Hammond-Blackstone family tree could provide enough juicy fodder to satisfy the greedy press for weeks. They wouldn't even have to get their hands dirty digging, since most of it had been emblazoned across the front page of every major scandal sheet at one time or another.

"How many cameras were outside the gates when you came in?" Garth asked him.

"Too many."

"Can't they leave us alone, at least for this one day?" Sonya asked.

"No," Ric said wearily, "that's not how they work. We'll

all have to be prepared for the intrusion and speculation and the rehashing of old history. This is going to get a hell of a lot worse before it gets any better."

Kimberley couldn't stomach any more. With an excuse of needing to stretch her legs after her two long flights, she stalked outside to the terrace. Minutes later Ryan came to the open doors and said he had some business to attend to, and unless any news came through in the meantime he would see her in the morning.

She'd noticed his distraction in the living room. Whoever's call or message he'd been checking his phone for every five minutes had not come through. No doubt he would chase that down with his usual ruthless determination.

Restless and wired, she strode over to the arced balustrade that presented Miramare's multimillion-dollar view of Sydney Harbour to perfect advantage. Reflexively, her hands fisted over the sun-warmed wall and she had to force herself to relax her steely grip. She'd escaped the unrelenting tension of the living room and the endless eddying conversation about Marise and Howard.

She didn't want to think about them, to picture them in cahoots, their well-groomed heads together, conspiring Lord knows what.

She didn't want to think about them at all. She just wanted to close her eyes and let the late afternoon sun seep into her body, to relax her whirling mind and melt the icy ache from her belly. If only she could conjure herself onto one of the yachts far below, flying across the sea-blue water with the wind at their backs.

Of course all that was impossible. When she closed her

eyes, she did see Marise and Howard together and she heard Perrini's blunt summation. *This is going to get a hell of a lot worse before it gets any better.* That comment had hustled her from the room before she exploded with a sharp rejoinder.

Worse? How could it get any worse?

A plane had crashed. People had died horribly, innocent people going about their everyday working lives. The pilot and copilot, a cabin attendant, a lawyer travelling with Howard—all real people whose families would be stunned and grieving and asking their own questions about fairness and fate. Perhaps some left loved ones with unanswered questions, but did it matter? Ryan was right about Marise. It didn't matter what she'd been doing that night in the restaurant or why she was on Howard's charter flight. What mattered was how Matt would suffer a brutal hammering from the press as they speculated over every aspect of his family history and his business and his marriage, at a time when he should be mourning the loss of his wife in peace.

What mattered was another child not understanding why his mummy hadn't come home. He would forget her face and her cuddles and her laughter, but later he would grow inquisitive and seek answers. Sadly they would be clouded by every scandalous supposition printed and gossiped about and adopted as truth.

Kimberley knew all about that and the thought of her godson going through the same distress chiselled open a chasm of pain in her heart. She'd been the same age as Blake when her mother hadn't returned from a break at their Byron Bay holiday home. Many years later she'd read all the conjecture over Ursula Blackstone's apparent suicide, her inability to cope with two young children while stricken with grief and remorse over the abduction of her firstborn son. How her depression had deepened over the rift between her brother Oliver and her husband following a loud and belligerent confrontation at her thirtieth birthday party.

At least Blake had a father who loved him unconditionally, who would protect him and explain the truth about his mother. Matt was a good man, a fair man, and a wonderful father. His only mistake was marrying the lethally beautiful Marise.

Familiar footfalls on the sandstone terrace broke into her reverie. *Damn.* After ten years she shouldn't remember such minute and significant detail, but her consciousness refused to forget the cadence of his stride. Or the intense scrutiny of his gaze on her face as he settled by her side.

"You can't enjoy the view with your eyes closed," he said after several seconds.

"I've seen the view a thousand times." Kimberley kept her eyes firmly closed. "I was enjoying the solitude."

"Pity."

Perrini fell silent, but she felt the brush of his sleeve against hers as he leaned forward. She pictured his hands planted wide on the balustrade, his azure gaze narrowed as he surveyed the amazing view. It always blew visitors away, this picture-perfect vista that stretched down the harbour to the famous bridge and beyond.

"I thought you might have been thinking," he said after a moment.

"About?"

"Marise and Howard. You didn't offer an opinion inside." He paused, a deliberate hesitation before delivering the million-dollar question. "Do you think they were having an affair?"

Reluctantly she opened her eyes and felt the impact of his

perceptive gaze—narrowed and as blue as the harbour—ripple through her senses.

Double damn. She couldn't escape this. She couldn't walk away.

"Anything is possible," she said, choosing her words with care.

Perrini's expression tightened. "Stop pussyfooting around, Kim. You knew Marise better than any of us. What was she doing in Australia these past weeks?"

"She came over for her mother's funeral. As far as I know she stayed to tie up some matters with the estate."

"Over Christmas and New Year's?"

"Her mother passed away in December—I doubt she had much choice. I believe her father isn't well and her sister was away on a modelling assignment."

"And if there was money involved in her mother's estate," he mused, "Marise struck me as a woman who'd be all over it."

Kimberley exhaled through her nose. She would not respond. Speaking ill of Marise now seemed uncharitable and purposeless. She'd survived a plane crash, spent terrifying hours in the water, only to pass away among strangers. No one deserved that, not even a woman who'd deserted her husband and child for weeks on end with scant excuse for her absences.

Not even a woman who might have done so as cover for an affair.

"I don't know Marise as well as you seem to think, so I don't know what she might or might not have done," she said. "But I do know what my father is capable of."

"You don't think your stance on Howard is slightly jaundiced?"

A humourless laugh escaped Kimberley's lips as she met his gaze. "You know it is. And you know why."

"Ten years is a long time, Kim."

Staring into his shadowed face, she wondered about that. So much hadn't changed, including the way he sparked her temper and her body's dormant hormones with equal ease. Just by standing a little too close. Just by looking into her eyes a little too long. Just by pressing his lips to her wrist and stirring insistent memories of other kisses, against other skin, far more intimate.

"Did he tell you about the last time I saw him?" she asked, regathering her concentration. "When he came to New Zealand to try and snare me back to Blackstone's?"

"I'd like to hear your side."

Oh, he was smooth. He wouldn't give away how much Howard had shared about that horrendous meeting. He'd been the same inside, she realised belatedly. Assuming control of the discussion, asking the leading questions, drawing opinion from everyone else but never offering his own.

She could call him on that—later—but for now she *wanted* to share her side.

She wanted him to know exactly what Howard Blackstone was capable of.

"When I refused his job offer," she said, getting straight to the point, "he sweetened the salary package. More than once. When I told him money wasn't the issue, he asked what it would take. I said an apology."

"I gather you didn't get one?"

"Have you ever heard Howard Blackstone apologise? For anything?"

Something tightened in his expression, but he simply said, "Go on."

"He rejected any notion that *he'd* done anything wrong, but then he accused Matt of stealing me from Blackstone's. He called him a thief like his father, and brought up the whole sorry raft of accusations from Mum's party." Shaking her head, she blew out a heated breath. "That was thirty years ago. I can't believe he still thinks Oliver Hammond stole the Blackstone Rose necklace that night."

"You don't think Oliver took the opportunity to reclaim what he believed should have been Hammond property?"

"No," she replied with absolute conviction. "Oliver wouldn't have taken that necklace if it was handed to him on a silver platter. He despised Howard for cutting up the Heart of the Outback stone and making it into such an ostentatious piece. He hated that he'd put the Blackstone name to the necklace, when it came from a diamond found by a Hammond. And he despised Howard for making such a blatant show of owning it, with all the magazine spreads and having Mum photographed wearing the necklace at every opportunity."

"From what I understand, your grandfather gave the diamond to Ursula. It was her prerogative to do with it as she wished. Eventually it would have passed to her estate," he said with emphasis. "If it hadn't gone missing, the Blackstone Rose would be yours, Kim."

She gave a strangled laugh and shook her head. "No, that was never going to happen. Howard was the sole beneficiary of my mother's estate. And as of last month, I believe I am no longer named in his will."

"He said he was striking you from his will?" Perrini

whistled softly through his teeth. "That must have been some argument."

"You might say that."

His lips quirked at her dry comment but his brows were lowered in serious contemplation as he caught her gaze. "Surely you didn't believe he'd go ahead with it once he cooled down?"

"Maybe not, but what about his other threat? He still doesn't accept that I walked away from Blackstone's—" *and you* "—because of his actions. He blames Matt for actively recruiting me. The last thing he said to me that day was 'Hammond will pay for this.'"

The portentous statement hung for a beat in the still evening air while Perrini made the connection. His blue eyes narrowed. "You think he was sleeping with Marise out of vengeance?"

"I don't know, but I wouldn't be surprised if that's what he wanted Matt to think."

She watched him consider that, his expression guarded. "Did Hammond have any reason to think his wife would cheat on him?"

"Matt didn't discuss his marriage with me."

"But it's possible?"

Kimberley ached to say *no, their marriage was as solid as the Sydney sandstone beneath our feet. Marise valued her husband and her child too dearly to stray.* But she couldn't say it. She looked away, her silence answer enough.

They stood like that for what seemed a long time, side by side at the balustrade, considering the shocking implications. Whether there'd been a clandestine affair going on or not didn't matter. If the tabloids ran with it, if Matt believed it, then Howard's job was done. Whether he was here to enjoy the fruits of his malicious game didn't matter. He'd won.

The thought chilled Kimberley to the bone. This was her father. The man she'd looked up to with adoration throughout her childhood; the person she'd set her sights on emulating when she'd focussed single-mindedly on a career in the precious gems industry.

Unconsciously she rubbed her arms. "How can I mourn such a man?" she asked bitterly. "How can anyone?"

Perrini didn't answer, but she sensed a change in his posture, a stiffening, and felt the warning touch of his hand on her arm. She swung around and saw Sonya standing just outside the French doors.

Had she heard that last comment?

Kimberley felt sick. She would never set out to hurt her aunt, who for some inexplicable reason had always stood by Howard with the same steadfastness as she'd defended him earlier. Over the years there'd been much speculation about their relationship, but Kimberley believed Sonya when she said there'd never been anything sexual between them.

Of course not. He's my brother-in-law, she'd said, sounding offended that Kim had asked.

But she still could have loved the bastard. Kimberley suspected she would mourn him more purely than anyone.

"I know neither of you have eaten all day," Sonya said now, in her customary mothering role, "so I'm going to start dinner early. You will stay, Ric?"

"Thank you," he said easily. "I will."

"Good." Sonya turned as if to leave, then paused. "Your room is made up, as always, so do consider staying over. We'd love the company tonight."

Your room? As always?

Kimberley blinked in confusion at the allusion to regular sleepovers. Her gaze shifted from her aunt to the ex-husband who seemed to have slipped right into her family during her absence. No wonder he'd known where to locate her bedroom when he'd taken her luggage upstairs.

"I'm not going anywhere," he assured Sonya with a smile, but when he turned his gaze on Kimberley the warmth of that smile didn't reach his eyes. They darkened with a message that felt like a vow.

I'm not going anywhere.

Four

True to his word, Perrini stayed that night and through Friday, as well. He left only once, following a call from his office Friday morning, and even then he waited until after Ryan had arrived before leaving.

"Does he think we womenfolk will fall apart without a big, strong man standing guard?" Kimberley asked Danielle across the remains of their breakfast.

"I would hardly call Ryan's presence *standing* guard. He hasn't stopped pacing since he arrived!"

Kimberley watched Ryan's impatient stride back and forth from shadows to sunlight at the far end of the terrace, the ever-present phone at his ear and a forbidding frown on his face. "He should go in to work," she said. "At least then he might feel like he's doing something useful."

"He *is* doing something useful."

Sonya's soft words came from beside Kimberley's chair, and she turned back around to find her aunt had brought fresh coffee. She set it down before continuing, her tone as close to a reprimand as she ever managed.

"Ryan is handling all the calls that are coming in, the same as Ric did during the night and early this morning, and which I know I can't deal with at the moment. He will ensure we hear any news as soon as it comes in. And if the police need to find us—" her eyes met Kimberley's briefly, her meaning clear in their tear-shrouded anxiety "—then this is where they will come."

With quiet dignity, she gathered up some of the breakfast dishes and walked away. Last night they'd learned that Sonya had given all the household staff leave. On Perrini's recommendation, of course.

So, okay, she understood the need for caution with the estate under siege from the media. Especially as Perrini already suspected someone in the know of leaking her flight arrival details to the Auckland press. She understood, but she reserved the right to feel snippy about his air of authority regarding all things Blackstone.

Ten years ago she'd stood toe-to-toe with Perrini and accused him of marrying her to become a Blackstone. She'd asked if he'd considered changing his name, since it was so obvious that Howard was treating him like a surrogate golden son. And she had felt like a meaningless pawn, her only value the Blackstone name and birthright.

To establish herself and to prove her worth she'd had to leave. And in her time away it seemed that Perrini had performed exactly as accused. He'd not only scaled the corporate ladder at Blackstone Diamonds, he'd become a part of the Blackstone family with a room at his disposal and the kind of easy rapport with Sonya and Danielle that only comes from constant contact.

She could only presume his relationship with her father had progressed to the same degree, and in her mind's eye she saw the self-satisfied look on Howard's face when they'd returned from that momentous vacation in San Francisco. When they'd decided, on a whim, to fly to Vegas for a weekend and he'd surprised her with the "impromptu" proposal.

She swallowed tightly, her throat constricted with raw, bitter emotion as she recalled Howard's words when they'd walked hand-in-hand onto this very terrace and told him their news.

"Welcome to the family," he'd said, jumping to his feet to shake Perrini's hand and clap him on the back. "You never fail to disappoint me, Ric."

Kimberley had felt the snub like a body blow then, and now it seemed as though her ostracism was complete. She was the outsider in her own family, and she'd made little effort to bridge that gap. Gathering up the rest of the breakfast plates, she pushed to her feet. "I'm going to help Sonya with the dishes."

Over her coffee cup, Danielle arched her brows. "You know how to do dishes? You have changed, cuz. Colour me impressed."

"Danielle has just suggested that I've changed." Straightening from packing the dishwasher, Kimberley met Sonya's constrained gaze across the impressive width of the Miramare kitchen. "But it seems you can still rely on me to say what I'm thinking, without thinking. I'm sorry, Sonya. I was feeling tetchy earlier when I made that crack about Ryan, but I wouldn't have said what I did if I thought you might overhear."

"The same as last night?"

How can I mourn such a man? How can anyone?

Kimberley blanched as she recalled what Sonya had overheard on the terrace the previous evening, but she refused to be a hypocrite even to spare her beloved aunt's feelings. "I'm sorry you heard that; although I'm not sorry I said it."

Sonya shook her head sadly. "He's not all bad."

"Why do you always defend him," Kimberley shot back, "when he's been such an utter bastard to so many people?"

"He's been good to me, always. He provided me with a home and paid for my education after my father passed on. And he's done the same for Danielle. I could not have wished more for my daughter than what's been provided in your father's home."

Kimberley thought about her cousin, with whom she'd chatted long into the night about her designs and the materials she worked with and her fledgling business in Port Douglas. They had so much in common. And how could she dispute Sonya's claim? "I want to disagree on principle," she said after a moment, "but Danielle is so warm and lovely and talented and smart. She is a credit to her upbringing. You must be very proud."

"I am, but it's not only my doing, Kim. Did she tell you that Howard helped her with the capital to set up her business?"

"Yes, she did." But Kimberley couldn't help thinking there must have been something in it for Howard.

"He would have done the same for you," her aunt said gently, "if you'd stayed."

"I never wanted my own business."

"Then he would have advanced you at Blackstone's, the same as he's done with Ryan and Ric. He loved you, Kim. Whatever else he may have done, whatever you hold against him, never forget that."

There was so much heart in Sonya's delivery, so much conviction, that Kimberley longed to believe her. Who didn't yearn for their parents' love? But Howard had too many strikes against him and the acrimony of their last encounter still burned in her stomach. He'd done nothing honourable, nothing to earn back the love he'd crushed like a worthless bug ten years before. And nothing in his attempted reconciliation suggested it meant anything to him beyond vengeance against the Hammonds.

Some of that resentment must have shown in her face because Sonya continued with the same earnest intensity. "I remember when you were born and Ursula told me how overjoyed he was to have a daughter. He chose your name, you know."

"After the location of his mining leases?" she asked.

"Honey, you know that's not the reason. When you came kicking and screaming into the world a week early—January twenty-sixth, Australia Day—he wanted a significant name, something fitting to mark our national holiday. He chose Kimberley because it's his favourite part of Australia, because of the region's natural beauty, and also because it is home to so many treasures. That's you, Kim. You were always his treasure. Don't ever forget that."

Early Saturday morning, the pilot's body was pulled from the water and AusSAR started making noises about calling off the search for survivors. Prepared for this eventuality, they had a team on standby to continue the search for the wreckage on the seabed. But Ric hadn't expected it this soon. Until now he'd managed to harness his impatience and frustration, but all morning he'd been on the phone to every official contact he could find or make, only to be quoted policies and procedures until he ached to shove them back down officialdom's collective throats.

He tossed the phone onto the armoire and dragged a weary hand over his face. He needed a shave. He needed sleep, too, not the restless minutes of shut-eye that were interrupted too soon by another phone call, another worried executive needing reassurance, another headline about the company's future to repudiate.

The spread of papers across the table he'd commandeered as a desk in the top-floor living room of the Vaucluse mansion told the tale. It *had* gotten worse, even more swiftly and viciously than he'd predicted two days earlier, and it wasn't all about scandal. Today's business pages speculated over who would lead the billion-dollar business and hinted at the possibility of a power struggle.

The buzzards hadn't even waited for a body to be found before starting their nasty work, damn them.

He needed a break from those screaming headlines, and when he paced onto the patio, he found the perfect distraction.

Kimberley lounging on the pool deck.

That she wasn't wearing a bikini was only a minor blip of disappointment because the sleek, black one-piece clung to her killer curves and exposed the tanned length of her legs as she settled on one of the loungers. Even more spectacular than the harbour view, he mused, leaning his hands against the railing and drinking in the sight.

She'd changed some over the years, growing into the sophisticated sexiness she'd only promised at twenty-one. Yet she'd lost none of the strong will. None of the firebrand that had snared his attention from the second they locked eyes across the Miramare dinner table ten years ago.

Watching her now whipped a new frustration through his veins—a resentment of every one of their years apart, of every barb aimed in vengeful anger, of the pride that prevented him from chasing her down and dragging her home where she belonged.

He didn't allow the feeling to take hold. She *was* here now, and getting her to stay was a mission he could sink his teeth into, one that wouldn't leave him floundering like this morning's exercise in futility. Right on cue his phone buzzed again, but he gave it only a cursory glance as he strode through to the bedroom he'd barely used the past two nights.

He was taking a break. Alone with Kimberley. She'd been avoiding his company, or distancing him with a cool politeness he figured was for Sonya's benefit. Ric preferred her sharp-tongued frankness, and alone on the pool deck he might just get a healthy dose.

If not, at least he'd get some exercise.

Swimming laps of the serene Miramare pool was a poor substitute for pounding through the Bondi surf. That was Ric's exercise of preference. Pitting himself against the unpredictability of the ocean's surge and pull every morning set him up for the volatility he faced at the rockface of business. He relished that challenge, in the water and in the workplace. Pity it had taken him this long, through too many dead-end disappointments, to realise he needed it in his woman, as well.

He turned up the tempo, churning the pool's surface with the power of a sprinter's strokes. Another lap, forging through his own wake, still wasn't the challenge of open water, but it dispelled the last of the morning's frustration and breathed life into his dulled senses.

He climbed from the water, those senses already honed on

the only occupied piece of poolside furniture. She was reclining, but not relaxed. Even from a distance he could see the tension in her posture, in the slender fingers curled around the edges of her lounger.

He knew she'd see his presence as an intrusion. A small grin tugged at his mouth as he recalled the evening she'd arrived, when he'd intruded on her solitude up on the terrace. His grin stretched when he imagined her outrage when he—

Still dripping from the pool, he stopped beside her and shook his head like a wet dog.

Kim didn't disappoint. With a gasp of shock she bolted upright and whipped off her water-dotted sunglasses. Her eyes fired with green sparks. "What the hell do you think you're doing, Perrini?"

He finished pulling a lounger right alongside hers and stretched out. "Drying off."

Damn, it felt good to see that blaze in her eyes. And to smile, genuinely, for the first time in days. Being around her always made him feel alive…in all kinds of ways, he added, as she began drying her dark lenses on the nearest soft cloth.

Which happened to be the softest part of her swimsuit.

Ric took full, unapologetic advantage of the show, even after she noticed the downward drift of his gaze and stopped polishing. "Nice suit," he said, meeting her eyes again. "I'm glad you packed it."

"I borrowed it from Sonya." She shoved the glasses back over her eyes, hiding the irritation in her expression although she didn't bother keeping it from her voice. "She told me you were working."

"I was."

"I assumed she meant at your office."

"I have a makeshift office upstairs," he said casually, closing his eyes and feigning his own relaxation. "In the living room next to my bedroom."

"Don't you have a home to go to?"

"I do. At Bondi."

She didn't answer right away, but he sensed a change in her mood and felt her alert gaze on his face for several seconds before she asked, "The same one?"

"Yes. Why do you ask?"

"I thought you might have cashed it in," she retorted. "Although if property values in the eastern suburbs are still on the rise, then I suppose it's a smart investment."

"That's not why I kept it."

"Why did you?"

Surprised she would ask such a leading question, he opened his eyes and turned to look at her. She'd pushed her glasses on top of her head, and her candid green gaze and the intimacy of lying side-by-side—as close as if they shared pillow talk—kicked him low and hard.

"Because I like living there."

Something flitted across her expression and was gone before he could catch it. And when she replaced her sunglasses and rolled onto her back to stare up into the blue summer sky, he knew that moment of connection was gone. Even before she sniped, "If you like your home so much, why do you spend so much time here?"

"Ahh."

Kimberley turned to glare at him through her designer lenses. "What is *ahh* supposed to mean?"

"Sonya mentioned you had problems with the 'standing guard.'"

That comment she'd made at yesterday's breakfast. She should have known he would hear about it. Not that she wouldn't have said the same to his face, but she hated the thought of her words being repeated behind her back. "Do you and Sonya discuss me often?"

"Would it be much of a disappointment if I said no?"

Damn him and the dark silkiness of his voice. Damn him for coming down here parading his assets in those Daniel Craig swimmers. Damn her foolishness for watching those powerful assets rise from the water, for wanting to know about his house, for longing to say yes, *I loved living there, too, even for such a short time.* For that split second of yearning for a place they'd once been, a time they could never wish back. Too much had been said, too much unsaid, too many years had passed.

"No," she said finally in answer to his question. "Not if it's the truth."

An uncomfortable silence stretched, broken only by the murmur of traffic from the streets far below and the mournful hoot of a distant ferry in the harbour. Kimberley closed her eyes but she couldn't shut him out. She felt his narrowed gaze on her face. Dissecting her expression, divining for emotion.

Damn him.

She shoved her feet to the ground, but he stopped any further retreat with one mildly delivered comment. "Walking away again?"

"That's a cheap shot," she snapped over her shoulder.

"A fair observation, I'd say." With a seriously distracting play of muscles across his abdomen, he pushed upright. "Care to tell me what's really bugging you?"

Kimberley's gaze snapped back to his knowing blue eyes.

Oh, yes, he'd noticed her distraction. "Do you mean what's bugging me right now?"

"About me being here."

He didn't mean here, now, on the pool deck. She knew that. And she was glad, because admitting she was bugged by his state of undress would seem petty in the least. Revealing at the most. She didn't mind telling him what bothered her about his continual presence at Miramare, however.

"It's not just you, it's the endless waiting." She lifted her hands and let them drop in a gesture of undistilled frustration. "You and Ryan and Garth—at least you're kept busy with taking calls and keeping up with what's going on with the search. I didn't realise how hard this would be, just sitting around and waiting and feeling…excluded."

"We've kept you updated."

"Exactly. *You've* had control, *you've* done the updating, which shuts me out no matter how much information you pass on. I can answer a phone. I can speak for the Blackstones. I wouldn't find it any hardship to say 'no comment' or 'no further news.'"

"And if the person on the phone is Tracy Mattera or Max Carlton or Jamie O'Hare. Would you have no-commented them?"

"How can I say? I don't recognise the names."

"Mining production manager, human resources manager, Howard's driver," Ric supplied matter-of-factly. All three had called him that morning. He hadn't plucked the names out of thin air, although the doubt on Kim's face suggested he had done exactly that. "All real people, all employees of Blackstone's."

"Which I am not," she said tightly. "I get the message."

Ric watched her turn away and get to her feet, her shoulders as tight as her voice, her backbone rigid. He could let her walk away again. This wasn't the time or place for this discussion, but she had provided the perfect opening. She wanted a purpose. She needed something to occupy her mind.

Perhaps this was the right time....

"It doesn't have to be that way, Kim."

She swung back around, her hands stilled in the process of tying a lime-green sarong around her hips. "Are you suggesting I return to Blackstone's? When I have a job I love and a home in New Zealand? Why would I even consider doing that?"

"Because you're a Blackstone."

"That hasn't changed."

"Other things have," he said with quiet resolve, coming to his feet and meeting her gaze across the width of the loungers. "The board of directors is seven strong. Currently that's Ryan, Garth, your uncle Vincent, David Lord, Allen Fitzpatrick."

"You—" she tapped finger against thumb, counting off number six "—and my father."

Ric inclined his head in confirmation. "Chairman, managing director...and, with Ryan and Vincent, one of three Blackstones required on any sitting board, according to the articles of constitution."

"And you're thinking about a replacement?" With her quick brain, she'd caught on immediately. But the dark flash of her eyes and the tone of her voice indicated that she didn't like the taste of that catch one little bit. "Isn't that a little premature?"

"The board is due to meet Thursday this week. I imagine we will have news by then, and the directors will look at appointing a replacement. That may sound callously quick, but as directors we have a duty to our shareholders and our staff—

at the moment that duty is projecting stability in the face of press that's suggesting otherwise."

"The power struggle between you and Ryan?"

Obviously she'd read today's business pages. Ric's jaw tightened. "Don't believe everything you read in the papers, Kim. The board will decide Howard's successor as head of the company, when and if it has to. There won't be any fight."

She had a comeback—something acerbic, by the flare of her eyes—but the melodic chime of a ringing phone distracted her. With a quick, "Excuse me, I'm waiting on a call," she ducked down to retrieve the flip phone from beside her lounger. The distraction in her eyes turned to something like relief when she read the caller ID.

"I have to take this," she said shortly, already turning away.

Hammond, Ric surmised, cursing the timing. *The last person he wanted in on this decision.*

Phone at her ear, she'd already started to walk away, but in several long strides Ric caught up and put a hand on her shoulder.

Kimberley whirled around as if she'd been scalded. "One minute," she said into the phone. Then to Ric, "Excuse me?"

He didn't allow her rapid turnaround to dislodge his hand. Instead he fastened his hold on her smooth, warm skin until her eyes widened slightly and he knew he had her full attention. Then he said, "When the board meets, your name will come up. Think about it. This is your chance to be on the inside, to shape something positive from this disaster."

Her deep green eyes snapped. "How?"

"As part of the force that determines how Blackstone's goes forward into the future."

* * *

Kimberley had so many questions, so many rejoinders, but Perrini silenced them all with the latent power of that last statement. She watched him stride back toward the house, her heart beating too fast and too hard as the implications raced through her brain.

She could make a difference. She could solder broken links. She could make up for her father's mistakes.

Then his long, decisive strides carried him inside and out of her sight, and she felt as though she'd walked into the shadows. Reflexively she rolled her shoulder, which still bore the imprint of his touch, and remembered the phone call. Matt. Damn. For the past three days they'd been playing phone tag, and now, finally, they'd managed to connect and she had left him on hold.

Just because Perrini had unsettled her again, first with the heat and the texture of his hand on her bare skin, then with the juicy enticement of righting the Blackstone wrongs toward her uncle and her cousin.

"Matt?" She swung around, phone to her ear. "Are you still there?"

"I'm here."

She released a soft gust of relief. "Thank you for holding. I was just in the middle of something."

"I can call back."

"No, no. It's okay. He's gone. I'm done. I'm just so glad I've finally found you with feet on the ground…your feet are on the ground?"

"I'm in Sydney," he said in short, succinct contrast to Kimberley's delivery. She was pacing, too, unable to stand still. "Landed this morning."

"Where are you staying? The Carlisle Grande? Why don't I come in. We could have coffee or even dinner, if you're free. Is Blake with you?"

"This isn't a trip I'd bring my son on."

His cold, clipped tone brought Kimberley's pacing to a brickwall halt. She palmed her forehead in her hand. How stupid and thoughtless. He'd come to identify Marise's body, lying cold and lifeless in a city mortuary. How could she have asked about bringing Blake?

"I'm so sorry, Matt." She didn't know what else to say, so she said it again. "So very sorry for your loss. Especially this way."

"Is there an easy way to lose your wife?"

"Good God, no, of course not! I meant the headlines and the tabloid frenzy. I can only imagine that's as bad for you as for us."

"No," he said after a heavy beat of pause. "I don't think you can imagine."

He was right, and she felt too choked up with emotion— and with the foot she couldn't seem to keep out of her mouth—to answer for several taut seconds. In person this would be easier, the same as it had been with coming home and seeing Sonya and Ryan. "Can we meet for coffee?" she asked again.

"I won't be here any longer than it takes to arrange a funeral."

The shock of that last word turned to ice in Kimberley's veins. She rubbed her free hand up and down her arm. How could her skin be so warm when she felt cold to the core? "When you've made the arrangements," she said stiffly, "please let me know when and where. I would like to be there."

"It will be a private burial. No cameras. No headlines. No Blackstones."

Kimberley understood his point. She knew pain had honed his voice to that diamond-hard edge but she still felt the rejection like a slap. It brought her head up and put a sting into her response. "I'm sorry I won't be there, for you, for Blake, for Marise. But with Howard gone, surely it's time to put this Hammond-Blackstone animosity to rest so we don't have to choose sides. I hate that—I'm sure Sonya does, as well. I've been approached about a possible position on the board of Blackstone Diamonds, and perhaps that is a good place to start mending the broken links."

"A conflict of interest with your position at Hammonds, wouldn't you think?"

"No, I don't think that has to be the case. The business rivalry has only come about through the old feud and personal bitterness, some of which was between Howard and me. With that over now—"

"No." Matt's objection was low, but delivered with such chilling finality that it sliced right through Kimberley's argument. "It's not over. After what Blackstone has done to my family, it can never be over. Not until everything the bastard took from us is restored to Hammond hands. Since one of those things is the wife I'm burying next week, I don't give that outcome a chance in hell of succeeding. Do you?"

Five

"That's all for now. Thank you, Holly."

Ric closed his office door behind the PR assistant who'd delivered the press clippings from Tuesday morning's papers. It didn't matter that there'd been no new developments in the search for the jet's wreckage or that no further bodies had been found, the headlines kept on coming. This week the focus had shifted from the present to the tragedies in Howard Blackstone's past, everything from the kidnapping of two-year-old James Hammond Blackstone thirty-one years ago to Ursula Blackstone's suicide and the disappearance of the Blackstone Rose necklace.

"This isn't news," Ryan said as he tossed a national broadsheet onto Ric's desk with barely concealed fury. "I expected better from them."

Ric didn't expect anything from the media except more

sensational headlines. They'd stalked Howard Blackstone throughout his life and now they haunted him in death, with the biggest scandal—the possibility of an illicit affair with Marise—still hovering over them like a fat black thundercloud. So far they'd reported nothing beyond her positive identification, running poignant photos of Matt Hammond's grief-ravaged face as he arrived in Sydney to claim her body, but following tomorrow's supposedly private burial the storm of speculation would build. As sure as thunder followed lightning.

They had to do more than wait it out. Ric owed that to Howard, to his staff, to the shareholders.

He didn't return to his desk but chose a central position where he could face the other two men, the seated Garth and the prowling Ryan, to explain why he'd called them to his office at the company's Sydney headquarters after days of monitoring the search from the Blackstone home. "We've waited as long as we can but in the absence of new developments, it's time to move on. We—"

"Move on?" The words exploded from Ryan's mouth. "No. We're not giving up yet, Perrini. Who are you to say we abandon my father?"

Ric met the sharp spear of the younger man's gaze without flinching. He'd been prepared for the hostility. Ryan wouldn't like him taking the initiative in calling this meeting any more than he'd like what Ric had to say. "I'm not suggesting we give up anything. Not the search and not this company your father built up from nothing but an exploration lease and his belief that diamonds were there to be found. Howard wouldn't appreciate us sitting on our hands, waiting for an outcome of a search that could go on for weeks."

Garth made a sound of agreement. He folded the paper he'd been scanning and placed it neatly on top of the others. "I can hear him now, growling in horror at the share devaluation."

"The price is still sliding today?" Ric asked.

"Down another five since opening. At this rate every second analyst will be tipping us as a prime takeover target by the end of the next week."

"It's not the raiders I'm concerned about."

Ryan turned in front of the window, hands on hips, framed by the city skyscape at his back. "Who are you concerned about?"

"Matt Hammond."

"Still holding him accountable?"

Ric's jaw tightened although the blow had been aimed much lower. He didn't give Ryan the satisfaction of responding. Instead he zeroed in on the reason he'd called them together. The threat of a takeover, not by an anonymous corporate raider or venture capital consortium, but at the hands of a man motivated by vengeance. "Howard holds fifty-one percent of the Blackstone Diamonds stock." He turned toward Garth, the company secretary, who was also the executor of Howard's will. "Can you confirm how that will be distributed?"

"Equally between you, Ryan and Kimberley."

"No chance he wrote Kim out of the will as he threatened?" Ric asked.

Garth shook his head. "He was set on that course when he returned from his November trip to New Zealand, but maybe he thought twice after he cooled down. Maybe I managed to talk him out of it. God knows, I talked long and hard enough. And maybe he took his lawyer along on this trip with a new threat of disinheritance. Whatever the reason, his will remains unchanged. That three-way split of his company stock still holds." The older man's eyes narrowed astutely. "I take it you're concerned about Hammond pursuing Kim's share, the way he went after William's ten percent?"

Two months ago Howard's older twin brothers, William and Vincent, each had owned a stake in Blackstone Diamonds. Then Hammond took advantage of rumours of a falling-out between the brothers. Needing cash in a hurry William had seized the chance to unload his stock at a premium price, and he'd been dirty enough on Howard to relish selling to his adversary.

"He wouldn't have to be that aggressive in chasing Kim's stock," Ric said. "She wouldn't be looking for instant profit. He would only need to spin a good story, convince her she was doing the right thing, and with those two bundles and whatever else he can pick up on this depressed market, it's conceivable he could acquire a majority share."

"We know he's not a player. He's only doing this for one reason." Ryan's expression was as hard and dark as black diamond. "The son of a bitch would gut the company."

Garth grunted in agreement. "We need Kim on our side. Any chance she would reconsider returning to Blackstone's?"

"I'm working on that," Ric said. His gaze shifted to Ryan. "As long as there are no objections."

"She's a Blackstone. She should never have left." There was a world of condemnation in the words and in the other man's expression as he faced Ric down. "Makes me wonder what you intend offering to bring her back from Hammonds."

"A fair question."

"Do you have an answer?"

"I'll offer whatever it takes," Ric said with steely resolve. "Leave it in my hands. I will bring her back."

"You're not wearing the new dress?"

Kimberley hesitated on the staircase, her gaze dropping from Sonya's arched eyebrows to the plain oatmeal linen sheath she'd changed into at the last minute. Okay, so she'd changed several times. Possibly half a dozen. And during that process the dress Sonya talked her into buying had been relegated to the very back of the queue. Not that she didn't like the soft, inviting fabric or the leopard-spot print—even the sexy touch of lace was growing on her— but it was just too unbusinesslike for a dinner that was all about business.

"This is more suitable," she said, lifting her head and continuing resolutely down to the foyer.

Sonya had paused, a stem of roses in each hand, in the middle of arranging a massive vase of freshly cut blooms from the Miramare gardens. She raised her elegantly shaped brows even higher. "I thought the purpose of today's shopping expedition was to choose a dress for tonight."

"That was our *excuse* to go shopping," Kimberley said with a wink. Then, over her shoulder, as she proceeded through to the living room, she said, "I would never have got you to agree to come along otherwise."

And they'd both needed to get out of the house. Kimberley hadn't thought she would miss the presence of Perrini and Ryan and Garth, after they'd taken their mobile phones and their constant grim-faced pacing and returned to the city megalith that housed the headquarters of Blackstone Diamonds.

Danielle had left, too, to apply the final touches to her collection for the annual Blackstone Jewellery show. Each year the event launched the latest in-house collections, as well as showcasing an emerging young designer. This year was Dani Hammond's big break.

This is what you've worked so hard for, Sonya had said, encouraging her reluctant daughter to return to her Port Douglas studio. *I have Kim here now, so I won't be alone. You still have work to do, so go, be inspired, be brilliant. Make me proud, make Howard proud...and make those critics who pooh-poohed his choice eat their words!*

Without them all, the house echoed its vast emptiness. Kimberley had felt the impact most acutely when she'd woken that morning. Wednesday. Marise's funeral day. Beautiful, headstrong, self-assured Marise was dead and for the first time Kimberley forced herself to face the reality that her father, too, was gone. This house, which had always been a reflection of the man and his taste for the grand, the opulent and the glamorous, would forever feel empty without him and the ever-present party of business and society acquaintances he brought home.

Sonya felt the emptiness, too. Kimberley had taken one look at her aunt's haunted eyes and restless hands as she fussed around preparing a breakfast neither of them would eat, and she'd decided they both needed a distraction.

Perrini provided it with a phone call and what had sounded like an off-the-cuff invitation.

"Dinner?" she'd asked. Her heart kicked up a beat and her free hand curled around her pendant charms. "I don't think that—"

"You need to eat? To get away from that house for a few hours? To discuss details of my proposal about the Blackstone's board vacancy...."

Oh, yes, he'd been clever. He'd known over the weekend that the waiting and inactivity were making her stir-crazy, and he'd picked the perfect time to lure her with the board position and the prospect of changing old animosities from the inside. Then he'd left her a day too long to think it over. Now she was hungry for more information, to find out exactly what was going on at Blackstone Diamonds…and why she'd been targeted for the Blackstone-only board position.

That's the only reason she'd accepted his invitation. That's why she'd gone with the plain business-meeting dress, despite playing along with Sonya's fancy to choose something fun, flirty, and way different from her usual classic style. The shopping trip to her favourite Double Bay boutique had been a game, a ploy, a distraction to take both their minds off the funeral in progress just a couple of suburbs away.

It had nothing to do with tonight's "date."

Now, as she wandered the living room unable to sit or stand or settle, Kimberley wished she'd insisted on meeting Perrini at the restaurant instead of letting him railroad her into the "more convenient" pickup. Being all dressed up and waiting for a man to arrive on her doorstep only played into the nerve-jangling notion of a real date.

She should have asked him to call when he left the office. Then she could have timed this better. Perhaps she still had time to go upstairs and change her earrings. Or to pin her ponytail into a chignon. At least that would fill some—

The chime of the doorbell echoed through the cavernous interior and startled Kimberley's jumpy heart. He was here. About bloody time.

"I'll get it," Sonya called.

Seconds later Kimberley heard the murmur of voices followed by the deep rumble of Perrini's laughter. She'd already taken several strides toward the foyer but the punch of that sound brought her up short. Laughter, so unexpected, so familiar to her female heart.

A hot charge of anticipation rocketed through her veins, tightening low in her stomach and tingling through her skin. She so wasn't ready for this. She needed a minute or two to compose herself, to restore her cool poise…time she didn't have as footsteps and the melodious notes of Sonya's voice heralded their approach.

At the last second, she scurried for the nearest chair and picked up a glossy from the side table. When Sonya said, "Kim, Ric's here," she managed to lower the magazine with surprisingly steady hands. Her smile was cordial, calm, controlled. Then she looked up into the deep sapphire of his eyes and her heart lurched like a poleaxed drunk.

"You're here," she said nonsensically.

Not the opening line she'd rehearsed—that was supposed to be a cool *you're late,* as she swept past him and strode out to the car—but better than thanking him for being here and bringing laughter into the emptiness.

"Ready to go?" he asked.

She put down the magazine. "For the past twenty minutes."

One of his brows rose marginally. "Nice to know you've acquired punctuality."

The subtle jibe at the past, referencing one of the flaws she'd fixed in the new grown-up version of Kimberley Blackstone, cooled the remaining impact of his arrival from her blood. Ignoring his proffered hand she rose to her feet and, after kissing Sonya on the cheek, swept past Perrini and out to his car. Marcie, the housekeeper, opened the front door and allowed her to proceed unimpeded. If only they had valet parking she could have swept all the way to his car and into the passenger seat.

Instead she was left beside the locked Maserati cooling her three-inch heels. She'd chosen them to help level out the height difference and therefore the power dynamic, although she still needed an extra couple of inches to bring her eye-to-eye with Perrini's six-one.

Why in heaven's name had he felt the need to lock his precious car?

Arms folded, she tapped her toe and frowned back toward the still-open front door. Several minutes later he appeared, and paused to speak to Marcie. Okay, she was honest enough to admit that he looked bloody good. Even though he'd likely come straight from the office after a twelve-hour day, his charcoal suit was immaculate, his white shirt crisp, his sapphire tie perfectly knotted.

But it wasn't only the expensive hand-tailoring, it was the way he wore the clothes. Whether he was striding into a meeting wearing one of his suits or sauntering by the pool in nothing but a brief pair of swimmers, he had a unique combination of cool authority and kick-ass confidence that drew attention to the man rather than the external trappings.

The effects of that long, open inspection were still rippling through Kimberley's body when he bent and kissed a blushing Marcie on the cheek, and peeled away to jog down the steps. The remnants of a smile softened his mouth and she had to work hard to maintain her irritation.

"Don't you trust our staff?" she asked, inclining her head toward the locked car.

"Force of habit." The doors popped with a scarcely audible snick. He opened her door, then waited until she'd slid inside before he leaned down to meet her eyes. His were no longer smiling. "For what it's worth, I wasn't expecting to see any staff."

Kimberley recognised the pointed dig. "I couldn't see the sense in keeping loyal, long-serving staff laid off for fear they may leak private information, when it is obvious the press is getting whatever details they want from their own sources."

"Are you referring to Marise's supposedly private funeral?"

"That's one instance." It had been mentioned in more than one of today's newspapers, which made her mad enough to spit. "They seem remarkably well-informed about everything."

"It's their job to be." Perrini's expression tightened with his own irritation. "Seat belt."

"I'm not a child. I know—"

She sucked in a breath as he short-circuited her indignant protest by leaning across to retrieve the belt. In the process his arm brushed the side of her breast and she felt the fleeting contact reverberate low in her belly and pull tight in her nipples.

Damn.

He stilled a moment—or perhaps that was just her, her heart, her senses—before clicking the belt into place. Then the dark heat of his eyes locked on hers and he spoke in a low and rough-edged voice. "I know you're not a child, Kim, despite indications to the contrary."

Indications to the contrary? What the hell did he mean by that?

The door thudded shut, leaving her quivering with suppressed wrath for the six seconds he took to round the car and slip into the driver's seat. Kimberley counted to six again, while he started the engine and she controlled her urge to shriek those questions.

"Indications to the contrary?" She managed to sound cool and composed. And adult.

"This decision to reappoint the household staff without consulting me—did you have a reason other than to thumb your nose at me?"

"Without consulting you? I'm sorry, but I didn't realise you were now the head of my household."

As he powered through the security gates and into the street, he cut her a narrow look. "I didn't realise you considered yourself a part of this household."

Touché.

Kimberley inhaled long and deep. Provoked by his remark about her childishness, that head-of-my-household comment had just slipped out. "You're right," she admitted in a more reasonable tone. "I'm only a visitor, but I did consult with Sonya before calling any staff back on duty. I didn't think she needed the extra work."

"Perhaps she does."

That perceptive comment deflated the last of Kimberley's resentment. How could she remain piqued when they were on the same wavelength regarding Sonya? "Yes, she does…to an extent, which is why I asked the cook to take an extra week of holiday leave. Sonya enjoys the kitchen and that's enough for the moment. Plus with Marcie in the house she has both help and company."

Another sidelong glance. "You aren't enough help?"

"In the kitchen?" Kimberley laughed dryly and shook her head. "You know what happens when I'm allowed access to a cooktop!"

For a heartbeat their gazes caught and a decade-old memory arced between them. Burning bacon, a shrieking smoke alarm and Kimberley hopping from one foot to the other, yelling for help.

Her husband of six days had picked her up fireman style and bundled her back to the bedroom. *In here,* he'd said, *you can burn and scream all you want.*

"Things change in ten years," he said now.

"Some things. Others stay the same."

Stationary at a traffic light, Ric leaned his forearm on the wheel and turned to study her profile more closely. She'd tied her hair back, worn minimal makeup and jewellery and one of those blend-into-the-background dresses whose only plus was the fact it ended short of her knees. Rather than diminishing her beauty, the austere look drew all attention to her face. With that amazing, contrary combination of fire and ice, of strength and vulnerability, of have-me mouth and hands-off eyes, Kim Blackstone would never blend into any background.

"What hasn't changed?" he asked softly.

For a moment he thought she would ignore his question, but then she rolled her head against the seat and the answer was there in her eyes, in that moment, in the crackle of sexual awareness.

This hasn't changed.

From the moment she'd strutted into his life, fresh from a two-year apprenticeship with a diamond master in Antwerp and bursting with a passionate impatience to overhaul the marketing of Janderra's rare coloured diamonds, she'd lit his senses with white-hot desire. For seven and a half weeks she'd kept him at bay with her sharp tongue and cutting lines. *That* hadn't changed, either. The same distrust, the same defence mechanisms, the same defiance that put her in the beige background dress instead of the stunner Sonya had described her buying today.

The light changed to green and Ric urged the Maserati forward. The engine's smooth growl reverberated low in his belly. If Kim didn't feel threatened by this undiminished sexual spark between them, then she wouldn't feel a need to employ those obvious defences. She was working to keep *him* at arm's length, he realised with a delayed jolt of perception. She tried to keep her own desires in check.

First time around he'd allowed her time and space while he enjoyed the challenge, the pursuit, the anticipation. This time the stakes were higher. He wasn't playing games; he was playing for keeps.

From the corner of his eye he caught the almost imperceptible lift of her chin. Defence mechanism number one. A precursor to speech, used when preparing for verbal battle.

Deep inside Ric smiled in anticipation. *Bring it on, babe. I'm ready.*

"I may not have learned how to cook," she said, circling back to her earlier comment about kitchen helpfulness. "But I have changed in other ways."

"How?"

"I'm more cautious now. I don't make snap decisions. I weigh my options so I can make an informed choice."

With the position on the Blackstone's board, for example. That's where she wanted to lead the conversation; that's why she'd taken her time in choosing her words so cleverly. A pity and a waste, since he wasn't ready to go there. They were within five minutes of their destination and an inevitable disruption.

Their long, involved and probably heated discussion was

for later, without interruption, so he let her leading comment take this conversation in another direction. "Such as deciding to wear that dress—" his gaze swept over her before returning to the road "—instead of the new one?"

"I beg your pardon?"

"The new dress you picked out in Double Bay this afternoon."

"Sonya," she said on an accusatory note. "I can't believe she told you about that!"

"Not nearly enough, as it happens. Why don't you fill in the gaps."

"You want to hear about our shopping expedition?"

The incredulous look on her face was priceless. Ric stifled a grin. "I want to hear about the dress and why you decided not to wear it." He let his eyes drift over her in lazy speculation. "Was it too short? Too low-cut? Too revealing?"

"All of those things," she replied without missing a beat.

"Then I can't wait to see you in it," he murmured.

"I doubt that will happen."

"Spoilsport."

The start of a smile lurked around the corners of her mouth but she looked away quickly, peering out the side window in sudden rapt interest. He noticed the exact second her pseudo-interest turned real. Her shoulders stiffened, her head snapped around. "Where are you taking me?"

"My place. Is that a problem?"

"You said dinner. I assumed you meant at a restaurant."

"I could get a table at Icebergs if you'd prefer," he said mildly. "Although I can't promise we'll have privacy to talk or that our tête-à-tête won't appear in a society column tomorrow."

Indecision ghosted across her expression.

"Which wouldn't be all bad," he mused. "It'd give them

something to talk about other than Howard and Marise."
Flicking on an indicator, he pulled over to the side of the road
and reached for his mobile phone. "I can call ahead and secure
a table if you don't mind being noticed dining with me. Or
we can eat at my place, as planned, with the privacy to talk
business and no risk of interruption.

"Your decision, Kim. What's it to be?"

Six

Perrini was too damn clever by half! Kimberley quietly simmered while she chose privacy, just as he'd set her up to do. They had business to discuss and if he tried baiting her again as he'd done over the dress and just now over the restaurant, then she might feel inclined to throw something at him. She would prefer if *that* didn't appear in any society columns, thank you very much.

Which didn't mean she felt comfortable returning to the house where they'd spent so many nights and weekends of their affair, plus their short, drama-filled ten days of marriage. During the days they'd worked side by side with cool, professional restraint, and in the evenings they'd driven into this street, this driveway, this garage, and torn into each other with a fevered passion that could not wait a second longer.

"You're not nervous about coming here?"

Kimberley blinked herself out of the minefield of memories. Carefully she relaxed her fisted fingers and moistened her lips. "Should I be?"

"I don't see why."

But there was a dangerous glint of heat in his eyes as they rested briefly on her mouth, and she wondered if he, too, was recalling the times they hadn't made it upstairs with all their clothes on. When they'd slaked their hunger for each other here in his car, or in the foyer leading off the garage, or in the slick elevator that glided between the three floors of this uniquely designed contemporary town house.

"Do you live here alone?" she asked.

The question had been brewing, unacknowledged and unspoken, ever since the day by the pool when he'd told her he still lived here. Now seemed the time to ask. Before he took her inside.

"At the moment," he said after a beat of pause, "yes."

Now, what was that supposed to mean? Had there been a live-in lover, one who'd recently packed her bags and departed? Or did he have someone waiting in the wings, all primed and ready to park her stilettos under his bed?

The thought crept up like a thief and ambushed her with unbidden images. Perrini with a faceless, nameless woman. Her hands sliding inside his shirt. Her mouth opening to his kiss. Her arms pulling him down to the bed.

No. Kimberley shut down the visuals with a vicious shake of her head. And while he opened the passenger door and ushered her from the car to the foyer and into the elevator, she struggled to tamp down the impact of her irrational possessiveness. She had no right to it. She had no claim on him.

Business, she reminded herself. *It's not about us.*

But in the confines of the closet-size lift, she became hyper-aware of the whipcord tension in his body and the heat emanating from his skin despite the layers of fine Italian tailoring separating their shoulders, their arms, their hips. Those ten-year-old memories of greedy mouths and impatient hands and swiftly shed clothes worked back into her consciousness, blurring the imagery until the nameless woman's face became hers.

Her hands, *her* mouth, *her* arms drawing him onto the bed and into her body.

"Hungry?"

The velvet murmur of his voice spent a moment meandering through her fantasy before Kimberley snapped her errant mind back into focus. "Yes, I am." Cool. Somehow she managed to sound very cool. "What are we eating?"

"Seafood. For expedience I ordered ahead. I hope you don't mind."

"That would depend on what you ordered."

"Blue swimmer crab. Roasted scallops. Ocean trout. Catch of the day with aioli and Murray River salt."

Although her taste buds had started to shimmy in anticipation, Kimberley merely nodded. The real test was in the final course. "And for dessert?"

"Ah, so you still start your order from the bottom of the menu? That hasn't changed?"

She tilted her head, enough that she could favour him with a silly-question look.

Amusement kicked up the corner of his mouth. "Zabaglione and Roberto's signature gelato."

"Which is?"

"Good. Very good."

Her taste buds broke into a dance just as the elevator doors slid open at the top level. And she realised with a jolt of shock how little notice she'd taken of her surroundings downstairs. Here the changes hit her full in the face.

Ten years ago the house had been newly built and decorated in stark white to play up the clean lines and irregular angles. But with the open plan and abundant windows, light had bounced off every wall with blinding impact. Many times she'd teased him about the need to don sunglasses before entering his house.

Not anymore.

Evening sunlight still beamed through the glass doors that opened onto a large curved balcony, but the effect had been softened with earthy tones of cream and pale salmon and rich moss green. Kimberley paused in the centre of the living room to take in all the changes. In the dining room one feature wall was painted with a mottled sponging of peachy cream. The artwork, the plants, the polished timber floors and terracotta sofas packed with plumped cushions, even the gilded shades on the unusual light fittings, all complemented the warm palette.

She finished her slow 360-degree inspection to find Perrini watching her from behind the kitchen bar. A bottle of wine and two glasses sat before him on the waist-high counter.

"What do you think?" he asked. "Did I get it right?"

There was something in his stillness, in the deliberate casualness of his question, that caused her heart to thump hard against her ribs.

He'd listened. The night she lay on one of the matched pair of snow-white couches with her head in his lap and described how *she* would decorate this area. He'd remembered.

She completed another turn as if she was still making up her mind, and then she lifted her arms and let them fall with the same fake casualness. "It works for me. Do you like it?"

"Overall, yes." The hawklike intensity of his expression softened as he switched his attention to opening the wine. "I could have done without the peachy colours but Madeleine insisted."

Kimberley's heart stopped for a beat. Of course he hadn't done it himself. How stupid to imagine him matching colours and cushions with her long-ago Sunday musings.

She wandered over to inspect a large abstract canvas, then on to the glass doors where she stared blindly out at the view. "Madeleine?" she asked.

"The decorator. She had her own interpretations on the brief I gave her."

Not the live-in lover stewing in her imagination, but a professional. It was nothing personal, nothing to do with Kimberley at all, which was a very good thing. It was bad enough that she still felt an intense sexual pull every time he got too near, she didn't need the emotional resonance of discovering he'd decorated to her specifications, to please her, to welcome her home. It was much better to acknowledge that he'd taken her overall idea and used it to inspire the overhaul. She couldn't be disappointed. She would not allow herself that weakness.

When Perrini arrived at her side and handed her a glass of white wine, she thanked him with a smile. "Even if you painted the walls lime-green, it wouldn't matter. This—" she raised her glass to indicate the view "—would always be the focus."

He opened the doors and Kimberley wandered out to stand at the wrought-iron railing. Low down to her left Sydney's most famous beach was littered with people despite the late hour. Some swam, some strolled, others sat on the golden slice of sand and scanned the horizon, as Kimberley did now, for a sailboat or a cruiser or a cargo ship chugging out to sea.

It wasn't quiet, thanks to the traffic on Campbell Parade and the summer tourists cruising the beach promenade—but Kimberley welcomed the sounds and sensations that regaled her body, even the sensual buzz when Perrini came to stand close by her side. The past week sequestered at Miramare and focussed so completely on the plane crash and its deadly consequences had numbed her to the wider world. She'd needed to get out, somewhere like this, a place that breathed life into her senses.

"I love this aspect," she said with soft reverence. "Not to mention the view."

"Is that why you bought your town house in One Tree Hill?" he asked after a moment.

Unable to make the connection, Kimberley shook her head. "What do you mean?"

"Its similarity to this place. The high aspect, the view, the architecture."

"I don't think they're even close to alike. My total floor space would fit on one of your levels with room to spare. And as for the view—" she expelled a breath that was part wry laughter, part disbelief "—how can you compare? You have a version of this postcard panorama from every window. I have to stand on tiptoes in my highest heels to get the tiniest glimpse of Manukau Harbour, and that's only from my deck."

Perrini didn't respond although she felt the long, warm drift of his gaze all the way down her body until it reached her leopard-print heels. And for that length of time she wished she had worn the new dress with its matching print and silk-cloud fabric. She wished the evening could continue in this easy harmony, that she could kick off these heels and indulge her sensual self with the wine and the food and the company and yes, even the dangerous tug to desire.

She wished she could forget her past hurts and everything that had happened this week and just live in the moment.

"I don't come out here enough." Perrini's voice, low and reflective, interrupted her reverie. "The view is a waste when I don't take time to enjoy it."

"Do you still work those punishing hours then?"

"When I have to."

"No one ever *has to,*" she countered with subtle emphasis. "They choose that course, for whatever motivation drives them. Ambition, money, ego, security, insecurity."

With Perrini she wasn't certain which applied. For all his charm and extravagant good looks, he possessed an inner toughness and a determination to succeed. She knew he'd been raised by a single mother, that he'd worked his way through school and a business degree, but he'd never really opened up about his childhood. That was just one more regret she'd taken away from their relationship. He'd only ever shared what he'd chosen to, withholding so much of the important stuff.

"Which is it with you, Kim? What motivates you?"

"The work," she said simply.

"Still?"

"Yes, still."

He studied her a moment, his blue gaze shadowed in the gathering dusk. "What about that ambition you used to talk about, that craving for a top-floor office at Blackstone Diamonds? You used to see yourself as your father's successor. What happened to that dream?"

"A dream is all that was ever going to be, Perrini. You know that."

"No," he contradicted, "I don't know that and neither do you. Everything is about to change at Blackstone's. If you haven't revisited that dream lately, then it's about time you did."

Kimberley's heart was beating hard. She hadn't revisited those old dreams, old ambitions, the stuff of her childhood, in more than a decade. Since her return she hadn't looked beyond the directorship proposition and the chance to end the old feud that had rent the two branches of her family apart.

Did she want to be part of the family company?

Did she harbour that leadership ambition anymore?

The chime of the doorbell broke the intense moment. Perrini straightened, lifting his head. "That will be dinner. Roberto's food is too good to keep waiting. Let's continue this discussion after we eat."

Ric kicked himself savagely for bringing up business prematurely and destroying the relaxed ambience established on the balcony. Dinner provided a temporary distraction. While they enjoyed the simply prepared but stunningly flavoured food, they talked about Roberto's restaurant, her recent holiday, the frustrating lack of progress with the search, Danielle's departure—everything but the unfinished business that hovered between them.

Now he watched her put down her spoon and push away the glass dessert bowl. "That's the best you can do?" he asked, eyebrows raised at her unfinished gelato.

"As hard as it is to believe, yes. Everything was divine but those scallops were my undoing."

"Would you like coffee?"

She shook her head.

"A liqueur? I have cognac or tokay—"

"Nothing, thank you. Let's just get on with why I'm here."

Ric inclined his head at her blunt request. It was time to get down to business, but not here at the dinner table. "Let's go through to the lounge. You can put your feet up and relax while we talk."

"Oh, I very much doubt that," she said softly, bringing a smile to his lips. But she set her serviette aside and pushed back her chair. "Still, let's do this away from the crockery. Just in case the discussion gets heated."

With that in mind, Ric suggested she sit at the far end of the sofa. "That lamp is damn ugly but it cost a fortune. Best keep it out of your reach."

Amusement softened the curve of her mouth as she took the proffered seat. "Wise decision. The base looks solid enough to make quite a dint."

"This doesn't have to be a confrontation," Ric said evenly.

"No, although our history suggests there is that possibility. Especially when the subject of Blackstone Diamonds enters the discussion."

Ric couldn't argue with that claim; he couldn't even say it was all bad. When they'd worked together on the business plan for Blackstone Jewellery, their heated debates had been more than intellectual foreplay, they'd sparked new angles and creative solutions. They'd complemented each other in the office, as well as the bedroom, and that's what he wanted again. That heat, that spark, that connection.

That's what he wanted and that's what he would have, but that didn't stop him wanting to prolong their current harmony.

He didn't want to wipe that glint of humour from her expressive eyes. But he did, as soon as he settled opposite her on the second of the suede sofas. The smile faded from her face even before he spoke. "Let me at least get my proposal on the table before you arm yourself," he suggested.

"Would that proposal be the board position or the dream job you dangled in front of me earlier?"

"Let's start with the directorship."

She nodded briefly. "I have given that some thought."

"And?"

"Matt suggests it would be a conflict of interest with my present position at House of Hammond."

No surprise that she'd discussed his preliminary approach with her boss. Ric had expected as much, but that didn't stop his jaw tightening in annoyance. "Your boss is right," he said shortly. "You couldn't continue to work for him if you took on this directorship."

"Why would I choose a board position over the job I have—a good job that I love?"

"Because that's all Hammond will ever offer you. A job. Second in charge," he stressed, when he saw an objection fire green sparks in her eyes. "But where is the future beyond that? Matt Hammond will never cede power to anyone but another Hammond."

"Not everyone craves power, Perrini."

He met the condemnation in her eyes head-on. "You used to. You came back from Europe, your head crammed with ideas and your heart fired with passion. You couldn't wait to make changes, to put it all into practice, and you couldn't do that from the sidelines. I recall you saying as much the day you stormed out of your father's office."

"I left Blackstone's for many reasons," she said tightly. "That was only one of them."

"You made those reasons crystal clear when you left, but things have changed. You have a personal stake in the company now."

Her forehead creased with a frown. "What do you mean?"

"When your father's will is read, you'll become one of three major stakeholders in Blackstone Diamonds."

"No." She shook her head adamantly. "Howard wrote me out of his will. He said—"

"Whatever your father intended when you had that row, a new will was never filed. I checked with Garth, who is executor of his estate. You *will* inherit a third share of Howard's stake in the company, and that is significant equity. With it comes the power to implement change. From the forty-third floor you can see dreams through to reality. You can heal rifts. You can right wrongs."

Ric watched the storm of possibilities flare in her eyes for several long, weighty seconds.

"That's powerful rhetoric," she said.

"It's not just rhetoric," he responded without hesitation. "This next few months will be a tough time for the company. The share price is already taking a beating on the back of this week's negative publicity. We can't sit tight and ride this out. We need to play the game smarter. We want you working with us to generate positive press, Kim. We want you back at Blackstone's."

"We?"

"Senior management. Ryan, Garth, myself."

"'Generating positive publicity' sounds more like a PR

specialist's dream job than mine," she countered after a moment's consideration. "Why don't you hire a consultant?"

"We don't want a slick consultant. We want you and your sharp brain and your industry knowledge and credentials." He leaned forward, hands linked loosely between his knees, but there was nothing casual about the insistent strength of his gaze. "We want to present a united front, Kim, to show we're not dwelling on the past but moving forward with the next generation. And we want your name quoted in the papers, your face in front of the cameras."

Her brows arched with a hint of derision. "I thought you were using Marise's supermodel sister as the 'Face of Blackstone's'."

"Briana Davenport is the 'face.' We're proposing you as the 'mouth', a role for which you're eminently qualified."

Unexpected amusement sparkled at the back of her eyes. "Aren't you concerned that my mouth will create more trouble?"

"Only for me," he acknowledged dryly, "and I'm big enough to take it."

It was an innocent remark, designed to show he appreciated that her mouthiest moments had always been reserved for him. But when she didn't fire back an instant retort, and when the glow in her eyes warmed with a different fire, the harmless jest grew teeth that gnawed through the thickened silence. There were all manner of things he ached to tell her about her mouth, how he'd missed the bite in these exchanges, how he lived for the moment it opened beneath his, how he dreamed of its sweet-spice taste.

This wasn't the moment. The only task that mattered right now was luring her back to Blackstone's, and he couldn't risk ruining his chances.

He shoved to his feet and strolled toward the open doors

to breathe the familiar, salty air, to clear the buzz of another seduction from his brain.

"If I took this position—" her gaze, direct and unwavering, met Ric's as he swung around "—who would I be working under?"

"That would depend on the project," he replied carefully, ignoring his libido's grunt of response to her wording.

"The projects being…?"

"The big one is the launch of the latest jewellery collections. I'm guessing Danielle would have told you about the gala show?"

"A little." She tried for cool, but failed to hide the sparkle of interest that lit her expression. "It's next month, right?"

"February twenty-ninth. Even without recent events, this year's show has special significance."

"The ten-year anniversary of Blackstone Jewellery," she guessed without hesitation. "So, the usual birthday celebrations, continuing promotions, ad campaigns?"

"All that."

"I'm guessing this would be well covered by the marketing department. What, exactly, would I be doing?"

Looking into her eyes, Ric felt an adrenaline punch of response. *This* is what he'd missed—her quick pickups, her sharp comebacks, the verbal duels that were never predictable but always stirred something vital inside him. "If I knew, then I wouldn't need you."

"I?" she countered. "Not the royal *we?*"

"Interchangeable." He figured she knew that anyway. It's why she'd asked who she'd be working under. "In this case, you'll be working with Ryan and his staff, supplementing the marketing plan to generate positive press for the Blackstone brand in general and the launch show in particular. As for how you do that—" he spread his hands expansively "—that's your job. To explore the possibilities."

"And answerable to Ryan?" she murmured after a moment's consideration. "He would be my boss?"

"On this project."

"And overall?"

"The new CEO, as appointed by the board."

"Meaning there's a fair chance it will be you."

"An even chance. Ryan is a Blackstone, a significant point in his favour. But if I am appointed—" Ric narrowed his gaze on hers as he closed the space between them "—is the prospect of working beneath me a deal breaker?"

She came to her feet and faced him with cool pride in her stance and etched in her expression. "I wouldn't return to work for my father, why on earth would I consider working for you?"

"Because we need you, Kim. Blackstone's, your brother, the company, each and every member of our workforce—we need you working with us. I sincerely hope you understand what I'm offering is on behalf of the management team, and that you won't let our past stand in the way of the Blackstone future."

Seven

Kimberley's heart drummed like a jackhammer against her rib cage. Poor, foolish, easily swayed thing wanted to believe in his sincerity even while her brain chirped a warning to beware his motives.

"I'm not a naive twenty-one-year-old now," she began, her voice surprisingly even given the rough cadence of her pulse. "I won't be taken in by your sweet rhetoric and I won't be used just because I'm Kimberley Blackstone."

"Used?" Perrini's eyes narrowed dangerously. "I've never used you, Kim. Not in any sense."

"You still don't see that pursuing and marrying your boss's daughter in order to secure a plum promotion—"

"Let's get one thing straight. I always wanted you, the woman, enough that it didn't matter that you were Kimberley Blackstone. From where I stood that was a big, fat strike against you, not just because you were the boss's daughter but because you inherited so many of Howard's pain-in-the-ass qualities."

She must have looked as outraged as she felt, because he expelled a harsh-sounding laugh and shook his head.

"You said you didn't want any of my rhetoric, so let's try some home truths. You're stubborn, cynical, opinionated, but on the flip side there's your quick brain and your passion for this business, your honesty and humour and the way you lift your chin whenever you take a stance on something you believe in. Yeah, just like that," he said in a low, rough-edged voice that resonated through her blood. "Whether it's right or wrong, it doesn't matter. You stand by your word and that's one of the many reasons I pursued you. Not with any ambition other than to have you. In any and every way that I could."

The silence following his speech crackled with the undis-tilled passion of his delivery. This wasn't the smooth charmer, the slick orator, the silver-tongued lover. This was a side Perrini showed so rarely that it stunned Kimberley into silence.

"That day in the Hammond workroom," he continued, "you said you should never have married me."

"And you agreed." Finally she found her voice, although it rasped with raw emotion. "You said our marriage was a mis-take."

That coldly conveyed summation had pierced her heart like a spear of ice, before shattering into a hundred frosty shards. The final, chilling end of that argument and of their union.

"It was a mistake," he said bluntly, stunning her all over again. "I married you for the wrong reason. I thought I was calling your father's bluff."

"What do you mean?"

"That Christmas, before we left for our holiday in San Francisco, he had a word with me over a quiet whisky. He knew we were lovers—maybe he had all along—and he played the outraged father. Said he didn't appreciate us creeping around behind his back and suggested, forcefully, that if I wanted to bed you, I could damn well marry you."

That was so like Howard, Kimberley couldn't summon a quarter-carat of shock. She'd known her father had orchestrated their marriage; she just hadn't known the details. At the time she'd been too outraged, too shattered, too betrayed to believe any explanations.

And now…at least now she knew what had prompted Perrini's out-of-the-blue proposal. "So you thought, why the hell not?"

"I wanted you here, in my home, every night, every day. So, yeah, I thought why not marry you? I sure as hell didn't expect we'd be welcomed home with open arms. I'd married his only daughter—the Blackstone heiress—in a Vegas chapel. I expected your father would be livid."

Instead Perrini had been rewarded hugely for taking the initiative. He'd passed the Howard Blackstone test. He'd proven he had balls.

And Kimberley, if she'd played along, would have been relegated to the subordinate role of wife and mother, a part she could never even pretend to play. Infuriated, she'd lashed out at them both. When Perrini sided with her father, she'd walked.

"It didn't quite work out how any of us expected," she said. "Even for Howard."

"Especially for Howard. He wanted you back at Blackstone's, Kim. He was just too proud and stubborn to admit it."

Perhaps, but now she would never know. Regret and sadness thickened in her throat. "It's history now. All of this. We can't go back and change anything we did or said."

"No, but you're letting that history influence your decision."

"And I shouldn't?"

"That's up to you. But just so everything is clear and aboveboard, let me say this." His eyes narrowed with a dangerous glint of purpose and challenge. "I want you back at Blackstone's and I want you back in my life. Whether you accept the business proposal will have no bearing on the personal. They are two separate entities."

"And if I say no. If I return to New Zealand?"

"Not far enough to keep me away."

Kimberley's mouth turned dry. Her heart was beating hard and fast, but she lifted her chin and met those determined blue eyes without a backward step. "I shall take that into consideration when making my decision."

Perrini inclined his head in acknowledgment. "Do that," he said shortly. "We'd appreciate an answer before next week's board meeting."

When will you be back to work? I need to know tomorrow, if not sooner. If you can't reach me, talk to Lionel.

Matt's message greeted Kimberley when she checked her phone that night, a cool, clipped reminder that Perrini wasn't the only man waiting on her decision. She couldn't sleep and pacing through the vast emptiness of the Vaucluse mansion, she had never felt more alone.

She longed for the familiar comfort of her Auckland town house…and then she didn't.

There, too, she would be alone and pacing with no one to

talk to. For the past decade Matt had been her sounding board, but she sensed their friendship would never be the same again, even if she chose to return to House of Hammond.

Paused outside the door to Sonya's suite, she raised her hand to knock but then let it fall away. Sonya would listen and might even dispense advice on her dilemma, but that guidance would not be impartial. There were two sides, the Blackstones and the Hammonds, with a yawning abyss of misunderstanding between.

The prospect of breaching that gap appealed more than ever after Perrini's potent speech. Kimberley's pulse kicked up a beat. For all his talk of dream jobs and the tempting notion of working on the Blackstone Jewellery show, healing the family rift spoke most directly to her heart.

But did she want to return to Blackstone's, to work for a business founded on her father's shady acquisition of the Hammond mining leases? To this day the Hammonds claimed Howard Blackstone wooed Ursula Hammond and befriended her father only to get close to the mines. The fact that Jebediah Hammond signed over the lease to Howard on his death bed only bolstered those claims.

Could she work for Blackstone's now that she knew the full story?

Could she separate the business and the personal and work with Perrini, knowing he aimed to pursue her with the same ruthless purpose he'd employed ten years before? Could she resist the powerful pull of their attraction…and did she even want to?

It was the hardest decision of her life and in the end the choice was hers to make alone. She would not be rushed into it; she would make an informed decision. To do so she needed to see the Blackstone Diamonds of today, to assess the current business structure, to determine whether she even fit anymore.

Did she want to work for Blackstone Diamonds?

Kimberley strode into the ground-floor foyer of the Blackstone Diamonds building the next morning and came to an abrupt halt. Her gaze skimmed from the manned security desk to the high-tech scanners to the ID tag displayed by an employee as he hurried through to the bank of elevators. The nervous anticipation that had swirled in her belly during the taxi ride to the city settled to a leaden weight.

What had she been thinking? That she could simply waltz in the door and wander around at her leisure? Stupidly, she hadn't thought ahead. She'd wanted to come here, to see what had changed, to test her instinctual response to the workplace she'd left ten years before.

Not that the new security checks were an insurmountable problem. At nine-thirty on a Thursday morning, Perrini, Ryan and Garth would all be entrenched at their desks. A quick phone call to any one of their offices and she would be whisked up to the rarefied atmosphere of the upper levels.

That wasn't what she wanted.

Belatedly, she recognised the implausibility of her goal. Blackstone Diamonds had grown into a gargantuan corporation, its multiple departments spread over scores of floors in the soaring tower. This was not an atmosphere that invited idle wandering. Imposing, isolating, impersonal, it was a world apart from the House of Hammond.

Kimberley rubbed the goose-bumped skin of her bare arms. In a moment of defiantly dark humour, she'd decided to wear the new dress. It wasn't nearly as daring as she'd allowed Perrini to believe, but in the air-conditioned confines of the building she wished she had at least grabbed a jacket. Not that she was staying. In fact—

"Can I help you?"

She turned, expecting to see one of the covertly uniformed security guys. Instead she found herself eye-to-eye with the most prettily handsome man she had seen outside the pages of the fashion magazines. Golden hair. Smooth tanned features. Vivid blue eyes rimmed by outrageously long lashes. And a dazzling toothpaste-commercial smile that widened as recognition sparked in his eyes.

"Miss Blackstone," he murmured. "I couldn't help noticing that you looked a little lost. Can I help you find your way? If it's clearance that you need—"

"No." Then, to soften the nerve-honed sharpness of her answer, she smiled. "Thank you, but I'm not going inside after all. I've changed my mind."

"Your prerogative." Amazing, but his eyes really did twinkle. Like a perfectly matched pair of brilliant-cut blue diamonds. "I hope we'll see you back here soon, and if you ever need clearance, call me. Max Carlton. Human resources manager."

He lifted his hand in farewell, and as Kimberley watched him pause to swap a short greeting and bring a smile to the stern face of the security-desk custodian, she couldn't help smiling herself. Perhaps she should have taken him up on his offer, but did she want the slick showman's tour? Not really. Although an hour or two of his pretty face and disarming smile would be no hardship.

Feeling infinitely better for the short interlude and inspired by Max Carlton's eyes, she walked outside and turned right into the morning sunshine. She hadn't given up on her day's task. She was just starting where she should have started all along.

Blackstone Jewellery's Sydney store was a short walk uptown from the office tower and occupied a prime corner site in a historic sandstone building that also housed the five-star Da Vinci Hotel. Kimberley had shied away from even a passing glance at this and all the Blackstone stores during her business travels. After watching the evolution of the latest over-the-top opulence across the street in Auckland, she'd expected similar here.

How wrong could she have been?

The building was grand, yes, but in a classic, traditional sense. The signage was discreet and window displays spare, spotlighting individual pieces against monochrome backgrounds. She paused, captured by the unique design of a gold-pearl-and-diamond necklace. Around the corner a larger display set a collection of retro-style diamond brooches and earrings against deep ruby velvet.

When she finally swung through the revolving door into the air-conditioned interior, her heart was beating thickly with a strange combination of pride and anxiety. *This* was how she'd visualised Blackstone Jewellery when she'd brought the plans to her father the very first time. She felt almost at home as she slowly circumnavigated the open downstairs gallery. The air of exclusive, expensive class reminded her of House of Hammond, although she doubted anyone at Blackstone's would appreciate the comparison.

The click of high heels brought her head up suddenly and snapped her mind out of introspection. A slightly built woman was descending the staircase from the first floor with hurried steps. When she caught sight of Kimberley, her eyes widened slightly in recognition and her worried frown turned tail into a welcoming smile. The smile transformed her face, although her silver-blond hair combined with an austere black dress to highlight her pale air of fragility.

"I'm Jessica Cotter, the store manager," the younger woman said, as she reached the ground floor. "Welcome to Blackstone Jewellery."

"I'm Kimberley Blackstone…although I sense that's superfluous information."

Jessica nodded. "You won't remember, but we were at school together," she continued, a hint of nerves clouding her pretty brown eyes. "You were a senior when I started P.L.C., which is why I recognised you and now I'm making a very unprofessional first impression."

"I caught you on the hop. I should have let you know I was coming in," Kimberley said with an apologetic smile. "I was just passing, and curiosity got the better of me." Which was only a small diversion from the truth. "Would you believe I've never been in a Blackstone store?"

"Then you have come to the right one. This is our flagship store, the first location we opened almost ten years ago. Let me show you around."

"Thank you." Kimberley smiled. "As long as I'm not keeping you from your work."

"Not at all. Is there anything in particular you would like to see?"

"The pearl-and-diamond pendant in the window. Is that by one of your in-house designers?"

"Xander Safin," Jessica said with a nod. "His last collection is one of my favourites. Earth Meets Sea. His aim was to offset the brilliance of diamonds from our Janderra mine with the lustre of coloured pearls."

"If the necklace in the window is any indication, I would say he succeeded."

Jessica's pretty brown eyes lit with warmth. "Come upstairs and I will show you some of Xander's other pieces."

They spent more than an hour poring over the various designs and designers, comparing their preferences for various cuts and settings. Although her name was familiar, Kimberley didn't really remember Jessica from school. After doing the math she'd calculated her age as midtwenties, which was young to manage such an important store. She wondered about the other woman's history, although she didn't doubt her knowledge of jewellery or her passion for the job.

A like soul, Kimberley thought. A woman she could work with if she returned to Blackstone's.

"Are you involved with the February show?" Kimberley asked.

A shadow crossed the other woman's face momentarily but then she looked up, her smile bright and fixed. "Yes. I have been working with Ryan...with Mr. Blackstone. We have some fabulous collections this year. Will you be coming to the show?"

Good question. Would she still be here? Or would she be back in enemy camp and struck from the invitation list? "Well, I hope I'm invited," she said lightly.

Jessica's eyes widened in horror. "Blackstone Jewellery was your idea, your vision. Of course you will be invited to the anniversary celebration."

"I will hold you to that, because I'm really looking forward to seeing the Dani Hammond collection."

"You are in for a treat," Jessica said, the glow of a secret smiling in her eyes. "Dani has such a talent for making her designs come to life."

"I don't suppose you have anything of hers in store?"

"No, unfortunately. The samples we have for the show are under lock and key and Ryan would have my hide if I showed them to anyone." Then, as if suddenly realizing what she'd said, her eyes rounded in horror. "I'm sorry, I didn't mean—"

"I know my brother well. You have cause to look out for your hide." Jessica looked even more dismayed by that reassurance, and Kimberley scrambled to ease her discomfiture by turning her attention back to the jewellery. "Could I possibly have a closer look at the necklace I pointed out downstairs? The Xander Safin?"

"Of course," Jessica said with obvious relief. "I will just go and get it for you."

She returned a minute later with the necklace, which was made up of three broad strands of pavé-set diamonds finished with golden drops of South Sea pearls. "This," she said, holding it up to Kimberley's throat, "would look fabulous with your dramatic colouring. With your hair up, a plain strapless gown. White or silver, I think. See?"

Kimberley saw. It was an exquisitely designed and crafted piece. And beneath the bright showroom lights and the gleam of enthusiasm on Jessica's face, she also saw the shadows beneath her eyes. Jessica Cotter. Suddenly she recalled why the name was familiar—not from school, but from the original passenger list for her father's fatal flight. This was the employee who had cheated death with a last-minute change of plans.

No wonder she looked fragile.

Something of her thoughts must have shown in Kimberley's

expression, because the other woman's smile dimmed. A hint of consternation crossed her face as she locked the necklace back in a display case. "I'm sorry. I get a little carried away when I find someone who shares my enthusiasm."

"Don't apologise. I was thinking of something else," Kimberley assured her. "My mind was miles away."

Jessica looked up, her eyes large and dark and troubled as she discerned where Kimberley's mind might have been. "Kimberley…please accept my condolences for your loss. I know with the lack of news and everything that's been written in the papers, this is a difficult time for you and…for all your family."

"Thank you." There was little else she could say, and when an awkwardness descended she grimaced at her watch. "I have monopolised you long enough for one morning. Thank you for your time and for showing me through the store. I enjoyed it very much."

"It was my pleasure."

"I will call in again." Kimberley smiled and tucked her bag beneath her arm. "Perhaps next time you can talk me into buying that necklace."

Jessica returned her smile but it didn't quite reach her eyes. Secrets, Kimberley thought, as she made her way downstairs.

The girl has something going on in her personal life, which is why she missed that plane and why she is still alive and why she has that haunted look in her eyes.

Immersed in her thoughts, she almost ploughed into Ryan coming out the revolving door and moving with his usual bulldog-after-a-bone tenacity. Steadying her with a hand on each arm, he scowled over her shoulder and up at the floor above before focussing narrowly on her face. "What are you doing here?"

"And hello to you, too, little brother."

The frown suddenly changed tenor, as if he'd shifted gears to finally take in the significance of her presence here at Blackstone Jewellery. "This the last place I'd expect to find you. What's going on, Kim?"

Eight

After Kimberley admitted that her visit to the Martin Place store was part of an inspection tour of the Blackstones' business, Ryan walked her back downtown for a tour of the office complex. Ryan, being Ryan, made it the potted version but that was all right with Kimberley. She preferred to make up her own mind, without the rah-rah rhetoric she might have expected from someone like Max Carlton. Or Perrini.

In the high-speed elevator they zoomed their way to the executive floors, and the sudden pitch of her stomach had less to do with that speed than the prospect of seeing Perrini. How adolescent. Kimberley gave herself a stern mental slap but her nervous anticipation only escalated with each passing floor. So much for keeping business and personal compartmentalised. Perrini had always been so much better than her at that distinction.

The lift slowed and stopped several floors short of their destination. Patrice Moore, an accounting whiz she remembered for her expert input on the jewellery store business plan, stepped on board. Her smile was instant, warm, genuine. "I heard you were in the building. Nice to see you back, Kimberley, despite the circumstances."

"Thank you. I'm glad you're still here."

"Why wouldn't I be?" the other woman said. "They look after me well."

The lift pinged open at the top floor, and Patrice offered a few sincere words of sympathy before striding off down the corridor. Ryan steered Kimberley in the opposite direction, away from the offices of the senior executives and toward the boardroom. As they walked she felt his inquisitive scrutiny of her face.

"I didn't expect to see so many familiar faces," she admitted.

"You thought we'd have driven them all away with our evil business practices?"

Kimberley laughed and shook her head. "Not exactly. I guess I just…I don't know what I expected."

"Our staff is a large and recognised part of our success. We're proud of our retention records and of our recruitment program."

They turned into the spacious vestibule outside the boardroom and Kimberley cast a quick eye over the comfortable seating, the low tables and the artwork, before returning to the issue of staff. "I have to tell you I was most impressed with your manager at Martin Place. Is she one of your recruits? She's quite young to be managing a store."

Ryan paused with his hand on the door to the boardroom. Kimberley couldn't see his face but she could see the stiffness in his shoulders for the brief moment before he turned around. "Jessica has been with the company since she left school," he said. "She knows our product inside out. She's earned every one of her promotions."

From his sharp tone, Kimberley wondered who might have suggested otherwise, but she didn't get a chance to ask. Ryan was already moving on, opening the door, and gesturing for her to precede him inside. For now she let it go, her mind and her heart and the nerves in her stomach distracted by the long, gleaming cherrywood table lined by tall-backed chairs.

"The many seats of power," she murmured, trailing her fingertips from chair to chair as she strolled the length of the room. She could imagine her father seated at the head of this table, completely in his element, the master of all he surveyed.

She snuck a glance at her brother, found his eyes on that same chairman's place, his expression fixed and forbiddingly stern. The rigid set of his shoulders as he'd paused at the door now made a different kind of sense. He'd been bracing himself for this. For seeing that chair and what its emptiness represented.

Quickly she closed the space between them and placed a hand on her brother's shoulder. Even if she had the words, she doubted her ability to push them past the lump in her throat, especially after she glanced up and saw Ryan's jaw struggling to contain his emotions. Lord, she thought she'd moved past this. That she'd accepted, with the news of Marise, that Howard was gone.

A mobile ringtone shattered the intense moment, and with a last comforting squeeze she stepped back to allow Ryan access to his phone.

"Yours," he said curtly, his gaze skating off Kimberley's as if uncomfortable that she'd witnessed his momentary turmoil. "I'll leave you to take it in private."

"Thank you." If this was Matt returning the call she'd

placed earlier, then she would need that privacy. "This may take a while," she told Ryan. "I've seen all I need for now so I will see myself out. We'll talk later, okay?"

"A word of warning. Don't let Ric Perrini under your—"

"I'm a big girl now," she cut in. "Rest assured, Perrini won't be getting under anything of mine."

Ryan nodded briefly and was gone in a dozen swift strides. When he closed the door behind him, Kimberley retrieved her phone and sucked in a breath. It was Matt. The moment of truth. Her stomach clenched as she put the handset to her ear.

"Matt. Thank you for calling back." Through the phone, she heard the high-pitched prattle of a child's voice and Matt's deeper response. "Is Blake with you?" she asked.

"Rachel—the nanny—brought him in on the ferry."

"He loves that ferry ride." Kimberley's voice thickened, remembering her godson's barely contained excitement as he recounted imaginative "sightings" of dolphins and whales and submarines. "Can I say hello?"

"He's on his way out."

Kimberley's heart dipped at Matt's cool reply. Her hand gripped more tightly around the phone. How could she leave and risk cutting herself off from her godson? Or was the damage already done?

"When are you coming back?" Matt asked. Then, when she didn't answer right away, his voice dropped another chilling degree. "*Are* you coming back?"

"I've been offered a job at Blackstone's."

"You have a job, at Hammonds. Surely you're not considering this offer."

"Considering, yes," Kimberley admitted. "But there is an

awful lot to think about and I hate the thought of leaving you short staffed at such a difficult time."

"Lionel is managing the shortfall."

She pressed her lips together for a moment, fighting the awful sense of being torn in two. The redoubtable Lionel always managed, and so did Matt…. "But that isn't the point. I don't—"

"No," Matt said, cutting her off cold. "The point is, you're contemplating this move after everything Howard Blackstone has done. Your decision should be simple—either you can work for that bastard's company or you can't."

"He's my father, Matt, and he's gone. Please respect that this is a difficult time for me, as well."

"If you're suggesting that you're mourning a man you spent the past ten years despising, then you're not the person I thought you were."

Stung by the frosty slap of those words, Kimberley lifted her chin. "If you can't understand my position, then you're not the man I thought you were, either."

"I understand," Matt said curtly. "You're a Blackstone. That's all that needs to be said. I shall take this as your resignation from Hammonds, as of last week."

Patrice Moore alerted Ric to Kim's presence in the building. "Any truth in the rumour she's coming back?" the accountant asked in her usual forthright manner.

"News travels fast," Ric said noncommittally.

"You're not kidding. It'll be in the gossip columns tomorrow."

Ric didn't doubt it. At least that would be a positive piece of press, unlike the rest of the current rumour-mongering about Blackstone's. For a good ten minutes after Patrice left his office, he fought the urge to hunt Kimberley down to find out if the rumour bore any truth, or if her tour of the offices meant she was closing in on a decision.

During the drive back to Vaucluse last night she'd asked for time and space to reach that decision, and he had no idea what she'd been thinking or if he'd miscalculated and gone too far in revealing his intentions toward her, the woman.

He'd wanted her to know where he stood, and where she stood, so there would be no misunderstandings when he made his move. When he brought her back from Auckland, he'd thought he could be patient. That he could wait until after her father had been laid to rest and the ensuing commotion had settled down.

That was before he'd taken her to his house…and let her leave without touching her.

He'd spent a restless night rueing the outcome of his self-control, and the restless heat in his blood had not been cooled any by his predawn plunge in the ocean. That heat surged again now, knowing she was here, on this floor, and not knocking on his office door.

With a low growl of impatience he shoved to his feet.

Ten minutes he'd given her, and that was all the patience he had.

He found her in the boardroom, and the first sight of her stopped Ric dead in his tracks. Dead but for the rush of arousal that quickened his pulse.

Beyond the long stretch of the table, she stood at the bank of windows looking out at the city. Sunlight slanted through the glass and burned ruby sparks in the loose fall of her hair. The same God-given rays sliced through her dress, silhouetting every curve of her body in mouthwatering detail.

That image, and his body's response, riveted him for several long greedy seconds before he took in the bigger picture. The tense set of her shoulders. Her absolute stillness. The fact that she was so lost in thought that she hadn't noticed his arrival.

It struck him then how small and isolated she looked against the expansive view of Sydney city that stretched beyond the boardroom windows, and his initial surge of lust thickened to a deeper, richer need. Gently he closed the door, but the quiet sound was enough to bring her swirling around, both hair and dress alive with that momentum. Their eyes met down the polished length of cherrywood, and he caught a glimpse of that same vulnerability he'd detected in her stance.

Then she lifted her chin. "Did Ryan tell you I was here?"

"I heard via the office grapevine."

"Word travels fast."

"All the way to the top floor." He paused halfway down the room, pacing his approach, checking the urge to charge forward and claim the softened curve of her mouth. "Is this the dress you didn't wear last night?"

"Yes," she said, sounding surprised. "How did you know?"

"You gave away the vital clue last night." He debated whether to continue, but what the hell. He felt prickly enough to tease her. Hang the consequences. "You said it was revealing."

She blinked once, slowly, realisation dawning in her eyes as she quickly looked down and then around at the light at her back. A hint of colour traced her cheekbones but she didn't rush away. She just raised her eyebrows a little and said, "In future I will be more careful about what I wear into this room."

"You see yourself in this room in the future?"

Her shoulders straightened with what looked like resolve and she nodded once, the gesture as tense as her posture. "Yes. I've decided."

"Good," he said simply. *Get the business done. Then celebrate.* "The job and the position on the board?"

"Both…if the other directors agree."

"They will." He halted his progress through the long room beside one of the credenzas parked along the wall. Close enough, for now. "What made up your mind?"

"A combination of factors," she said carefully. "I do regret cutting myself off from my family, and you were right about my dreams and my future and the difference I can make. I want to be part of shaping the future of Blackstone's."

"Your tour through the building helped?"

"Yes, and visiting the Blackstone Jewellery store. I felt at home there, seeing the heart of the business."

Ric shook his head. "Those polished gems aren't the heart, Kim—they're just the pretty face. The heart and soul of Blackstone Diamonds is way up north, in the red Kimberley earth."

"The Janderra mine," she conceded softly. "Of course." Then she blew out a rueful breath. "Would you believe after all these years in the diamond business, I've never visited a mine?"

"Easily fixed."

She straightened slightly. "Oh, I wasn't fishing for an invitation."

"I didn't think you were. But as a director you need to visit Janderra to get the full scope of this business, to meet the key personnel, to be able to do your job."

"Then, thank you. I would like to do that."

"I'll make the arrangements."

"For when?"

"I was planning to fly out there early next week, to address concerns about new workplace agreements and about the future management. That'll be the ideal opportunity for you to look around." Ric's gaze fastened on hers, straightforward and challenging. "If you don't mind an overnight stay."

Something flared in her eyes, a sign that she felt the low simmer of awareness between them. But she didn't acknowledge it. She moistened her lips and fixed her gaze resolutely on his. "Why would I mind?"

"With the ongoing wait for news on your father, I thought you might prefer to stay close to Sydney."

"If we're using the company jet, we can turn around and come back if necessary. We'll only be three hours away at most."

"Four."

She nodded. "So, what's next? What do I need to do to get started?"

"I'll organise an office for you."

"Which department?"

"You'll be working from this floor."

"No," she said, shoulders straightening. "This is the territory of senior executives. Hardly appropriate for the position you offered me."

"Suit yourself." Ric spread his hands expansively. "But you'll be in close consultation with those executives. Having you nearby would be convenient."

"Perhaps, but I'll also be working closely with the other departments—PR, marketing, the jewellery division. To be honest, I would rather if my office weren't up here on this floor."

Ric considered her answer. Cool, logical, matter-of-fact. But there was something else, something that tinged her high cheekbones with warm colour and deepened the green of her eyes. "Too close to me?" he asked.

"That shouldn't be a factor."

"But it is, isn't it?"

She pressed her lips together, a hint of annoyance flitting across her expression before she replied. "You're right. That shouldn't be a factor. I will consider whichever location you deem appropriate, as long as it suits my workspace requirements."

Her tone was formal and stuffy and so unlike Kim, Ric had to suppress a smile. The prospect of an office too close to his unsettled her. Good. "When do you want to start?"

"Yesterday."

Ric unleashed a smile as he straightened and pushed away from the credenza. "Monday might be more convenient, but we can get started on the formalities now." In half a dozen businesslike strides, he closed the space between them. "Welcome back to Blackstone, Kim."

He took her hand in what started as a formal handshake, but when he felt the faint tremor in her fingers and saw the stirring of emotion in her eyes, his grip on her hand tightened. "You've made the right choice," he said softly. "You belong here. You—"

"Don't." She shook her head abruptly. "Please, don't go all understanding on me now. That is not what I need."

"Perhaps you do."

"Oh, no. I definitely don't." She expelled a little burst of air.

"It's been quite a day. Seeing Blackstone Jewellery for the first time and talking to Ryan. Then making my decision. I spoke to Matt just before you came in, and Blake was there—"

Her voice cracked on the boy's name and so did her composure. He saw something like desperation in her eyes as she tugged her hand free and swung away. Nothing could have hit Ric as hard as that wounded fracture in her voice or the sign of tears looming in her eyes.

He put his hand on her shoulder. A gesture of comfort, he told himself, but it wasn't enough. He shifted closer, his simple touch expanding until his palm cupped her shoulder and his fingers encountered the smooth warmth of her skin. Dipping his head, he pressed his lips to her sunwarmed hair. Perhaps that would have been enough if she hadn't made a choked sound of distress.

It sounded like, "Don't," but he paid no heed. With a hand on each shoulder, he turned her into his chest and tucked her close. The tickle of her hair against his chin, the scent of orchids and spice in each breath, twined around his senses and thumped in his pulse.

This was where she belonged. Right here. In his arms.

He would hold her, just hold her, while his hands soothed the bare skin of her arms and the delicate fabric that cloaked her shoulders and her back. Leopard print. With lace peeping from the shoulder straps and the hemline. Underwear aside, it was one the sexiest things he had ever seen her wearing and with each stroke of his hand his control slipped another tenuous notch.

"This dress," he muttered thickly, his fingers giving up the fight and tracing the delicate line of lace down one shoulder blade, "is not coming on the Janderra trip."

He felt the flutter of her breath against his throat, the tension in her shoulders, the live-wire jolt of his fingertips on her skin.

"Of course not." Her voice sounded low, breathy. Turned on. Or at least that's how Ric's body interpreted the husky edge. "It's completely not appropriate for work."

"Then it's lucky you're not yet on the payroll."

She went perfectly still, and he knew exactly what was ticking through her agile brain. *Inappropriate. Work. My boss's hands on my skin.*

Beneath those hands he felt her gathering control. Every cell in his body growled a fierce objection. No way in this life or the next was he letting her go.

When she started to pull away, his hands slid to her upper arms and held her in place; his eyes on her face did the same.

"And since you're not," he said, low and dangerous, "I'm not bound to let you go."

Her nostrils flared as she drew a quick breath, and a new awareness shivered in the air between them. "Even if I ask?"

"Are you asking?"

A beat of pause, the green-diamond flash in her eyes, the quick lick of her tongue to moisten her lips, was all the time Ric allowed for her answer. Then he lifted a hand and touched his thumb to her mouth. He felt the warmth, the moisture, the shudder of her exhalation, and was lost.

He lowered his head and took her mouth with the hunger of years of wanting and the ache of the past week's emotion. It was no gentle exploration, no tender assault, not once she responded with her own longing, with her hands at last on his arms, his shoulders, twining around his neck to draw him more fiercely into the kiss.

With a low growl, he changed the angle of contact so he

could have more of her, more of the sweet heat he craved. When she welcomed him into her mouth, he tasted the impact all the way to his groin. It was sharp, intense, an exquisite surge of lust that he wanted to assuage, here and now.

Hands on her back, he pulled her closer until their bodies were flush and the kiss exploded with a silken savagery. Thigh to thigh, hip to pelvis, breasts to chest, she was everything he remembered of raw heat and unrestrained passion…and still it was not enough. He cupped her buttocks and lifted her against him, all the while turning and backing her toward the credenza.

Breaking the kiss, he lifted her onto the sleek cherrywood surface and her hands slid forward to cradle his face. Her thumbs stroked the corners of his mouth, the effect a gentle contrast to the rough rasp of their breaths. Their gazes locked for a long moment as he palmed the smooth warmth of her thighs, his thumbs circling inward with the same erotic motion as hers.

At first he thought the vibrating hum was her response to his touch. Then she touched a finger to his lips in a shushing gesture, her mouth turning down in a frown. "That's your phone. Don't you think you should answer it?"

"No," he growled against her throat. "I don't."

But she slipped her hand into his jacket pocket and retrieved the phone. "Ryan," she mouthed, hitting the answer button and holding the receiver to her ear.

Ric's growl turned into an internal groan…until she sat up straight, her eyes big and stark in her suddenly pale face.

"What is it?" he asked.

With a trembling hand she passed over the phone. "He's just taken a call from the search area. They've located the wreckage."

Nine

Closure, finally, Kimberley rationalised once the initial spear of shock had dulled. The interminable waiting was over. They could mourn Howard's passing, make arrangements for his funeral service and burial, satisfy the press with final statements, move on at a personal and business level.

Unfortunately it wasn't that simple.

An initial inspection located only three bodies in the wreckage, meaning one of the men—and the marine police couldn't even speculate on whether this was passenger or crew member—remained missing. Due to the depth of the water and adverse weather conditions brewing off the coast, the recovery operation could take several days. The process of formal identification would require the use of dental records and DNA matching, which, their police contact warned them, could take weeks rather than days.

Looming over it all was the real and sobering possibility that the lost body might never be found…and that it could be Howard.

The waiting continued. Kimberley appreciated being included in the inner information circle this time, and for that she thanked Perrini. Or she would once they got through the weekend and the incessant phone calls. As the Blackstone PR mouthpiece she'd decided to be more open with the press, in the hope that regular statements and updates would result in more factual stories and less speculation.

So far it seemed to be working. Several business and social commentators had already reported on the prodigal daughter's return to Blackstone Diamonds, and she'd taken a deep breath and agreed to an interview for a magazine piece at a date to be fixed. Positive press, she reminded herself, when her heart palpitated at the thought of such public exposure of her private self.

"Good start," Perrini said, in one of their few moments alone. It was late Saturday afternoon and the official gatherings and press updates had given way to the personal. Garth, her uncle Vincent and two of Howard's yacht club cronies had called at various intervals during the afternoon to offer sympathy and support. None had left. Sonya's tea had given way to Howard's best whisky, and Kimberley had retreated to the terrace for a brush with solitude.

That's where Perrini found her and those small words of praise resulted in an inordinate rush of satisfaction. Perhaps because his expression conveyed more than words, perhaps because she was enjoying their stolen seconds of privacy a little too much. Perhaps because, for a whisper of time, their incendiary boardroom kiss sizzled the air between them.

She liked that it wiped her mind of the deathly images imprinted in the past forty-eight hours, that it melted the icy weight of angst in her stomach, that it focussed everything on this moment, this connection, this enlivening flame in her senses.

"I hope it's the right start," she said in response to his comment…and because she couldn't resist the thinly veiled allusion to what lay unfinished between them.

"It is." Arrogant, supremely certain, his gaze lingered on her mouth for a telling second before drifting back to her eyes. "I like that you seized the opportunity and ran with it."

"I gather you're talking about the magazine article?"

"Of course…unless you prefer to talk about us."

Did she? Her heart skipped an erratic beat as she met the still intensity of his gaze. Asking too much, too fast, too soon, that look sizzled through her, charging her senses with renewed memories of their white-hot kiss and the press of his body hard against hers. A loud burst of laughter from inside the house broke the connection, reminding her they weren't alone. Reminding her that she'd given no thought to discretion in those crazy lost-to-the-world moments when he'd lifted her onto a cherrywood sideboard.

And that she'd given no thought to what was next.

"No." She lifted her chin and shook her head resolutely. "Not yet."

"When you are ready—" for a scant second his fingertips skimmed the back of her hand, a touch as dark and hot and double-edged as his words "—you know where to find me."

He left soon after, but those final words and his dark, velvet touch kept Kimberley intimate company throughout a night of little sleep. She woke early, out of sorts with herself for chickening out of that talk, not just the previous evening but ever since she learned of his intentions. He wanted her. Five minutes of hot magic in the boardroom had demonstrated that desire. But on what terms?

And what of tomorrow?

Did she even want to know, when the answer might reveal future needs she could not deliver?

Her heart constricted with an aching trepidation that sent her rocketing out of bed, too antsy to lie still any longer. She pulled on three-quarter yoga pants and a sports singlet, comfort clothes that made her feel no less comfortable in her own antsy skin. She needed to get out, to escape the claustrophobic press of this house and her restless mind.

What she needed was a long, energetic walk. Her mind conjured her favourite jaunt of old, the path that dipped and rose from beach to clifftop between Bondi and Bronte. Open air, the sea breeze on her skin, the challenge of attacking steep rock stairs and on a leisurely return trip, sinking her toes into the silky Glamarama sand...

Yes. That's exactly what she needed.

It was early, so early that she beat the notoriously early-rising Sonya downstairs. If she left now she might also beat the Sunday crowds who flocked to the popular coastal walk. Although she'd been given carte blanche access to the extensive Miramare garage, she dithered several minutes before jotting a note and grabbing the keys to Sonya's compact Mercedes.

Fifteen minutes later she parked at the northern end of Bondi Beach and attacked the mile-long stretch of sand at a testing pace. Despite the early hour she wasn't lonely, passing steady walkers and being overtaken by the serious exercise nuts. At the top of the first steep rise she paused to catch her breath and to absorb the stunning moment of daybreak over the Pacific horizon. Far below, waves crashed and foamed against the dark shelves of rock; far above, real estate battled for a share of the compelling view.

One of those houses was Perrini's.

Would he be up, enjoying his first coffee on the deck outside his bedroom? Or was he still asleep, long limbs spread-eagled across the king-size bed, covers kicked free by a restless, over-heated body?

The image took root in her brain, and she couldn't pry it loose. Nor could she prevent herself turning back and then taking the detour up the steep hill to the headland. When she turned into his street her heart was pounding, not from exertion but with nervous tension.

She didn't know what she was doing here. From the street-side, a privacy wall and the steep drop of the site protected most of his house from view. She had no clue if he was home or not. The sensible course of action would be to turn around and hotfoot it back to the car. The nonsensible, risky, spur-of-the-moment thing involved her mobile phone and a speed-dialled number.

A light came on in a second-floor window. His bedroom. Her stomach tightened with a new and different tension.

"Kim." The deep morning huskiness of his voice curled through her, tightening to a stark ache low in her belly. It was desire. It was loneliness. It was the lure of a light in his bed-room window and the sound of her name on his tongue. "It's hellish early. Is everything all right?"

"Yes." No. *Not exactly. Why hadn't she composed some-thing to say before hitting that button?* "I was just wonder-ing if you were home," she finally managed to say. "I'm in the neighbourhood and I just—" She closed her eyes, her fingers tightening in a deathgrip around her palm-size phone. "I seized the opportunity and ran with it."

He opened the door before she rang the bell, and for several electric seconds they stood in silence, their eyes locked. Kimberley did notice that he wore trousers and nothing else— nothing except a narrow-eyed look of intense, primal concentration that would have knocked her off her feet if he hadn't snaked out a hand and pulled her inside.

Vaguely she registered him reaching out to push the door shut behind her. Mostly she registered the scent that clung to his skin, the unique combination of expensive soap and male heat she'd labelled Ricaroma way back then. It still had the power to make her hormones sit up and pant.

For a long, thick beat he studied her face, her heightened colour, the jut of her tightened breasts in a top not designed for aroused nipples. "Do you want to talk?" he asked, and those female hormones rolled over and begged.

"No." She met his hungry look, direct, honest. "Not talk."

One of the things she'd always appreciated in Perrini was his ability to judge the moment. He could match words with the smoothest orators on the planet, but he knew when talk wasn't necessary, when action spoke with the greatest eloquence.

Without a word he led her by the captured hand to the elevator. From ground floor to second, he kissed her with the exact intensity she needed to eat away the last flutter of nerves. As he backed her toward the master bedroom, those first greedy seconds eased into a sultry meeting of lips, tongues, mouths.

Oh, yes, the man knew when and how to use his mouth to devastating effect.

In the doorway he paused, to tug the elastic from her ponytail, to drag her singlet over her head, to hold her arms trapped while he took her in with a low, thorough look that screamed through her senses. This was her chance to slow things down and rethink, to step away from temptation and think this through.

From the moment she'd turned on the clifftop path and caught a glimpse of the ivory stucco walls, the jutting balconies, the glint of daybreak on bedroom glass, she'd been steel to a magnet, powerless to resist the pull. She didn't want to think. She wanted to feel, to drive the past days from mind and body with the purest, most absolute, life-giving pleasure. The kind she had only experienced in this man's expert hands.

Stretching up, she kissed the raspy line of his jaw, the indent in his chin, the velvety fullness of his mouth, and they sunk into another long, deep soul kiss that waltzed them in perfect, thigh-brushing synch toward the bed. She lapped up the dark flavour of his mouth, savoured the heat and texture of his hands as they palmed her shoulders, her upper arms, the blades of her shoulders.

Eventually he eased the connection with a delicate trail of nips from her bottom lip to her jaw and earlobe. "Shave," he muttered, demonstrating the need with a momentary brush of his whiskery cheek against hers.

"Shower," she murmured, thinking about her earlier exertion and then his beautiful, big, shower-with-friends-size room.

Thinking about him, naked and wet, his hands sliding over her skin, filled her veins with a heavy, languid beat. Their gazes connected and the same primal drumming burned in his eyes and tightened his expression. He lifted a hand, knuckles skimming over her hair before he twisted a hank around his fingers and urged her closer. When her taut nipples came into scorching contact with the hard wall of his chest, all the air left her lungs in a fractured gasp.

Eyes locked on his, she shifted her hands from his waist to the front fastening of his trousers but he stilled her fingers beneath the flat of one hand. "It's been too long," he told her bluntly, "to stand much play."

"Too long…without?"

"Without you." The honesty of that statement and its inherent message—this is you, this is different—resonated through her blood and into her heart. When he released her hair and his fingertips teased across the rise of her breasts, she swallowed a lump of hot, desperate desire.

"Same," she said, stepping out of her shoes, her hands already peeling down her pants until she stood naked before him. "I'll turn on the shower."

He didn't let her shave him but he joined her beneath the double showerheads. He stepped straight into her arms and into a kiss that was strong and bold and without pretence. They explored each other's bodies with the same intense, unhurried thoroughness, until his hands moulded her bottom and drew her up against his thick arousal. Their mouths came apart but their gazes held the connection as he rocked her slowly, deliberately, stoking the restless fire and testing the tenuous limit of their control.

For a second Kimberley could do nothing but ride the wave of erotic pleasure that flooded her, then he lifted her and she wrapped her arms around his neck and her legs around his sleek, wet flanks. She felt him, hard and hot between her legs, and need—unbearably intense—swelled in her breasts and in her female core and in her heart.

Eyes linked with his, she saw the momentary hesitation and felt the slight withdrawal, and guessed its cause.

"No," she whispered, not wanting to break the moment, only wanting him inside her like this, with nothing between them. "There's no need."

"You're protected?"

"I'm…yes. There's no risk of pregnancy."

Something fierce flared in his eyes, a blaze of possessiveness that caused her heart to contract and ache with the truth of the statement. *No risk of conception, unless by some miracle.* Then he carried her from the shower to the dressing room. He set her down on the vanity, the cool marble surface a shockingly erotic contrast to her overstimulated skin and to the heat of his hands. They spanned her waist, drawing her forward while he fed on her mouth, her throat, her breasts.

When he fingered her slick heat, she moaned into his mouth and then his hands on her thighs opened her and anchored her when the first measured thrust of his body filled her with unbelievable heat and sensation and with a vicious jab of regret for their years spent apart.

In the supercharged intensity of that intimate coupling, Kimberley saw the same complex mix of sensual awe and conflicted emotion in his eyes. She lifted her fingers to his mouth and felt the warm slough of his breath when he spoke low and ardent. "Welcome home, babe, where you belong."

She wrapped her legs higher, drawing him deeper and pulling him into a kiss that strengthened their intimate connection. Beneath her hands the harshly etched muscles of his back reflected his restraint as he started to move with a slow, controlled cadence. The pleasure was exquisite, immense, impossible.

Her hands slid lower, relearning the shape of him as her

body relearned the power of his restrained strength with each deep thrust. She traced the long planes of muscle, the dimples at the base of his spine, the taut muscles of his behind.

And when she reached lower still, a deep shudder racked his body. His head lifted, eyes fiercely hooded as he dragged her bottom lip between his teeth and changed the angle to rock deeply against her pelvis. He didn't need to touch her anywhere else, didn't need to do anything except look at her. He drove her to a climax that shattered into a spray of vivid brilliance in her blood and in her flesh and in her heart.

Ric leaned his unashamedly bare hip against the doorframe and watched her come awake with the quickness he remembered from the past. No slow stretches and yawns for Kim, her eyes opened clear and focussed, her brain already geared for action. Despite the second thoughts he imagined ticking through her agile brain right now, he smiled with satisfaction, not only because he'd taken her to bed and made love to her another time with complete, inventive thoroughness, not only because she was still here and he was thinking about a third time, but because she looked so right in his bed.

"I wondered if you'd ever wake."

"Worn out," she murmured. The contented light in her eyes as she found him watching her was a kiss to the heart. "What time is it?"

"Quarter after midday."

"You're kidding." A frown formed between her brows. "I didn't expect to be away so long."

"That's a problem?"

"Only that I took Sonya's car. She might wonder…."

When she swung her legs out of bed, Ric abandoned his

nonchalant stance and moved swiftly to prevent her exodus. He sat on the edge of the mattress, trapping the sheet beneath him. Unless she wanted to slide butt-naked from under that sheet gripped across her breasts, he had a captive audience. He intended having that talk now, and finding out what prompted her surprise visit.

"How long did you expect to be gone?" he asked.

"When I left home, it was to do the Bronte walk. That's all."

"And this—" he gestured between them with his fingers "—was a spur of the moment impulse? Alternate exercise? What, exactly?"

"An impulse," she admitted, hunching her shoulders into a tight shrug. "After this weekend, everything about the crash seemed a little too real and…graphic. I wanted to take an hour to forget about searches and victims and means of identification. I wanted those images out of my mind."

"Did it work?"

"Yes." Her gaze lifted, stark and luminous with the same emotion that coloured her voice. "Thank you…not only for this morning, but for everything this weekend. I appreciated being included in the meetings, even though Ryan disapproved. And thank you for allowing me to make the media statements."

"That's your job."

"I'm not officially on the payroll until tomorrow," she pointed out. Then said, "Thank you for calling Danielle and getting her back so swiftly. Sonya needed her family around her this weekend."

"No need to thank me," Ric said quietly. "She's the closest I have to family."

"I noticed."

"And you don't approve?"

"I don't *understand*," she clarified. Then she shook her head and blew out a breath. "No, that's not quite right. I think I understand all too well."

Alerted by the edge to her voice, Ric's gaze narrowed on her face. "What is it you think you're seeing here, Kim?"

"My father welcomed you with open arms when you married me, and it wasn't only as an approved son-in-law. He'd always looked on you as a surrogate son, a replacement for the one he'd lost."

This revelation wasn't news to Ric, he'd always suspected that part of Ryan's antagonism toward him was based on a similar belief. But that didn't make it any easier to swallow. Not when coming from Kim. Not when it was just plain ludicrous. "Howard never saw me as a substitute for James. Why would he, when he believed James was still alive?"

Eyes wide and appalled, she sat up straight and stared at him. "Are you crazy? My brother was taken thirty-two years ago. Despite all the investigations and all the reward money my father offered, there were no leads that didn't peter out a mile down the road. How could you suggest that he's alive?"

"I don't believe it any more than you do, but Howard refused to give up hope. That was his one weakness. His inability to let that go."

"His inability to let go," she said fiercely, "was always his weakness."

She had a point. And if his reason for being on that plane was tied up in his vengeance against the Hammonds, then it had turned into a fatal weakness.

"What about you?" Ric lifted a hand and threaded a loose

tress of hair behind her ear, leaning in to follow with his lips. "Are you able to let go of the past? To start again here and now? Will you stay?"

Ten

Ric couldn't talk her into staying Sunday night, but before he finished kissing her goodbye he had convinced her to fly to Janderra with him on Monday afternoon. With the crucial board meeting on Thursday and concerns about the still-depressed share price spreading edgy malcontent through some factions of the company, this wasn't the best time to be out of the office. But he didn't want Kimberley there, or at the Vaucluse house, when the police brought in the bodies. For once Ryan agreed with him.

They took off late afternoon in the company's Gulfstream, and this time she sat beside him and accepted the comforting grip of his hand at takeoff. Although she didn't miss the chance to point out, "I'm not a nervous flyer, you know that. It's just that last flight from New Zealand, I couldn't get out of my mind that we were flying over the same stretch of water where the jet went down. That I could look out the window and see—" She blew out a rough laugh. "Silly, because given the expanse of the Tasman the odds would be miniscule."

"Not silly." Ric lifted their linked hands and pressed a kiss to the delicate skin on the inside of her wrist. "FYI, I'm using this excuse to hold your hand. Humour me."

"FYI, humouring you is not part of my job description."

"Can be added. It's fluid."

She gave him a look.

"So, how did you spend your first day?"

"Meeting staff, reading annual reports, getting the lay of the land. There's been a lot of change, a lot to catch up on."

A helluvalot. And businesswise he would allow her to catch up. As for everything else, he stood by what he'd told her in his bedroom. There and then they'd let the past go. They were starting over. "Did Max get the formalities sorted out?"

"Ah, Max, a bright spot in the middle of all those balance sheets," she said with a grin. "The man should come with a warning."

Ric's gaze narrowed. He knew Carlton's reputation as a charmer. Everyone east of the Great Divide knew, but hell—

Laughing at his grim expression, Kim shook her head. "Relax, Perrini. He didn't offer to hold my hand or anything. We just met over coffee and talked for a while. He was very helpful, clueing me in on staff politics. Oh, and he recommended Holly McLeod as my assistant."

"Good choice."

"I met her and I agree, except I don't need a permanent PA."

"You are entitled," he said, "as an executive and a director."

"Which doesn't mean I need to take up the perk," she retorted. "I will utilise Holly when necessary. She impressed me already, putting together a dossier on the jewellery show at short notice."

"Have you had a chance to look at it?"

"Briefly."

Something in her expression focussed Ric's attention on her face instead of his contemplation of how much she'd changed. Ten years ago she'd taken every perk as her due as a Blackstone. He approved this change. Very much. "Problem?" he asked.

"Briana Davenport," she said, a frown between her brows and in her voice. "The model used in all the promotional materials for the show. I haven't worked out if she's a problem or an opportunity yet." After a moment's hesitation she asked, "How well do you know her?"

"I've met her at a number of functions and from everything I've seen and heard, we couldn't have chosen a harder-working or more amenable model as 'the face of Blackstone's.' Are you concerned because she's Marise's sister?"

"Precisely. I'm worried about what spin the media might put on that, now that they've started chewing over the juicy prospect of a Howard-Marise affair."

Ric swore silently and succinctly. "You saw that column, then?"

"It's my job to see columns like this morning's," she said matter-of-factly, shaking her head at his question. But he saw the anger darken her eyes. "It's also my job to think about future ramifications. What if Briana sells family secrets to one of these gossip magazines?"

"She wouldn't do that. She isn't the type who chases attention."

"She's a model…she's a Davenport. Are you sure about that?"

"Briana may be Marise's sister," Ric said with conviction, "but that is where the resemblance ends."

Kimberley made a mental note to call Briana Davenport on their return from the outback, to arrange an informal meeting where she could form her own opinion. Then she turned her focus to the trip and to renewing her opinion of the man at her side. Until now she'd acted impulsively, in succumbing to his kiss, in going to his home, in falling into his bed, but from here on she needed to be honest with herself about where this was leading and what she expected from their relationship. And the first step to honesty was acknowledging that Perrini could never be a casual lover. He was her ex, her boss, the only man who had ever owned her heart…but was he the same man ten years later?

Today he was more relaxed than she'd seen him since her return from New Zealand, and she liked to think that present company had something to do with his upbeat mood. They'd always connected in conversation, in ideas and interests, which stimulated their exchanges—both verbal and physical—with an extra element of excitement. That hadn't changed.

But the following day at the mine, as she watched him roll up his sleeves and don hard hat and boots to go onsite at the gaping open pit, she realised that his laid-back demeanour might have as much to do with Janderra itself. This was a Perrini she'd never seen before, equally at home addressing the site managers or leaders of the indigenous community or climbing into one of the huge ore trucks to chew over the concerns of the mine staff. Recalling the day in the boardroom when he'd told her that this was the heart and soul of Blackstone's, she wondered about *his* heart and soul.

When Kimberley first met Ric Perrini, she'd judged him as the perfect Blackstone representative, as eye-catching and expensive and charismatic as the stones at the company's foundation. Now she was intrigued by his hidden facets—and by the original, rough diamond from which he'd been hewn. What drove his ambition, his love of the beautiful and the exclusive, his loyalty to a man who'd manipulated him into an ill-fated marriage? By the end of their first day at Janderra, Kimberley's curiosity had not only been reignited. It flamed blue-hot with her need to know.

Tracy Mattera, one of the mine executives, had invited them to a barbecue dinner at her home in the Janderra township. Having met the all-business, khakis-and-boots-wearing Tracy at the mine site, Kim hadn't pictured her as a mother. So it came as something of a surprise when they were greeted at the door of an unprepossessing, ranch-style home by another version of the thirty-something woman.

This Tracy looked younger, softer, prettier in shorts and bare feet and freshly washed blond curls, with a baby perched on one hip. She greeted Kimberley with cool politeness and Perrini with a big welcoming smile, and Kimberley gained the distinct impression the other woman had pulled back from greeting him with even more enthusiasm.

That initial prickle of knowledge was barreled over by another stronger rush of female response when Perrini scooped the toddler from Tracy's arms and swung her high in the air. The sound of the little girl's giggles, the sight of Perrini's wide grin, the fierce tug of longing as their eyes met over a mop of baby-soft blond curls, arrowed straight to her heart and to an emptiness deep at her woman's core. And it only intensified when a little boy of six or seven shuffled into the room, skinny legs weighed down by full-size cricket pads, bat and ball in his hands. Tracy's expression clouded. "Oh, Cam, no backyard cricket tonight. Ric has brought a…friend."

"Kim won't mind," Perrini said easily, and still tense from that awkward introduction she didn't realise his intent until her arms were filled with wriggling baby girl. She didn't mind—the proposed game of cricket, the baby, anything—but she had been caught off guard and that unpreparedness must have shown on her face. Uttering a hasty apology Tracy reclaimed her child.

"Please, I don't mind," Kimberley reassured her, but it was too late. With a cool smile Tracy hurried off to fix them drinks and Kimberley was left feeling oddly bereft after one token moment of sweet-scented baby in her arms. Hugging her arms lightly she looked up and her gaze collided with steady blue perception.

He'd paused at the ranch slider, one hand tossing and catching the well-used red cricket ball, the other resting lightly on Cam's shoulder but his attention was fixed entirely on her, catching her unguarded, her emotions stripped bare. For a moment she thought he would say something, but Cam tugged at his shirt, recapturing his attention, and they continued on to the backyard, a picture of man and child that reached into her emotional heart and squeezed it like a vise.

"You were quiet tonight," he said later, driving back to their accommodation. For a second she felt the sidelong touch of his gaze, felt its perceptive impact shiver through her. "Should I have warned you about the kids?"

"I'm that transparent?"

"Usually, no."

But at that one moment, yes. Since then she'd had plenty of time to collect herself and to prepare an answer that, while not the complete truth, wasn't a lie. "I am going to miss Blake. Tonight I realised just how much."

"I wondered if I'd done the wrong thing thrusting Ivy on you."

"Only from Tracy's viewpoint." Then, when Perrini looked puzzled, she shook her head. *Men. Perceptive one second, clueless the next.* "She didn't exactly approve of me, did she?"

"She didn't approve of you breaking my heart," he said lightly. "Give her time. She'll get over it."

He was kidding; she knew it in her mind and yet that didn't stop her heartbeat thickening with a longing. *Follow his lead,* she cautioned herself. *Keep it light.* "I gather you've been friends a while?"

"Twenty years, give or take. We started at the mine together, the same day, same shift. I've known her kids since birth."

Another part of his life she'd known nothing about. The knowledge irked. "It might have helped if I'd known some of this history beforehand."

"Helped, how?"

"I don't know. Maybe if I'd known you were close friends I wouldn't have been taken aback when she all but kissed you at the door and when you grabbed hold of Ivy. Instead I was left wondering about your relationship—"

"You thought I might be their father?" he interrupted, his voice a rough rasp of astonishment.

"No. *No,* that didn't even cross my mind. I meant your relationship with Tracy. I thought you might have been lovers."

"You were jealous?"

"Yes," she admitted after a moment. "If she knows you better than I do, then I'm jealous of that."

"You know me."

"No," Kimberley countered, shaking her head. "Whenever I've asked about your background, you provide the minimum of facts with a what-does-it-matter shrug. What do I know about you? You were born in Italy, and came to Australia with your mother when you were a baby. You grew up in West Australia. After your mum died, you worked to pay your way through university. One of those jobs was here at the Janderra mine. And after finishing your business degree you got an entry-level job in the marketing department at Blackstone's."

"That's my background, not me." His words might have been deliberately dismissive, but the determined set of his features and the long sidelong glance he cast over her face were anything but casual. "If you want to know me, move back to Bondi. Live with me. Work with me. It's as easy as that."

"No, that's easy for *you*. Tell me just one thing," she continued quickly when his blue gaze snapped in protest. "Why did your mother come to Australia? Why did she stay, when she had no family here? That must have been difficult for her, especially as a single mum."

"Just *one* thing?"

His tone was dry, one eyebrow lifted in sardonic query, but Kimberley wouldn't be put off by semantics. "One thing in several parts," she justified. "Why Australia?"

"My father was Australian. Mum came out here to find him."

"And did she?"

"Apparently." He hitched a shoulder, the what-does-it-matter gesture exactly as she'd described. "I was too young to remember. That didn't work out but Mum decided to stay. She had no reason to go back to Italy."

"She didn't have any family?"

His mouth thinned with impatience or irritation. "There is Perrini family, but they didn't approve of the pregnancy or her decision to keep me. They wouldn't have welcomed her back."

Perrini family. That she'd never known about, that he'd never mentioned. Family that had cut him out. Her heart beat hard with renewed curiosity and with silent empathy. "Have you met any of your family?" she persisted.

"No. Nor do I ever want to."

Kimberley turned in her seat, better to study the hard set of his profile. "You aren't curious about your grandparents and…are there uncles, aunts, cousins?"

"I called once, when Mum was dying. Her father didn't want to know her, he didn't want to know me. That's not family."

"Your grandfather," she murmured on an appalled breath. "Is he still alive?"

"I don't know. I don't care. The only relevance is how that little episode taught me to appreciate family that does care."

"Like the Blackstones?"

"Like Sonya. Like Tanya and her kids." His eyes were Antarctic cold, but beneath the frosty expression was more, the kind of emotion that told her this mattered. Very much. "Just so you're clear—I've never aspired to be a Blackstone. If I wanted that kind of a family, one that picked and discarded its members like Howard has done with his family, then I have Pappa Perrini in Turin."

The previous night she'd insisted on sleeping alone in her room, citing Perrini's words—which annoyed him to no end—about keeping their business and personal relationships as two separate entities. Tonight he showed her to her door and after a kiss that claimed complete possession of her mouth and her heart, she took his hand to lead him inside. Something snapped tight and intense in his expression.

"No," he said, low and rough-edged. "Not tonight. I am not a man to be pitied."

It's for the best, she told herself as his retreating footsteps echoed through the hollow corridor of the executive accommodation complex and found a matching resonance in her heart. If she called him back, if she made love to him now with her emotions so exposed, he would question her motives and any words of love that crept from her tongue.

Instead she stripped and showered and fought the impact of his rejection by chewing over all she'd learned, her heart analyzing the impact of his family's callous abandonment. He'd only been fifteen, damn it, and watching his mother—his only parent, the only family he knew—dying of cancer. No wonder he'd never mentioned his family. No wonder he'd reacted so heatedly when, in the dustup of their marriage, she'd accused him of wanting to become a Blackstone. No wonder he'd bonded with Sonya and retained a strong friendship with Tracy, both single mothers doing a wonderful job with family, just as his own mum had done.

She couldn't help wondering if his ambition—his near ferocious drive to succeed—stemmed from a need to prove himself to an old man in Turin who'd not thought his grandson worth knowing. And when she left her bed and wavered by the door, wanting to go to him, to hold him, to make love with the whole man she now recognised for all he'd overcome and all he could be, she heard his closing words and her hand dropped away from the doorknob.

Pity was not something Perrini's pride would ever accept,

and the next morning she sensed a barrier—a subtle coolness in his eyes, a focus on last-minute business he conducted alone—that prevented her broaching the subject until they were airborne on their return to Sydney late in the morning. And then she had to lean across the table between them and place her hand on the papers he was reading and weather the irritated slice of his frown.

"This won't take a minute," she assured him, lifting her chin and meeting the blue reserve in his eyes. "Thank you for bringing me out here. You were right—Janderra is the heart and soul of the business."

He inclined his head in acknowledgement. "Is that all?"

"I wanted to thank you, also, for sharing what you did of your past…although you were wrong to claim it irrelevant. It all matters. It all made you the man you are and you were right—that is not a man to be pitied." In his eyes she saw the look of rejection, and quickly she leaned forward to trap his hand beneath hers on the tabletop. "Tell me one thing before you pull away. This last week—when you kissed me in the boardroom, when you pulled me into your foyer last Saturday morning—was your desire driven by compassion or pity over Howard? Is that why you wanted me?"

"You know it wasn't."

"Then can you accept that I wanted you last night? That I want you now?"

Something shifted in his expression, his eyes flared with heat, and Kimberley's heart breathed a heavy sigh of relief.

"Now?" he asked softly, turning his hand beneath hers to capture her fingers and draw them to his lips. "On a business trip?"

"Now," she said, "on our lunch break."

* * *

By the time they arrived back in Sydney Kimberley knew she was ninety-nine percent back in love with him. She fell the final one percent during the board meeting held on the following day. It wasn't only how he introduced her, not as Howard's daughter but by acknowledging her standing in the industry and her creative vision, which had spawned Blackstone Jewellery ten years earlier. It wasn't just the standing ovation he led when the board formally accepted her as the new interim director. It wasn't even his decisive leadership of the meeting, or the overwhelming vote of confidence that led to his appointment as interim Chairman and CEO of the company.

No, the moment when she allowed herself to fall that final percent came in a singular second after the announcement of Howard's successor was made, when he sought her eyes as if her approval was all that mattered. And in that instant of connection and clarity, she saw the man he'd become and it didn't matter where he'd come from or what had brought him to this point.

In all his facets he was the perfect cut for her, and the knowledge thrilled her and soothed her and scared her in equal measures.

As Ric anticipated, the remains of the crash victims were recovered from the wreckage while he and Kim were returning from Janderra. The exhaustive identification process had commenced and despite the dark pall cast over proceedings by Howard's as-yet-unresolved fate, the meeting ended on an optimistic note. Rick had wanted to take Kim out for a celebratory dinner… after she'd packed her things and moved into his house.

To his chagrin she'd agreed to neither.

"Let's not rush into anything this time," she'd said. "And wearing my PR hat, I would suggest that any celebration of your appointment is done in private."

"That's not what I want to celebrate," he'd pointed out. "But since I can't toast your move into my home, how about we enjoy a quiet dinner from Roberto's?"

She'd agreed. They'd eaten. And since she now sat on his sofa, her feet curled up beneath her and a second glass of Dom Pérignon in her hand, Ric couldn't complain about the outcome.

"Do you think Ryan will stay on?" she asked.

Halfway to sitting down beside her, Ric paused. "Has he mentioned leaving?"

"No, nothing like that. But he can't be happy with your appointment."

"Which is interim," he reminded her. "If he doesn't think I'm the right choice, then he can lobby for change."

"Do you think? The other directors made it clear that they believe Howard handpicked you as his successor. It must have been tough for Ryan to hear that his own father preferred another man for the job he coveted."

"That's not why Howard or the directors chose me. Your brother's still young. I have a solid eighteen-year history with Blackstone's. I started in the mines—I've worked across the divisions, from marketing to retail to export. Today's vote was an issue of experience and seniority, not preference."

"But is that the way Ryan will see it?" she asked, her voice soft with empathy. "I know how he feels. I've been in that position."

"Howard chose me back then for the same reason, Kim."

"Seniority and experience. I know." Her shrug was casual, belying the whirl of emotion in her eyes. "But that didn't help soften the blow." With a shuddery sigh, she leaned her head against the back of the sofa to stare up at the ceiling. "I wonder what *he* thought of today's events. If he's sitting there with a smug look on his face because you're in charge and I'm back here as he always intended."

The pensive edge to her voice as she conjured up that spirit of their past loosened a great knot of emotion in Ric's gut. He watched her sitting there beside him, with the mahogany gleam of her hair and the smooth tan of her bare arms and the sweet curve of her hip... Hell, she was so damn beautiful it hurt.

"I'm pretty sure he would approve of us."

Slowly she turned her gaze on him. "Ironic, isn't it? In life he tore us apart, but his death has brought us back together."

"He won't come between us again," Ric promised. "Not Howard or Blackstone's."

For a long moment his resolute words hung in the night between them, a solid vow, a promise he would keep. Kim moistened her lips, her gaze shadowed as she dipped her head to take a sip of her champagne. "Is that all that was wrong between us back then?"

"We were young. What we had—" he didn't know how to describe it, what words would encapsulate that potent passion "—hit us quick, before we'd worked out what we wanted."

"*I* was young," she corrected in a rueful tone. "You always gave the impression that you knew exactly what you wanted."

"I knew I wanted you. The first time I saw you. I knew."

"Despite the hard time I gave you?"

"Despite Ryan's disapproval and the threat of career suicide." He waited a beat, expression serious before continuing. "You accused me of getting everything I wanted when I married you."

"And did you?"

"Yes." The shock of that admission registered in her eyes and when she would have looked away Ric leaned forward and captured her chin in his hand. "I got the advancement, the prestige, the chance to prove myself. And while I wasn't ever a substitute for your brother, I did get to feel like I was part of a family. Sonya has that knack."

A hint of disquiet shimmered in the depths of her eyes. "That mattered?"

"Family is everything. Yes, it mattered. It all mattered, until you were gone."

For a long moment she sat in silence, a faint tremor of emotion in her eyes and in the skin beneath his fingers. Then she murmured, "And now I'm back."

"Then let me know you are. Move in with me. Come out to dinner, have your photo taken on my arm. Let me know I'm not just an impulse or a distraction. Let me know, and let the world know that you're back and you're mine."

Let's not rush, Kimberley said in careful answer to that heart-stoppingly ardent declaration, but four hours, three glasses of Dom and two orgasms later she had agreed to move into Perrini's house. And to accompany him to a formal Sydney Festival event the following Tuesday night, not only as a representative of Blackstone's, but as a date.

And to start calling him by his given name.

Ric. Ric. Ric. She practiced in time with the tap of her heels as she hurried through the Pitt Street Mall en route from the designer floor of David Jones' city store to Martin Place. *Ric. Ric. Ric.*

The repetitive cadence triggered memories of the night

before, when he'd held her on the edge of release, their fingers joined high above her head while he stared into her eyes and insisted she call him Ric.

"Only when I come?" she'd asked.

"That'll do nicely for a start."

The mere memory coloured her skin as she shouldered through the revolving door of the Blackstone's store, her hands filled with shopping bags and the hangered gown she'd chosen for the reception. Only five minutes late. Which, given the way she'd been chasing her tail all morning, was something of a miracle.

She'd called Jessica Cotter yesterday to make the appointment, right after Perrini—*Ric*—had reassured her that attending the reception was a good idea.

"A Blackstone presence won't be expected," she'd argued. "We're in mourning."

"Not expected," he'd countered, "which makes it a sound promotional ploy. The rags are buzzing with Marise and your father. Let's give them something else to talk about."

Resigned to becoming society-column fodder, Kimberley decided to make the best of it. She would wear Blackstone jewellery and a designer gown to set it off. Hence her shopping expedition and her appointment with Jessica, who met her at the top of the stairs. Her curious eyes took in Kimberley's plastic-protected burden. "You brought the gown with you? Perfect."

"I've come straight from DJ's," Kim admitted. "Where I came perilously close to calling you and begging for your help in deciding."

"You should have," Jessica said with a warm smile. "I would have been happy to help."

"Oh, you did. When I was here last week, you described a gown—strapless, white or silver." While she spoke, Kimberley unzipped the bag to reveal her choice. "And here it is."

"The dress looks divine," Jessica said softly. "This reception you're going to…is it the one at Warralong House?"

"I'm not sure. It's for one of the highlight acts at the Sydney Festival—the dance company performing at the Opera House."

"That's the one."

There was something in the younger woman's voice—a note that sounded almost wistful to Kimberley's ears. "If you would like to go," she said with a smile, "you can have my ticket. I'm really not a fan of these affairs."

"I don't think my presence would be appreciated, even if this gorgeous dress fit me. Now, let's see what we can find for you. Are you looking for something subtle? Classic? Sophisticated?"

"Something that photographs well," Kim said, putting aside her curiosity about Jessica for a moment. "That is the main thing. And since I'm representing Blackstone's, it definitely has to be diamonds."

Eleven

Even though coloured stones—especially the rare Janderra pinks—were the Blackstone trademark, Jessica put her in white diamonds.

"Better for my colouring," she told Ric as he took his sweet time about fastening the fabulous multistrand necklace. "What do you think? Enough bling for a Blackstone?"

His fingers lingered on her throat, a deliciously warm contrast to the cool weight of the stones against her skin, but he didn't answer right away. Seated at the dresser applying a final brush of bronze to her cheekbones, Kimberley looked up and caught his gaze in the dresser mirror. Then he let his eyes do the talking with a long, lazy sweep over her near-backless gown, her bare arms and shoulders, the hint of cleavage above the silvery sheen of her fitted bodice.

"You don't need the bling, Kim." Leaning forward, he

covered the necklace with his hands. His thumbs blocked out
the fat diamonds in her ears. "See?" he whispered at her ear.
"You dazzle without them."

Wow. The impact of his inspection, his words, his breath
against her skin, pooled low and hot in Kimberley's belly. She
drew in a breath that wasn't quite steady, closed her compact
and set it down on the top of the dresser. "Do you want to go
to this party?"

"Not particularly."

His voice was as casual and deliberate as the drift of his
fingertips to the sensitive skin beneath her earlobe.

Kimberley shivered deep inside. "We could stay home."
She leaned back against his black dinner suit and felt the
erotic imprint of his arousal in every female cell. "I've never
made love in a quarter million dollars' worth of diamonds."

"We will rectify that," he promised, and his mouth replaced
his hands, trailing a string of delicate kisses to her hairline.
"After we've let the world know you're going home with me."

She pointed out the flaw in his logic while they drove to the
glamorous Point Piper venue. It helped distract her from what
she saw as an ordeal ahead. She'd never liked society soirees,
and she had a feeling she would hate being studied and whispered about when she appeared on her ex-husband's arm.

But after the first half hour and the obligatory pose for a
society snapper, she found herself enjoying the evening much
more than anticipated. Part of that pleasure was due to the
outdoor setting, in the terraced gardens of a historic harbour-
side mansion. Part was knowing she had the party's hottest
date at her side, feeling his hand at her back, catching his
rescue-me glance when he'd been shanghaied by yet another
predatory female. She might have felt sorry for him if he

wasn't inviting the interest, with his killer smile and smooth conversational skills.

But her biggest delight came from the knowledge she would be going home with him, and the expectancy that built with every touch and every captured glance. The pleasure bubbled away inside her, a secret smile couched in optimistic hope that this time around things might just work out.

They'd already started to wind their way back up the garden toward the house and the exits, taking their time, heightening the anticipation, when she saw her brother's familiar tall frame. She did a double take. "I didn't expect to see Ryan here. I wouldn't have thought this would be his thing," she murmured, although how would she know what Ryan's thing was? She knew nothing about his private life. She studied the statuesque blonde at his side. "Is that his date?"

"No, that's the wife of the one of the festival directors. I met her earlier."

"Is he dating anyone?" she asked after a moment.

"I have no idea. That's not information your brother would share with me," Ric replied dryly.

But Kimberley was recalling Jessica's odd reaction to tonight's party and the vibes Ryan had given off when she mentioned Jessica's name the day he showed her around the office complex. "You don't think he might have something going on with Jessica Cotter?"

"An employee? Hell, no. You know his opinion on that issue."

Ten years ago she'd known his disapproval of her and Ric's relationship, a distaste born from Howard's affairs with several secretaries. But that didn't stop her wondering and besides that curiosity, she'd wanted to catch up with him ever since last week's board meeting. To say what, she didn't quite know, but she didn't want that old enmity resurfacing. Her return was supposed to heal rifts, not drive a wedge in them.

"I'm going to say hello."

"Uh-uh." He hooked his arm around her back and pulled her snug against his side. The promise in his eyes and the heated spread of his fingers against her bare back smoked through Kimberley's senses but she made a valiant attempt to rally.

"I won't be a minute."

"You can say hello to your brother tomorrow. It's time to go home," he said, dipping in to melt her objections with a short but devastating kiss. "I have a hankering for diamonds."

It was just a line. As he loosened his bow tie and flipped the studs from his dinner shirt, he met Kimberley's eyes in the mirror of her dresser and told her he only hankered for her, unadorned. Drawing her to her feet with the sensual power of his words and his voice and his cobalt gaze, he carefully, deliberately, went about unadorning her.

First, he unzipped the platinum gown and let it fall in a pool at her feet. Next, the lacy slithers of underwear, the sky-high heels, every diamond pin in her hair, and last he removed each glittering piece of jewellery until she stood naked before the full-length mirror. Then he stripped her completely bare by looking into her eyes and telling her that this was how he wanted her—just her, Kim, without a glimmer of Blackstone's between them.

When he vowed to kiss every inch of bared skin, she felt a momentary ripple of disquiet but he chased that away with the moist touch of his lips at the base of her spine. When he turned her in his hands, one kiss following the next over her flanks and hips and belly, he noticed the scar in her belly button for the first time. Although she tensed momentarily, the velvety brush of his thumb and then the moist heat of his kiss against the tiny mark released the last vestige of self-preservation.

"Keyhole surgery," she explained on a whisper of breath because his mouth shifted lower. "Women's stuff…it's okay."

His hand stilled on her belly, enveloping her emptiness with heat and a reverent pressure, and in that moment it was okay for the first time in a very long while.

"You've stopped." She stretched, a sinuous movement designed to distract and provoke. "If you do manage to kiss every inch, then I promise to reciprocate."

Distracted and provoked, he fulfilled his promise and so did she, and the memory of that amazing connection—when he was inside her, reminding her of what mattered and what didn't—still steamed through her senses three days later.

"You left suddenly the other night."

Ryan's voice cut into her sensual memory and Kimberley turned, letting the elevator she'd been about to board go without her. The smile that was never far from her lips these past days bloomed to full effect as she greeted her brother. Not smiling, but that was Ryan, and despite his unwelcoming expression she was glad they'd finally caught up. "We were on our way home when we saw you. Did you enjoy the reception?"

"No. Going up?" He indicated the vacant lift with a nod, then followed her inside. "I didn't expect to see you there."

"Part of the strategy," she said, "to demonstrate that Blackstone's is hail and hearty and moving forward. We want to show we're not stalled by grief or backpedaling due to the negative press."

"And moving in with Perrini…is that a strategy for the good of the company?"

Quiet words, but their implication froze Kimberley's smile. "No. That would be a strategy for the good of me."

"I hope so, Kim."

"Look," she said tightly, reading a wealth of meaning behind those words. "I understand your grievance with Ric and I know you're feeling raw at the moment. Perhaps this isn't the best time for this conversation."

"The best time would have been before you got involved with him again. I shouldn't have let him assume control of this deal."

The lift glided to a smooth halt at her floor, but Kimberley's stomach kept on moving. She hit the button to hold the doors shut and looked into her brother's eyes. Not hard, cold, hostile, as she'd expected, but churning with something that looked like self-recrimination. "What do you mean?"

"We all wanted you back here, Kim—none of us liked you working for Hammond—but Perrini always held him accountable for busting up your marriage. That gave him extra motivation." He expelled a harsh breath, and the sound shivered like a chill of precognition all the way to the marrow of Kimberley's bones. "That, and his need to have a Blackstone at his side at that board meeting."

No. *No.* She shook her head, rejecting the awful clawing sense of déjà vu. "He didn't have me at his side. My return to Blackstone's has nothing to do with my personal relationship with Ric." But the words sounded hollow, booming with the memory of that day when he'd introduced her, when he'd sung her praises, when he'd sought her gaze across the boardroom table.

Had everyone noticed that connection? Was she such a blind fool?

"Your return was the talk of the office," Ryan confirmed. "Especially after you took off to the outback."

Just the two of them. In the company jet. Of course there would have been talk, talk that was only confirmed by the society columns' pictures of them together—a reunited couple—in this week's papers.

But that didn't mean Ryan was right, or that Perrini had used her to further his own ambitions. "He would have won that vote," she told Ryan, "with or without my support."

"You're wrong. He needed you as leverage in that board-room. He said he'd do whatever it took to get you back, and it seems that you let him."

Her brother's words struck like a slap, bringing her head up and washing the blood from her heart. "Then perhaps you should have warned me of this earlier."

"I did."

That day in the boardroom, when she'd said she was a big girl, that she wouldn't make the same mistake again.

She sucked in a breath, struggling to hold herself together and managing to do so by repeating those same words in her mind. She would not make the same mistake again. She would not assume too much. She would find out the whole story, from Perrini, before making any rash judgements.

Ric wasn't in his office and his PA knew nothing of his whereabouts other than he was not due back until midday. Kimberley knew he had a lunch meeting with several depart-ment heads, he'd told her that morning, after he'd returned from an early swim and they'd talked about their plans for the day over breakfast on the deck.

At the time she'd been smiling, thinking *I could get used to this start to every day, this routine, this simple bond of sharing. This man who filled my heart.*

Right now that same heart was knotted and tense over Ryan's disclosure. Quite likely she was overreacting or Ryan had misinterpreted. He saw Ric as his adversary and had always been a little too keen to point out the negative aspects of his ambition. That reasoning didn't ease her anxiety.

Too restless to settle, too tied in knots to concentrate, she paced to her window. The lunch meeting would keep him tied up for most of the afternoon and if she left this discussion until after work she feared it would grow and fester and explode in a heated volley of accusations. She didn't want that. She wanted a calm, controlled conversation.

Tomorrow was her birthday. Ric was taking her to a private retreat in the mountains, where the staff and he would pander to her every need. If she didn't get this sorted now, she feared the fallout might cast a shadow over their plans.

She tapped her phone against the palm of her hand for a moment before turning it over, decision made. With a finger that quavered only slightly, she dialled the number of his mobile phone.

Ric's phone buzzed as he was leaving the car dealership in the newly purchased Porsche. He could have taken the call handsfree but when he saw Kim's name on the caller ID he chose to pick up. Her voice he preferred in his ear, private and intimate, a gift to his hormones.

He grinned as he steered the sports car over to the kerb with a gentle caress of the wheel. She handled superbly—smooth, responsive, amenable, with a fiery strength beneath the sleek, sophisticated exterior. Pretty much like the woman he'd bought it for, as part of the birthday package. He aimed to make her very, very happy and very, very appreciative.

He flipped open the phone. "Any chance you can take a quick break?"

"I…yes." She sounded slightly taken back, the frown obvious in her voice. "I need to talk to you. That's why I called."

"Sounds ominous," he said lightly. The beat of silence afterward sounded even more so. His grin faded. His hormones subsided. He switched gears instantly, to the implications of her need to talk. "Meet me out the front in fifteen minutes. Look for the silver Porsche."

She hesitated beside the kerb, a frown drawing her brows tight. *Jump in,* he'd said, but by her expression he might as well have said *jump into the shark tank.*

She drew a breath, snapped her gaze to his. "Can we go somewhere private, somewhere we can just…talk?"

Everything about her, from her choice of words to her troubled eyes to her fingers tapping the frame of the opened door—to the fact that she hadn't seemed to notice he was driving a strange car—stirred a warning in Ric's gut. This wasn't business. This was about them. "If you get in before I score a ticket for loitering in a no-stopping zone, then I'll find somewhere private. We'll talk."

That got her moving. Although once she'd slid into the low seat and buckled up, she sat tense and motionless while he negotiated the midmorning traffic.

"You want to give me a hint?" he asked, stopped at a red.

For a second he wondered if she would answer. If she'd even heard. But slowly she turned her head to look at him. "I ran into Ryan this morning."

The alarm in his gut shrilled. He should have guessed this would be a Blackstone doing, that Ryan wouldn't take his defeat last week lying down. The light changed and he scooted ahead of the traffic, picking a route to a quiet residential area close to the city centre.

"And he's told you something to sour your perception of me?" he guessed. His voice sounded mild, matter-of-fact, his question measured—a surprise when his blood rankled with a mix of anger and disappointment. Forget mild. He cut her a sharp look. "Why the hell would you even listen to him?"

"I'm not taking his word, Ric. I want to hear your side of the story."

She used the word *story*. A piece of fiction. Good choice of word, he thought. He turned down a dead-end street and found a park outside a neat row of terraces. He switched off the engine and turned in his seat. "Then you'd better spell out the charge I'm answering to."

She nodded, her gaze not quite steady on his. He could tell she was collecting herself, choosing her words carefully, and the idea of that self-censorship fired his irritation like an accelerant.

"No pussyfooting," he said shortly. "Just say what you have to say, Kim."

Her chin came up. "Did you say you would do 'whatever it takes' to get me back to Blackstone's?"

"Yes," he said without hesitation. "That's exactly what I said."

She blinked, the shock of disillusionment bright in her eyes. Before she could respond Ric leaned closer and captured those wounded eyes with the resolute strength of his.

"I said it and I meant it, Kim. When I went to New Zealand, I had a simple agenda. Getting to you before the media, doing whatever I could to soften the blow of the news about your father and bringing you home to your family. But as soon as I climbed in that car with you and you turned those eyes and that tongue of yours on me, I knew I wanted more.

"Make no mistake, Kim," he said, low and serious, "I was always going to do whatever I could to get you back."

"Even offer me a directorship in the company?"

"That had nothing to do with my personal agenda. I told you the night you came to dinner. Business and personal, two separate entities."

Nearby a small dog started to yap, distracting her attention. He could tell she remained ambivalent, chewing over his words and searching out the argument points.

"I thought we covered all of this that night," he continued brusquely "If there's anything else I didn't make crystal clear, or if your brother passed on any other information for the purpose of creating trouble, he—"

"That wasn't his purpose. His concern over your motives is genuine. And so is mine."

"You choose to believe him over me?"

"I want to understand, that's all. Everything that led to your offer and why you targeted me. No one has convinced me why I was so indispensable. Why me and not Uncle William? He has the necessary Blackstone name, plus he's spent a lifetime in the mining industry. He invested start-up capital in the company and yet his name didn't come up once at the meeting last week as a prospective director. Why not? Did he turn the offer down? Or was it Howard's daughter you needed on your side at last week's meeting?"

Ric heard the last sentence loudest. It hung between them, heavily shaded with the true nature of her distrust. "William had a falling-out with Howard last year over selling his stake in the company. He would have been our last choice."

"Because he sold his shares?"

"Because he sold to Matt Hammond."

That bald pronouncement shocked a disbelieving laugh from her mouth. She started to say something, then shut her mouth and shook her head before trying again a second later. "Matt isn't a market player. And he despises Blackstone's. William owned a substantial holding. Why would Matt outlay such a significant sum on opposition stock?"

"For the joy of sending Howard apoplectic."

This time she didn't laugh in either shock or incredulity. She looked away, staring blindly out the side window. When she finally turned her eyes back on him they shimmered with more than disbelief. Wounded disillusionment dimmed their dark beauty, but not the spark of her voice or the pride that held her chin high. "So this all comes back to vengeance. Matt acquired Blackstone shares and you couldn't risk me siding with him, not if I'm to inherit a sizeable parcel of shares."

"That's only the business equation."

"Wasn't there an element of payback in the personal, too?" she asked, bitterness sharpening her tone. "Because Matt took your new plaything?"

"No. I always wanted you. For me. For what we are together. Hasn't this last week meant anything to you? Hasn't it shown you what I want with you? I don't know what else I can say to convince you."

"Perhaps you can't. Perhaps the mistrust and the doubts have been eating away at me too long. Perhaps the scars are too deep. Perhaps what you told me last week in Janderra explained too well why you have to keep climbing that ladder, doing whatever it takes, to prove yourself better than the Blackstones or the Perrinis back in Italy. To show your mother did the right thing and that you're the equal of everyone in this world. Perhaps I'll never be able to trust that you want me—just *me*—not the Blackstone name and all the power and privilege that comes with it."

The resonance of her passionate declaration engulfed them in the long, weighty aftermath. It was reminiscent of another time, another place, another fight, one Ric had made a prideful mess of, but this time he wasn't letting go as easily. He was all out of words but he had one remaining weapon, and he aimed to wield its power ruthlessly.

With a decisive efficiency of movement, he turned, buckled and started the engine. "Buckle up," he said shortly. "We're going for a drive."

"Take me back to the office," she said. And when he ignored her, joining the link road to the Harbour Bridge, she sat up straighter. Indignation coloured her cheeks and desperation edged her words. "You can't make me go with you. Let me out."

"You're coming with me. You're listening to me. Then you can make up your mind."

"And if I won't listen?"

He cut her a sideways look of lethal intent. "If you can look me in the eye and say you don't love me and that I don't have a chance to prove myself worthy of you and your Blackstone name, I will let you out right now, here or wherever you demand."

Eyes blazing, she stared him down, but when she opened her mouth to speak, the words didn't come. The truth glimmered in her eyes, rare and precious as green diamond, for one unguarded second before she looked away. And Ric's heart started beating again.

After he forced that silent admission, Kimberley was too wrapped up in miserable anguish to care where he was taking her. It didn't matter. He could talk about wanting her until he was blue in the face and she would listen and it would make no difference. Wanting her had never been in dispute. Respecting her, trusting her, seeing her as more than a Blackstone and a boardroom asset to be won back from the enemy—those were the things she needed and which she feared she could never earn from Ric Perrini. He'd played her again, using her to get the result he needed for his future at Blackstone's, and her misery was compounded knowing how swiftly and easily she'd fallen into his plans.

And now he knew that she loved him.

Could this hurt any more? Was there anything left to bring her right to her knees?

Dimly she heard the rumble of his voice as he spoke on the phone, and with a sharp mental slap, she forced her mind back into focus. She was pitiful, wallowing in the pit of despair she'd dug for herself while he'd moved on, calling his PA and cancelling the lunch meeting.

"Do you need to clear your schedule at the office?" he asked.

Ah, yes, her handcrafted position at Blackstone's. A paste

job. And not even a good one, she realised, now that she saw it with the clarity of hindsight. Yet she'd been seduced by the dazzle of Perrini's description, by the picture he'd painted… the one she'd wanted to see. It was her own contemptible fault, because she'd wanted it to be the real deal. She'd wanted that youthful dream, engraved into her heart the first time her father took her into the Blackstone's workrooms to see the magical transformation of rough diamond to polished gemstone.

"If you do, Vina can make the calls," Perrini continued.

Kimberley shook her head. She didn't need his PA. There wasn't much to cancel. "I'll call Holly. I have an appointment late this afternoon. Do I need to cancel or will we be back by then?"

"Cancel it."

She did, not because of that terse demand but because the appointment was to meet Briana Davenport for the first time at the Da Vinci's elegant Louvre Bar. Whatever the outcome of this mysterious drive, Kimberley knew she would be in no mood for polite small talk over drinks with Marise Hammond's supermodel sister.

"What is this about?" she asked after flipping her phone closed. While she'd been wallowing they'd crossed the bridge and turned east through the affluent middle harbour suburbs, heading toward the northern beaches.

"I'll tell you when we get there."

Twelve

When was fifteen minutes later.

Where was a cul-de-sac high on a bluff overlooking the Manly peninsula.

He killed the sports car's engine, and before Kimberley had a chance to take in more than a first impression of peace and space and elevation he'd strode around and opened her door.

"Come on," he said, leaning down to unbuckle her seat belt. "I have something to show you."

For a split second his eyes met hers, and if she didn't know better she would have read the shadows in their depths as nervousness. Then he straightened with his usual smooth efficiency and she huffed out a breath. Not nerves, just determination to turn her around with whatever smoke-and-mirrors show he had planned.

Gathering her cynicism around her like a cloak, she stepped

from the car's cool interior into the late morning heat. His hand at her elbow steered her from the paved footpath toward a thickly grassed block that rose from street level to meet the brilliant blue of a cloudless sky. Kimberley's heart fluttered into an edgy beat that rippled like goose bumps over her skin despite the summer sun. Either nerves or the steep slope they climbed turned her knees wonky, but he steadied her with a grip on her arm.

"You should have told me we were hiking. I would have chosen more appropriate foot—" Her breath caught on a gasp as they crested the rise and she caught sight of the view. Not just harbour, not just beaches, but bushland and treetops. "Who owns this land?" She turned on him, regathering her resolve to deflect whatever he threw at her. "Why have you brought me here?"

"It's mine." A muscle jumped in his cheek. "I bought it nine years ago, after my wife left me."

After she'd left…Kimberley shook her head, not comprehending. "Why?"

"When I first joined Blackstone's and when you met me, my ambition was all about proving myself, just as you said."

"Proving yourself to whom?"

"The boss at BJ Resources who tossed my application aside because I didn't attend a GPS school. Every pizza shop and liquor store I ran deliveries for. The family who excommunicated my mother when she disgraced the Perrini name with her pregnancy." He turned away suddenly. Hands on hips, he stood surveying the view for a long, breathless moment. Then he exhaled and turned back to face her. "The Blackstone directors. Howard. You."

Every one of those telling revelations punched a huge chip

out of Kimberley's resolve. *This* was the Perrini he'd never exposed, the real man beneath the polished facade. Although a part of her ached to pick apart each of those clues, another recognised that the details didn't matter. Concisely and eloquently he had told the complete story.

"And this?" she asked, gesturing at the land around them. "What is this to prove?"

"When I came to New Zealand to bring you home, I had the deeds to this block of land in my pocket. Proof that I wanted a future together, that I was looking forward to the time when we'd build a home here. I chose this land with that future—*our* future—in mind. I could see us bringing up our children here. There's a school right down there." He pointed off to their right, and Kimberley closed her eyes, her heart pounding so painfully hard she felt it in every cell of her body. "And over there is the beach where I'll teach them to swim and surf.

"I bought this block as a proof of my commitment to our future and the only thing that's changed is that the future is now. I want everything I see here—the home, the kids, the family—and I want them with you."

She squeezed her eyes shut in a vain attempt to block out the picture he painted, but she couldn't block out his low, gruff-voiced intensity. She couldn't block out the realisation that *this* was his dream—not success in the business world or chairmanship of the board òr her return to his life and his bed, but this family that he'd never had. It seemed so simple, so attainable, and yet it was the very thing she could not give him. That knowledge drove a shard of pain right through her heart, as she lifted her chin to face him.

To tell him.

"I'm not the woman in that picture, Ric."

His head came up, jaw rigid with determination. "Why not? Is it this place?"

"No. This block is— God, you know what it is!" He might as well have reached right into her heart and plucked it out. "I can't give you everything you see here. I am not your future, Ric. I *can't* be. I can't have those children."

Kimberley thought she'd reached rock bottom when forced to acknowledge her love, but that was before Perrini revealed the future she would share with him in a heartbeat if she thought that future could be happy. That was before she told him that any conception would be a miracle pregnancy and he couldn't disguise the shock of raw regret that crossed his features.

Then she struck rock bottom.

Recovering rapidly he demanded details of her surgeries, first for endometriosis and then to remove the resultant adhesions, and she recited facts and statistics. True to form he steamrolled over medical opinion, stating they would see fertility experts, investigate IVF, whatever it took.

Kimberley was starting to despise that phrase. "And if I don't want to have babies?" she asked, her heart breaking with the lie. "Have you considered that I might not share your vision of happy families? That my dream may be something else entirely?"

His head came up, and his gaze narrowed. "Because of your mother's postnatal depression? Are you afraid of history repeating itself?"

"No," she said softly, unable to latch on to that ready-made excuse. "My mother lost a baby. She must have suffered incredible guilt."

"Then what?" When she would have turned away, he

closed in on her, taking her stiff shoulders in his hands, forcing her to face him. "The truth, Kim."

"I can't give you what you want, Perrini. Can't you accept that?"

His grip and his features tightened with a combination of frustration and determination. "Our future isn't dependent on you having my babies," he asserted. "You can't chase me away that easily."

Chin high, she gathered together the tattered shreds of her resolve and faced him down. "I have fulfilled my end of the deal. I came here. I listened. And I've made up my mind. Now, please take me home…to Miramare."

Ric took her to the Vaucluse mansion, as she demanded. When he parked the car and handed her the keys, she gave him a bewildered look. After the tense silence on the drive back from Manly when she'd shut down his every attempt to discuss her stance, he figured any look she gave him, other than total acquiescence, would have set his teeth on edge.

Unfortunately doe-eyed bewilderment didn't.

"The car's yours," he said roughly, folding her stiff fingers around the keys. "Happy birthday."

She puffed out a breath. "I…I don't know what to say. I can't—"

"'Thank you, Ric,' would do for a start," he said over the top of her protest.

There was only so much rejection a man could hear in one day and Ric had reached his limit. If he hadn't just handed her the keys to the only ready transportation, he would have turned and walked away. Not for good—he was far from done with Kimberley Blackstone—but for now.

Turning on his heel he took the steps to the mansion two at a time, ignoring the protests that followed in his wake, and greeted Marcie with a strained smile as she opened the door. "Is Sonya in?"

"She's out the front, in the garden." The housekeeper shot a worried look out the front door. "Is Miss Kimberley all right?"

"She'll be in shortly. She's just deciding what to do with her new car."

As he strode inside he took his phone from his pocket and switched it on, frowning at the list of missed calls. Ryan, more than once. He checked the text messages and stopped in his tracks.

Halfway back across the foyer he met Kim coming in. Her phone was in her hand and her eyes sought his, wide with the unasked question. He nodded. *Yes, he'd got the same message.* Although he saw the shield come up in her eyes, he kept on walking and took her resistant body into his arms.

They'd identified Howard's remains. The waiting was over.

He helped her through the formalities with the coroner's counsellor, stayed for the family meeting to discuss funeral arrangements, and for the dinner Sonya insisted they eat. Afterward Kim suggested he looked tired. He ignored the thinly veiled hint. He wasn't going anywhere.

"Kim's right," Sonya said, reaching across to place her hand over his. "You do look worn-out. Why don't you go home? It was lovely having your company for dinner, but you don't have to stay and babysit me. In fact, I'll be going upstairs myself soon. So, please, both of you, go home."

"I'm staying here tonight," Kim said after a beat of awk-

ward silence. Then, for the first time since they'd received the
news six hours earlier, she met his eyes. "You can take the
Porsche. Please."

"The Porsche?" Sonya asked, looking between them with
curiosity. "Do you have a new car?"

"An early birthday present." His eyes locked on Kim's,
daring her to disagree. "Thank you for the offer of its use, but
I don't need a car. If you're staying, then so am I."

Her eyes flared, her lips thinned, but in front of Sonya she
said nothing. Several minutes later, while he answered
Sonya's question about why he'd chosen that particular car,
she quietly excused herself. Suspecting she would lock her
bedroom door, he didn't allow her too much start and caught
up on the first-floor landing.

"I will see you in the morning," she said stiffly, turning to
her door as if she expected him to continue upstairs to the
room he normally used.

"No." He closed the space in six easy strides. "You'll see
me now."

"Don't do this," she whispered. "I can't handle this fight,
not tonight."

The fragile edge to her request cut him to the quick. He
lifted a hand and touched his knuckles to her cheek, to the
dark fall of her hair, and then he bent and kissed her forehead.
"I'm not here to fight, baby, I promise you that."

Too drained by the day's emotional seesaw to resist, Kimberley let him into her bedroom. The idea that he might use
sex as a weapon to wear down her defences should have
stirred her to anger, instead it only deepened the ache in the
middle of her chest.

She showered quickly and when she unlocked the bathroom door to an empty room, she breathed a sigh of relief. He stood outside the French doors on her small balcony, out of reach of the one bedside lamp, and when she slipped into bed she turned that off, too.

Four nights she'd spent at his Bondi home, and already she felt the strangeness of lying alone in bed. In the dark her heartbeat sounded too thick, too fast, too needy. She heard him come inside, heard the rustle of clothes as he undressed, and she held her breath. But he didn't come straight to bed. He showered, too, with the door open and the light slicing across the bedroom while the air filled with the sound of running water and her body softened with images of his naked body and her heart ached with the pictures he'd painted on an impossible future.

Then the water shut down, the bathroom light went out. Tension held her limbs rigid, her fingers curled into her pillow, while she waited for the dip in the mattress, the flutter of the sheet, the heat of his body behind hers, his arm closing over her and drawing her back into the spoon of his body.

"Relax," he murmured near her ear and she shivered at the touch of his hair still wet from the shower. "I'm just going to hold you."

She closed her eyes, willed her body to relax. He didn't just hold her. He held her and he talked to her, random memories of her father that were in turn funny and infuriating, irreverent and respectful. When the tears finally came he held her more tightly and soothed the tremors with long, calming strokes of his hands.

Afterward she tried to turn away, but he wouldn't let her. Patiently he broke down her defences and made love to her with heartwrenching tenderness, filling the hollowness with his healing heat, and opening her heart to a deeper, stronger ache. This was the man she wanted, the only man she had ever loved, and she could not give him what he most wanted.

Much later, when his body felt slumberously heavy against hers, she hugged his arms tight to her chest and whispered into the dark, "I can't give you what you want."

And she felt the press of his lips to her neck, the stir of his breath as he spoke. "Let me be the judge of that."

The following days swept by in a blur of activity, with ongoing funeral arrangements and the preparation of press statements and the continual stream of condolence calls. Kimberley smiled graciously through each and every one until her cheeks ached with the effort. Through it all Ric remained at her side, a source of solid support and extra despair.

"What am I going to do with you?" she whispered on Monday night, after he'd stormed her defences again with his body and his sweetly destructive tongue.

"You could give up this intransigence," he replied sleepily. "You will in the end. You know it, I know it. I'm not going away."

Perhaps he was right. Perhaps she was being falsely stubborn, obstructing what was meant to be. But there was something holding her back, a complex combination of the babymaking issue and her lingering mistrust of his motives in wanting her back.

"I need a sign," she muttered as she traipsed along Pitt Street on Tuesday morning. She'd been on her way to the jewellery store when Garth called and asked if she could meet him at his office. Another detail to sort out for the funeral, no doubt. She'd turned back and had almost reached the Blackstone building when she caught sight of Ric crossing the street, his stride long and purposeful, his expression creased in concentration. Her heart did a little bump, just from the unexpected sighting. Ridiculous really, when she'd seen the man step naked from her bed that morning.

Perhaps this was the sign she'd asked for. As infinitely simple as that *I-see-you* bump of her heart. Her heartbeat accelerated with the thought, wanting with a painful kick of intensity to believe that it could be this simple.

As straightforward as him crossing the street on this block at this precise moment.

She stopped, a smile starting to curve her lips as she prepared for the moment when he stepped onto the sidewalk and saw her. Perhaps she should walk right up and kiss him—not a quick hello peck but a passionate embrace right here in the middle of Tuesday morning. Her smile kicked up, contemplating his surprise, but then a woman pushing a stroller brushed past her, blocking Ric from view momentarily.

When she saw him again he was picking up something from the footpath—a tiny, pink shoe—and handing it to the young mother. The woman's harried expression turned to a smile when he hunkered down to put it back on the toddler's foot. Then he straightened and the expression on his face— a concentrated dose of purest longing—trampled Kimberley's heart to the street.

The sign she'd asked for was simple after all. As simple as a baby's dropped shoe.

Ric saw her ahead of him hurrying into the Blackstone's lobby, but when he called her name she kept on moving. He increased the length of his stride, concentrating his effort on intercepting her at the elevators. He didn't know how much detail Garth had given her, if any, and before she stepped into that office she deserved some warning.

As he passed through the security scanner he called her name again, but her sage-green dress and the swing of her dark ponytail disappeared into a lift. With a last Herculean dash he managed to get his hand in the gap between the rapidly closing doors, reversing their direction at the last second. As he stepped into the car, she sucked in a breath that flared her nostrils and widened her big green eyes.

He swore softly. "Garth's told you already."

"I'm on my way up to this office now, so, no. What is this about, Ric?"

"Your father's will," he said shortly. "There's been a new development."

"New development?" she echoed.

"A lawyer from Ian Van Dyke's firm called Garth this morning."

"The lawyer who was on the plane."

Ric nodded. "That's right. An estate lawyer who's been doing work for your father for some time now. Apparently a new will was drafted and signed that day, before they got on the plane."

"And they've just found it?" She choked out a laugh. "Did it fall behind a filing cabinet?"

"I don't know what happened. I imagine this meeting will shed some light on why this document took so long to come to light, and its contents."

"I don't think the second part is too much of a mystery, do you? He told me he was writing me out."

"Don't jump to conclusions, Kim. This could be anything from a complete shake-up to a few cosmetic changes. I think the second is more likely, given the thing was signed and witnessed in an airport lounge."

"The documents that delayed the flight," she said softly.

The lift stopped at the top floor. The doors glided open, but he could see by the pallor of Kim's face and her white-knuckled grip on the charm pendant around her neck that she wasn't ready for this meeting. "Ryan's not here yet," he said, turning her toward the boardroom. "Come and sit down for a minute."

A minute probably wasn't going to do it, Kimberley thought, as she sank into a chair in the director's lounge. Ric had gone to let Garth know she'd arrived and where to find them when Ryan showed up. Whether it was a minute or ten, she appreciated the chance to collect herself.

She knew in her heart what this lawyer would tell them, but it wasn't the threat of imminent disinheritance that had knocked the wind from her lungs. It was the sum of all that had happened this month, and the realisation of all she'd changed and all she stood to lose. She'd left the job she loved at House of Hammond, thinking she had a personal stake in the future of Blackstone's. In the process she'd lost the respect and friendship of her cousin Matt. She might never see her godson grow up.

And she'd learned what had forged Perrini into the man he was today, a man with a mark to make on the world and a need for family, a man she loved for all he'd become and all he could be. A man she didn't believe she could ever make truly happy.

The door opened and he came back into the room, his eyes instantly finding hers. Whatever he saw in her face meshed his brows into a tight frown. He pulled a chair over in front of hers and sat, close enough that their knees bumped when he leaned forward to take her hands in his. He held them tightly for a moment until the trembling stopped.

"If I'm not a stakeholder in Blackstone's," she said finally, picking the one thing she could focus on without falling apart, "this whole month has been for nothing."

He studied her silently for a second. "Let's assume that this new will is what you suspect. That doesn't have to change your position or your directorship at Blackstone's."

She huffed out a breath. "How can I stay on knowing my father didn't want me to have any part of the company?"

"Do you want to stay?"

"It isn't that simple."

"It can be," he said, gripping her hands more firmly and shaking them with a quiet insistence. "If you would just accept that things don't always have to be difficult."

"Things, such as?"

"Let's start with this will. *If* your father has disinherited you, it's because you had a blow-up row. He hated that you wouldn't play by his rules in his sandbox. He hated who you chose to play with instead. That doesn't mean he didn't love you or that he wouldn't be damned pleased to see you back here."

"It would seem I have a problem recognising love."

"It would seem," he said dryly, but his expression tightened with his trademark strength of purpose. "I gave everything I thought I could offer the other day, but maybe I should have stuck to the simple, and the simple truth is this—I don't care if it's Manly or Bondi or Janderra or the moon, I just want to make a home with you, a life with you."

"And if I don't believe it's that simple? If I believe it's a family you yearn for?" Her voice grew thick, choked with emotion that swelled in her chest and squeezed her heart. "I saw your shock when I told you I couldn't have babies."

"Hell, yes, I was shocked. You were telling me about surgery, about your inability to conceive, about big things in your life and your body that you'd never mentioned before. Of course I was shocked and concerned—for *you,* not for me."

She shook her head slowly, not wanting to reject the sincerity of that message, but not ready to accept. "I *saw* you out in the street before, when you picked up the little girl's shoe. I saw your face when you held little Ivy, when you bowled a cricket ball to Cam. You say you just want a home and a life, but I *saw* the look on your face. I can't give you that, Ric, and that's about me, not you. I want to be able to give you happiness. Maybe that's what love is. It tears me in two because I can't give you what you want."

"Kids? A family? Yes, I want, I'm not going to lie about that, but there are other means, other methods, and if that doesn't work out we foster or we adopt from overseas or we do whatever it takes, because you're the only woman I've ever wanted as my wife and the mother of my children. No one else can give me what you do."

"Difficulties?" she asked on a hoarse exhalation, not quite a laugh, not quite a cry. "All those pain-in-the-backside qualities you mentioned I'd inherited? I guess no estate lawyer can take those from me!"

A spark that looked something like triumph and something like love kindled the sapphire depths of his eyes. "Wouldn't want to try," he murmured, and his clasp on her hands changed tenor, softening, deepening, along with his voice and the thickening thud of her heartbeat. She so wanted to believe him, to take that final leap of trust. "I went ten years without you making my life more difficult and more of a delight. I don't want that again. Ever."

"How do you do that? How can you make this sound so easy?"

"It's as simple as trusting our love and deciding you want to marry me again, for the right reasons this time."

"The right reasons?"

Lifting their joined hands, he tapped her knuckles to his heart. "I love you, Kim. It doesn't matter what Howard's will does or doesn't say, whether you choose to stay at Blackstone's or not. Nothing will change the simple truth of my love. Your choice—do you want to marry me, love me, give me everything I could ever want?"

The lingering spectre of doubt shadowed her face and her eyes as she started to shake her head. He stopped her with the most effective move of all, leaning in to take her lips in a kiss more eloquent than any words.

"You, babe," he said against her mouth. "You're all I want, all I need, all I cherish."

His next kiss started gentle, and was everything his words promised. Honest, direct and everything she could ever want in a kiss and in her man. Dizzy with the heady promise of a simple future, she leaned nearer and closed her eyes and he took the invitation to deepen the contact, to taste her capitulation on her lips and her tongue.

She could have gone on kissing him forever but a knock at the door interrupted and brought them crashing back to the present. Kimberley didn't mind. She smiled into his eyes and said, "Yes, I will marry you, for the right reason. The simplest reason. I love you, Ric Perrini."

He kissed her again to celebrate that moment and that admission, then he pulled her to her feet. "Are you ready for this?"

Kimberley nodded, the smile in her heart spreading to her lips. "Let's go and see if you've made a very poor choice of bride."

"I haven't," he said with absolute conviction. His hand tightened on hers, linking their fingers, sealing their bond of love. "That's the simplest truth of all."

* * * * *

Don't miss the next
DIAMONDS DOWN UNDER *title,*
Tessa Radley's
PRIDE & A PREGNANCY SECRET,
available February from Silhouette Desire

Silhouette®

Desire

NEW YORK·TIMES BESTSELLING AUTHOR

DIANA
PALMER

A brand-new Long, Tall Texans novel

IRON COWBOY

*Available March 2008
wherever you buy books.*

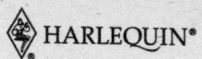

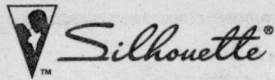

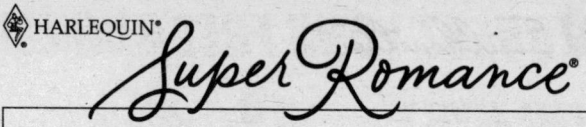

Texas Hold 'Em

When it comes to love, the stakes are high

Sixteen years ago, Luke Chisum dated
Becky Parker on a dare…before going
on to break her heart. Now the former
River Bluff daredevil is back, rekindling
desire and tempting Becky to pick up
where they left off. But this time she has
to resist or Luke could discover the secret
she's kept locked away all these years.…

Look for

TEXAS BLUFF

by Linda Warren

#1470

*Available February 2008
wherever you buy books.*

REQUEST YOUR FREE BOOKS!

2 FREE NOVELS
PLUS 2
FREE GIFTS!

Passionate, Powerful, Provocative!

SDES07

You can lead a horse to water...

When Alyssa Barkley and Clint Westmoreland
found out that their "fake" marriage was never
rendered void, they are forced to live together
for thirty days. However, Clint loves the single
life and has no intention of being tamed, but
when Alyssa moves in, the sizzling attraction
between them is ignited and neither wants the
thirty days to end.

Look for

TAMING CLINT WESTMORELAND

by

BRENDA JACKSON

Available February wherever you buy books

COMING NEXT MONTH

#1849 PRIDE & A PREGNANCY SECRET—
Tessa Radley
Diamonds Down Under
She wants to be more than his secret mistress, especially now that she's pregnant with his heir. But she isn't the only one with a secret that could shatter a legacy.

#1850 TAMING CLINT WESTMORELAND—
Brenda Jackson
They thought their fake marriage was over...until they discovered they were still legally bound—with their attraction as strong as ever.

#1851 THE WEALTHY FRENCHMAN'S PROPOSITION—
Katherine Garbera
Sons of Privilege
Sleeping with her billionaire boss was not on her agenda. But discovering they were suddenly engaged was an even bigger surprise!

#1852 DANTE'S BLACKMAILED BRIDE—Day Leclaire
The Dante Legacy
He had to have her. And once he discovered her secret, he had the perfect opportunity to blackmail his business rival's daughter into becoming his bride.

#1853 BEAUTY AND THE BILLIONAIRE—
Barbara Dunlop
A business mogul must help his newest employee transform from plain Jane to Cinderella princess...but can he keep his hands off her once his job's done?

#1854 TYCOON'S VALENTINE VENDETTA—
Yvonne Lindsay
Rekindling a forbidden romance with the daughter of his sworn enemy was the perfect way to get his revenge. Then he discovers she's pregnant with his child!